OPERATION

NAVAJO

Award-Winning Tracker Novels by Author
Anita Dickason

Au79

"I wasn't quite ready for the dizzying speed when the storyline took off and the action didn't stop. I loved it!" *Amazon top 500 Reviewer*

"Riveting action thriller. Terrific dialogue, amazing intrigue and intense action keep you turning pages." *Readers' Favorite*

GOING GONE!

"Excels at ratcheting up the tension and developing well-nuanced characters." *Book Viral*

"If you like action-thrillers, this one has murders, covert agents at risk, car chases, explosions, ex-special forces good and bad guys, paramilitary action, gun battles, etc." *Amazon top 500 Reviewer Vine Voice*

SENTINELS of the NIGHT

"Will have serial killer mystery fans and paranormal urban fantasy junkies alike getting excited over a new series which has something for just about everyone. A compelling debut novel." *Readers' Favorite*

"A riveting high stake read—*Sentinels of the Night* proves an edgy and notable debut for Dickason with the promise of more to come." *Book Viral*

www.anitadickason.com

OPERATION
NAVAJO

Anita Dickason

Mystic Circle Books

Publisher: Mystic Circle Books
Cover Design: Mystic Circle Books & Designs, LLC
Editor: Jennie Rosenblum, www.jennierosenblum.com

ISBN
978-1-7340821-2-8: Paperback
978-1-7340821-3-5: Hardback
978-1-7340821-4-2: eBook

Library of Congress Control Number: 2020913869

ACKNOWLEDGMENTS

To my daughter
Julie
Thank you for the many hours you listened,
and your help with the plot.

To my daughter
Christy Kay
Thank you for helping to create the cover,
and the idea for the plot.

To my friends
Pat Pratt & Beth Vansyckle
Thank you for all your suggestions and help.

"Whoever controls the *flow* of the supply of money, irrespective of whether it is fiat or gold currency, is the *one* to fear."

CHAPTER 1

WASHINGTON D.C.

SOMETHING WAS WRONG, terribly wrong. Uneasiness morphed into a deep-seated foreboding. Unable to contain the nervous energy, she paced, occasionally pausing to push aside the corner of the drapes, only to stare at the deserted street. She typed a coded message and hit send. Nothing. Rick was never late or failed to answer a text. His silence spoke volumes.

Every possibility, down to the smallest detail, had been analyzed and answered, except ... this one. With the safety of the packet utmost in her mind, she had to assume the worst. Even if it meant breaking her cover, she had to deliver it without delay. If they had Rick's phone, it might already be too late.

Thoughts raced as she glanced around the empty apartment, leased for one reason, her meetings with Rick. There was nothing they could find, not even a fingerprint. The thin, leather gloves she'd always worn had been a wise precaution.

She quickly dismantled her phone, shoving the pieces into the pocket of the hooded jacket. She'd find a place to dump them after she left.

Under her t-shirt, a small, padded envelope was taped to her rib cage. Her fingers smoothed the edges of the tape before giving it a hard push. Reassured it was firmly in place, she checked the holster pressed against her side. Though it was secure, she tightened the belt another notch, then tugged the jacket around her hips.

After flipping the inside lock, she stepped out. She hesitated, searching the shadows before walking down. When her feet hit the sidewalk, she broke into a slow lope, her eyes watchful as she passed the apartment buildings. At this time of the evening, most residents had arrived home. To all appearances, she was out for a jog as she headed toward a nearby shopping center, an easy run, a mile or so. One she'd done before. There she could catch a cab.

A light tinkle of metal alerted her. Ahead, shadows at the edge of a building shifted. Not one to ignore an instinct of danger, she altered her direction. Her pace steady, she crossed the street, turned back, planning to circle the block. A faint whistle floated in the night air.

She rounded the corner, then ran flat out. At the next street, she turned again. Behind her, the pounding of heavy, fast-moving footsteps grew louder. A bullet, then a second struck the side of the building, spewing chips of brick as she raced by. *Silencers!* Whoever was hot on her tail and bent on killing her were professionals.

Fueled by fear and adrenaline, her stride lengthened as she kicked into high gear. The packet rubbed against her breasts. Tape tugged her skin as she sucked in air. Leg muscles burned.

Another ping echoed when a bullet struck a parked car. One slammed into the sidewalk near her foot. Her head whipped around for a quick glance. Two men were less than a block behind her. Soon, one of their shots would find its mark.

Zigzagging around parked cars, she desperately searched for a way out. Ahead was an alley. She raced toward it.

Once she was out of view, she spun, jerking the Glock from the holster. She leaned around the corner and fired. A man stumbled. A second shot missed when they ducked behind a car.

Would the few precious seconds she gained be enough? Maybe

so, when she spotted a ladder mounted on the wall at the far end of the alley. Even as she ran toward it, she knew it was a risk. If they caught her on it, a bullet in the back was an easy shot. But it was her only chance. The roof evened the playing field.

She shoved the gun in the holster, grabbed the rail, and scrambled to the top. There, she dropped, then scooted to the edge. Lungs heaved with deep breaths to slow the pounding of her heart as she focused on the entrance to the alley.

Barely visible in the shifting moonlight, a head appeared at the corner of the building. The man paused before stepping into the alley. He crept forward, then motioned. The second man followed, limping as he tried to keep up. Their movements cautious, they eased their way toward the other end.

A look of grim determination crossed her face. Elbows braced, gun firmly gripped, she aligned the sights center mass, then fired. The lead man dropped like a bag of sand. The second man hesitated, swinging his weapon in a futile attempt to find her. Double-tapped, he landed alongside his partner.

Certain the shots had been heard, she didn't waste time. Sliding down the ladder, she jumped the last few feet. On one knee, she leaned over the bodies. Both were dead.

In the distance, sirens echoed. As she trotted out of the alley, her hand brushed her chest. The package was secure.

CHAPTER 2

ROUSED BY THE ring of the phone, Scott glanced at the clock. For the head of the Tracker Unit, a call at three in the morning was never good news. "Fleming," he answered.

"Scott, this is Frank Littleton."

Apprehension surged, wiping out Scott's lingering remnants of sleep. Littleton was the Federal Reserve Chairman.

He added, "I need to speak with you. There's a diner at," and rattled off an address.

"Why?" Scott asked as he rolled out of bed.

"I can't explain over the phone." The line went dead.

Disturbed by the cryptic call, Scott threw on his clothes, then grabbed his keys, phone, and gun.

When he rushed out of the elevator, the security guard seated behind the lobby desk jumped up. "Agent Fleming, is something wrong?"

"No," he answered, knowing it was a lie. Outside, he hesitated, scanning the street and buildings. A light breeze churned the muggy air, but nothing stirred in the deep shadows. While it was a relatively safe neighborhood, it didn't pay to take chances, especially at this time of night. Scott kept a sharp lookout as he hurried to the parking garage.

Traffic was light, so he made good time. He tried not to speculate, but the sight of a parking lot with more gravel than concrete and a rundown building didn't ease his tension. On the roof, a weather-beaten, faded sign proclaimed, JOE'S DINER. A neon sign glowed in the front window. The E in OPEN intermittently blinked.

What the devil was the Federal Reserve Chairman doing here? Exiting, his gaze studied the parking lot, a car, two cabs, and the pickup parked in front and didn't like what was missing.

As he stepped inside, a bell mounted over the door tinkled. The smoky odor of charred meat, fried onions, and spices mingled with freshly brewed coffee. A counter with stools extended across the back. In the middle, tables sat on a stained linoleum floor. Booths lined the front. Two cabbies seated at the counter shot a look of disinterest over their shoulders before turning back to the wall-mounted TV.

A man, his back to the door, sat in a booth. Scott muttered, "Where the hell is his protection detail?"

Littleton's head turned at the sound of Scott's footsteps. His grim expression shifted to one of relief as Scott slid onto the bench opposite him.

He extended his hand across the table for a brief handshake. "You made better time than I expected."

"It's not every day I get a three o'clock wake-up call from a high-ranking government official. A powerful motivator. What happened to your security team?"

A wry look crossed Littleton's face. "Do you think I can't drive? Though I must admit, it's not something I often do."

"No sir, not at all. I didn't expect to see you here by yourself."

"Let's get past the sir business. It's Frank. I have a feeling we'll get to know each other a lot better in the coming days. I dismissed my security detail. They believe I'm safely tucked in for the night."

As he stared at him, Scott wondered, how do you chastise the Federal Reserve Chairman?

Frank said, "I know what you're thinking, it's foolhardy to take this kind of risk. But when needs drive, sometimes you don't have a choice. I made sure I wasn't followed."

"Why here?"

With a nostalgic sigh, Frank glanced around before saying, "At one time, I was a frequent visitor. In my early days as an attorney, this place was a popular hangout. I figured we could talk without being recognized." He picked up the chipped cup and took a sip.

The kitchen door swung open. A beanpole of a man stepped out. Tied around his middle, a dirty apron hung to his knees. He picked up a coffee pot, hooked his little finger around a cup handle, and ambled toward them. After setting the cup down, he filled it before looking at Scott. "You want a menu?"

Scott shook his head. "Just coffee."

He grunted. "If you change your mind, holler. Name's Barney."

Scott picked up the cup and studied Frank over the rim as he took a swallow. He'd first met him at the White House when President Larkin requested his presence during a meeting. At the time, the Tracker Unit was investigating the disappearance of an ATF agent along with several thefts of explosives in Texas.

In Scott's opinion, Frank Littleton was the second most powerful man in the federal government. Though, banking advocates might argue, putting him ahead of the President. As the Federal Reserve Chairman, he was responsible for the country's central banking and monetary system. His plump face and short, pudgy body didn't convey a perception of authority. Even more so now, unshaven, and wearing a stained, frayed jacket. Scott wondered where he'd acquired the garment as he couldn't imagine it hanging in the closet of the usually dapper, high-powered executive.

Still, most people wouldn't give him a second glance until you looked into his eyes. The intelligence in his penetrating gaze conveyed a clear message. He wasn't a man to underestimate. The first time they shook hands, Scott felt an unusual awareness of like-mindedness. One of Scott's unique abilities was analyzing patterns in human behavior and what they meant. A handy advantage when applied to a criminal's actions and the reason for his unprecedented number of arrests as a field agent.

He suspected Frank had a similar ability in his dealings with the financial sector. Despite the man's casual comments, Scott sensed he was troubled, uneasy.

Once Barney was out of earshot, Frank leaned forward, his voice dropped. "I received a death threat."

Scott's uneasiness spiked. "When?"

"Yesterday, I had a meeting with several colleagues at the Greystone Hotel. I gave my overcoat to the bell captain. When I left, I found this in the pocket." He reached inside his jacket, pulled out a plastic bag with a folded piece of paper inside, then slid it across the table. "After reading it, I put it in the bag."

"What does it say?" Scott picked it up, flipped it over to examine the other side, then shoved it into his coat pocket.

"It's a warning telling me I'll be killed and not to trust anyone in the Federal Reserve."

"Anyone else touch it?"

"No."

Nerves buzzed with a familiar sense of intrigue as Scott picked up his cup and drank. Certain of the answer, he still had to ask. "Why didn't you notify your security personnel?"

"I didn't dare." Anger sparked in Frank's voice. "If I've got rats on my staff, I want to find out who, not drive them underground to strike another time. Since reading that damn note, I've debated my options. If I inform Captain Hayes, the head of my security team, it won't take long for word to spread. We both know you can't keep something like this quiet. It's a risk I'm not willing to take."

"Which is why we're meeting at Joe's Diner," Scott said.

"I knew you could take the ball and run with it."

Scott's hand scrubbed his face as he considered, not a ball, but a political bomb he'd just been handed. The bell over the door tinkled. The cab drivers left. He shifted to stare out the window, watching until they drove out of the parking lot, then turned back to Frank. "Any idea why you'd be targeted?"

"A reason is something I haven't stopped thinking about. Other than the obvious, my position as head of the Federal Reserve, I don't have a clue."

"When was the meeting at the hotel scheduled?"

"It's a standing meeting, once a month."

"Is your schedule posted online?"

"No, it's not."

"Who knew you'd be there?"

"Any number of people. The meetings aren't secret. Been going on for several months. Even had a few reporters show up."

Footsteps approached. The two men eased back.

"Want a refill?" Barney held out the coffee pot.

Frank waved his hand over his cup, but Scott pushed his to the edge of the table. While Barney poured, he pondered his options, which were damn few, and none were good. How could he protect the man when it wasn't his jurisdiction? Hell, he couldn't even interface with Frank's security team. He picked up the cup and swallowed a large gulp.

Coming to a decision, he set the cup down. "I need a copy of your itinerary and a list of your personnel. Anything out of the norm on your schedule?"

"Nothing I haven't done before, meetings here in Washington, a banking conference in Wyoming."

"Wyoming? Odd place for a banking conference."

"Not really. Every year the Federal Reserve sponsors the Teton Economic Conference."

The odor of fried bacon emanating from the kitchen meant time was short. Scott told him, "We have to get out of here. The breakfast crowd will be arriving. I need a way to contact you that won't create suspicion. I don't want to use your landlines or cellphone. On the way here, I passed a convenience store. We can pick up a couple of prepaid phones. I know you're friends with Vance Whitaker. He's another option. If necessary, we can use him."

Through the course of several investigations, Scott had learned a great deal about the head of Homeland Security. The man would probably relish the role of a middleman.

Headlights flashed across the window as a car drove into the parking lot. Scott picked up a napkin. After scribbling on it, he slid it toward Frank. "My fax number and email address. Your home computer, is it linked to the one in your office?"

"No."

"Good. Use it instead of your office computer."

Three more cars pulled into the parking lot.

Scott pulled a ten-dollar bill from his wallet, then dropped it on the table. "Let's go."

As they approached the door, Scott stepped in front of Frank. Opening it, he walked outside. His eyes scanned the lot before moving to the side to let Frank exit.

"I'm following you home."

With a frown, Frank stared at him. While not loud, his protest was forceful. "It's not necessary. I'm sure no one would expect I'd be alone in a car."

His tone grim, Scott said, "I'm not taking the chance."

For the short distance to the store, Scott took the lead. After purchasing two phones, he programmed the speed dials, then walked to Frank's vehicle. He handed one through the open driver's window. "Don't go anywhere without it."

Despite the build-up of traffic from early morning commuters, Scott managed to stay behind Frank's vehicle. Though he didn't expect trouble, his eyes continually shifted from the road to the rearview mirror. When Frank pulled into his driveway, a feeling of relief swept over him. As a field agent, working a protection detail had never come his way.

On the way home, his thoughts grappled with the complexities of the conundrum Frank had tossed him. Who warned the Chairman? Who planned to kill him, and why? Uppermost in his mind, how the hell was he expected to protect him?

While he showered and dressed, he discarded idea after idea. By the time he walked out the door, there was only one possibility.

CHAPTER
3

AFTER FLIPPING THE bank of light switches by the front door and deactivating the alarm system, Scott walked across the deserted reception area to his office. He laid the briefcase on his desk, opened it and pulled out the plastic bag. He unzipped it, then tilted the bag to let the letter slide out. With the end of a pen, he unfolded it. Bent over the desk, his hands braced on each side of the paper, he studied the typed words.

IMMINENT PLAN TO KILL YOU TRUST NO ONE INSIDE RESERVE

From the number of creases, it had been folded into a small square. It would easily fit inside a coat pocket. Not an impromptu drop, the messenger came prepared. He turned it over. Nothing.

After making multiple copies, he slid the message back in the bag. He'd have Adrian process it for prints but doubted they'd find any other than Frank's. He glanced at his watch, then hit the speed dial for his boss.

When Paul answered, he said, "Scott, an early call from you isn't good. What's going on?"

"I hate to spoil your day before it's even started. I need to talk to you. My office, not yours."

When Scott arranged for office space for his team, he'd selected a location away from the FBI building. His foresight had come in handy, as it kept the interest down on the team's activities.

"What's so urgent?"

"I'd rather wait on explanations until you get here."

"I'm getting ready to walk out the door. I'll stop there on my way into town."

After disconnecting, Scott headed to the breakroom to get the coffee started. One of his contributions to the new office was a large coffee machine with every gizmo imaginable. His agents would be arriving any time now. A team meeting was first on his agenda.

While he waited, he logged onto his computer, pulling up the website for the Federal Reserve. The chatter of voices broke his concentration. When he stepped out, his gaze skimmed the three agents clustered in the outer office. If the red-rimmed eyes were any indication, Adrian Dillard had another late night. As always, Blake Kenner looked as if he was ready for a military inspection.

A laugh rang out. "Coffee. Thank all the gods, I smell coffee." Nicki Allison's eyes twinkled with merriment as she added, "Morning, boss man." A cheeky smile lit up her face.

"Grab some coffee. Paul's on his way. Once I've talked to him, plan on a meeting in the conference room."

Their expressions turned serious. If Paul Daykin, the FBI Director, was headed their way, it meant trouble in capital letters.

The front door opened. Paul walked in. After greeting the agents, he followed Scott into his office. "I'd say good morning, but I doubt it's one. What's happened?"

As Scott sat, he said, "Frank Littleton received a death threat."

Paul stared at him for a moment before dropping into a chair. "Hell! You didn't just ruin my day, you destroyed it."

Scott handed him a copy of the letter.

As he quickly scanned it, a short huff was his only reaction.

He started with Frank's call, then detailed their meeting, ending by saying, "It's why I asked you to come here. I felt it was better if I wasn't seen walking into your office."

Paul voiced the same thought Scott had earlier. "What in god's name was the man thinking? He gets an assassination threat, decides to get in his car, *by himself*, then takes off to a damn diner in the middle of the night."

"As Frank put it when needs drive, sometimes you don't have a choice. While I didn't like it either, I've had time to consider his actions. I believe he took the only route open to him. If he's got rats in his organization, his term not mine, he doesn't want to alert them."

"I wonder if it occurred to him, someone might be watching his house?"

"Whether it did or not, my impression of Frank Littleton is he's an individual who carefully evaluates every situation and weighs the consequences of his actions before coming to a decision. If I had been in his shoes, I'd consider the meeting a minimal risk."

"I don't like the idea the Federal Reserve Chairman plans to play the role of a tethered goat," Paul told him. "That's what he's doing by hushing this up."

"Not the best of scenarios. But I agree with Frank. I don't want to alert whoever it is either."

"Damn, I've got to notify Vance, who will call the President. I doubt they'll like it any better than I do. Any idea why he's a target?"

"No."

With a deep sigh, Paul asked, "What do you need?"

"Key in Vance to his possible role as middleman. I don't want to be seen with Frank."

"Vance will love it." Paul chuckled. "Assuming, of course, he buys into your agenda. What's your plan?"

"Nothing yet, but I'll have a better idea after I meet with my team."

"You have a lot of faith in them." It wasn't a question.

A note of pride in his voice, he answered, "I do. Since I don't know how long it will take Frank to get me a list of his staff, I need the names on his protection detail. Nicki can get started with her dungeon sweeps."

Paul interjected, "Dungeon sweep? Should I even ask?"

A rumble of laughter erupted from Scott. "Probably not."

"There are several Special Agents in Charge across the country who'd gnaw off their right arm to get Nicki on their team."

Scott grunted. "Tell them, it's a waste of an arm. I do need clearance on another request. A couple of weeks back, I interviewed an agent. I planned on sending a copy of the transfer papers next week for your approval. I need her here as soon as possible."

"Agent Roth?"

"Yes."

"Why the rush?"

"Still working out the kinks on something. I'll let you know later."

"I'll contact Clint Jackson, the SAC for the New York office, and get her on a plane. We can catch up on the paperwork later. Clint's not happy over losing her. I had to listen to a litany of complaints on how your unit is scarfing up the best agents."

Scott couldn't disagree. He considered the agents in his unit were the elite of the elite.

"Anything else?" Paul asked.

"Not right now. Do you want to sit in on the meeting?"

As he stood, Paul smiled. "While I would enjoy it, I doubt your agents would. I'll call Vance. Might as well ruin his day too."

Paul stopped in the doorway, looked over his shoulder, then took one last shot. "You do realize, you probably bought yourself another trip to the White House." With a decidedly malicious smirk, he walked out.

He groaned at the thought as he grabbed his file folder and headed to the team meeting. On several occasions, he'd been summoned to the Oval Office. He'd never become comfortable with the rarefied atmosphere of power he felt each time.

In the conference room, a sense of *déjà vu* settled over him as he remembered his first meeting with his new team of agents. At the time, there were only four, Cat Morgan, Adrian Dillard, Ryan Barr, and Nicki Allison. Since then, Blake Kenner and Kevin Hunter, Cat's husband, joined the team. Another name, Savannah Roth, was about to be added to the roster.

This morning, only Nicki, Blake, and Adrian were present. The other three agents were in Ohio hunting down a serial killer responsible for twenty-eight murders. As he took his place at the front of the table, the conversation died. The agents waited with expectant expressions.

"What I'm about to tell you is classified. When I finish, you'll understand. At three this morning, I received a phone call from the Federal Reserve Chairman, Frank Littleton. He asked to meet with me."

Their gaze never wavered as he reiterated the discussion inside the diner. When he finished, he passed out a copy of the letter.

Adrian whistled as he scanned the document. "Looks like the Chairman has a guardian angel."

"Check it for prints." Scott slid the plastic bag with the letter toward him. "I've asked for his personnel list and itinerary. He said he has several local meetings plus a trip to Wyoming."

"What the hell is the Federal Reserve Chairman doing in Wyoming?" Blake asked. "Somehow, I can't picture him standing in the middle of a stream and fly fishing."

"It's a bank conference held there every year and attended by the who's who of the international banking community."

"I'll start the backgrounds on his personnel," Nicki said. "Many are probably listed on the Federal Reserve website. Once I get his list, I'll cross-reference the entries to be sure someone wasn't missed. Full dungeon sweeps, boss man?" Since she knew he didn't like her nickname, her lips twitched upward in a sassy grin.

Nicki's nicknames were a constant source of amusement to the team. One of the latest was the dungeon sweep, a background check that far exceeded the typical searches. She'd often joked if someone had been treated for a hangnail as a kid, she'd find it.

As usual, he ignored the provocation. "We need to go deep with this one. These people have already been vetted."

"I'll head over to the hotel," Blake said.

"Adrian, go with him. Get a copy of the footage from the security camera system. Everyone start researching the Federal Reserve and news articles. There's a reason why someone wants to take out the Chairman. Let's find it."

"We sure could use Ryan on this one," Blake said.

Since Ryan was the unit profiler with an uncanny ability to get into a criminal's thoughts, Scott said, "Can't disagree. But I can't pull him off the Ohio case. Which brings me to my next point. Another agent is joining the team. Her name is Savannah Roth, though she goes by Savvi. She's out of the New York office. Paul is contacting her boss to expedite the transfer."

"Hot damn!" Nicki exclaimed.

With a wry tone, Scott said, "I take it, you know her?"

"I do." Her eyes twinkled with an impish look.

"Care to explain?"

"We roomed together at the academy."

Adrian said, "I've heard of her. She headed the investigation in the takedown of a Ponzi scheme run by a banking group in New York City. Millions of dollars were involved. With her financial background, she'll be an asset."

"I suspect we're going to need all the help we can get with this one," Scott told them. His phone rang. As his agents filed out of the room, he hit the answer button.

Paul said, "Scott, I talked to Vance. As I expected, he doesn't like Frank's position. For the moment, he'll go along with it, but he told me, you damn well better come up with a solution to safeguard the man. You're on a short leash. If Vance decides to cut it, there's nothing I can do."

"I still believe it's the right approach, but I also understand the Secretary's concerns."

"On the positive side, Agent Roth is on her way to the airport. As soon as she lands, she's been told to report to your office. My admin reserved a room at the Marriott."

"Thanks for the foresight."

"The least I can do, considering you're sitting on a ticking time bomb."

CHAPTER

4

ADRIAN STOPPED IN the doorway to Blake's office. "Ready?"

Blake pushed back his chair and grabbed the cellphone on the desk. "You driving, or am I?"

"Flip for it," Adrian told him.

"Nah, I'll volunteer. The hotel's only a few blocks from here," he said, following Adrian out of the office.

As he backed out of the parking space, Blake asked, "Ever been to the Greystone?"

"The closest I've come is driving by the place," Adrian said. "You?"

Blake chuckled. "It's high dollar, way out of my league."

"Any ideas on this deal with Littleton?"

For several seconds Blake thought, before saying, "I think we've been handed a live grenade and the pin is missing."

"Damn good analogy," Adrian said.

Ahead, the Greystone Hotel, a historic landmark, came into view. The prestigious hotel had played host to the rich and famous for over fifty years. Blake parked in a spot marked reservations, waving off a valet as he exited.

Heels clicked on the marble floor as they strode toward the reception desk. Overhead, magnificent chandeliers sparkled in the light streaming through ceiling to floor windows overlooking a patio and garden. Massive marble columns crisscrossed the large room. Strategically placed sofas and armchairs, along with an assortment of tables, provided a sense of privacy or to accommodate larger groups. A curved staircase led to conference rooms on the second floor.

Dressed in black uniforms, the waitstaff mingled among the seated guests, filling glasses or cups. Behind an elegant, marble-topped counter, similarly attired desk clerks stood.

As they approached, Blake's gaze alternated between studying faces to scanning the ceiling for security cameras. An evenly modulated voice caught his attention. "May I help you?"

At the end of the counter, an older man eyed them with disdain.

Impeccably dressed in pressed jeans, boots, a plaid shirt, and a lightweight jacket, Adrian had taken advantage of Scott's elimination of the FBI dress code. Not comfortable with the casual style, Blake clung to the traditional Bureau standards. Still, their appearance didn't scream money, and the desk clerk knew it.

Edging close, Blake rested his elbow on the desk as he leaned forward. He hoped it wouldn't be necessary to identify himself. In a low voice, he said, "We'd like to speak with the General Manager."

With a soft sniff, the clerk looked at Adrian, then back at Blake. "I'm sorry. He's not available. If you would like to leave a message, I will give it to him."

With a look of irritation, Blake pulled out his badge case. Using his body to block the view of anyone nearby, he flipped it open. "Find him. Tell him we want to speak with him in private."

Eyes widened as the clerk studied the badge. He gulped, then said, "Please follow me."

He led the way along a hallway to a double set of doors. Opening one, he said, "Please wait here. I'll tell Mr. Porter."

Centered in the middle of the room, the conference table could comfortably seat twenty or more people. Another set of ceiling to floor windows overlooked the garden. Blake strolled over and pulled the cords to close the drapes.

Adrian plopped into a chair. "When you said this place was high dollar, you weren't kidding."

The door opened. A tall, distinguished-looking man, his silver hair brushed back from a broad brow entered. "Gentlemen, I'm Harold Porter, the General Manager. I understand you are FBI agents. Would you care for coffee or a soft drink?"

Blake stepped forward. "No thank you. I'm Agent Blake Kenner. This is Agent Adrian Dillard." He opened his badge case and held it up.

His open case in his hand, Adrian stood.

After a quick glance, Porter nodded, then motioned to the chairs. "Please, be seated." He stepped toward the windows.

Blake's voice stopped him. "We'd appreciate it if you would leave them closed."

The man turned. A worried expression settled over his face. "Why are you here?" He pulled out a chair and perched on the edge of the seat.

"We are investigating an incident involving your hotel yesterday," Blake told him. "I'm not at liberty to divulge specific details. It is vitally important you do not discuss our visit with anyone. It includes your desk clerk."

"All right. This incident, is there any danger to the guests or hotel?"

"No. If it changes, you will be notified immediately."

Satisfied, Porter relaxed in the chair. "What do you need?"

"What is the recording cycle for the security cameras?"

"One month, but we retain copies for six months."

"Then, we'd like copies of the tapes for the last thirty days along with a schematic of the locations of the cameras. Please don't destroy any tapes until further notice. Also, a copy of yesterday's reservation list for the dining rooms. Do you require official author-ization?"

"Since I'm acquainted with Paul Daykin, it won't be necessary. There is one problem. I've got to contact the administrator of our computer network to obtain a copy of the tapes. He'll want a rea-son. The rest of your requests I can download from my computer."

Adrian spoke up. "Tell him the police are looking for a pick-pocket who's been working hotel lobbies."

"It will take an hour or so to gather the material you've re-quested. Are you certain you wouldn't like refreshments?"

Blake shook his head. "No. We would, however, like to speak to the coatroom attendant."

A curious look crossed Porter's face, but he only nodded his head.

Porter led them to an area under the staircase. On the way, Adrian asked they be introduced as police officers. Over the door behind a counter, a discreet sign identified the cloakroom.

A young woman, in her middle twenties, looked up as they ap-proached. Her eyes immediately locked onto Porter. She straight-ened, throwing her shoulders back. "Mr. Porter! May I help you?"

From her demeanor, Blake suspected Mr. Porter seldom deemed it necessary to speak to the young woman.

"Ms. McCommas, these police officers would like to ask you a few questions."

Startled, her eyes darted to Adrian, then to Blake, who leaned against the end of the counter.

"Have I ... did I do something wrong?"

"No," her boss reassured her. "They are investigating a series of thefts at other hotels and asked to speak to you."

He nodded to the two men before walking away.

"Ms. McCommas, my name is Adrian Dillard. This is my part-ner, Blake Kenner. How long have you worked here?"

"A little over a year."

"Were you working yesterday?"

"Yes."

"When a guest walks into the hotel, what happens if they want to check their coat?"

"Uh, sometimes, the person walks over and hands it to me, or the bell captain will bring it over."

"Do you provide a receipt?"

Her eyes darted between Adrian and Blake. "Yes! Always!" Her voice rose with indignation. "Each hanger has a double set of small tags. I give one to the guest or the bell captain. Are you accusing me of stealing?" Her hands fluttered in the air.

"Not at all," Adrian said in an emphatic tone, hoping to calm her fears. "I am comparing the procedures at this hotel to the other hotels. Who has access to the cloakroom?"

"The bell captain, of course, housekeeping, the desk clerks, I guess that's it."

"Do you get breaks?"

"An hour for lunch and two fifteen-minute breaks."

"Does someone replace you?"

"Only for the lunch break. One of the desk clerks takes my place. For the short breaks, no. I have a small sign letting people know I'll be back in a few minutes."

"What time do you take your breaks?"

"The first break is midway through the first half of my shift, then lunch, and another break in the second half."

"As an example, how many coats did you check yesterday?"

She hesitated, then said, "I think … ten or eleven. This time of year, not everyone checks their coats. The evening shift does more business than I do."

"Did the guests bring their coats to you?"

"The bell captain brought two."

"Did you take a break after that?"

"Yes, it was the last break of my shift."

"One last question. Did you notice anything unusual or see someone loitering who looked out of place yesterday?"

She thought for a few seconds, then shook her head no.

After thanking her for her time, Blake and Adrian casually strolled around the hotel.

"That was some fast thinking with Porter," Blake commented. "How'd you come up with a pickpocket?"

"This hotel reminded me of an incident in another investigation. It seemed like a good ploy to use. I had more questions but didn't want to draw attention to Frank and his coat. If we don't find what we're looking for on the tape, we may have to have a second go at her."

While their meanderings appeared pointless, by the time they returned to the main lobby, they knew the hotel's layout and had spotted many of the cameras.

Porter approached with an envelope in his hand. He handed it to Blake. "If I can be of further service, please let me know."

Blake said, "We appreciate your cooperation," and gave him a business card.

On their way out the door, Adrian said, "It's going to be damn interesting to see what's on the tapes."

CHAPTER
5

TICKING TIME BOMB, my ass, as if he didn't already know. Scott slid the phone into his pocket, picked up the file folder lying on the conference room table, and headed to the breakroom.

At the sight of the dark look on Scott's face, Nicki paused in the doorway. On the high-side of thirty, at six-foot, he was solidly built with an impressive breadth of shoulders. A small scar split an eyebrow, another curved over his cheekbone, adding a raffish look to his angular, rough-hewn face. A watchful intelligence gleamed in his dark, hooded eyes. At times, with a disturbing intensity that seemed to pierce her very thoughts.

"Why the grim look, boss man?" Nicki asked.

As the steamy brew flowed, he said. "I've just been informed I'm sitting on a ticking time bomb."

"Not surprising. This is a high-risk deal. The Chairman sent you his itinerary. You also have an email from Director Daykin with the names of the security detail. I dropped copies on your desk. Any ideas yet?"

"Hmm … that's the problem. I don't. Start the backgrounds on the protection detail." He took a swallow of coffee while he watched her refill her cup. "I'm curious. How'd it go, rooming with Savvi at the academy?"

A roguish laugh erupted. "The woman is a walking, talking

human calculator. I could tell you some stories …" When she spotted a gleam of avid interest, she stopped. "Then again, maybe not. Sometimes, it's better when the boss man doesn't know every detail."

"Humph," he grunted.

"Savvi is one tough lady. The guys soon learned not to mess with her. By the way, never play poker with her. She'll strip you of every cent you have."

He laughed. "I'll keep it in mind." With his file folder in one hand, the cup in the other, he said, "Be in my office."

Scott glanced over the names on the protection detail, then studied the Chairman's schedule before propping his feet on the desk. His fingers idly picked up a pen—tap, tap, tap. A long-time habit that helped him think but drove his agents crazy. Once, he'd overheard Adrian threaten to take away all his pens. At the memory, his lips curved in a smile.

Then, his thoughts slid into the question that had plagued him from the start, how to safeguard the Chairman. Since it was impossible to protect him from the outside, Scott had to go inside. His only option, one he'd considered since leaving the diner, had slowly jelled in his mind.

With a thud, his feet hit the floor, and his hand reached for the phone. When his boss answered, Scott said, "I've got a solution."

"Let's hear it."

"Assign Roth to the Federal Reserve on some pretext. With the restrictions Frank's laid on us, we need an agent on the inside. There's the added advantage of her financial background. Finding a motive is crucial."

"Makes sense, though there is a problem—jurisdiction. The U.S. Federal Reserve Police agency won't be amenable to our dropping an agent in their playground. Plus, there's already going to be hell to pay when they find out we cut them out of the loop on this."

"It's why we need another reason for her presence. There must be a way we can use her financial background."

"I still don't believe Captain Hayes, the head of Littleton's security team, will buy into it."

Scott paused, then said, "I have an idea. I'll call you back."

Disconnecting, he picked up the burner phone from his desk. The Chairman answered on the second ring.

"Littleton."

"Are you in a position to talk?" Scott asked.

"Yes."

"I want to assign one of my agents to your office, but in a way, it won't arouse suspicion. It's doubtful Captain Hayes will be receptive to an FBI agent joining his team. The agent is Savannah Roth, who is currently assigned to the New York office."

"Roth ... Roth. Of course! The Shelby Financial case."

"She was the lead investigator."

Frank said, "From what I heard, she set off a few ripples in the financial circles."

"We need a pretext to get her on your staff. Agent Roth will be your personal bodyguard, though you're the only one to know it. I need a reason along with a nudge from you."

"I'll call Paul to make an official request. As you are probably aware, the Federal Reserve is about to launch a gold-backed currency system. There's been considerable dissension over the new currency. A simple explanation that I'd like a temporary liaison from the FBI to assist in the implementation should suffice. When will she arrive?"

"She's flying in today. She can be at your office in the morning."

"I have another suggestion. Vance and I are meeting for lunch tomorrow. I assume he knows."

"Paul briefed him."

"Good. I'll ask Paul to join us and bring Agent Roth with him. Where is she staying?"

"Paul booked her into a hotel near the Tracker office."

"Cancel it. She can stay at my home. We've got plenty of room. I'll drop a vague comment here and there that my wife, Amelia, is friends with her family."

"Does your wife know about the threat?"

A wry laugh sounded. "Scott, after thirty-seven years of marriage, there aren't any secrets. She'll be fine with it. We'll work out the details after I've met Agent Roth."

"This certainly exceeds my expectations."

"I'm fully aware of the untenable position I've put you in. Assigning an agent is a smart move. I'll do whatever is necessary to accommodate your requests. I also have a somewhat underhanded reason. Vance and I go back a long way. With witnesses tomorrow, I won't have to endure his pithy remarks over what I'm doing."

"Then, one more word of caution."

"Yes?"

"I've been informed by a very reliable source, don't play cards with her."

Laughing, Frank disconnected the call.

Not much astounded him these days, but the ease with which the Chairman solved a very tricky situation was slightly unnerving.

The next call was to give Paul a heads-up. When he answered, Scott said, "Problem solved. You'll get a call from Frank requesting Savvi be assigned to his staff. It takes Hayes out of the picture. She's staying at his house."

"Son-of-a-gun! How the hell did you pull it off?"

"I can't take the credit. Frank's idea, not mine. He's also going to ask you and Savvi to attend a lunch with him and the Secretary tomorrow."

With a dry tone, Paul said, "Anything else I should know?"

"No, other than he's going to put out the word about being friends with Savvi's parents."

"Have her at my office in the morning. I'll call Vance to clue him in on tomorrow's agenda."

Scott told him, "With Savvi in place, he may not need to play middleman."

After a wry chuckle, Paul said, "Good try, Scott. I doubt very much you're going to get him out of the picture. I'll contact Clint to let him know Frank just nabbed your latest agent."

"Since I want to keep a low profile on this one, it will help."

"Knowing Clint, he'll spread the word you didn't get her. You're in for some good-natured gloating, might even throw a party to celebrate your loss."

Yeah, but I'll have the last laugh, he thought as he disconnected. His team was extraordinary. He was probably the only person who knew just how special they were. As a kid, he'd always excelled in games requiring an analysis of each move. The first time he'd picked up a Rubik's cube, he'd solved the enigma of the colored blocks in minutes. He soon learned he could apply his uncanny talents to unravel the twists and turns of criminal behavior. What he always referred to as connecting the dots in an investigation had led to many arrests. It was the reason he was tagged to head the Tracker Unit.

Scott had applied those same methods to the initial selection process for his new team. He'd spent months evaluating agent profiles, their case closure rate, and conducting interviews. In a select few, he'd found anomalies in their investigations, unexplained gaps that hinted of unidentified abilities.

Savannah Roth was another find. From a stack of files, he selected one, leaned his chair back, then propped his feet on the corner of the desk. Flipping the folder open, he stared at the picture stapled to the inside. Bureau personnel photos were never flattering. The image failed to portray the vibrant fervor in her demeanor.

He'd flown to New York for the interview where he met Savvi along with her boss, Clint Jackson. When she greeted him, he'd felt an unnerving probe of a razor-sharp gleam, a look that assessed, then judged. As she shook his hand, she smiled. Her eyes warmed, the strange glimmer gone. If he hadn't felt the prickle along his neck, he would have believed he imagined it.

After the introduction, Clint left. While Scott had several questions, Savvi had more. Her profile failed to convey the force of her acuity as she zeroed in on the Tracker Unit. Once she was satisfied with his answers, she eagerly accepted the new position.

The aroma of pepperoni enticing his taste buds broke his concentration. Someone had remembered they needed to eat.

Blake stepped into the doorway. "We picked up several pizzas on our way back. We've got the tapes."

He scrambled out of the chair, dropping the folder on his desk. Inside the conference room, boxes littered the table. Adrian sat at a small desk, fiddling with a computer, then glancing at the large wall-mounted monitor. It was a twin to the one in Nicki's office.

When the unit moved into the new office, Scott had a wall removed to create one large room for Nicki's computers. She'd been given carte blanche on her equipment, a decision he'd never regretted. The wall monitor covering half of one wall was her latest toy. With one tap on her keyboard, she could change the picture from a single screen to a split-screen, one for each of her systems. The use of the monitor quickly became a source of contention as the other agents wanted to use it, leaving Nicki to grumble like a mama bear protecting her cub. While he suspected they were just pushing her buttons, he had requisitioned a second one.

Blake pointed toward the screen as images flashed by. "The tapes from the hotel security camera system."

Adrian picked up the remote and stopped the feed. "While we eat, we'll bring you up to date on what we discovered."

Paper plates were soon filled with hot slices of pizza. In between bites, Blake talked about their visit, with an occasional comment from Adrian.

Intrigued, Scott said, "Pickpocket?"

"I'd never have thought of it. It was Adrian's idea. It worked."

Once Blake finished his report, Scott said, "There's been a change in plans with Savvi." He explained her new role in the investigation.

Nicki said, "Dang, boss man, it's brilliant! Knowing Savvi, she'll be the bird dog that won't stop."

Waving a pizza slice that sent cheese sliding to the edge, Adrian asked, "Just how well do you know her?"

Nicki chewed, washed it down with a swig of Coke, then said, "Pretty damn well. I'll tell you ..."

A melodious voice tinged with amusement said, "Just what do you plan on telling them?"

A squeal erupted. Nicki shoved back her chair. "Savvi, my god, it's so good to see you."

With a look of keen interest, Scott watched the reunion as the two hugged. When he met Savvi in New York, she was dressed in the typical anonymous Bureau attire, her hair neatly coiled into a knot on her neck.

Now, dressed in stiletto heels, skin-tight jeans, and shirt, the mass of reddish-blond curls tumbled down her back. Her statuesque figure towered over Nicki's petite build.

They were as different as day and night until they turned toward Scott. A similar look of alertness gleamed in their eyes that conveyed a powerful perceptiveness.

CHAPTER 6

SCOTT STOOD AS Savvi stepped toward him, her hand extended. "Nice to see you again, Agent Fleming. I hope I haven't interrupted. Since there wasn't anyone in the main office, I followed the sound of voices."

"Not at all. It's Scott. Welcome to the group." After introducing Adrian and Blake, he motioned toward the table. "Help yourself. We've got plenty."

With a curious glance toward the image of a hotel lobby on the large screen, she said, "I grabbed a bite at the airport while I waited for my flight."

"Then, let's go to my office."

As he stood, Scott glanced at Blake. "Go ahead with the tapes. If you find anything, let me know."

In his office, Scott motioned toward a chair, then propped a hip on the corner of the desk. "You must be wondering why you were hustled onto a plane."

Savvi settled in a chair. "It *was* a surprise when Clint called, told me to pack a bag, and head to the airport." A hand waved across her body. "He didn't leave me much time. I apologize for the informal attire, but I'd taken a couple of vacation days."

Scott brushed-off her concern. "If you haven't already noticed, this unit doesn't conform to the Bureau's dress code. In fact, I eliminated it." He opened a folder lying next to him and slid out a copy of the note.

"What I'm about to tell you is classified. You can't discuss it with Clint or any of your fellow agents in New York."

Though she eyed the paper in his hand with a sharp look of interest, in a calm tone, she said, "Duly noted."

Just as he did with his team, he detailed his meeting with Frank Littleton. Though she didn't comment, her attentive gaze intensified.

He handed her the message. "This is a copy of the note left in the Chairman's coat."

She studied it for a few seconds, then passed it back. "The image on the monitor, the hotel lobby. Find the messenger, and you have a shot at locating the assassin."

Not surprised by the quick assessment, he nodded in agreement.

"In the meantime, how do you protect the Chairman when you can't inform his security team?"

"You're about to become his personal bodyguard."

Stunned, Savvi stared at Scott, then leaned forward. "*I'm* going to protect the Chairman of the Federal Reserve?"

"Yep. The only way to protect him is to put an agent inside his organization. You're the logical choice. Chairman Littleton has already agreed and is looking forward to meeting you. He's familiar with your last case."

In disbelief, she asked, "Ah ... um, how is it going to work? If I'm his bodyguard, what about his security detail? They'll have to know."

"Not really. We've worked out a cover story. While you'll still report to me, Paul Daykin is transferring you to his staff. You'll be on temporary assignment, loaned out might be a better phrase, to the Federal Reserve. With your financial background, you're there as a liaison for the implementation of the new currency system. Only a select few, including my team, will know the real reason."

He waited for her to absorb the details before he hit her with the next salvo. "You're going to stay at his house."

This time, shock overrode her calm self-control. Disbelief battled against a growing look of excitement. The "Oh, my, god," she softly whispered, didn't escape his notice.

He stood, then walked around his desk. "Tomorrow, you'll be attending a luncheon with Secretary Whitaker, Director Daykin, and the Chairman. It's a public setting to start the process. I've got a car for you. It's in the parking lot."

He reached into a drawer, picked up a set of keys, and slid them across the desk. When he spotted her tightly clasped hands, his lips thinned to stop a grin.

"Uh." She cleared her voice. "What do I tell people? How do I explain staying at his house? What about his wife and family?"

"From what I understand, his wife, Amelia, is wholly in the know. When you get there, I'm sure you can work out a story. Old family friends or something. It'll add plausibility to why the Chairman asked for you. One other point. Besides protecting the Chairman, we've got to find a motive. Talk to his staff. Listen for disgruntled comments. Study their work habits, assignments, etc. We need to learn everything we can about the personnel."

"How do I communicate with you?"

"Through Nicki. Let's head back to the conference room. I want the team involved in the rest of this discussion."

"You mentioned your agents." She stood, picking up the keys. "How much do they know?"

"Everything," Scott replied. "You'll soon find out, I run a different type of ship. Besides, the Trackers have unusual abilities, which makes it difficult to conceal secrets. A trait I look for in new agents."

He stared into her deep blue eyes. The odd look of intensity sparked for an instant. *You didn't expect I'd know,* he thought as she turned to walk out the door.

Excited chatter filtered into the hallway as they approached the conference room. Inside, the agents clustered in front of the monitor. At the sound of footsteps, they turned.

Blake said, "We've found the person who left the note."

While the agents took their seats, Scott walked to the monitor for a closer look. The camera angle had captured the front of the coat check counter. On top, a small sign indicated the attendant would return in a few minutes. A person attired in pants and hooded jacket stood at the end. The hood had been pulled up, blocking a view of the face.

Blake said, "This is after the bell captain gave the attendant two coats. The attendant was on her break."

A click sounded. Blake slowly advanced the film. The person walked into the coatroom, then a few minutes later emerged, sidled around the corner of the counter, and walked out of view. A hand pressed the hood against the face.

Scott said, "Whoever it is, knows where the cameras are located."

"It's the same conclusion we came too. We also think it's either a woman or possibly a boy," Adrian added.

"Back it up," Scott told Blake. When the figure came into view again, he said, "Stop. Enhance it." Blake enlarged the frame.

"A woman," Scott said. "The tennis shoes aren't what a boy would wear, and she's wearing gloves." He turned to face the table. "Did you find her anywhere else in the hotel?"

"Not yet, but we haven't finished reviewing all the footage," Adrian answered.

"How far back do the tapes go?"

Blake said, "A month. I told the general manager not to destroy any tapes in case we needed to request earlier dates."

"Keep looking. How did the woman know the location of the cameras or the attendant would be gone? Here's another point, how did she know which coat? Find out if the answers are on those tapes."

"Boss man, another batch of documents arrived from Chairman Littleton. Personnel list and an updated copy of his itinerary." As she passed a copy to everyone, she added, "Note the addition to the Chairman's calendar."

Scott dropped into a chair, flipping through the pages until he reached the Chairman's schedule. A meeting with Secretary Whitaker, FBI Director Daykin, and Agent Roth at the BroadBank Club had been added.

Nicki slapped Savvi on the back. "Dang, lady, 'you're moving on up' as the old song goes."

In a dry tone, Scott said, "Nicki, before you get carried away, you may be on the same ladder. After today, I don't want Savvi to have any contact with our office. You are our go-between. The two of you getting together will be perfectly normal. Anyone looking for a connection will find you were in the same class in the academy."

He picked up his pen—tap, tap, tap. Scott pondered the Chairman's schedule lying in front of him. Local meetings, Wyoming—tap, tap, tap.

At hearing a faint groan, he looked up. With an air of innocence, Adrian stared at the ceiling. Scott bit back a grin. "If you are going to assassinate the chairman, how would you do it?" he asked.

Blake laid the remote on the table. "Two ways, an explosive device or shoot him. Of the two, I'd lean toward a rifle."

Adrian said, "I'd agree. A bomb means getting in close, and he has protection. A sniper can reach out, take the shot, then easily disappear. The place I'd pick would be Wyoming."

"I agree," Scott said.

"The Wyoming trip has red flags all over it," Blake mused. "But I don't believe we can negate an attempt closer to home. We need to find out where he is vulnerable. How extensive is his protection outside of home and office?"

Savvi looked up from the documents she'd been studying. "Since I'll be with him, I'll find out."

Adrian asked, "Is his schedule public information?"

Scott answered, "No. But the meeting in Wyoming is common knowledge. It happens every year. Blake, plan on heading to Wyoming. Savvi will be with the Chairman. I want you in place to back her up."

"When do you want me to leave?"

Scott looked at the itinerary. "At least a day ahead of the Chairman. It could change depending on how this goes down. In the meantime, dig into the background on the symposium. Adrian, reach out to some of your contacts in the financial crimes unit. See if any rumors are floating. Whatever you find, coordinate with Nicki. Give her ammunition for her fancy new program. Do we have a name yet?"

He'd created TRACE to identify peripatetic serial killers who moved around the country, their victims never linked to a common killer. The result was they flew under law enforcement's radar. Once police departments were connected to the TRACE system, details of unsolved homicides for the agency were loaded to the program. Nicki had been brought on board to take over the implementation. In typical Nicki fashion, she added improvements, extending the program's search algorithms beyond anything he'd imagined. She was also an avid gamester with a penchant for assigning gaming descriptions. The team had a betting pool on when she'd change the name.

"Not yet, boss man." A snarky smile lit up her face.

He suppressed a groan. What the hell was she up to now? Before he could ask, his phone rang. It was his boss. Instead, he said, "Let's get to work," then answered the call as he walked out.

"Scott," Paul said. "Everything's set for tomorrow. Your leash isn't quite as short as it was earlier. Vance was quick to point out he'd be keeping a close eye on the situation. You're still sitting on a ticking time bomb."

CHAPTER
7

AFTER SCOTT LEFT, Blake looked around the table. "Ready to get started?"

Adrian said, "Go back to the beginning. This time in slow motion."

Blake tapped the remote to restart the tape. Images of people strolling around the first floor or seated in chairs rolled across the screen.

"Stop." Adrian hopped up. "Back up a couple of seconds. There." He stepped to the corner of the screen and pointed. "In the corner by the column. I caught just a glimpse."

Blake reran the tape, slowed it down even further as they studied each person's movement. For an instant, a figure partially hidden by a column near the front doors moved out of sight. Isolating the single image, Blake froze it. The face was turned away, but the clothing matched the person at the coat check counter.

Savvi said, "Five-six, a hundred and twenty-pounds give or take a pound or two."

Astonished, Adrian and Blake stared at her. Knowing what was coming, Nicki just grinned.

"How'd you come up with that?" Blake asked.

"Umm ... an estimation based on a comparative analysis of her body to the size of the column and coat check counter."

Laughing, Blake said, "You won't get an argument out of me."

"By the time stamp, it's more than two hours before she left the note," Adrian noted.

"If we go by when the bell captain handed the coats to the attendant, she was already in the hotel." Blake picked up the documents from the packet Porter gave him. "According to the list of reservations, the Lindell Room was reserved from 1 p.m. to 4 p.m. It's a standing reservation and the only one matching Chairman Littleton's description."

Adrian said, "It answers one question, how she knew which coat."

"Check the other camera feeds. Maybe one picked her up in the parking lot or another section of the hotel."

After the third run-through, they admitted defeat. Nothing. It was as if the woman was a ghost moving through the hotel.

"I'll get Scott," Adrian said. A few minutes later, Scott followed him into the room.

Blake cued the tape to the woman behind the column. "Savvi estimates her weight around one-twenty, height five-six."

With a questioning look, Scott glanced at Savvi. A glint of mischievous humor glinted in her eyes, oddly reminiscent of Nicki.

"Column and counter?" he asked.

She nodded, yes.

Scott asked, "Find her anywhere else?"

"No, this is it," Blake answered. "It's more than two hours before she was at the coatroom. From the paperwork we got from the hotel, it appears the Chairman's meeting ran from one to four, which means she was in the hotel when he arrived."

Leaned against the wall, Scott thought for a second. "Nicki, if you had access to the hotel's computer, could you find out if someone hacked into the system to get a layout of the cameras?"

Her look of astonishment changed to one of annoyance.

Scott waved a hand in the air. "Okay, okay. Scratch the question. In the morning, you and Blake head over to the hotel. I'll call the general manager so there won't be a problem giving you access to their system. Pick up the tapes for the last two months."

He glanced at his watch. "Go home. We've done all we can today. Savvi, do you need directions to your hotel?"

"Thanks, but I canceled the reservation. I'm bunking with Nicki tonight."

"In the morning, head to Paul Daykin's office." He picked up a paper from the table and scribbled a number on it. Handing it to Savvi, he said, "Don't call this office. I don't want any outgoing calls on your phone. If it's an emergency, this number will reach me day or night. Otherwise, to contact me, call Nicki on her cell phone."

Savvi scanned the number, then handed it back. "Got it."

Scott stared at her, wondering how many people knew Savvi Roth had a photographic memory, along with an incredible mental ability to perform complex calculations. After reviewing her case files, it was the only explanation for the unusual results she'd achieved. Though he had to admit, she'd cleverly disguised how she came up with the information. Estimating the size of the woman was probably child's play to her.

The agents trooped toward the front office, where Adrian grabbed a sizeable rolling suitcase from the stack piled near the door. Blake got another. Savvi took the two smaller cases.

Scott headed to his office to get his briefcase. A phrase Frank used kept popping into his mind—dissension in the ranks. What had he meant? Scott dropped into his chair, pulled the keyboard towards him, and typed. Immersed in banking articles, he forgot he planned to go home.

★★★

Outside, Blake asked, "Nicki, where are you parked?"

Savvi interrupted, "Scott gave me a set of keys, said the car was in the parking lot."

"Okay, we'll find it."

Once they were inside the garage, Savvi hit a button on the key. Halfway down an aisle, lights flashed.

As they headed toward it, Adrian asked, "Well, what do you think of the unit?"

"At the moment, I'm a bit overwhelmed. Give me a day or so to get my head wrapped around this, then I'll let you know."

Adrian chuckled. "Fair enough. Trunk or backseat?"

After the men left, Nicki went to get her car. Savvi relaxed for the first time since walking into the Tracker office. *My god, what a day*, she thought. When she'd received the phone call from Clint, there was nothing to forewarn her. Of course, as she soon realized, he didn't know.

Nicki tooted the horn as she drove past. Delighted to be spending the night with her friend instead of in a hotel room, Savvi pulled behind her. About a mile away, Nicki drove into another garage and parked near the elevator. Savvi pulled into a nearby space. When Nicki hopped out of her car and dashed toward her, she was reminded that Nicki operated in one gear, high speed.

Exuberant, she exclaimed, "I'm so glad you get to stay at least one night. I didn't know you were coming until Scott announced it in the meeting today." She opened the rear door. "I'll grab the big ones."

"Slow down, girl. I only need the carry-on. It has everything I need." She reached across the front seat, grabbing her tote bag.

"Can you believe where you'll be working? My god, the Federal Reserve. Considering you'd originally planned on a banking career instead of one in law enforcement, this must seem really weird."

In the elevator, Nicki pushed the second-floor button.

"I'm not certain weird adequately describes the sensation. I wasn't kidding when I told Adrian I needed time to let it sink in."

When the doors slid open, Nicki led the way to the end of the hall. "Hold onto this while I find my keys," she told Savvi, handing her the carry-on. Digging through her bag, she pulled out a set and unlocked the door.

Savvi stepped into a room, bursting with color. It was so Nicki. A large rug with multi-colored squares, circles, rectangles, and triangles covered the center of the hardwood living room floor. Colorful geometric shapes adorned pillows scattered across a dark blue sofa and two burnt orange, easy chairs. Vivid abstract art hung on the walls.

In the middle of the coffee table, the inevitable computer. Nicki was never far from one. Even in the academy, she'd lugged two in her backpack.

"Let me have the bag. I've got two bedrooms, so you're not stuck with the couch," Nicki said, before striding toward the hallway.

Slowly, Savvi strolled around the room, studying the artwork hanging on the walls.

Behind her, Nicki said, "Those are by a local artist. He recently had a showing at a gallery in Georgetown. I couldn't resist. You ready for a glass of wine with some girl talk?"

"Oh, god, it's the best offer I've had today." Savvi sank into a chair, then toed off her shoes. Fingers massaged her feet while she moaned in relief.

Nicki handed her a glass, then settled onto the couch.

"Umm … this is good." With a sigh, Savvi leaned back. "I didn't get a chance to comment earlier, but it's one humdinger of an office you've got. How the devil did you wrangle all the equipment? In my office in New York, we have to beg, borrow, or steal, just to get a decent desk."

With her feet tucked under her, Nicki curled in the corner of the couch. "Sometimes, when I look at it, I'm afraid I'll wake up and discover it's all a dream." She took a sip. "Before we moved in, Scott had a wall removed to make one office out of two. Then told me to give him a list of whatever I wanted." With a wicked grin, she said, "Boy, did I take advantage."

"Your reputation in the Bureau is growing by leaps and bounds. I've heard about some of the cases you referred to other divisions after your fancy software program identified serial killers active in their area."

"I didn't design the original program. Scott did. Don't underestimate him, Savvi. Before I accepted his offer to join the Trackers, I did some checking. He's a genius, IQ's 164. He created TRACE to track serial killers. To get the program up and running was my first assignment with the unit." She took another sip.

"Wow, I wasn't aware of Scott's computer expertise."

"The man's good, damn good."

"High praise, indeed, coming from you."

Another smirk crossed her face. "Of course, I've fiddled with the software, enhancing the algorithms used to search the internet. The program can come up with details that standard backgrounds miss."

"The last time we talked, you raved about the Trackers. Odd, I never expected to end up here, with both of us on the same team."

"You'll find out this unit is different, more so than you can imagine."

"Okay, enough on work, tell me what's going on in your love life," Savvi said.

"Hah, what love life. I am beginning to think I'll become the proverbial bridesmaid, never the bride, since I've been in two weddings in the last several months."

"What happened to the guy who worked for Dallas PD?"

"Ah, Lieutenant Ted Phillips. We still talk, say we ought to set up a meet, but it never happens. Maybe one day, who knows. How about you? Leaving anyone behind in the Big Apple?"

"Had a good fling a few months back, but then the Ponzi case came along with long hours and weekends. He decided he didn't like to compete with my job. It was probably a wise move."

"Do you want a refill?"

"Nope. Time to call it a night. I have a feeling tomorrow's going to be a long day."

Nicki uncurled from the couch, then picked up the glasses. "Anything you need?"

"No, I'm good. Thanks for letting me stay here tonight."

In the bedroom, as Savvi prepared to go to bed, her thoughts drifted over the events of the day. After slipping an oversize t-shirt over her head, she curled under the covers. The one question burning in her mind after reading the note left in the Chairman's coat was why. Assassinations were driven by money, revenge, or a political statement. Which one was the motive?

★★★

A sound, the repetitive tap of a pen, echoed in the deserted office. Feet propped atop his desk, Scott's head rested against the back of his chair. Eyes closed, his thoughts circled around what he knew and didn't know. After reading a multitude of articles, he hadn't found anything more than the typical rhetoric which surrounded high-ranking government officials. No matter which side of the fence one was on, there was always someone else on the other side who complained.

Where was the pattern in the random bits and pieces of information, the dots in any investigation? Finding it wasn't any different than solving the Rubik's cube. The initial step was to set the first layer, then move the other layers or pieces into place.

One word, voiced by the Chairman, repeatedly played in his mind. Dissension. Might it be the first layer?

CHAPTER
8

BLAKE ARRIVED EARLY and walked into a brightly lit office. So much for wondering if he'd get there first. It didn't happen often. Though this time, he didn't expect to find Nicki asleep on the couch, not with Savvi in her apartment. The last time it happened, Scott threatened to toss it out the door. She flipped him one of her cheeky grins, a "yes, boss man," comment, before strolling out of the breakroom.

As he headed to his office, Nicki's voice stopped him. She leaned out of the doorway. "Got a minute?"

"Sure. What's up?" he asked.

"I found our mystery woman in the parking lot."

Pulling a chair alongside Nicki, he watched as she manipulated the images on the wall monitor. A hazy picture of the parking lot scrolled across the screen. Nicki stopped the tape and moved her pointer to a corner where a figure stood between cars. "I merged the feed from different camera angles. This is what I found."

She tapped again. Another tape started. The figure slipped along the row of cars before stepping onto the sidewalk. Then she sprinted and disappeared.

"She didn't come in a car," Blake said.

"Uh, huh. Smart move. A car is a lot harder to hide from cameras."

"She must have one parked nearby."

"It's what I'm thinking. I'm running a search for camera systems in the immediate vicinity. It's a longshot."

"Good idea. Are you ready?"

"Let me refill my coffee mug, and I'm good to go."

★★★

"Wow, this is some impressive place." Nicki's wide-eyed gaze scanned the hotel lobby. "Way above my paygrade."

Blake led the way to the hotel's administrative offices. Inside, he introduced himself and Nicki to the young woman seated behind a reception desk.

"Oh, yes. Mr. Porter is expecting you. May I get you coffee or something from our kitchen?"

Blake glanced at Nicki, who shook her head. "No thank you."

"I see you've brought different reinforcements this time."

Blake turned to greet the man standing behind him.

After meeting Nicki, Porter said, "John Adamson is head of the hotel's IT department. He's expecting you."

As they walked along the hallway, Blake asked, "What did you tell him?"

"I hired a security company to examine our security and recommend any improvements."

In an office further down the hallway, Nicki gazed with interest at multiple camera screens monitored by a security guard.

From behind another desk, a man stepped forward. Porter said, "John, this is Blake Kenner and Nicole Allison."

"Nice to meet you both. Which one of you is going to look at our system?"

With a wave of her hand, Nicki said, "Me."

"I have a computer in our communications room you can use." With a set of keys pulled from his pocket, he unlocked a door, then swung it open. Nicki followed him inside.

Blake stopped in the doorway where he eyed double bays of

communication and computer equipment, a couple of desks, and monitors. Once he realized the conversation between Nicki and John had evolved into technical details way over his head, he said, "Nicki, I'll be in the lobby once you're finished."

Engrossed in her conversation about firewalls, she waggled her fingers in the air.

Porter chuckled as they left the office. "I feel the same way when John explains why he needs a new program or gadget."

"Be prepared then. Nicki's the best in the Bureau. By the time she finishes, you may be hit with a list of costly expenditures."

"An upgrade might be in order. I'm sure her suggestions will be quite helpful. If you'd like to wait in the dining room, please feel free to order anything on the menu, compliments of the hotel."

"I appreciate the offer, but I'd like to use the time to study the hotel layout in more detail than I did yesterday."

Blake meandered around the ground floor, then took the stairs to the second floor. From inside conference rooms, voices sounded as he passed. Unable to account for his odd sense of restlessness, he ambled down the stairs and headed to the front doors. Uncertain what he was looking for, he strode toward the parking lot where Nicki found the woman.

At one point, he stopped, slowly turning as he examined the position of the parking lot lights and trees bordering the street. Satisfied he'd found the right spot, he followed the woman's path onto the sidewalk, turning to look in the direction she ran. While stately homes surrounded the hotel, not far away were apartments and a shopping center. That was where the woman had headed.

★★★

Not finding Blake inside, Nicki walked out the front door. Across the parking lot, she spotted him standing on the sidewalk. As she drew near, for a moment, she paused to study him. Stocky of build, he carried himself with a military air, a holdover from his army days. Short hair, clean-shaven, with a spit and shine style, he hadn't taken advantage of Scott's elimination of the Bureau's dress code. Blake still clung to tailored suits with pants hemmed to fall at a precise line on his high-gloss wingtip shoes.

Of all the Tracker agents, he was the most remote. It wasn't that Blake was standoffish, quite the contrary. He'd usually be found in the middle of whatever was happening. It was the weary look in his eyes at times, as if an unbearable sadness weighed on him.

"Blake," she cried out.

He turned, the slow, easy smile crossing his face. "You didn't take as long as I expected."

"The system isn't complicated. It was hacked. Easy to find the breach. I made a few recommendations on ways to improve their security."

A roar of laughter erupted.

"What's so funny?" she exclaimed.

"I warned Porter to be prepared to spend money. Did you get the tapes?"

She shot him a look of disdain. "Of course, I did, though I expect we won't need them."

✯✯✯

Voices echoed in the outer room. Nicki and Blake were back. Nicki rushed through Scott's doorway, a look of elation on her face. Fingers drum rolled the air, a favorite mannerism when she had a piece of news to convey.

Blake stopped behind her, leaned against the doorjamb with crossed arms and a wide grin.

"System was hacked." Then her eyes narrowed as she looked at Scott with a soulful expression. "You thought I couldn't do it."

"Nicki, you know I took it back, so cut out the theatrics."

In a flash, the look was gone, replaced by a mischievous grin. "Just so it doesn't happen again." After plopping into a chair, she said, "They've got an okay system. It needs to be updated. Access to the mainframe is in a small locked office. A guard monitors the cameras in an outer room, but it's not twenty-four seven. The breach was through an inventory program used to order everything from soap to milk. Once the hacker was into the system, it only took a few seconds to download the schematics. The department heads have access to the inventory program."

"Then someone got to one of the supervisor's computers," Scott said.

"It's what I figure. The administrative offices are locked at night. But getting past one of the locks would be child's play."

"What about the tapes?"

"Got the last two months, but I don't think they will be any help. The breach happened the night before the note was left in Littleton's coat."

He looked at Blake, who was still propped in the doorway with Adrian behind him. "Damn. Well, take a look at them anyway."

"I'll get started," Blake told him.

Adrian spoke up. "I'll help. I'll get the tapes set up in the conference room. Blake, there's a package on your desk. It was delivered this morning."

Blake headed to his office. Atop his desk was a small, padded envelope. Stuck to the front was a mailing label with his name and address. Odd, there was no return address.

Using a letter opener, he slit it open. Inside was a flash drive. A tingling tightened his gut. Upending the envelope, it slid onto his desk. He flipped it over with a pen, but it was an ordinary style, a type available in most office supply stores. He double-checked the inside of the envelope. Nothing.

Though he didn't believe they'd find a fingerprint on it, he couldn't risk it. Blake carefully inserted it into his computer. A click on the keyboard, and it opened. It contained two folders. He opened the first. A page appeared with a few short sentences. At first, the text looked like gibberish, a foreign language. Recognition slowly dawned. A cold wave of shock rippled through him. His chest tightened. He couldn't breathe. The words blurred.

It was impossible, but it was there—a message from the dead.

CHAPTER
9

AN UNEXPECTED TWINGE of nerves rippled through Savvi as she and Paul Daykin entered an old, well-known haunt for movers and shakers of the political world. The BroadBank Club, located near the Lincoln Memorial, reeked of money and power. Rich, dark wood walls shone under the ornate chandeliers. Autographed images of former presidents, ambassadors, and heads of state tastefully hung on the walls. Tables, covered with white linen, filled the room. Waiters moved discreetly from table to table as a low hum of conversation resounded.

A waiter led them to a table in the corner. Two men stood as they approached. Neither of whom Savvi had met. Mentally, she straightened her shoulders. She'd stepped into a rarified stratosphere, a place she'd never expected to play.

Homeland Security Secretary Vance Whitaker nodded to Paul, then extended his hand toward Savvi. "Agent Roth. What a pleasure to meet you. I'm familiar with your impressive resume."

"Thank you, Mr. Secretary," Savvi murmured.

Vance turned toward the other man. "Agent Roth, this is Chairman Frank Littleton."

"I'm pleased to meet you. Please have a seat," Frank said as he pulled out a chair. Then he turned to greet Paul.

A waiter stepped forward, handing Savvi, then Paul a menu.

Her questioning glance prompted a comment from Vance. "We've already ordered."

Perusing the menu, she looked for something not messy or difficult to eat. She decided on baked salmon with steamed vegetables, then eased back in her chair.

Once the waiter was out of earshot, Frank said, "I'm pleased you are joining my staff. I'm even more delighted you're staying at my home. My wife, Amelia, is looking forward to meeting you." He broke a roll apart and smeared it with a small portion of butter.

"It was very gracious of you to invite me. I'm certainly looking forward to it," Savvi said before taking a sip of water to ease the dryness in her throat. She already decided to pass on the bread, too many crumbs.

"I followed your investigation of the Shelby Financial Corporation with a great deal of interest. It's why I contacted Vance. With the implementation of the gold-backed currency looming, I felt having a liaison with the FBI would be advantageous. We'll get into the details of your new assignment later." His gaze held a clear warning.

A glance around the room told her why. People gazed at them with a curious look while the ones seated nearby could overhear their conversation.

"Fortunately, we were able to respond quickly," Paul said. "Scott Fleming had already requested Agent Roth's transfer, which is why she arrived yesterday from New York City."

Frank chuckled. "I hope my request didn't upset Scott's agenda."

"Not at all." Paul grinned. "He took the news with his usual stoicism. Not much rocks his boat," then took a bite of a roll.

"May I call you Savannah?" Frank asked.

"Please do, though, I usually go by Savvi."

Interspersed with bites of food, their discussion centered around events occurring in Washington with a few questions tossed her way about working in New York City.

As Savvi ate, she slowly relaxed. The laidback manner of both Vance Whitaker and Frank Littleton put her at ease.

★★★

From across the room, Senator Charles Halston, III, watched. He'd noted Daykin's arrival with a woman in tow. Dressed in typical Bureau attire, he guessed she was probably an agent. Despite an unrelieved black pantsuit, low heeled shoes, and hair pulled into a bun, she was a damn good-looking woman. Tall, with curves the suit couldn't hide, she strode across the room as if she owned it. Who was she? Why was she with Whitaker and Littleton?

After an impatient glance at his watch, he idly kept his eye on the group as he sipped his martini. When a man dropped into the chair across from him, he grumbled, "Why the hell can't you ever be on time? You know I hate to be kept waiting."

Remy Chabot stared at him. His cold gaze sent a tingle of uneasiness rippling down Halston's back. With a mocking tone, he said, "I don't operate by your schedule. I'm here. What do you want?"

The Senator's eyes flicked in warning as a waiter approached. His voice louder, he said, "I'm glad you were able to make it on such short notice. I want to discuss those new projections with you."

"Are you ready to order, Senator?"

He replied, "My usual, Sanders."

When the waiter turned to him, Chabot said, "Just coffee. I won't be here long."

"As you wish," the elderly man said, before walking away.

Shifting his attention back to Halston, the impassive look on his face hid the contempt he felt for the man. Wealthy and overindulged all his life, Charles Halston believed he was entitled to whatever he wanted. His present position as a Senator added to his sense of entitlement, and now, he had a different target in sight.

Halston's gaze skimmed the room. Assured no one was within hearing, he laid his arm on the table, leaning forward. "I want an update."

"This isn't the place to discuss it."

"No, it's perfect. Who would suspect this is anything other than an innocent business lunch?" He raised his martini glass to acknowledge a wave from a man seated several tables away. "After all, one of my campaign pledges was honesty with transparency." He looked at Chabot and laughed as if to emphasize the unimportance of their discussion. "By now, you should have had confirmation."

"A slight delay. I don't, however, anticipate it will affect your deadline."

Halston's only reaction was a slight narrowing of his eyes. "What delay?"

At the approach of the waiter, Chabot leaned back. A plate with grilled shrimp and vegetables along with a cup and coffee decanter was set on the table. After acknowledging Halston's request for another martini, the waiter turned to Chabot. "May I pour for you?"

With a wave of his hand, he said, "No, I'll do it."

The Senator cut the tail from a shrimp, then shoved the rest in his mouth.

After filling his cup, Chabot took a sip of the rich brew as he stared at Halston. The man's portly figure and a faint trail of broken blood vessels across his cheeks bespoke of his indulgence for food and alcohol.

Setting the cup down, Chabot said, "It's under control. Nothing for you to worry about."

Halston waved his fork. He refused to be intimidated. After all, he was the power in this arrangement. "Oh, but you see. I do worry. I don't like being kept in the dark."

"There's no cause for alarm. Even if I told you, you can't do anything about it."

Chewing on a mouthful of food, Halston shot him a look of irritation.

Ignoring him, Chabot shifted to study the individuals seated at the other tables. When his gaze swept a table in the corner of the room, a spark of interest glinted.

Noticing the direction of Chabot's stare, Halston said, "Interesting meeting. Do you know the woman?"

"Never met her," he answered. As if aware of his scrutiny, her head turned. For an instant, their eyes met before she looked away. In the brief contact, his casual curiosity shifted to an acute desire to learn her identity.

Halston said, "I'd like to know what the hell it's about. From her attire, I'd say she's an agent. Why would she be involved in a meeting with Whitaker and Littleton? They're out of her league."

In a bored tone, Chabot said, "I can't imagine it's anything significant." While it appeared he had shuffled Halston's interest aside, he had every intention to find out.

After swallowing the last of the coffee, Chabot pulled a twenty from his wallet, dropped it on the table and stood. "I'll be in touch."

Halston glared. With a mouth crammed with broccoli, all he could do was nod. As Chabot weaved around the tables, Halston's eyes followed. Seeing the ardent looks of interest from women he passed, Halston's intense dislike bubbled to the surface. All his money couldn't buy him what Remy Chabot had, rugged good looks along with a dominating, arrogant presence.

Still, he mused, the man was nothing more than a pawn. Shrugging his shoulders, he polished off the last of the martini as he eyed the group in the corner. By the end of the day, he'd know who the woman was and why she was having lunch with Frank Littleton.

★★★

As they prepared to leave, Frank said, "Savvi, if you prefer, you can accompany me back to the office. I'd like to introduce you to my staff."

"I appreciate the offer, but my car, with all the belongings I have at the moment, is in the Bureau's parking garage."

Paul spoke up. "If you'll give me your keys, I'll have it delivered to Frank's office."

"Let's make this easy," Frank said. "Paul, have your agent take it to my home."

As everyone stood, Vance said, "Savvi, I'll look forward to your progress reports from Paul." His eyes twinkled with a suppressed humor.

As they walked out, her gaze drifted toward the table across the room. The man was gone, though Senator Halston was still present, glad-handing a woman who stood next to his table.

Outside, she handed her car keys to Paul as they waited for the Chairman's limousine to arrive. When it pulled alongside the curb, the man in the front seat hopped out, then opened the backdoor. Savvi motioned for Frank to enter. He hesitated before stepping into the car. As she slid inside, she glanced out the window. The man she'd spotted with the Senator watched from across the street. She wondered why.

★★★

Fixated by the sight of the group emerging from the club, Remy Chabot paused, his hand on the door handle. When the woman slid into the Chairman's vehicle, the puzzle jolted his instincts. He didn't like the sensation. With what was at stake, he couldn't ignore the feeling.

CHAPTER 10

PAPER SPEWED FROM the printer. Fingers trembled as he reached to pick up the stack. Blake stared at the top page. His mind wanted to deny what his eyes couldn't. It wasn't possible, but even as he grappled with the mind-numbing shock, deep memories stirred. Memories he'd locked away. Words from the past slowly emerged, deepening his sense of trepidation.

He laid the paper aside to look at the rest of the documents—bank statements. What was he looking at, and more importantly, why had they been sent to him? Gathering the papers together, he headed to Scott's office. From the look of concentration on his boss's face as he stared at the computer screen, Blake figured he was deep into his research.

When Blake rapped on the door, Scott's gaze shot upward.

"I need a few minutes of your time."

At the sight of the grim look on his agent's face, Scott's momentary irritation at the interruption vanished. "Come in." He waved his hand toward the computer. "More research, but it can wait." When Blake closed the door behind him, it set off a ripple of disquiet.

"I received an envelope." He handed the papers to Scott. "Inside was a flash drive with these documents."

Scott flipped through the pages, noting most dealt with bank reports, then looked at the front sheet again. "Any idea who sent it to you, or what's on this page?"

While Scott studied the documents, Blake had stepped to the window to stare at the busy street. "I'll answer your second question first." His voice faded as he added, "I'm not really sure I can answer the first." Gathering his thoughts, he said, "Know anything about the Navajo Code Talkers in World War II?"

Arrested by the implication in the question, Scott's eyes flashed toward the stiff-shouldered man in front of the window. "Not a lot, other than the Japanese were never able to crack their code."

With a sigh, Blake turned and dropped into the chair in front of Scott's desk. "During the war, several Native American tribes, Lakota, Comanche, Hopi, Crow, and others served as Code Talkers. They coded and decoded messages based on their native language. The Navajo were recruited by the Marines to serve in the Pacific theater. Their code was the most intricate of all the Code Talkers. It became the only spoken military code never to have been broken."

He paused, staring at the paper in Scott's hand. "What's typed on the paper is a variation of the Navajo Code used in World War II."

Scott laid the paper on the desk as he studied the meaningless words. Nerves hummed as his obsession with enigmas flashed into high gear. "You know this ... how?"

When Blake didn't answer, he looked up. The man seemed to have retreated inside himself, something Scott had noticed on more than one occasion. He waited.

After several minutes, Blake began to speak, his even tone belied by a bleak expression. "During my stint in Afghanistan and Iraq, I hunted bombs, to be more precise, IED's deployed by the enemy. I had an affinity for finding them. Didn't matter how or where they were hidden. The running joke was, send out Kenner, the human bloodhound. One day, my unit swept a roadway. After we finished,

I had an uneasy feeling. I'd noticed a group of men clustered around a small shop not far from the road. Something about their watchful gaze didn't seem right." Too restless to sit, Blake rose and paced.

Scott knew Blake's background. Before he offered him the position in the Tracker Unit, he'd requested Blake's military file. Scott was also aware there was more to Blake's explanation of his ability to find explosive devices.

"I turned back, and sure enough, after we passed the shop, someone planted an IED. As we were diffusing it, their intended target, a convoy of military vehicles pulled up. A woman hopped out, Navy Lieutenant Jaimie Marston. I recognized her immediately. We'd met at a function at Ft. Bragg. We struck up a conversation. By the time I shipped out, we were engaged."

There was nothing in Blake's file about a fiancée. Scott wondered how it had been missed. As he listened, he learned why.

"We hadn't told anyone. Fraternization is frowned on in the military. Since Jaimie still had a year to go, she wanted to keep it secret until she was stateside. She was a Navy cryptographer, assigned to the Marine Corps as an interpreter. She spoke several languages. It was her cover story. Her real mission was implementing a code similar to what was used in World War II. Jaimie was the great-granddaughter of one of the Navajo Code Talkers. The code had been passed down through the family. She knew it as well as the English language."

Scott felt a pattern forming, but it only deepened the mystery.

Blake dropped back into the chair. "I came home and applied to the FBI. Jaimie was super excited over it. She'd laugh, tell me I'd fit right in with the Bureau's rigid mentality. One night, two Navy personnel showed up at my door." He sucked in a deep breath. "Jaimie had been killed, along with four other people. Their vehicle hit an IED. I didn't know she'd added me to her emergency contact list."

"I am sorry. When did it happen?" Scott said.

Blake's shoulders straightened. "Right before I transferred to the Tracker Unit."

Scott remembered the leave of absence Blake had taken around the time he'd interviewed for the Tracker position. He leaned forward. "Do you think there's a chance she didn't die in the explosion?"

"I don't know what to believe." His hand rubbed his face. His voice harsh, he said, "God Almighty, Scott. I helped carry her coffin from the plane when it landed, at the funeral, and to her gravesite. She's buried in the National Cemetery in Arlington."

"Is there any other explanation to explain this letter?"

"If there is, I can't get my brain to come up with one."

"Is it possible it's someone from your days in the military? Someone who would have known the code?"

"I thought about it. But how would they know to send it to me? There's something else. I chalked it up to my imagination. Did Nicki show you the tape she found of our mystery woman in the parking lot?"

"Yeah. She nabbed me the moment I stepped into the office this morning."

"When I saw the woman run, she reminded me of Jaimie, who had the same fluid motion. Running was something she loved to do and even ran marathons."

Scott leaned back. His fingers reached for his pen—tap, tap, tap. "This is a tough question, but it's one I have to ask. Did you see her remains?"

"No. For obvious reasons, the casket was sealed."

"Let's assume she is alive. Why would her death have been faked?"

"In one of her letters, she mentioned a new assignment, but couldn't tell me the details."

Scott brooded over the paper. "Can you translate it?"

"I don't know. The program was highly classified. It was run on a need to know basis. After training, a translator worked from memory to code and decode messages. I learned a few phrases from Jaimie, but I couldn't keep written notes."

"Did you know any of the translators? Someone we could contact?"

"No. Their identities were also a closely guarded secret."

"Any ideas on the bank reports?"

"None."

Scott studied the strange message for a few seconds before saying, "Until we learn otherwise, we're going on the assumption Jaimie Marston wasn't killed. We have to find out where she's been for the last few months. The bigger question is why? This has to be shared with the rest of the team."

Blake nodded. "I'll tell them."

"Get the others into the conference room. I'll be there in a minute."

As Blake walked out the door, Scott was already on the phone. When his boss answered, he said, "Paul, I may have a lead on who left the note in the Chairman's coat. I need the military records for Navy Lieutenant Jaimie Marston, officially listed as killed in action. I suspect it's going to take someone higher than my pay grade to get access to the file." He went on to explain why.

"While I understand your rationale, it's a big jump for an assumption," Paul told him. "I'll put out some feelers, see what kind of reaction I get, then go from there. Any idea about the financial reports?"

"Not yet. I'll let you know when I do."

With a thoughtful expression, Scott hung up. He picked up the documents and headed to the conference room.

The chatter died as Scott stepped to the end of the table. "New developments. I'll let Blake explain."

"I received a USB drive today. Sender unknown. These are copies of what's on the drive." He slid stapled copies of the documents across the table.

Nicki was the first to react. "Good lord, what's this mishmash of letters on the first page?"

"A variation of the code used by the Navajo Code Talkers in World War II."

"Really," Adrian exclaimed, and eyed the document with a great deal more interest. Military history was one of his hobbies.

In a few succinct sentences, Blake summarized his discussion with Scott, ending with the details about his fiancée.

As Nicki stared at his grim expression, it was painfully clear what he'd been hiding all these months. Her voice, uncharacteristically somber, asked what everyone was thinking. "Do you think the Chairman's guardian angel is Jaimie?"

His hand lying on the table fisted. "Christ, I don't know. But it's the only explanation that makes sense. Jaimie would know I'd recognize the code."

Adrian asked, "Can you decode it?"

"Scott asked the same question. I don't know. I learned a few phrases and words from Jaimie before I left Iraq. Maybe."

"Blake, I want you to concentrate on decoding the message. We've got to know what it says. Next are the financial documents. Nicki, see what you can do with the information. Any progress on the Chairman's staff?"

"The dungeon sweeps are still running. There are a lot of employees."

Scott looked at Adrian. "Anything from your research?"

"I talked to a couple of agents in the financial crimes unit. Nothing of any significance floating on the rumor mill. As for the rest, there is a mega overload of articles to wade through. The Feds and President Larkin have created quite an uproar within the political arena and banking community with this new gold currency. It could certainly qualify for motivation. The only problem is narrowing down a suspect from a multitude of possibilities. I'm not sure why taking out the Chairman would solve anything."

"I'm finding the same in the research I've done," Scott said. "Too many candidates. Everyone from bankers to politicians to heads of government. The rhetoric makes Brexit look like a romp through a playground. Let's get back to it."

As Blake headed to his office, the turmoil churning in him pushed his control to the edge. While listening to Scott, he'd stared at the phrases of code on his copy, and suddenly realized—he recognized one of the words.

CHAPTER
11

INSIDE THE MARRINER S. Eccles Federal Reserve Board Building, the surreal feeling Savvi had experienced since entering the BroadBank Club swelled as she walked alongside Frank Littleton. Certain he'd notice, she ignored the urge to pinch herself. She suspected not much escaped his attention.

"I've arranged for an office for you. Though I'll be here for the rest of the day, Director Ben Sutter is in charge of the program. He can answer any questions. Unless something unexpected occurs, I plan on leaving early."

Aware the security officers accompanying them were likely listening, she thought a bit of gush might be appropriate. "I really appreciate the opportunity you've given me. It's an honor I never expected to come my way."

"When Vance and I came up with the idea of a liaison between my office and the Bureau, you were a perfect fit. I've followed your handling of the Shelby case with a great deal of interest." A twinkle sparked in his eyes as he glanced at the guard, walking ahead of him. "I'm certain your presence will be an asset in the coming weeks."

As the two security guards peeled off in another direction, Frank led the way to an elevator. On the second floor, he stopped in front of an open doorway and motioned for her to enter. "I hope this is satisfactory."

After a quick glance around the small office, she set her briefcase and tote bag she'd retrieved from Paul's car on the desk. "Absolutely." She turned, nodding toward the door.

Frank stepped further into the room, closing it behind him. With a quick flick of a finger, she popped the locks on the briefcase, then removed a small digital device along with her laptop.

Making small talk, she quickly swept the room before dropping the scanner back into the case, then asked, "How often are your offices swept for bugs?"

"Daily."

"Where else?"

"The boardroom used by the Federal Open Market Committee. Since the FOMC is tasked with the Federal Reserve's monetary policy, any premature disclosure of the committee's decisions would adversely affect the country's economic system."

"Your home?"

"No. I never thought it was necessary as I seldom conduct business there."

"Maybe not business, but I expect you do discuss your travel plans and itinerary with your wife. I'll take care of it tonight."

A troubled look crossed his face. "It's difficult to accept one of my staff could be involved."

"We're running backgrounds on everyone who works here. Nicki Allison is our computer guru in the Tracker office. If there's anything to find, she'll be the one to do it. Since we were in the academy together and it's known we're good friends, she's my contact to reach Scott."

Frank glanced at his watch. "I have a conference call coming up. I'll introduce you to Director Sutter."

Savvi followed him to another suite of offices where he introduced her to the young woman in the outer office before asking, "Is Ben busy?"

"No, sir. I'll let him know you're on your way in."

Frank lightly tapped the door before opening it.

After scanning an office not much bigger than the one she'd been allotted, Savvi turned her attention to the man standing behind the desk. From her initial research, she was familiar with his background. In his early sixties, he'd been with the Federal Reserve for over thirty-five years. A heavy man with a round face, his small eyes stared at her with a curious look.

He extended his arm across the desk to shake her hand. "Agent Roth, your reputation has certainly preceded you. Welcome to the Federal Reserve."

"Thank you. Please, it's Savvi. I'm looking forward to working with you."

Sutter motioned to a chair as he glanced at his boss.

"Ben, I've got a conference call. I told Savvi you could answer any questions."

After Frank walked out, Ben settled into the chair. "While I am delighted to meet you, it was somewhat of a surprise to learn you were coming on board."

As she sat, Savvi chuckled. "No more so than I, Director Sutter."

"I'm Ben. We're rather informal around here. What do you plan to do?"

Savvi told him, "Right now, I'm not certain. I was informed by Director Daykin my role is more of an observer than outright involvement. What the Federal Reserve plans to implement is a game-changer in the country's economic system. Chairman Littleton wants to stay on top of the implementation to ensure there are no unanticipated complications."

As she talked, he studied the young woman. After learning she was to be added to his staff, his concern over the FBI's involvement had prompted his own research. What would an agent know about the complexities of the PGS project? What he discovered surprised even him, and he wasn't easily impressed.

Agent Roth had graduated at the top of her class from Harvard with a master's degrees in finance and economics. Instead of going to work in her father's bank, she elected to join the FBI. After graduating from the academy, she'd been assigned to the Financial Crime Section. She was known to be brilliant and ruthless in her pursuit of white-collar crimes.

"How familiar are you with the parallel gold standard, or what we refer to as the PGS project?" he asked.

"I've followed the financial reports. I know the gold-backed currency will co-exist with the current system, the fiat dollar. It's a move that has a lot of people upset."

Leaned back in his chair, with his hands resting on his belly, he chuckled. "You're right about the game-changer. A fiat dollar has no intrinsic value other than the declared worth by the government issuing it. Ever since the U.S. abandoned the gold-backed dollar in 1971 and switched to the fiat system, the debate has raged. Proponents clamored for its return, but no one seriously believed it would happen until Arthur Larkin was elected President. When he campaigned on building a strong economic system, I don't think anyone truly understood what he had in mind."

He smiled. "But, of course, these are details I'm sure you know."

Avid interest gleamed in Savvi's eyes. The intricacies of the country's monetary system had always been a source of fascination. One of her essays at Harvard dealt with the creation of the Federal Reserve. Most individuals weren't aware that in 1907, the banking industry was a fragmented mishmash of banks and states using their own currency. The bankruptcy of two brokerage firms triggered a run on the banks resulting in a push for a reform of the banking system that set the stage for what happened three years later.

On November 22, 1910, in the dead of night, six men, high-powered politicians and financiers, climbed aboard a private train in Hoboken, New Jersey. Their destination, a private club on Jekyll

Island off the coast of Georgia. The Jekyll Island Club's exclusive membership included the world's wealthiest families, the Vanderbilts, Rockefellers, and Morgans. Shrouded in secrecy, the men used only their first names and a cover story of duck hunting to allay any interest from reporters.

During the week-long stay, they drafted a bill to reform the country's economic system that would ultimately become the Federal Reserve Act. It was signed into law in 1913 by President Woodrow Wilson. The bill also gave the newly created agency the power over the nation's currency.

A monetary system that was now in a state of economic chaos as proponents and antagonists argued over how to shore up the American dollar. The proposed solution was a return to the gold-backed currency. The thought of being in the middle of a historic event intensified Savvi's captivation.

Ben said, "When Larkin was elected, Frank Littleton was already on the Federal Reserve's Board of Governors. Once the President appointed him as the Chairman, he had an ally in his vision of monetary reform. It was the culmination of a plan they'd discussed on many occasions."

"I remember Chairman Littleton's appointment met with a great deal of contention during the confirmation process."

"I've been with the Federal Reserve for most of my career. Served under four chairmen. The debate over Frank's appointment was surprisingly acrimonious. At the time, many of us who work here wondered whether he'd get the necessary votes."

"Any internal dissension?" she asked.

A surprising look of discomfort crossed Ben's face. He hesitated before he said, "Anytime, there's a radical change, there's bound to be some disagreement." He shrugged, then added, "Just part of the job. Now, what can I do to help you?"

Savvi wondered why the question seemed to strike a nerve. "I would like to learn more about the specifics of the PGS project and the timeline."

He nodded. "There's a computer in your office. Someone from the IT division will stop by to set up your security clearance. Once you're online, you'll have access to the project file. If you have any questions, please don't hesitate to let me know."

Ben stared at her for a few seconds, then added, "There is one other issue. Since I'm in charge of the PGS project, I'll need to be kept informed of your activities."

While she had no intention of telling him anything, now was not the time to broach the issue—no point in pissing off the natives until she had a reason.

Ben stood. A signal the meeting was over. Savvi thanked him, though she still had several questions. On the way to her office, she replayed the encounter in her mind. Though she didn't understand why, she had an uneasy feeling.

When she reached her door, it was open. She distinctly remembered closing it. As she stepped inside, a man was bent over her laptop. Her tone edgy, she said, "May I help you?"

He straightened and turned to face her. With an insolent grin, he said, "You must be the new cop everyone is talking about."

With a pointed glance at her open laptop, which had also been closed when she left, she said, "Yes. I'm FBI Agent Roth."

"I'm Darren Holcomb, the IT guy around here."

"Is there a problem with my computer?"

Holcomb glanced down at it before saying, "Oh, no. Routine check. Computer security is a high priority, including personal computers in the building."

While she didn't like his explanation, she let it pass. "Director Sutter said somebody would come by with my security clearance."

"Yep, it's me. I handle most of the computer issues around here." He picked up a clipboard, removed a piece of paper, and handed it to her. "Login name and password. Once you're in the system, you can change the password. Any questions, I'm down-stairs. My extension number is at the bottom of the form."

He stepped around her. Savvi turned, a thoughtful expression on her face as she watched him walk out of the office. It was the second encounter with a Federal Reserve employee that left her with an uneasy feeling.

CHAPTER
12

BLAKE STARED AT the gibberish typed on the paper. One word stood out--BILH-HE-NEH! *Warning.* Used as a keyword in military dispatches to signal an immediate threat, it was one of the first words he'd learned. It left little doubt someone had sent him a message. But was it Jaimie? He still couldn't wrap his thoughts around the possibility she was alive. It seemed to be beyond incredible.

At the sound of a loud knock, his eyes darted upward. Nicki stood in the doorway. "Can I help?"

He shook his head even as he said, "Something I've got to work out."

"Don't forget. The team is here for you."

An unexpected sense of warmth filtered into the darkness inside him. Since joining the team, he'd felt like an outsider. Blake couldn't even say for sure where he did belong. He had no family. His parents died in a car accident not long after he graduated from high school. Ostracized for his strange ability, he'd been a loner in the Army—until he met Jaimie. She filled his life, gave him a purpose. Her death left a black void from which there seemed to be no escape.

"I'll run the text through the enhancement software I've been working on for translating languages."

A wry smile crossed his face. "Good luck. The code the Navajo

Talkers used was declassified in the late '60s. It's why Jaimie wrote a new code."

"Send me the files on the flash drive."

"Nicki! You're not planning on staying late again?" The tug of war between Nicki and Scott had become a source of amusement for the rest of the team.

A sassy grin flashed as she shrugged her shoulders, then walked away.

Blake sighed. Sometimes, he'd wondered whether her defiance wasn't a way to distract Scott from sinking into one of his introspective moods. Whenever the sound of his tapping pen echoed from his office, the team knew he was brooding. He could relate as he considered how he planned to spend the evening.

✯✯✯

Scott dropped his files on his desk, then headed to Nicki's office. A goblin danced on the wall-mounted screen. As Nicki's fingers flicked across the keyboard, the screen split into multiple sections, each displaying the status of the program she was running. The strange assortment of letters from the coded message appeared on one of the screens.

"Do you think you can decipher it?" Scott asked.

She shot a wry look at him. "Boss man, anything's possible."

He dropped into the chair alongside her desk. "I saw Blake heading out the door. He looked like he was carrying the weight of the world on his shoulders."

"This has hit him hard. Did you know about the fiancée?" It wouldn't have surprised her since Scott could be tight-lipped at times.

He picked up the copies of the bank reports lying next to Nicki's keyboard. "Umm ... not until he walked into my office with the contents of the flash drive." As he flipped the pages, perusing each one, he said, "I'm not making any sense out of these. Impact of losses on pro forma earnings and capital, derivative and balance statements. There's nothing to identify whose report it is."

"I can't make heads or tails of it either. This may not be an easy answer to find."

"Call Savvi."

Nicki picked up her phone, pushed the speed dial, then tapped the speakerphone icon. A few seconds later, Savvi answered, "Nicki, I was going to call as soon as I got settled."

"Can you talk?"

"Yes. I'm headed to the parking garage. The Chairman is getting ready to leave."

Scott said, "I'm here too, Savvi. Anything to report?"

A chuckle echoed. "I must say, today will go down in the record books as one of my more memorable and unusual days. I've already had a couple of disquieting encounters with two of the staff. For some reason, they seemed a bit off, but nothing I can articulate as to why. Right now, it's just vibes."

Scott brought her up to date on Blake's packet, and their suspicion it was connected to the person who left the note, then added, "I'm sending the reports to Frank. Find out if he has any idea what they are. What's on the agenda tomorrow?"

"I plan on getting acquainted with more of the staff. I've got to go. I'll be in touch."

After disconnecting, Scott asked, "How long are you planning on staying?"

"Not long. I just want to input this data, get the programs started."

"Nicki." He stood, waiting until she looked up at him. "Do not spend the night. We may be in this for the long haul. Go home. Sleep in your own bed, not on the damn couch."

She grinned.

"I mean it."

"I hear you, boss man. I won't be here long."

He grunted as he walked out the door. Scott didn't believe a single word of her reassurances. At the sound of his office phone, he rushed into his office.

"Fleming,"

"Scott, you should have received a copy of the Marston file from the Navy's personnel office," his boss told him. "My copy just arrived. After reading it, if this is a coverup, it's very well done."

Scott checked his emails as they talked. "Yeah, I got it."

After hanging up, he opened the file and scanned the contents. Lieutenant Jaimie Marston was a hell of a lot more than a Navy cryptographer. She'd graduated in the top ten of her class from the Naval Academy with a finance degree. After graduation, she was assigned to the office of Naval Intelligence Operations. From there, she was sent to Iraq.

The section detailing the investigation of her death caught his attention. Jaimie and four officers were headed to Baghdad. The vehicle struck an IED. Due to the ensuing fire, the investigator noted it was impossible to obtain a positive identification of the victims.

Scott leaned back, picked up his pen—tap, tap, tap. No positive ID. He wondered how the investigator knew Jaimie had been in the vehicle. Only one way to find out, talk to the guy. He glanced at the name on the screen, Captain Randy Tidwell.

After a fast bit of research, he found him. He was back stateside, assigned to the Marine Corps Air Ground Combat Center in California. If Blake knew this guy, it might be better to have him make the call.

When Blake answered, Scott asked, "You home yet?"

"Just walked in. Why?"

"Do you know a Captain Randy Tidwell?"

"Sure do. We were stationed together in Iraq. Why are you interested in Randy?"

"I received Jaimie's Naval file. He was the officer who signed off on the investigation of her death."

"I'll be damned. I didn't know. I'm surprised I didn't get a call from him."

"Did he know about your engagement?"

"No, though he knew we were more than good friends."

"Your Jaimie is one impressive woman. You didn't mention she'd graduated from the Naval Academy."

"It didn't seem pertinent. Is it important?"

"Maybe, since she has a financial management degree and was assigned to Naval Intelligence."

"It wasn't something we ever got around to discussing."

"Tidwell mentions in his report there was no positive identification of the victims."

A soft whistle echoed in his ear.

Scott added, "He's stationed at 29 Palms. I figure he'll be more open with you than if I call."

"I'll get back to you," Blake said and disconnected.

Before leaving, Scott faxed the bank reports from the flash drive to Frank. Stuffing his copies in his briefcase, he planned to spend a few hours on his own research once he got home.

★★★

After several calls, Blake finally tracked down a contact number. As he stared at what he'd written on a notepad, a familiar sick churning settled in his gut. Could he hope it was all a lie? If he did, then found out Jaimie was dead, it meant living through the grief again. The first time was close to his undoing. Could he survive it a second time?

Blake pushed back from his desk. Before he called, he had to get his thoughts under control. He walked out of the small bedroom he turned into a home office. Stepping into his living room, he stared at his simple accommodations, a chair, sofa, coffee table and TV. Hell, all he'd been doing was biding his time. Most of his stuff was still boxed, piled high in a closet and stacked in his office. While he had a new job with the Tracker Unit, his life had been on hold since the day his doorbell rang, and two men waited on the other side.

With a can of beer he grabbed from the fridge, he walked back to the office. Popping the top, he took a long swallow, then looked down at the number. It was a call he wanted to make but didn't. The contradiction of his feelings had to be pushed aside. He didn't have a choice. More was at stake than his life.

He dropped into his chair, took another swig, then picked up the phone. It rang several times before a gruff voice barked, "Tidwell."

"Is this the sneaky s-o-b who still owes me for a bet on the Superbowl?"

"Son-of-a-gun! Blake! Blake Kenner! A voice I never expected to hear again. If you'd stuck around instead of hauling your ass back stateside, you'd have collected."

"What the hell are you doing in California? You always said it was the last state you'd ever want to live in."

"Hey, you know how the Corps works, doesn't give a man an option. As it turns out, it's okay. Some hot looking babes around here."

"Randy, you haven't changed one bit, still chasing women."

"I heard you'd gone with the feds. How's it working out?"

"Not bad. I'm assigned to the Washington office, a new unit, the Trackers."

Raucous laughter erupted. After several chortles, Randy said, "You're putting me on, right? Kenner, the human bloodhound, is working for some unit called the Trackers?"

"Absolutely the truth. It's the name of the unit."

"Jeez, wait until I see some of the old crowd. Several of our buddies are stationed here. We'll tip a few beers over that one."

"Randy, do you remember Jaimie Marston?"

His voice turned somber. "I sure do. Why?" he asked, then added, "If I recall, the two of you were tight before you shipped out."

"We were engaged."

"Jesus H. Christ! Blake, I didn't know. If I had, buddy, I would have called. I was the investigating officer."

"Jaimie wanted to keep the engagement secret until she left Iraq. No reason to beat yourself up over it. I managed to get a copy of your report. I've got a few questions if you don't mind my asking."

"Fire away. I'll answer whatever I can."

"Your notes indicate you couldn't make a positive ID on the victims. How do you know Jaimie was in the vehicle?"

"Blake, there was never any doubt. I saw her climb into the Humvee. We'd had a briefing just before she and four other officers left for Baghdad. When the call came in, I headed to the scene." He paused for several seconds. "When I got there, what was left of the vehicle was engulfed in fire. They didn't have a chance. I'm sorry, man ... so sorry."

Blake took a deep breath, trying to dispel the image in his mind. He'd seen far too many bombings not to know what it would have looked like.

"Where'd it happen?"

"Outskirts of Baghdad. We had to shut down the highway and reroute traffic. Why?"

Since Blake couldn't tell him the real reason behind the call, he fobbed him off. "Just trying to settle it all in my mind. Did you find who planted the bomb?"

"No, wish I could say we did. It was a bad day, losing five of our own. They weren't the only casualties. Do you remember Kathy Lincoln? She went missing the same day."

A surge of adrenaline shot through him, destroying the grey mist encasing his mind. Kathy had been an Army medic. "I do. What happened?"

"No one really knows. She was making a run for medical

supplies. Her vehicle was found abandoned in Baghdad, but she'd vanished."

"Is she still listed as MIA?"

"Afraid so, unless they found something after I left."

"Thanks for the answers, Randy."

"Anytime. If you get out this way, stop. I'll show 'ole sobersides Kenner the nightlife," then laughed.

"Yeah, maybe I will."

As he disconnected the call, his thoughts whirled. Was it possible Kathy and Jaimie had somehow switched cars? He tapped his speed dial.

"Blake, what did you find out?" Scott asked.

"Another female officer went MIA the same day." Blake went on to explain what he'd learned from Randy.

"It certainly stirs the pot if the two women switched cars."

"But it doesn't get us any closer to finding her if she is alive."

"Not yet," Scott answered.

After terminating the call, Blake opened the door to the closet. One of the boxes contained Jaimie's letters. One of them he'd never opened. Since it arrived several days after the visit from the Navy, Jaimie must have mailed it just before the bombing. He couldn't bear the thought of reading it and had filed it with the rest. He tugged the box from the shelf and felt the hope he could no longer deny.

CHAPTER
13

FRANK'S DRIVER STOPPED in front of a modest two-story home. Savvi spotted her car on an extension of the driveway along the side of the house. The officer in the front seat stepped out, opening the rear door. As she exited, she grabbed her briefcase and tote bag before following Frank.

Behind them, the car eased out of the driveway. Since Frank wasn't inside the house yet, it was another security breach to add to her list of items to discuss with Frank. An attractive woman, early fifties, had opened the door.

When Savvi stepped inside, the woman said, "You must be Agent Roth. I'm Frank's wife. Let me help you," and plucked the briefcase from her hand. "I'm so delighted to meet you," she said, closing the door. "Since I had the keys to your car, your suitcases are already in your room. I hope you don't mind."

A bit overwhelmed by the effusive greeting, Savvi stammered, "Uh ... not at all. I'm pleased to meet you, Mrs. Littleton."

"No, no. Please, it's Amelia. I understand we need to come up with a reason for you to stay with us. I, for one, am totally grateful to have an FBI agent in the house. We can discuss all of that later."

"Amelia, give her a chance to settle," Frank said with a laugh, then kissed his wife's cheek.

"Oh, absolutely. Do you need to freshen up?"

"I would like to drop my briefcase and bag in my room if you don't mind."

"Not at all, my dear. Come along. I'll show you to your bedroom. Then you can join us in the library. We like to relax before dinner."

Savvi glimpsed a large living room through an arched doorway as she followed Amelia toward the stairs. Sofas and several chairs made an attractive, comfortable grouping in front of a large fireplace.

Upstairs, Amelia ushered her into a bedroom with an attached bath. "If you need anything, just let me know. We want you to feel right at home. There's no need to stand on ceremony. Frank is going to give you a key, so you can come and go."

As her gaze swept the room, Savvi said, "It's lovely. I'm sure I'll be very comfortable."

Amelia's parting comment was to turn left at the bottom of the stairs. The library was at the end of the hall.

Still bemused by the cordial welcome, she set her bag alongside the briefcase Amelia had dropped on the bed. After washing her hands, she followed Amelia's directions and walked into a spacious room lined with bookshelves. The windows along the rear wall overlooked a patio. Positioned in front of the windows were a large desk and several armchairs.

With a warm smile, Frank stood as she stepped through the doorway. "All settled in?"

"Yes, thank you."

Amelia, seated in one of the chairs, said, "We were just discussing a reason for you to be here. Would you like a glass of wine or a cold drink, soda, iced tea? Frank said your nickname is Savvi. Do you prefer it to Savannah, my dear?"

As Amelia took a breath, Savvi quickly interjected, "A glass of wine would be nice. Even though my mother still insists on Savannah, for most everyone else, it's Savvi."

"Have a seat." Amelia's hand patted the arm of the chair next to her. "Frank, she'd like a glass of wine. I would too."

"White or red?" Frank stepped toward a cabinet topped by decanters and glasses.

Amelia said, "Now, dear, tell me all about yourself."

"Uh, white," Savvi told Frank as she tried to keep up, then turned toward Amelia.

Casually attired in jogging pants and a sweatshirt, Amelia's grey eyes twinkled in a heart-shaped face. An attractive salt and pepper shag cut hairstyle cupped her chin line.

Already captivated by the charming woman, Savvi couldn't stop a chuckle from erupting. "I'm not sure what you want to know."

As Amelia accepted the glass of wine her husband handed her, she said, "Just … everything."

With a loving look at his wife, Frank handed Savvi the glass in his other hand. "I should have warned you. Amelia is the inquiring mind, who wants to know it all. She is right, though, we do need to come up with a cover story."

Before she could respond, Amelia said, "Let's start with your parents. Where do they live? What do they do? Then we can move on to you."

With another chuckle, Savvi gave in to the inevitable. "My dad is the CEO of Garner National Bank in Peekskill, New York. Mom is the director of a local non-profit organization."

Amelia looked at her husband, who held a highball glass. "Are you familiar with the bank?"

"Actually, I am. Don Roth?"

Surprised, Savvi stared at him for a second before saying, "My dad. How do you know him?"

"I should have connected up the name, but I haven't seen him for maybe fifteen years or so. He was on a committee of bankers representing mid-sized banks during the era of the Dodd-Frank legislation."

Amelia let out a sigh of satisfaction. "Now see, we've already got a connection. We know your family. When you were assigned to Frank's office, well, it's just the most natural thing to ask you to stay with us." She smiled and sipped her wine.

Frank chuckled. "I knew Amelia would find a way to explain your presence."

"I truly do appreciate the invitation. I'm looking forward to picking your husband's brain over the new monetary initiatives he's implementing."

"Dinner will be ready soon. Afterward, you two can talk as long as you like. Umm … your mother. I should know her name."

Savvi laughed. "It's Rebecca."

"Did you attend college? Something else I should probably know."

"Harvard."

"How wonderful!" She clapped her hands. "Another connection. Frank graduated from Harvard." She turned to look at Frank. "My dear, this just isn't going to be a problem at all."

Frank said, "I do believe we've got a game plan as the saying goes."

"Oh, my!" she exclaimed, hopping out of the chair. "Look at the time. Cook will be setting our dinner on the table. Come along and bring your wine glass."

Feeling slightly battered by an invisible force, Savvi stood. With a wry smile at Frank, who astonishingly winked back, she followed Amelia.

It wasn't until after dinner Savvi had a chance to talk with Frank. As they settled in chairs in the library, Amelia walked in, carrying a tray with a coffee carafe and cups.

She set it on a table beside Savvi's chair. "Frank, go easy on the caffeine, or you'll be up all night," then turned to Savvi. "Feel free to rummage in the kitchen. Now, I'll leave the two of you to whatever it is you need to discuss."

The door closed behind her. Savvi poured a cup, then motioned toward a second.

Frank laughed. "Amelia's right, but I'm still going to have a cup." While Savvi poured, he slid several papers across the desk. "This came in from Scott, with a note to be sure to get a copy to you."

She moved to set his cup on the desk, then picked up the papers. Settling in her chair, Savvi quickly scanned them.

"I knew he was sending several documents. Do you have any idea what they are?"

With a grim tone, he said, "Yes, I do. I'd like to know how he acquired them."

Startled, Savvi glanced up.

"These are bank stress test reports," he told her. "Each year, large banks conduct tests using the Federal Reserve's disaster criteria. The purpose is to discover if the bank can survive. This year, thirty-six banks are involved. How did these end up in Scott's hands?"

"Blake Kenner, one of our agents, received a flash drive in the mail. These documents were on it. Scott thinks they may have been sent by the same person who left the warning in your coat."

"How could a bank stress test be involved?" Frank asked.

"It's what we have to figure out." Her gaze dropped back to the reports. "Any idea which bank these belong too?"

"No, but the reports are on file. It shouldn't be hard to find. I'll check into it tomorrow."

A concerned look settled on her face. "No ... I don't think it's a good idea. I'll do the research."

He frowned. "I see. It could alert someone."

"Maybe. We don't know who is involved. It could be a risk. No one will give me a second thought since my cover is to learn more about the Fed's operation."

She also had another concern to broach. Uncertain how Frank would react, Savvi eased into it. "Your safety is my first priority. Since we don't know from which direction the danger will come, a few security precautions need to be added."

"I'm not sure what you mean."

"I want to minimize your exposure. Instead of using the front door, I'll have your driver pull in front of the garage. You'll exit and enter the house through the kitchen."

He leaned back. With a thoughtful air, he mused, "Sniper."

"It's a possibility. Another one is a car bomb. Since your car is stored in a locked building, it would be difficult, but not impossible. When I asked your driver if the car was swept for explosives, he said, no. It's another change I plan to initiate. Next item. I don't want you wandering around outside, even in your backyard."

He sighed. "I don't like it, but I know it's necessary. What else?"

"While it's a gentlemanly gesture to step out, then help a woman out of the car, from now on, I go first. It lets me get into a position to protect you. Same on getting back into the car. You go first, then I enter."

What she didn't say was that she wasn't impressed with his security personnel. "Once I'm more familiar with your schedule, there could be other changes."

"Captain Lloyd Hayes has been out of town. He'll be back tomorrow. I'll arrange for you to meet him."

"Good. Now, what about motivation? Any ideas on why someone wants you out of the way?"

"None. And believe me, since finding the letter in my coat, I've spent considerable time thinking about it. If anything happens to me, the President will appoint another chairman."

Savvi nodded. "Tell me more about the gold currency project. It seems to be a polarizing event, both inside and outside of the Reserve."

Frank started with the fateful trip in 1910 to Jekyll Island. In 1913, Congress approved the Federal Reserve Act. The law created the Federal Reserve System to include twelve regional Federal Reserve Banks. He referenced the addition of the FOMC, Federal Open Market Committee, in 1935 to manage the country's money supply. The committee consisted of the seven members of the Board of Governors, the President of the Federal Reserve Bank of New York, and presidents of four of the remaining eleven Federal Reserve Banks.

He segued into his early days as an attorney and a growing friendship with Arthur Larkin, another enterprising attorney. He recounted the nights spent arguing the merits of the current fiat system, and as all young men do, envisioned if they had the power, what they would change.

Frank laughed as he stood, then walked to the coffee pot. "Who would have ever believed one day he'd be President, and I'd be the Federal Reserve Chairman? Refill?"

"Please."

He filled her cup, then his before sitting back in the chair. "Over the years, Arthur and I became increasingly concerned over the declining value of the dollar and the effect on the global economy. The U.S. no longer stands alone but is part of an international financial network integrating every country in the world. Attempts to boost the U.S. economy and international confidence in the dollar have failed. Many countries have entered into currency swap agreements to bypass the utilization of the U.S. dollar."

As he talked, Savvi realized Frank Littleton was more than a brilliant economic theorist; he was also a visionary.

His eyes held a distant look as he said, "There are only a few individuals who understand our economy is in dire straits. Continuing to flood the market by increasing the supply of fiat currency isn't the answer. Confidence in the American dollar must be restored. The only avenue is to resurrect the gold-back currency."

Enthralled, Savvi had asked numerous questions, most dealt with the implementation.

Frank told her the success of the program consisted of two key elements. The first limited the printing of new bills unless the gold existed to back it. The second was controlling the conversion. In 1971, in an unprecedented move, President Richard Nixon stopped the exchange of dollars for gold due to the depletion of the U.S. gold reserves by foreign central banks.

To ensure it didn't occur again, the exchange of fiat dollars for the gold currency would be monitored and controlled. It was the reason the fiat and gold currency systems would co-exist. Foreign central banks and banking institutions would be limited to the number of fiat dollars they could exchange for the gold currency.

Once someone possessed the new currency, it could be redeemed for gold. Hence the concern to avoid another depletion of the U.S. gold reserves. He also explained how the U.S. had slowly purchased gold bullion, shoring up the gold reserves for when the new system launched.

When Frank finally stopped, over two hours had passed, the coffee pot was empty, and Savvi had been treated to an economic lesson from the leading banking authority in the country.

After a quick glance at his watch, he exclaimed, "I certainly didn't intend to turn your question into a lengthy monologue."

"I highly enjoyed listening to your explanation, plus, the more information I acquire will help to find the why and who."

"It has been a contentious process. Your assessment of a polarizing event is absolutely correct. Elected officials, bank executives, finance experts, even regional Federal Reserve Bank presidents, who serve on the FOMC committee, have been quite vocal in their objections. It's a new realm of strict controls and accountability since the gold reserves must proportionally increase for every gold dollar printed. Of course, there are the doomsayers, predicting the transition will throw this country into a depression, unlike any we've experienced."

"If you were, let's say, taken out of the picture, what would happen?"

With a wry smile, he said, "It's a picture I don't want to envision, but for argument's sake, nothing."

"Nothing?" she echoed.

"Getting rid of me won't stop the process. It's moving forward. Oh, the implementation might be slowed down because the process to replace me would take time. But in the end, it wouldn't make any difference."

With a sigh, he rose. "I'd better turn in." He chuckled. "Amelia will be waiting with an 'I told you so' for the coffee. But it was enjoyable."

During their discussion, Savvi's questions revealed an analytical process that deepened his respect. Too bad she'd decided on a law enforcement career. He wondered, if when this was all over, whether he could woo her away from the FBI.

In her room, she slowly undressed as Frank's comments rolled in her head. While his safety was her top priority, sniffing out a reason to kill him was a close second. After slipping on her night t-shirt, she picked up her phone. Nicki answered on the second ring.

"I was hoping you'd call. How'd the evening go?"

"It was amazing. Listening to him talk about the U.S. and world economy was an incredible experience. The man is brilliant."

A chuckle sounded. "Scott's pretty impressed by him. In my books, it says a lot."

A spooky laugh echoed in the background. "What the hell was that?"

"Oh, it's my goblin, letting me know I have incoming."

"Your goblin! Nicki, where *are* you?"

"Umm ... at the office. I'm running the backgrounds."

"Don't tell me you've set up official FBI programs like a dang computer game."

During their stint at the academy, Nicki turned many of the courses into games. To the delight of the other recruits, the instructors ignored her underground computer network.

"Now, would I do something so dastardly?" Nicki quipped.

"Hell, yes, you would."

All she got was another chuckle from Nicki, oddly similar to the goblin's laugh.

"Pass this on to Scott. The documents on Blake's flash drive are bank stress test reports. Tomorrow, I'll look for a match in the Federal Reserve computer program. I wonder why our guardian angel didn't tell us?"

"Dang! Good question. Maybe it's in the message we are trying to decode. And what the hell are stress tests? Never mind, I'll find out. What else is on your agenda?"

Savvi laughed, knowing that by the time Nicki finished her research, she'd know everything from A to Z about the reports. "I've beefed up Frank's security. Tomorrow I'm meeting Captain Hayes. Got a feeling the man's not going to be happy I'm sticking my nose into his business."

"What reason did you come up with for staying at Frank's house?"

"You're not going to believe this. Frank knows my father."

"Creepers, it's weird. How'd that happen?"

Savvi explained, then said, "Make sure Scott knows in case of any questions."

After disconnecting, Savvi slid under the covers. Sleep eluded her as she stared at the moonlight creeping through a slight gap in the drapes. She couldn't blame the caffeine. Her mind didn't want to shut down as she sifted through what she'd learned. Somewhere, there was a nugget, one that would break the case wide open. But could she find it in time?

CHAPTER
14

UNLOCKING THE DOOR, Scott sniffed as he stepped inside. No coffee. No sounds in Nicki's office. Just because they were missing didn't mean she'd gone home. He dropped his briefcase on his desk before walking to the breakroom. The couch was empty. Wonder of wonders, she'd followed one of his edicts. Pleased, he punched the buttons on the coffee machine. He heard the outer door open, followed by footsteps along the hall.

"Hey, boss man."

Scott turned. His gaze skimmed her from head to toe. A sorrowful look of reproach settled on his face as he sighed. Attired in leggings, a t-shirt with a weird multi-colored flying creature on the front, she looked alert and bright-eyed. It was the hair. The long braid was still wet.

After leasing the office space, he'd contacted the owner of the gym on the first floor. His agents had full use of the facilities along with lockers for extra clothes.

"Nicki. Ah, hell," he muttered.

A cheeky grin crossed her face. "Got some good info, some bad," she said, knowing it would divert his thoughts. He'd forget her slight transgression, again.

"Okay, you got my attention. Give me the bad first."

"So far, nothing on decoding the message. Even working with the original code, I still get gibberish. I've got an idea for a new algorithm, but it will take a few hours to set up." Then she drum-rolled the air with her fingers. Her eyes twinkled. "Savvi identified the reports."

"She did!"

"Frank recognized them, bank stress tests."

"Stress tests. What the hell is a stress test, and how does it play into this?" The machine pinged. He picked up her cup and filled it.

"I can't answer the *how*, but I can tell you the *what*. I've already done some research. Check your inbox. It's not all." She explained the connection between Frank and Savvi's father, then added, "Sometimes, the capricious gods are on our side."

He handed her the cup, then filled his own. "Damn good cover story. I won't have a problem selling it to anyone."

Blake walked in. "I could smell the coffee from the front door," he said as he grabbed a cup from the counter. While attired as ever in neatly pressed pants and shirt, his face was drawn, eyes red-rimmed.

"Doesn't look like you got much sleep," Scott said.

"After talking to you, I went through all the letters from Jaimie. Then I spent most of the night on the message. Even though I don't understand it, I've made some progress."

"Hell, Blake! You've done better than me," Nicki exclaimed. "I've got diddly squat."

Adrian walked in. His voice grumpy, he said, "Hi," and headed straight to the pot.

Scott grinned, but only said, "Conference room, new developments."

Once everyone was settled, Scott motioned to Nicki.

She said, "Savvi called. Frank identified the documents on Blake's flash drive. They are bank stress test reports."

With a more alert air, Adrian piped up, "What the hell are stress tests?"

Blake said, "Whatever they are, they're part of the message. How this works is each letter of the alphabet represents a Navajo word for an object or animal. The Navajo word would be substituted for a letter in a word. For example, if a letter was S, the Navajo word for snake would be used."

As he explained, he passed everyone a sheet of paper. On it, he'd typed,

WARNING
   2) S _ _ _ S S
   3) _ _ S _ S
   4) _ _ M _ _ _ M _ S _ _
   5) _ _ _ _ _ M A _
   6) _ S S _ S S _ _ _ _ _ _ _
   7) _ M M _ _ _ _ _

"In the message, there are seven words. The first is Warning. It was a phrase used to signal an immediate threat. I've substituted the letters for the other six words from what I remember. What I didn't are the blanks."

Scott looked at the typed print. He began to fill in the missing letters, but Blake was ahead of him.

Rising, Blake stepped to an erasable board mounted on the wall. Picking up a marker, he wrote what he'd typed on the paper, then started to fill in the blanks.

"Considering the subject matter, the sixth word was easy to identify. Several letters in assassination are common to the other letters, A, I, N, T, and O." He added the letters to the missing spaces. "From there, it was easy. After what Nicki told us, it makes sense."

WARNING
  STRESS
  TESTS
  COMPROMISED
  CHAIRMAN
  ASSASSINATION
  IMMINENT

"Damn good work," Scott said.

"So, what the hell are stress tests?" Adrian asked again.

Nicki told them. "Basically, banks run a what-if scenario like a hurricane, bombing, or some other catastrophic disaster to find out if the bank can survive. It's actually a two-step process. First, the bank conducts the stress test based on the Fed's scenario. The results are then submitted to the Federal Reserve for an analysis of the results and the bank's capital plans."

"What happens if the bank fails the test?" Adrian interjected.

"All sorts of bad stuff, stopping payment of dividends to shareholders, participation in mergers and acquisitions, along with fines. Since the reports are made public, depositors can identify weak banks, and avoid a potential loss by moving their accounts to another bank."

"Are the reports Jaimie sent to Blake jury-rigged, or are they the correct ones?" Adrian asked.

Blake cringed at his ready assumption Jaimie was responsible. After all the months of believing she was dead, he couldn't just flip a switch to wipe out the grief that had consumed him. He didn't want to hope.

"Good question, but I don't have an answer yet," Scott told him.

"Nicki, did Savvi find out the name of the bank?" Adrian asked.

"She said Frank didn't know, but she'd try to find out."

"Why did Blake get a copy?"

Scott answered, "I surmise it's because she knew Blake would investigate."

Blake's surreal feeling deepened. Even his boss accepted she wasn't dead. When he realized Scott was staring at him, he said, "Scott's right. What he didn't tell you is Jaimie graduated from the Naval Academy with a degree in finance. If there's something hinky in the reports, she'd spot it." He paused, taking a deep breath before relaying the details of his conversation with Tidwell.

Adrian said, "Sure sounds to me like she's alive. I wonder how the two women traded places?"

Scott said, "The bigger question is, where has she been for the last few months?"

"Last night, I read all the letters I'd received from her. There was a reference to a new assignment in the next to the last one. She said she couldn't tell me about it yet. The last one didn't arrive until several days after I found out she'd been killed. I couldn't ... I ... uh, packed it away with the rest of her letters."

Nicki was seated next to Blake. He felt the warmth of her hand cover his clenched fist, giving it a light squeeze. Some of the tension faded as he continued, "Jaimie mentioned the new assignment again. She said she still couldn't share any details, but I shouldn't worry if she didn't send any letters for a while."

Adrian, who had worked more undercover assignments than he cared to remember, said, "She went undercover. It's the only reason for no communication. Been there, done that."

"I came to the same conclusion," Blake added.

Scott said, "Then someone knows where she is. Whether we can find out is another issue. I'll make some calls. Blake, where do we stand on Wyoming?"

Shoving aside his worries about Jaimie, he said, "Every year, the Federal Reserve Bank sponsors the Teton Economic Conference. It's attended by personnel from foreign central banks, finance ministers, and major players in the financial markets around the world. Typical attendance is around a hundred and twenty people. In other words, in the banking world, it's a big deal. The Grand Mountain Resort, where it's held, is in the Grand Teton National Park. It has over 400 rooms, restaurants, retails shops, and even a museum. The conference is pretty much contained within the confines of the lodge."

Blake glanced at Nicki. "The next time you talk to Savvi, ask for a detailed list of the Chairman's activities."

"Adrian, what about the tapes?" Scott asked.

"Just what you figured, nothing."

"Unless someone has something else, let's get back to it." On his way to his office, Scott refilled his cup, then stood at his window, staring at the gloomy wet day, and brooded. While the hot brew sliding down his throat felt good, it didn't do a damn thing to relieve the tension that had built since getting a call at three in the morning. His mind's eye could see a pattern starting to form in the jumble of dots, the bits, and pieces of information. He still didn't have a clue where they led. Time was not on their side. The killer could strike at any moment. He wasn't at all certain they could prevent it.

He picked up the burner phone he'd laid aside his cell. Dropping into the chair, he waited for Frank to answer. When the rings rolled to voice mail, he disconnected. A few minutes later, it rang.

"Scott, I had someone in my office. He's gone. Has something happened?"

"Yes. Blake Kenner, the agent who received the documents, also received a coded warning. He managed to decode it." He read it to Frank.

In a thoughtful tone, Frank replied, "So much for my wishful thinking this would all be for naught. It appears as deadly of a reality as any I might face."

"It's why I'm calling. Secretary Whitaker wasn't in favor of keeping this quiet, even though he agreed to put Savvi in place for additional protection. I also know President Larkin has expressed his concern. I'm getting ready to call Paul to inform him of these new developments. He'll be calling the Secretary. I need to know if you want to change your position and bring your security team on board along with additional protection from the Bureau."

For several seconds, there was silence.

"No. I don't want to make a change. If I do, we may lose the opportunity to get ahead of the curve on this one. The threat is still there. You can't protect me forever. I believe our best course of action is to continue with the one we've set in motion."

"Okay, I'll let Paul know. Don't be surprised if you get a call from Vance."

Frank chuckled. "I have no doubt I will, even one from the President. I'll handle it."

"What does the phrase, stress tests compromised, mean to you?"

"An interesting question. This year, a new condition was added. The assets reported by the bank establish the baseline for what the bank can exchange for gold currency. As a result, banks have been scrambling to complete their stress tests before we drop the new currency in place. If the report isn't received before the deadline or the bank fails the stress test, it could mean a loss of billions of dollars for the bank. The only reason to alter a test would be to cover up losses that could cause the bank to fail the test."

"Aren't there safeguards in place to prevent a false report?"

"Absolutely. Once the report has been submitted, there is a computer-generated analysis, then a manual review. Anything else?" Frank asked.

"We need a detailed list of your activities in Wyoming."

"I'll give it to Savvi."

His thoughts as he disconnected circled around the bank stress tests.

The insistent ring of his phone broke his concentration. He considered letting it go to voice mail until he saw the caller ID.

"Fleming."

"Scott, it's Clint in New York. I hear Savvi's taken a detour since landing in Washington."

"Is that a gloat I hear in your voice?" Scott asked as he leaned back, prepared for a little good-natured ribbing.

Laughter, with a derisive undertone, burst out. "Now, why would I be gloating? It seems she's taken a step up from the Tracker Unit. Guess the Federal Reserve Chairman trumps a lowly FBI supervisor any day of the week." Another laugh erupted.

"Go ahead, take your pokes. I'll get even another time."

"Okay, all jokes aside, I do have an odd bit of information. I got a call from one of Senator Halston's aides. He asked about the Shelby Financial case and whether my office had closed the file. He was a little too interested in the lead investigator, which, as you know, was Savvi."

His tone casual, Scott asked, "Did he say why he was asking about the case?"

"The typical reply about an update to the Senate Banking Committee. Halston is a chairman of one of the sub-committees."

"I thought the case was closed."

"It is unless the defense attorneys decide to go the appeal route. I told him Agent Roth finished the last set of depositions a couple of weeks ago. When I asked specifically what details he needed for the report, he said the Senator only wanted to know if the case was still open."

"You mentioned the interest in Savvi."

"He asked if she'd been reassigned to another case."

Scott's senses tingled. "Did he give a reason?"

"When I asked, he said Senator Halston was considering a commendation and wanted to know her status. I told him she'd been reassigned to FBI Director Daykin's office, and Senator Halston should contact the Director."

"Could be legitimate considering Halston's position. A commendation in her file would be a nice addition. The next time I talk to Paul, I'll pass on the information."

"What's the deal with the Federal Reserve?"

"The result of a meeting between Whitaker and Littleton. The two of them cooked up the idea to have an agent act as a liaison for the implementation of the new currency. Littleton brought up Savvi's name. Evidently, he liked how she'd handled the Shelby case, and he knows her father. Net result, she gets to play liaison for the next few months. She's even staying at his home." He hated lying to a fellow agent, but he had to allay Clint's curiosity. He didn't need any idle speculation hitting the Bureau's gossip mill.

"Humph, small world. I'd forgotten her father has a bank in upstate New York. Savvi certainly deserves recognition. She did a hell of a job on the Shelby case. This assignment will look a lot better on her resume than a commendation from Halston. Can't say I'm sorry. Your loss is Frank Littleton's gain," Clint said with another laugh.

As Scott tapped the disconnect button, his thoughts zeroed in on Halston's inquiry. He didn't like it. He didn't believe in coincidences, not in his line of work. This was a whopper to swallow.

CHAPTER 15

HE PRESSED THE speed dial. When his boss answered, Scott said, "New developments. Got a call from Clint."

Paul chuckled. "Was he gloating?"

"Big time. But Clint also passed on a disturbing piece of information." He explained about the call Clint received from Halston's aide, which prompted a strong reaction.

"Halston!" Paul exclaimed. "Ever since he was appointed to the Senate Banking Committee, his staff has hounded my office, demanding reports from the Financial Crimes Section, then complaining when we can't provide details in ongoing investigations."

"What's the reason?" Scott asked.

"Senator Halston likes to keep his subcommittee updated."

"Hmm …. same excuse his aide used. If Halston is serious about the commendation, expect a call from him. Under other news, the reports Blake received are bank stress test results."

"I've heard of them. How'd you find out?"

"From Frank. I'll forward Nicki's research to you. Frank couldn't identify the bank, but Savvi's working on it. Blake decoded the message."

After Scott read it to him, Paul said, "Hell, it puts a new spin on everything. Vance isn't going to like it, which translates into the President won't either. I suspect your leash may get yanked. Vance isn't going to take any chances with the Chairman's life."

"I ran those concerns by Frank. He's adamant. Doesn't want to change the existing arrangement."

"Something else that won't go over well."

"I also believe Lieutenant Marston is still alive." He covered the details of Blake's phone call to California, adding in Adrian's undercover comment.

When Scott finished, Paul said, "If she's undercover, we've landed in a quagmire. For her to send those documents means something has seriously gone wrong. She's reaching out to the one person who can help her. But why didn't she come forward?"

"It may be part of the problem. She can't. Paul, any idea who might have recruited her?"

"No. Finding the answer won't be easy. From the sounds of it, the military didn't know they made a mistake. It let her slide into another identity without any fuss."

"Since we're dealing with a threat to the Chairman, bank stress tests, and taking into consideration Jaimie's financial background, I'd say money is the place to start." He added what he'd learned concerning the consequences of a bank missing the deadline or failing the test.

"I still don't get what advantage there is to take out Frank. I can't understand it," Paul said.

"I don't either, but my gut tells me we're getting close. Would Vance or the President know about an undercover bank investigation?"

"I'm going to find out."

After disconnecting, Scott sat for a few minutes. The pen in his fingers idly tapped the desk as he pondered the Halston connection.

Shoving his chair back, he headed to Nicki's office. Stopping in the doorway, he said, "Nicki?"

No response. Nicki often laughed about her ability to tune out everyone and everything around her. She referred to it as being in the zone. Oblivious to his presence, her gaze focused on the monitor while her fingers flashed across the keyboard. From the lines of code scrolling across the screen, it was part of her dungeon sweeps.

When Scott stepped alongside her chair, the movement caught her attention. Her head turned, fingers stopped.

"Sorry to interrupt."

"It's okay. Still running down the personnel at the Federal Reserve."

"I have more names to add to your list."

"Good. I run enough people, somewhere I'll find the dirt. Who are they?"

"Senator Charles Halston and his staff."

"Getting big time here. Where'd they enter the picture?"

Scott explained what he'd learned, then asked, "Have you heard from Savvi?"

"No, but then I don't expect too. She planned to talk to the staff today, and the head security guy."

"Hmm ... I wonder how that will go?" Scott mused.

✬✬✬

At the moment, Savvi was facing a pissed off, Federal Reserve cop. From the biography she'd found online, she knew Captain Lloyd Hayes was in his forties, though his lined face looked older. A heavyset, broad-shouldered man with beefy arms, when he stood to shake her hand, his gun belt rode low on his hips under a protruding belly. Seated behind his desk, he stared at her with a look of hostility.

Before leaving the house, Savvi suggested she should inform Hayes of her assignment. Frank disagreed until Savvi explained she wanted to assess the man's reaction.

After she introduced herself and explained she was assigned to the Federal Reserve, his shock had been immediate and vocal. His attitude didn't surprise her. Cops didn't like to play nice when it came to interagency cooperation, especially when the playmate was the FBI. When she added the changes to the security procedures for the Chairman, anger radiated in his voice.

"There's no reason the FBI should be involved with the Chairman's security arrangements. Quite frankly, I don't like it. Who authorized it? Why wasn't I informed?"

Seated in a chair in front of his desk, she leaned forward. "Captain Hayes, I was as shocked as you are. I was in New York City, then the next day, I'm in Washington at a luncheon with the Chairman, Director Daykin, and Secretary Whitaker."

Taken aback by the name dropping, a look of disbelief, or was it fear, flashed in his eyes. His fingers drummed the desk. While seemingly relaxed, Savvi's gaze never left his face as she analyzed every nuance of his behavior.

Evidently, Hayes realized he needed to reevaluate his position as he moderated his tone. "What is it you're supposed to do?"

"I'm a liaison between the Bureau and the Federal Reserve for the implementation of the gold currency system. I will be working with Frank."

His face relaxed. "Then you're not taking over his security?"

"Not at all, though, I will be with him most of the time. I can be considered as another asset in his protection, which is why I am making changes."

"What the hell are you referring too?"

"I'm staying at his home and will be traveling with him."

Stunned, his elbows slammed the desk as he leaned forward. "If you're not taking over his security, why are you living in his house? What is this? Some kind of run-around bullshit on being a liaison?"

Her gaze hardened as she stared at him. "There's a simple explanation. My father and Frank are old friends. Since this is a temporary assignment, Amelia invited me to stay with them." *This should start the rumor mill buzzing,* she thought.

"Humph. Looks like I'm stuck with you."

A spurt of anger raced through her. "No! You are not *stuck* with me at all. I am not under your command, nor do you have any say over what I do. We need to be very clear about this. I work for Paul Daykin, the Director of the FBI, not you."

"Then, as long as you don't get in my way, we should get along fine."

"I do expect to get in your way along with your officers who are assigned to guard the Chairman. If you don't like it, I suggest you take it up with your boss. I'm sure Chairman Littleton or Director Daykin won't mind a phone call."

The look of dislike intensified. "Is there anything else?"

"Not unless I encounter resistance from your team. Then I expect we will have another discussion."

Savvi stood. "I won't say this was a good meeting. I had hoped for your cooperation. Still, I can do my job without it. It doesn't bother me one iota to cut *you* out of the information loop."

As she turned, it finally dawned on him what he'd done. "Hold up, Agent Roth, let's reconsider this."

Ignoring him, she kept walking, resisting the urge to slam the door behind her. In the hallway, she took a deep breath. The anger slowly dissipated as she viewed his behavior. Hayes had certainly done nothing to remove himself from her list of possible suspects. If anything, he'd moved up on her radar of people to watch.

Instead of returning to her office, she wandered the halls, stopping when she saw an open doorway to introduce herself to the occupant. Everyone was friendly and receptive to talking to her. Making a mental note of each person's name and responsibility, she continued to ramble through the building.

As she passed Sutter's office, he called out. When she stepped inside, he said, "Since I didn't find you in your office, I hoped you were still here."

"I've been getting acquainted with the building's layout and enjoying the architecture." She didn't think it was necessary to add, along with spying on the employees.

"Um … please, have a seat. I got a call from Captain Hayes. He's quite disturbed over his meeting with you."

I bet he is, she thought. Interesting, though. It was Sutter he called, not his boss, the police chief. "Umm, yes, it didn't go well," was all she said.

"I hope your presence isn't going to create any discord here. When Chairman Littleton first broached the subject of your assignment, I did have reservations. Our security staff has always been well equipped to handle any issues concerning the operation of the Federal Reserve. It seemed unnecessary to assign an FBI agent here. Even one as qualified as you. Now it seems, there's already some sort of controversy between you and Captain Hayes."

"Oh, I believe we had a meeting of the minds by the time it was over. There won't be a problem."

"Not according to Captain Hayes. It's my responsibility to keep personnel issues on an even keel, you might say. Captain Hayes oversees the security of this building and the personnel who work here. Which includes you. I need to be informed of your activities, so does Captain Hayes."

She stared at him while her lips twisted in a smile that never reached her eyes. Leaning forward, she said, "Therein lies the problem. I don't report to you. I don't report to Captain Hayes. While I might consider it a courtesy to discuss certain issues with you, it is by no means required. I'm here in an autonomous position to help ensure a smooth transition to the new monetary system. I hope *you* understand, and I can count on your cooperation."

Savvi rose and walked out of his office. She'd certainly stirred the pot. What bubbled to the top had set off a familiar tingle. Hayes and Sutter, both pushing the same agenda, wanting to know what she was up too.

Inside her office, she took a bottle of water from the compact refrigerator located in a wall cabinet. Dropping into her chair, she twisted the cap and took a deep swig. The chill helped ease some of the tension. After a second swallow, she pulled her cell, then pushed the speed dial.

When Nicki answered on the first ring, Savvi said, "Do you have the dang phone chained to your wrist?"

"What!" Nicki exclaimed.

"For normal people, it usually takes a few rings for them to get to the phone. Not you. It's either the first or second ring. I figure it's a chain, or you've managed to hardwire your brain to a device."

On the other end, a ripple of laughter erupted. "I'll never give up my secrets. Is there a purpose to this call?"

"Oh, yeah. What are you doing this evening?"

"I planned to work on the backgrounds and research the Wyoming gig. Why?"

"I need your help."

"For what?"

"To buy an evening gown." Silence on the other end. "Nicki, did I lose you?"

"No, wasn't certain I heard right. You did say evening gown?"

"Yep. I figure you know the stores around here. I don't."

"You're putting me on, aren't you?"

"No, I need an evening gown. All I brought with me were work and casual outfits. This morning Amelia told me they are attending a reception at an art gallery tomorrow night. It's formal attire, which means an evening gown."

"Holy crap. Does Scott know?"

"Not yet. It's been a busy day."

"Anything I need to pass on to him?"

"Maybe later."

"Oh, I get it. You can't talk?"

"You're right. What if I pick you up around six, go shopping, then grab a bite to eat?"

"I'll be ready. I'll pass along your upcoming jaunt into the upper echelons of the political arena."

Savvi could hear Nicki laughing as she disconnected.

Hearing footsteps, she rose and quickly walked to the door. Looking out, she saw a man at the end of the hallway. As he turned the corner, she recognized him, Darren Holcomb. Had he been listening outside her door?

CHAPTER 16

SCOTT EASED BACK in his chair, his hand rubbed his forehead. For over two hours, he'd read and evaluated a surfeit of articles flooding the internet on the new currency.

In 1944, forty-four countries met and signed the Bretton Woods Agreement. Countries could settle their international accounts by converting dollars to a fixed exchange rate per troy ounce of gold. By 1971, foreign central banks had depleted U.S. gold reserves. President Nixon's suspension of the conversion of dollars to gold created the current fiat system.

Now, in a similar move, President Larkin had resurrected the gold currency, one that would co-exist alongside the fiat system. His action overrode the objections of politicians and finance experts, setting off a wave of protests, even within the Federal Reserve System.

While Scott had gained a better understanding of the issues, he wasn't any closer to finding a motive or suspect. The ring of his phone was a welcome relief, even though it was his boss.

"Scott, I've got bad news. Neither Vance nor the President knows about any undercover operation."

"It was a long shot at best. I'll run it by Frank this evening. See if he can shed any light on the topic. Otherwise, we'll have to hope Jaimie surfaces again."

"Vance said to tell you, he's holding pat for the moment."

"It's all I can ask. I've got Nicki running Halston and his staff."

"Let me know if she finds anything. That's one politician I wouldn't mind nailing his hide to a wall," he said before disconnecting.

A chirpy voice sounded. Nicki lounged against the doorway. "I heard my name. Any progress?"

"Keeping my boss in the loop," he said as he eyed her with suspicion. She had her smirky grin, the one he learned usually preceded some outrageous announcement or devilment.

"You'll never guess where I'm headed tonight?"

With a wry look, he said, "Obviously, it must be somewhere other than the couch in the breakroom."

After scrunching her nose at him, she said, "To buy an evening gown."

Startled, he said, "For what?"

"Oh, it's not for me. Savvi is headed to some shindig at a gallery with the Chairman and his wife. She needs an evening gown."

He winced. The closer Frank stayed to home or his office, the easier it was to safeguard him.

Nicki's grin vanished. She plunked in the chair.

"Are you going to get him to cancel?"

His eyebrow twitched upward, though, he shouldn't have been surprised. Nicki had a way of reading his thoughts.

"No, it would be a dead giveaway something was up. But I don't like the idea. Where is the gallery?"

"All Savvi said was a reception at an art gallery."

"Hmm … shouldn't be difficult to find out where. When is it?"

"Tomorrow night."

"At least, we'll have time to check out the location. Anything else?"

"No, she wasn't where she could talk, though I know she's got more information. I'll get it tonight."

"What time are you going?"

"She said she'd pick me up at six," she answered, then looked at the wall clock. "Yikes! I've got to get going."

She raced out, hollering as she left. "I'll call."

An uneasy feeling roiled inside him. It only took a few minutes, and he was looking at the photos on the gallery's website. The artist, one who had taken the art world by storm, was exhibiting a new collection. To get through the door required a $500 donation to a local charity. An event of this type would draw a large crowd. His uneasiness grew. How was Frank's security detail handling this?

"What's got her revved up?" Blake asked.

Scott looked up. Blake and Adrian hovered in his doorway.

After hearing the reason, Adrian commented, "Not sure the stores are ready for Nicki and Savvi, the dynamic duo."

An idea sparked in Scott's mind. Before he acted on it, he needed to talk to Frank.

"Hmm ... either one of you free tonight? I'd like one of you to check out the gallery."

Blake sensed Adrian tensing beside him. Knowing he had plans, Blake said, "I am."

Still, Adrian protested. "I'll flip you for it."

"Nah, you've been planning on attending the blues festival for weeks. I've got this covered."

Writing down the address of the gallery, Scott handed it to Blake. As they walked out of Scott's office, Adrian said, "Hey, man, thanks. I owe you one."

Overhearing their conversation, Scott grinned. Seldom was Adrian found at home. He glanced at his watch. If Savvi was picking up Nicki around six, Frank should be home. He retrieved the burner phone from his briefcase.

When Frank answered, he said, "Scott, didn't expect to hear from you again today."

"I found out you are attending a reception tomorrow night."

Frank sighed. "It's Amelia's doing. She's enamored with this new artist and has been haranguing me for weeks to go. Since Savvi's arrival, she's stepped up her campaign. I finally gave in this morning. Is it a problem?"

"No, not at all. When you attend this type of event, where is your security detail?"

"I usually have two. The driver stays with the vehicle. The other officer is inside with me."

"Would it be possible to add another member to your party? I'd like to include Nicki Allison. Since she and Savvi are good friends, her presence won't spark undue interest. It puts two agents there to guard you."

"You don't seriously believe something could happen?"

"Frank, I've learned not to take anything for granted. I would much rather err on the side of caution."

"I'll let Amelia know. Do we need to pick up Nicki?"

"I'll get back to you. Are you aware of any agency running a covert banking investigation?"

"Not to my knowledge."

"What about foreign agencies? Any rumblings?"

"The answer is an unequivocal yes. It's the nature of the banking beast. There have been several bank investigations over the last few years. A couple are still ongoing. But nothing I could attribute to our problem. Do you want me to put out some feelers? I can call some of my contacts in the international market."

"No, not yet. I don't want to raise suspicions."

After disconnecting, he called Nicki. When she answered, she said, "I hope this is important boss man, because Savvi is parked in a no-parking zone downstairs. She said a mounted officer has ridden by twice, giving her the evil eye."

"I'll make this fast. You're going to the reception with Savvi. If you need a new dress, turn in the receipt on your expense account. Tell Savvi the same."

Her squeal had him holding the phone several inches from his ear. "I'll let her know. Got to go, so little time, so many dresses."

Laughing, Scott disconnected. After tossing a few file folders in his briefcase, he walked out. After setting the alarm, he flipped off the lights, then locked the door behind him.

Inside the elevator, he punched the ground floor button. A tall, rangy built man slipped between the doors as they started to close. He leaned in the corner. Once the elevator started down, the man hit the stop button. It slowly shuddered to a stop.

Scott shifted, knees flexed, his hand slid toward the butt of the gun on his belt.

The man held out his hands, palms up. In a mocking tone, he said, "Agent Fleming, no cause for alarm. I simply find it has become necessary to have a private conversation with you."

Scott snorted. "Couldn't you find a better place than an elevator? I do have an office."

With an amused look, the man glanced around the small space. "You must admit an elevator provides an illusion of security." His hand moved toward his pocket.

Scott tensed.

"Only my phone." He tapped the screen, then held it to his ear. "Make the call," he said, before sliding it back in his pocket.

Intrigued, Scott leaned against the wall. With arms crossed, his hand was inches from his gun. While seemingly unconcerned, every instinct tingled. "Since you know me, then who are you?"

"For the moment, let's just say a friend."

Scott detected a slight accent. "Why is it necessary to have a private conversation?"

"Ah, Americans, cutting right to the heart of the matter. There is a concern about a recent request for a military file."

Despite a sharp jolt of anticipation, his calm, even tone never changed.

"How would I know?"

"Agent Fleming," he mocked. "Let's not play games. We know it was sent to you."

Interesting, he thought. Paul's request must have triggered an alert, which meant someone in the military was involved. Still, how did the man know he'd received a copy? "Who is we?"

"Someone interested in Lieutenant Marston."

"Why would you be interested in a dead woman?"

"We've reached the crux of the matter. Why would *you* be interested?" He glanced at his watch. "Are you a football fan?"

What the hell! Whatever was going on, all he could do was play along. "I enjoy the games."

"Hmm ... American football, certainly more exciting than soccer in my country."

"What country is that?" Scott asked.

The mocking half-smile reappeared. "The hallmark of a true agent. Never let a slight slip pass you by. Do you have a favorite team?"

Though the man didn't answer his question, Scott's tone was unconcerned. "I can't say I favor one more than another."

"No favorite. Ach! Then, you cannot be considered a disciple of the sport."

Inside Scott's pocket, the cell phone rang.

"I suggest you answer it."

Scott pulled out the phone. "Fleming."

"Scott," Paul said. "I received a very odd call from Louie Bisset, head of Interpol. He gave me a code word to identify the man you're talking too. He said you'd explain, then hung up."

Scott's watchful eyes never shifted. "What is it?"

With a mocking gaze, the man stared back.

"Navajo. Does this have anything to do with your earlier inquiry on investigations by foreign agencies?"

"I'm not certain. I'll contact you later." He disconnected. After a thoughtful look at the man leaning in the corner, he asked, "Codeword?"

With another mocking half-smile, the man replied, "Navajo." He straightened, restarted the elevator, then extended his hand. "Remy Chabot, Interpol. Sorry for the cloak and dagger routine, but it was vital you had instant confirmation of my identity."

"I had the accent narrowed down to French or Brit. What are you doing here?" Scott said as he shook the man's hand.

Chabot evaded another question, saying instead, "Close. French Canadian. Why don't we continue this conversation in your office." When the elevator reached the ground floor, the man pressed a button, sending it back up. Before stepping out, he leaned forward, his eyes skimming the hallway.

A cautious man, Scott thought as he led the way to his office. Once inside, he turned off the alarm, then looked at the agent. "Coffee?"

"Most definitely." As Chabot glanced around the room, he said, "When I attempted to locate you, I was surprised to discover your offices weren't in the FBI building."

"These are temporary," he hedged. Despite the unorthodox manner to establish his identity, Scott still had an edgy feeling about his presence.

In the breakroom, Scott started the coffee machine. He motioned toward a stack of cups. "Milk's in the fridge."

"Black's fine." Chabot dropped onto the sofa. "Now, why did you request the Marston file?"

"She's alive, isn't she?"

The flash of surprise in Chabot's eyes was quickly suppressed. If Scott hadn't been watching, he'd have missed it.

"Then you know more than we realized."

"Why is Interpol involved?"

The machine beeped. Scott filled a cup and handed it to the man, then filled his.

Chabot took a sip. "Several months ago, Interpol recruited Jaimie for an assignment."

"Why her?"

"Two reasons, her financial background and the Navajo code she created for the U.S. military."

"Okay, go on."

"We had a plan to quietly remove her from Iraq. When the vehicle she was supposed to be in blew up, everyone assumed she'd been killed. My superiors decided to continue with the fiction."

"How did another woman take her place?"

"An unforeseen circumstance. Jaimie was on her way to Bagdad for a meeting with an Interpol agent. After her vehicle left the compound, a medic flagged them down."

"Um ... Kathy Logan," Scott interjected.

Chabot's hand, raising the cup, stopped. "Once again, Agent Fleming, you have surprised me. With me, it is not so very easy."

"It's Scott. I've a feeling we'll get to know each other very well."

Chabot's lips twitched with his mocking smile. "Remy. Now, how the hell did you find out about Logan?"

"Talked to the man who investigated the explosion."

"Ach, another surprise. Anyway, something was wrong with Logan's car. She said it was urgent she get to Baghdad. Since there wasn't room in the Humvee for another passenger, Jaimie stayed behind with the car. Another convoy was leaving, and she intended to hitch a ride when they came by. Instead, she managed to get Logan's car started and drove it to Baghdad."

"What was the assignment?"

Chabot swallowed the last of his coffee. He motioned with the cup. "A refill?"

Scott moved away from the machine. "Help yourself."

Once he'd filled the cup, Chabot settled back on the couch. "I can't discuss details until I know why the FBI has landed in the middle of an Interpol investigation. I've answered your questions. It's time for you to answer mine."

Scott pondered for a few seconds. "One more."

The man sighed, then nodded.

"Where is she?"

"We've lost contact with her."

"What!" Scott exclaimed.

"Her handler was killed."

"Sounds like a BS answer."

"Sadly, it does, but it's true. Now, why did you request her file?"

Scott stuck his cup under the spigot. How much should he tell the agent? As the coffee flowed, he said, "The Federal Reserve Chairman, Frank Littleton, received a warning he would be assassinated."

Behind him, a whistle echoed. "Mon Dieu! His assassination would rock the international financial community. Especially with what's at stake with this latest move, the gold currency."

Scott turned. "I believe the warning came from Lieutenant Marston."

Chabot's eyes narrowed. "How did you come by such a conclusion?"

"Bits and pieces from different sources, which together pointed to Marston. It's why I have a copy of her personnel file. What was her assignment?"

Chabot rose, walked to the sink, and rinsed out his cup. Setting it on the counter, he said, "I must speak with Louie Bisset. The threat to Chairman Littleton changes everything. I assume you have adequate protection in place for him."

With a grim look, Scott said, "You assume correctly. The clock is ticking. I need information."

"I understand, but I can do nothing without authorization."

He headed for the door.

"How do I contact you?"

"You can't. I'll contact you." Chabot stopped to glance over his shoulder. "A caution, Agent Fleming. I have no doubt you'll sic the hounds on my track as soon as I walk out of your office. I would appreciate it if you would exercise ... a degree of restraint." With a sardonic look, he added, "I don't want to end up dead in some alley," then walked out.

Scott turned off the coffee machine and set his cup in the sink. Before leaving, he picked up his briefcase where he'd dropped it, reset the alarm, then locked the door. No sign of Chabot, and he hadn't left by the elevator. It was still on his floor. *Yes, a very cautious man*, he thought.

Paul said they'd stepped into a quagmire. Scott suspected it was deeper than either of them had envisioned.

Chapter
17

L AUGHING, SAVVI FOLLOWED Nicki out the door of Esmeralda's Boutique. Their arms laden with boxes and bags, they headed toward Savvi's vehicle parked several blocks down the street. For the last two hours, they'd traipsed in and out of stores. After adding their purchases to the stack on the backseat, Nicki hopped in front, and Savvi slid behind the wheel.

"We've must have walked miles, and I'm starving." Nicki slipped off a shoe to massage her foot.

"So am I. Where are we going to eat? I need directions."

"If it's okay with you, let's go back to my apartment. A Chinese place across the street delivers."

Savvi started the engine. "It's more than okay. I'd much rather relax there than sit on a hard chair in a restaurant."

"Straight ahead and take a left at the next red light. I still can't believe Scott said the Bureau would pay for this little jaunt. When did you ever have carte blanche for shopping?"

"Never." Savvi chuckled as she merged into the heavy traffic. "How could I resist buying a few more items when I didn't have to pay for an outfit for tomorrow night? I've got to start thinking about where I'll live when this is over. I already need another suitcase."

"You can always stash it in my spare bedroom until you get settled."

"Thanks, I may take you up on it. It's been a whirlwind since I got the call from Clint." She shot a fond look at Nicki. "The best part is you are going with me. I'm glad to have the back-up."

A somber look settled on Nicki's face. "You think someone might make a try at the Chairman?"

"Hmm ... I don't know. A gallery doesn't seem a likely place, but crowds haven't stopped assassins in the past. While this interlude has been fun, bottom line, tomorrow night, we're working."

Waving her hand toward the backseat, she added, "Since we can't show up in Bureau attire, it's all window dressing and subterfuge. Anything yet on the backgrounds?" She tapped the brakes to slow for the turn.

"No. With hundreds of employees, it's a time-consuming process. If we could narrow it down, it would help."

"Remember those vibes I mentioned?"

"Yeah, why?"

"They got stronger today." She relayed what happened with Hayes, then Sutter. "Maybe Hayes is pissed because I'm FBI, but his reaction was a little too forceful. If he wanted to lodge a complaint, why didn't he go up his chain of command? Instead, he talks to Sutter. Then there's the IT guy."

"Turn right at the next corner. What's up with him?"

"Holcomb, Darren Holcomb. Yesterday, I caught him in my office, looking at my laptop. He blew if off as a security issue. Today, I think he may have listened to our conversation."

"I knew a computer nerd named Darren Holcomb. I wonder ..." Nicki's voice faded.

"I'd like to know what you find on them."

As they approached the apartment complex, Nicki said, "Park in the garage. Easier than tromping through the lobby with all the boxes."

Savvi pulled into a spot near the elevator.

Nicki hopped out and opened the back door. Eyeing the stack on the backseat, she said, "Dang, we did get a lot."

Savvi laughed as she exited. "I know. I didn't really need the last pair of shoes, but I couldn't resist."

As Nicki leaned into the vehicle, they heard the squeal of tires.

Savvi looked up. An SUV raced toward them. A man holding a gun hung out the window. She screamed, "Gun! Get down!" and darted to the front of the car. Shots rang out. Savvi jerked the Glock from the holster clipped to her belt. The gun bucked in her hands as she repeatedly pulled the trigger. One bullet shattered the windshield. The passenger ducked back as the vehicle skidded around the end of another row of parked cars, heading toward the entrance.

Fear clawed her insides. She screamed, "Nicki!" and dashed around the car. Sprawled across the boxes, Nicki's legs protruded from the vehicle. "Oh, god! Nicki?" Shoving the gun in the holster, her hands reached to feel her friend's body.

"I think … I'm okay." Nicki groaned. "Give me a minute to restart my heart." She slowly slid backward until her feet hit the ground, then stood. After several deep breaths, Nicki asked, "Did you hit one of them?"

Savvi leaned against the car. "I don't know, though the driver will have a tough time. I took out the windshield."

"If you hadn't shouted, I'd have been a sitting duck, or at least my butt would have been since it was sticking up in the air."

With a wobbly chuckle, Savvi said, "You idiot." Pushing away from the car, she turned to look at the damage. Bullet holes raked the side.

Nicki stepped beside her. "Holy crap! All those jokes I made about you carrying while shopping, I take them all back." She pulled her phone from her pocket.

When Scott answered, he said, "How's the shop…"

Nicki interrupted. "Boss man, we've got a bit of a problem. Savvi and I are okay, but someone decided to use us for target practice."

With a harshness Nicki had never heard, he asked, "Where are you?"

"Parking garage at my apartment building."

"I'm on my way."

★★★

Scott clipped his gun to his belt, pulled on a jacket, and ran out the door. Once he pulled out of the garage, he goosed it. While grateful the traffic was light, nothing would have slowed him down. Someone tried to take out two of his agents. Why? Anger boiled inside him as he tapped the speed dial.

Adrian's voice, muffled by loud music, said, "Scott, what's wrong?"

"Someone tried to kill Nicki and Savvi tonight."

"Holy hell! Did I hear right? Give me a minute to get out of this place." His voice louder as the music faded, he said, "Did you say someone tried to kill them? Are they okay?"

"Nicki said they are. It happened in the parking garage at Nicki's apartment building. Do you still have the evidence kit in your car?"

"Yeah. I'm on my way."

As Scott pulled in, he spotted the two women beside a car near the elevator. He screeched to a stop and jumped out. His gaze raked them, needing to be reassured they hadn't been hurt.

Though pale, Nicki's lips curled into her smirky grin.

The panic faded as relief rushed over him.

"Sure glad to see you, boss man," she quipped.

For once, the irritating nickname didn't faze him. "Who wants to give me a rundown?"

After glancing at Nicki, who nodded, Savvi began. For the next several minutes, she walked him through what happened. "I got off four shots. I'm certain all hit the vehicle. One took out the windshield."

"Description?"

"A black, four-door SUV. I only caught a glimpse of the license plate. I think the last two numbers were 06."

A car stopped behind Scott's vehicle, and Adrian jumped out. As he ran up, Nicki whistled, "Dang, dude, don't you look hot tonight."

He looked at Scott, then grinned. "Here I was, worried sick. Someone shooting at her hasn't slowed her down one iota. So, what happened?"

Once again, Savvi went through the process.

When she finished, Scott asked, "Nicki, where were you again?"

Oh, boy, Savvi thought. She'd glossed over the bit where Nicki was bent over to save her friend embarrassment. She might as well have saved herself the effort.

"If you must know, I was leaning into the car, trying to grab a box from the other side." At the gleam sparking in the men's eyes, she added, "And, yes, my ass was in the air. If either of you laughs, remember the old saying about payback."

Adrian, fighting the grin tugging at his lips, waved his hands in the air. "Mum's the word."

Savvi asked, "Do either of you have an evidence bag? We found the shell casings, nine mil. I'll show you." While Adrian retrieved the camera and bag from his trunk, Scott walked along the side of the car. Six holes. Most were located toward the front of the vehicle, where Savvi had taken cover.

He turned. She was helping Adrian bag the casings. "Savvi, are the Littleton's expecting you tonight?"

"Yes."

"I'll follow you, just to make sure someone doesn't try again. I suspect you were the target. Tomorrow, I'll have someone from the auto pound swap cars with you."

"Waiting for you, we came to the same conclusion. But why the hell would I be a target?"

Unable to answer, he shrugged his shoulders as he watched Adrian snap pictures. Once he'd finished, Scott said, "Adrian, help Nicki get her packages up to her apartment." He motioned to a camera mounted on a column near the elevator. "Then check the security office. Since the cops or a security guard haven't shown up, it's doubtful there's anyone there."

"If there isn't, I'll check in the morning," Nicki said.

"Who knew you were going out tonight?" Scott asked Savvi.

"There's a couple of possibilities—Darren Holcomb, the IT guy, for one. After I talked to Nicki about the shopping trip, I spotted him in the hallway. He might have been listening. On the way home, I discussed it with Frank. The officers would have heard. Does this change anything for tomorrow night?"

"No, it's still a go. But I don't like the timing of this attack. Anything else I need to know?"

"Yes. I already passed this onto Nicki to tell you in the morning, which reminds me." She turned to Nicki. "Let me have the packet I gave you."

Then she looked back at Scott. "Nothing on the identity of the bank. I had two disquieting conversations with Captain Lloyd Hayes and Director Ben Sutter. Both were overly insistent I keep them in the loop on my activities and very displeased at my refusal. One other point was troubling. Hayes called Sutter to complain. I'm not impressed with Frank's security team."

As she detailed the changes she'd made, Nicki handed Scott an envelope. Savvi added, "A list of Frank's activities in Wyoming."

He tucked it under his arm. "Don't mention this to the Littleton's."

"I hadn't planned on it, but I'm glad to know we're on the same page on hushing this up."

"Okay, we'll go back at this in the morning. Let's get you out of here."

After looking at the pile of boxes and sacks on the backseat, Adrian groaned. "Anything left in the stores? Nicki, how many of the damn things are yours?"

Her fist thumped his shoulder. "What! Too wimpy to carry a few measly boxes and sacks?"

Once Nicki and Adrian had left, Savvi backed out. When she pulled onto the street, Scott was behind her. During the drive, her brain clicked into overdrive as she replayed the shooting. One question endlessly circled. Why would she be a target?

As she drove into the Littleton's driveway, Scott flashed his lights as he sped by. The porch lights came on. As she stacked the boxes in her arms, Amelia rushed out.

"Oh, Savvi, let me help you. My, from the looks of these, I'd say you didn't have any problem finding what you needed."

With a wry chuckle, Savvi said, "And some I didn't."

"But that's what makes it so much fun. Frank's been pacing the floor wondering when you'd make it back."

Inside, Amelia asked, "Did you have any dinner?"

Belatedly, Savvi realized she hadn't. The Chinese takeout never materialized. "No, I didn't get a chance."

"I had a hunch, and I always follow my hunches." Amelia smiled over the top of three shoe boxes. "There is a plate of roast beef, garlic mashed potatoes, and sautéed green beans in the oven."

Just listening to the description set off a rumble in Savvi's stomach. "I'll gladly take you up on your offer."

"We'll drop these in your room. While you freshen up, I'll get the tray ready for you. If you like, you can eat in the library. Frank will be able to talk about whatever has him on pins and needles."

When she left the bedroom, she followed the aroma of roasted meat and onions into the library. Perched on the arm of a chair, Amelia said, "Much better, my dear. I was telling Frank you looked a bit peaky when you got here."

Someone shooting at you would do it, she thought, but only said, "Nicki's a very determined shopper."

Frank laughed. "I would suggest then you never go shopping with my wife. You'll be worn to a frazzle."

"Now, Frank. You know it is so totally untrue." Hopping off the couch, she pointed to the tray on a small table. "Come, don't let it get cold."

Amelia fussed until she was satisfied Savvi was comfortable and didn't need anything, before tripping out of the room, saying, "I'll leave you to your discussions."

As Savvi took a bite of the roast, she moaned with pleasure. "Absolutely delicious," she said as she forked up potatoes.

Frank had settled behind his desk. Several files were strewn across the top. "Do you mind if we talk business while you eat?"

She waved her fork in the air and swallowed. "Not at all."

"I had a very odd call from Scott earlier, wanting to know if I knew of any covert bank investigations. I told him I didn't. Any idea what he was talking about?"

Intrigued by the question, her eyes darted up. When her gaze met his, he said, "Exactly, my dear. Precisely the same thought I had. The plot thickens."

"It would seem so, though Scott didn't mention it."

"I'll have to wait to have my curiosity satisfied." He picked up one of the documents lying in front of him. "I've been going over these bank stress reports. Did you have any luck with them?"

"Not yet, though I did spend several hours looking for a match. I'll go back at it again tomorrow."

"If the reported figures are faulty, it does raise a serious concern over the legitimacy of the testing process. The consequences …" His voice trailed off as he grimly stared at the documents.

"What would be the fallout?"

"If the unthinkable, the catastrophic scenario used for the test, became a reality… massive bank failures. A financial tsunami of shock waves would ripple around the world. Not a single country would escape the impending economic destruction."

CHAPTER 18

SMILING AT THE dour-faced guard behind the scanner, Lois Barnett dropped her briefcase and backpack in the small bins on the conveyor belt. The guard was new. Her cheery, "Good morning," didn't crack the hard gaze raking her from head to toe. After stepping through the metal detector, she retrieved her items, uneasily aware his eyes followed as she walked away.

With a casual stride, which belied the tingle of nerves along her spine, she crossed the lobby of the Federal Reserve building, heading to the bank of elevators. Inside, she tried to relax as it glided upward. Stepping out, she greeted several people in the hallway. By now, she knew most everyone in this section of the building.

"Lois, hold up a minute."

Reluctantly, she turned. At the sight of the man walking up, her shoulders braced as Ed Deegan's smarmy gaze slid over her. For weeks, she'd dodged his advances, suggestions for a drink or dinner.

"Have you finished the analysis of the report for Butler Bank and Trust?"

"Almost. I should have it to you later today," she said and turned to open her door, hoping he'd keep going. No such luck as he followed her inside.

"The review should have been completed by now," he grumbled. He watched her drop the briefcase and backpack on the desk. "I know you've been working late. So, what's the hold-up?"

She turned to face him. "I reviewed the report again, just to be certain of my results before I sent it to you."

"Your insistence on checking, then double-checking, isn't necessary. The computer does the number crunching. I told you before, the only time you need to examine the figures is when an alert is triggered. If the program green lights the report, then sign off on the review and send it to me."

"Yes, sir. I will."

"The deadline for the reviews has been moved up, which means overtime. I've been told to clear the backlog. You've got three bank reports stacked up. Starting tonight, we'll be working late."

"I'm sorry. but I can't."

His eyes narrowed with displeasure.

She rushed to add, "I have a commitment I can't change. Tomorrow night won't be a problem. Any idea why the new deadline?"

With a curt tone, he said, "It's not important." His phone rang. "Plan on working tomorrow night," he said, giving her a stern look. "Deegan," he answered as he walked out.

Agitated by the encounter, she followed, closing the door behind him, then leaned against it. Why the sudden rush to approve the bank stress reports? Another troubling piece of news she couldn't send out. Hell, with Rick dead, her phone destroyed, she was flying blind, with no way to contact her team.

When Interpol set up Operation Navajo to insert an agent inside the Federal Reserve, keeping the point of contact to one person made sense. But no one anticipated he'd be killed. The news report of Rick's murder had sent her spiraling into a sea of fear and uncertainty, not only for herself but also for the safety of the Chairman.

Since racing out of the alley, she'd been looking over her shoulder. Had someone discovered Lois Barnett was Navy Lieutenant Jaimie Marston? Deegan's comment about her working late had set off another tingle of alarm, adding to her paranoia. Was someone watching her? Did they know she'd been searching offices?

From the start, her new persona seemed rock solid. Even the Fed's background check hadn't found any discrepancies. A U.S. citizen, she'd grown up in Switzerland and had worked for the Bank of International Settlements. Her resume even included references from bank personnel.

What did surprise her was the unexpected transfer to the stress test division a few weeks back. At the time, she'd chalked it up to Deegan's interest since he'd already started hitting on her. Now, she had to wonder if there was another agenda, one she knew nothing about.

Jaimie pushed away from the door and slowly walked to her chair. Even though a limited number of people were involved in Operation Navajo, surely by now someone in Interpol had to know he'd been killed. Why hadn't she been contacted?

All she could do was continue with her regular routine though her gut churned with foreboding. She'd already done what she could by warning the Chairman, then sending her last dispatch to Blake. It was a longshot he'd be able to decode the message, but the only one she had. Even though she'd toyed with the idea of calling him, the risk was too high. A phone call could jeopardize the entire operation, though, she might not have any other option. Who else could she trust? No one in the Federal Reserve.

Unless—the FBI agent? The rumor mill was abuzz with the news the agent had been assigned to the PGS project. It struck her as a little too coincidental that right after she left the note in the Chairman's coat, Agent Roth appeared on the scene. Did she dare take another chance and contact the agent?

With a deep breath, Jaimie shifted her focus back to the latest discovery. After finding a second set of jury-rigged reports, she realized the problem was the software program. It didn't trigger the alerts. Not only were the stress tests compromised, but also the Federal Reserve computer system.

How many reports had already been rubber-stamped? Was it the reason for moving up the deadline? When you factored in the assassination of the Chairman, this place would be thrown into an instant turmoil. Was the plan to use the confusion to ensure the rest of the stress tests received the seal of approval?

Jaimie needed to stay tonight. Every approved report had to be checked, but it would have to wait. Protecting the Chairman had become her top priority. Last night, she had slipped into Captain Hayes' office to check the assignment log for the security officers. It wasn't her first visit. The first time, she discovered the Chairman would be attending a meeting at the Greystone Hotel. This time, it was a reception at an art gallery.

★★★

Adrian was unlocking the office door when Scott stepped off the elevator. After greeting his boss, he said, "You were right on the security office in Nicki's apartment building. It was locked up tighter than a drum. I'm hoping Nicki will learn something when she talks to them this morning."

Following him inside, Scott said, "We might get lucky, but I didn't like the location of the cameras." As he gazed around the deserted office, he added, "At least one positive from last night."

"Oh?"

Scott grinned. "Nicki didn't sleep on the couch. Once she and Blake get here, head to the conference room. The hits keep on coming."

As Adrian strode to the breakroom, his laughter echoed along the hall.

Scott dropped his briefcase on his desk, then booted his computer, checking his messages. Nothing that couldn't wait. However, there was one call he had to make. When his boss answered,

Scott told him, "Interpol's running an investigation. The man I met last night is one of their agents."

There was a pause before Paul reacted. "They'd better have a damn good reason for the secrecy—otherwise, this will get ugly."

Scott explained what he learned, then added, "Don't run up the red flag yet. I want time to find out what the hell they're doing. It gets worse. Someone tried to kill Nicki and Savvi last night."

The pause was even longer before Paul exclaimed, "Son-of-a-bitch! What happened?"

Scott ran through the details, adding his belief Savvi was the target.

Paul snapped to the same conclusion Scott had. "Someone is getting nervous. Has Savvi discovered anything at the Federal Reserve?"

"Some suspicions, but nothing concrete."

"Hmm ... not going to tell me, are you?"

"I will, when it is more than supposition."

"Scott, let me remind you that you are still on a short leash. Don't let this get away from you." The line went dead.

As he laid the phone down, Nicki rapped on his door, saying, "Morning, boss man." Her tone was decidedly unfriendly, an unusual occurrence for her.

She plunked in a chair. "Frigging camera system is on the fritz. The manager said he'd meant to get it repaired, but it wasn't high on the maintenance list. After I ripped him a new one over the security, or lack of, in his building, he decided to move it up."

Scott nodded. "Not surprised. Adrian made coffee. When Blake gets here, we're meeting in the conference room."

Her face perked up. "Coffee. It's what I need to get rid of the bad taste from dealing with a weasel of a manager. I may have to find another place to live." Grumbling, she marched out of his office.

After making the arrangements to trade out Savvi's vehicle, he gathered his files. He'd heard Blake's voice, so his team was here.

When he walked into the conference room, a steaming cup of coffee sat on the table in front of his chair. He looked at Nicki. She shot him a mischievous look. Glad she was in better humor, he settled in the chair, then raised the cup with a toasting motion in her direction.

"I'll kickstart this. Interpol is involved." After the outcries of surprise from the three agents, Scott went on to explain his encounter with Remy Chabot. When he reached the part that confirmed Jaimie was alive, he paused to glance at Blake.

"It's okay. I finally accepted it was true," Blake told him.

"Nicki, he made a curious comment about ending up dead in an alley. See what you can find."

"Got it, boss man."

His grimace only sparked an unrepentant smirk. Turning to Blake, he caught the flash of a grin before it vanished. "What did you find out about the gallery?"

"Three entrances, front, a back door in the kitchen, and a side door for deliveries." He handed out diagrams. "Here's the floor plan. The catering company provides the waitstaff for the evening."

"Security?" Adrian asked.

"A couple of rent-a-guards. There is a parking lot adjacent to the gallery with valet parking. Across the street is a small park with a few trees and a couple of two-story buildings."

"Any metal detectors?" Scott asked as he perused the floorplan.

"The gallery director squawked in outrage when I asked. I was informed they'd never had a problem. He was emphatic that he wasn't going to subject his patrons to the indignity."

"I don't suppose any of the persons hired to work the event have been cleared with a background check."

Blake told him, "Nope. Another question that prompted an outcry of annoyance."

"I don't like it," Scott said. "Too damn many ways to get to the Chairman." His pen tapped as he thought.

"Nicki, have you been able to eliminate any of Frank's security personnel yet?"

"Nothing conclusive so far. While they seem squeaky clean, I wouldn't take a chance."

"Good enough for me. Adrian, Blake, I want both of you there. You two take the outside. Savvi, Nicki, and I will be inside. I want one of us with him at all times."

"Adrian, let's do a drive-by today. I'd like to have a plan on patrolling the outside," Blake said.

"Good idea. Let me know when you're ready to leave."

The pen still tapped. "Nicki, I don't want Frank picking you up. Instead, meet him at his house. Find out if he has a Kevlar vest. If he doesn't, take one with you. Make sure no one sees it."

Nicki nodded. "I'll have Savvi find out. I'll take my dress along with a bag for my accessories and change there. I can hide the vest inside the bag."

"You might hit resistance from Frank."

"Don't worry. Between Savvi and I, we'll make sure he doesn't leave the house unless he has it on."

"Clue her in on Chabot. Let's move on to the attempt to shoot Nicki and Savvi last night."

"What!" Blake roared.

"Sorry, forgot you didn't know." Scott explained, then added, "Savvi was the target. I'm not sure why, but someone is getting nervous. She could also be a target tonight."

"With the dress she bought, we can't put her in a bulletproof vest," Nicki grimly added.

"Where do we stand on the rest of the backgrounds?" Scott asked.

"Some interesting stuff, though I don't know of what value it is right now," Nicki said. "First, there's Senator Charles Halston. He's old money. His family dates back to the late 1800s. Edgar Halston was a banker who hobnobbed with the likes of the Vanderbilts, Morgans, Carnegie, and Rockefellers. Rumor has it, Edgar was involved in the infamous meeting at Jekyll Island. It's when the six men met to write the bill President Roosevelt signed in 1913 to create the Federal Reserve System. The problem is the history books make no mention of Edgar, though Charles loudly proclaims he was there."

She stopped to drink her coffee before continuing. "Over the years, the family maintained their interests in several key banks across the country. They eventually extended into politics. Charles Halston was a senator, and his grandson followed in his footsteps. Here's where it gets interesting. Most of the top dogs in banking are opposed to the changes at the Federal Reserve. Not Charles. He's been out front, leading the charge, waving the flag, so to speak, in favor of the new gold currency."

Scott said, "It tracks with what I've found. Anything else?"

"When he became a Senator, all his bank holdings were placed in a trust, and he allegedly has no say over the investments. He claimed he didn't want to be accused of double-dipping, especially after he was appointed Chairman of the Securities, Insurance, and Investments, a sub-committee under the Senate Banking Committee. I did discover a number of iffy donations to his political campaign."

"What about his staff?"

"Nothing there, run of the mill gophers, college grad types. Over at the Federal Reserve, though, it gets a bit more noteworthy. Turns out Director Ben Sutter has an interesting background. By the way," she looked at Adrian, then Blake, "he's on Savvi's list of persons of interest. Not that I found any dirt, quite the contrary. He's a respected economist, has published several papers on trade laws. In fact, several years back, his name was thrown into the hat for a position on the Board of Governors for the Federal Reserve, though it came to naught."

"Any signs of discontentment because he was passed over?" Scott asked.

"If he does, he's hidden it well," Nicki told him. "Savvi also mentioned Captain Lloyd Hayes. I don't have the results on him yet. But there's one more on her list I found intriguing. When Savvi mentioned the name, I wasn't certain if it was the Darren Holcomb I knew until I got the background results. Holcomb was three years ahead of me at MIT."

Adrian said, his voice filled with awe. "You graduated from MIT?"

With a look of puzzlement, Nicki nodded. She'd never kept it a secret, it just never came up in a conversation. She assumed they all knew.

Adrian looked at Blake. "Did you know?"

Blake shook his head. "Nope."

Adrian glanced at Scott.

With a shrug of his shoulders, Scott said, "Right after Nicki graduated, the FBI recruited her."

"Hey, it's not a big deal, let's get back on topic here," Nicki told them.

Adrian rolled his eyes. "The woman says it's no big deal ... MIT is no big deal." Seeing the glare from Nicki, he grinned. "Okay. I'm done. I'm listening."

"Thank you! Now, as I was about to say, Darren Holcomb is brilliant and made quite a splash with some of his computer innovations. One of them was a revolutionary firewall security system MIT still uses. The system's claim to fame is that it's hack-proof. For all his brilliance, he couldn't stay out of trouble, liked to live on the edge of danger. Darren was suspected of hacking the computer networks of a couple of prominent financial institutions, but nothing was ever proven. He didn't need money. His family is wealthy. He just liked to jack with systems for the hell of it, to prove he could do it. After he graduated, he evidently settled down and went to work for a computer firm. About two years ago, he was hired by the Federal Reserve. Darren could manipulate the Fed's computer, and no one would know."

She paused, gathering her thoughts. "Remember the iffy donations I mentioned. Halston received a hefty contribution from a company owned by the Holcomb family."

"And, Savvi also has Holcomb on her list," Scott mused.

His phone rang. Looking at the screen, it was his boss. Rising, he said, "I've got to take this. Let's plan on another meeting after the two of you get back," nodding toward Blake and Adrian.

After Scott greeted him, Paul said, "Vance called. He's found out about tonight's event, doesn't like it, wants to know what the hell you're doing to protect the Chairman?"

"The team was just hashing out a plan of action."

"I told Vance you'd be on top of it."

Scott explained the precautions they were taking. He added, "I'm curious. How did Vance find out?" The answer wasn't surprising.

"From the President. Evidently, he and the Chairman regularly discuss the status of the PGS project. Frank happened to mention his plans to attend the art exhibit, which prompted the call to Vance. I'll pass on your precautions."

Scott hoped it would satisfy Vance and the President. He'd been called to the Oval Office on previous investigations and didn't want to spend the time on another trek.

CHAPTER
19

POSITIONED IN A bank of trees in the park across from the gallery, Blake watched cars pull to a stop in front. Passengers exited. The keys were handed to one of three valets hired by the gallery.

Scott was already inside. On the roof of an adjacent building, Adrian waited. They'd flipped to see who went where. Quite frankly, Blake felt more comfortable on the ground than lying behind a rifle on a rooftop.

Dressed in black, Blake was barely visible in the dark shadows cast by the rising moon. He'd already made several passes around the park and the surrounding buildings. His earpiece crackled. "Littleton's limo is headed your way," Adrian said. Blake tapped the mic twice to acknowledge.

Slowly, the limousine inched forward, until it was parked by the red carpet running from the edge of the sidewalk to the front door. The valet who rushed up was waved back by the security guard climbing out of the front seat. After he opened the backdoor, Savvi exited, then Nicki.

A whistle echoed in Blake's ear. "Damn, they clean up really good," Adrian snickered. A dark red dress clung to Savvi's curvaceous form, the bottom flowing around her ankles. Nicki was equally striking in a blue dress with a narrow white stripe on each side. It topped her knees, showing off an impressive set of legs that ended in spiked heels. Side by side, the two glittered like bright jewels.

"Where the hell do they have their guns stashed with those outfits?" Adrian scoffed.

Knowing the women were listening, Blake grinned when both shifted the small handbags with a long strap draped over their shoulders. As they stepped forward, Frank's wife exited, then Frank.

"I sure hope to hell he's wearing the vest," Adrian said as the driver pulled away.

As Savvi and Nicki moved to flank Frank and Amelia, Nicki raised her hand to fix her hair. Two taps echoed.

"Guess he is," Adrian said.

★★★

Inside, Savvi gazed around the crowded room. People clustered in groups, while a few wandered, stopping to study the pictures hung on the walls. Dressed in a tuxedo, a slim man with hair held in place by a liberal application of styling gel, rushed toward them. With a broad smile, he stopped, airbrushed a kiss toward Amelia, then extended his hand to Frank. "What a pleasure to have both of you attend this little event."

Frank grinned as he looked around. "Carter, how can you ever classify this as a little event?"

The man tittered. "The turnout is quite remarkable, but then this new artist is amazing, don't you think, Amelia?"

"Oh, I do. I am so looking forward to seeing his new paintings."

A sly look crossed Carter's face. "Frank, I do hope it means you'll be breaking out your credit card."

Frank grinned back. "Something which remains to be seen."

"Who are these gorgeous women?" Carter asked, turning his attention to Savvi and Nicki.

"Friends of the family," Frank said as he introduced them.

"Please, wander, gaze to your heart's content, but if you're interested, buy quickly. I don't expect it will take long for Arturo's paintings to sell." With a wave of his fingers, he trotted away to greet another patron.

Amelia laughed. "Carter, always the salesman, but that's why his gallery is so successful."

"Shall we, ladies?" Frank said, with a gesture toward the walls.

At the sight of an approaching waiter carrying a tray of champagne glasses, Savvi eased in front of Frank. With a quick wave of her hand, she motioned him away. Another decision Scott had made at the afternoon meeting, nothing to eat or drink.

In a far corner, Scott held a champagne glass. He'd noted the arrival of Frank's group. The bodyguard had moved to a nearby chair. A look of boredom on his face, he crossed his legs and leaned back.

While Scott waited for the gallery director to walk away, he savored the icy chill of the champagne and gazed at multi-colored streaks across a white canvas titled *Morning Sunrise*. Next to the title, a very discreet price tag read $3500 along with a sold sticker.

A man stepped alongside him. "Not quite what I would expect to see in a morning sunrise."

Scott turned his head. The mocking gaze of the Interpol agent stared back.

Chabot gestured with the glass he held. "But still, it has a certain appeal."

"Can't say it does for me."

"Ah, a pragmatic man. What do your tastes lean toward?"

"I've always had a partiality for Native American Art."

A ripple of laughter erupted. "How so very American. Remy Chabot. To whom do I have the pleasure of comparing artistic styles?"

"Scott Fleming."

Chabot's gaze shifted around the walls. "I don't believe you will find any pictures this evening to suit your fancy. But then, again, you never know what might be waiting around the corner. Au revoir, Mr. Fleming."

Scott watched Chabot stroll across the room. What he discovered in his research only added to the mystery surrounding the Interpol agent. His gaze shifted, searching for his agents.

Nicki had spotted Scott in the corner. She nudged Savvi. With a nod of her head toward him, she said, "I'll be darned. He did show up. Scott said he might attend, but knowing him, I didn't expect he'd follow through."

Hearing Nicki's comment, Amelia said, "Your boss is here?"

"Umm … yes, and he's headed our way."

"Wonderful. I've wanted to meet the man."

"Chairman Littleton, what a pleasure to see you again," Scott said as he stopped in front of the group.

Frank shook his hand. "What an unexpected surprise."

"After listening to Nicki's enthusiastic description of Arturo's paintings, I decided to check them out myself."

"Scott, this is my wife, Amelia. Sweetie, this is Scott Fleming, head of the Tracker Unit."

Amelia smiled. "I'm delighted to meet you. Since the conclusion to your investigation into the gold heist, Frank has raved over you and your team. Even used words like brilliant, dedicated."

With a wry smile, Scott said, "You truly don't want to make a grown man blush, now do you?"

A tinkle of laughter erupted before Amelia added, "Let's say then, he was impressed."

He motioned with his glass. "I do have a bone to pick with you, Mr. Chairman."

"We agreed it's Frank. What have I done that puts me on your hit list?" He laughed.

"Stole one of my agents right out from under me."

Frank's eyes gleamed with humor. "As I recall, Vance did mention Agent Roth had been assigned to your unit. Don't worry, it's only temporary."

He figured he'd set the stage for anyone listening to their conversation. After a few idle comments about the exhibition, Scott moved away. As he walked along the walls, seemingly engrossed in the pictures, his watchful gaze never lost sight of the Littleton's or his agents. He also noted the number of people who stopped to visit with them. One was Senator Halston and his wife. Then to his utter amazement, Agent Chabot joined them, and it was Halston who introduced him.

Adrian's voice echoed through the tiny receiver in his ear. "Movement, at the limo." His thoughts immediately shifted away from the French agent.

Savvi and Nicki tensed, discreetly shifting to each side of the Littleton's who were still talking to the Senator. Nicki glanced toward Scott. In the event they needed to make a fast exit, the plan was to take them out of the building using the kitchen door.

With a slight shake of his head to indicate not yet, Scott slowly weaved through the crowd as he worked his way to the front. The aggravation of the slow pace to avoid any suspicious looks boosted his sense of apprehension.

He whispered, "Driver?"

Adrian said, "Damn fool got out of the car, then headed to the back of the building. I'm guessing he's in the kitchen."

Swearing under his breath, Scott sidestepped a couple who stopped in his path.

Outside, Blake had sprinted out of the park. He slipped around the cars parked on both sides of the street. The limo at the back of the lot was barely visible in the dim light cast by parking lot lights.

"He's crawled out from under the car," Adrian said.

As Blake raced toward it, a dark figure ran toward the back of the lot. A van waited on the street behind the galley. The side door was open. The man leaped inside, and the vehicle sped away.

A muffled shot echoed, then a second.

"What the hell! Adrian?" Blake cried out.

"Someone is running across the side street. Might be the shooter. Whoever it is, just disappeared behind a building."

Blake slowed his pace and holstered his gun. As he neared the car, he knew an explosive device had been planted.

Scott ran up.

"Scott, there's a bomb. I need a flashlight." He yanked on the driver's door handle. "Damn thing's locked."

"I've got one in my car. Do we need to evacuate?"

"No. I don't expect it to go off until the Littleton's are inside." Blake dropped and scooted under the car.

A few minutes later, Scott squirmed next to him and handed him a flashlight. "If I can help, tell me."

"Already found it." The light flashed across a small device lodged in a metal brace near the fuel tank.

"Can you disarm it?"

Blake studied the cell phone detonator attached to a small block of C-4 for a few seconds before answering, "Yeah." He passed the flashlight back to Scott, telling him where to keep the beam pointed. Clipped to the inside of his pants pocket was a switchblade. He flipped it open. With two fingers, he gently eased the wires apart. Sliding the blade under one, he tugged to sever it. Then cut a second wire.

"All clear."

"Man, you've got nerves of steel," Adrian said.

Blake rolled his head toward the sound. Adrian was alongside Scott.

"Handled ones a lot more complicated than this."

As Scott and Adrian crawled out, Blake pulled the device free from the metal bracket. He set it on the concrete, slid out, then reached back to retrieve it. Once he was on his feet, he laid it on the hood. "Well, damn, this car's not going anywhere." He stared at a flat tire. "This is what the shooter hit."

Adrian said, "I'll call the bomb disposal unit and a tow truck."

Blake said, "Hold up. I'll handle the disposal."

Various options on how to keep this quiet had been running in Scott's head. At Blake's words, a solution fell into place. "Okay, but first." Scott tapped his mic. "All clear, hold the Littleton's inside." Two taps acknowledged. "Tell me what happened."

Adrian covered what he'd observed from his perch on the roof. Blake filled in the rest.

"Adrian, did you get a good look at the shooter?"

"No, by the time I zeroed in on him, all I saw was a shadowy figure hauling ass."

"He used a silencer, which is why we're not swimming in cops," Blake said.

"What about the guy who planted the damn thing?" Scott asked.

"Wore a ski mask, no help there. The van was black, but I couldn't see the plate."

Adrian added, "Too dark for me to see the number."

"Did the two of you come in separate cars?"

When they nodded yes, Scott said, "Good. Blake, take the bomb and get out of here. We'll let the driver discover the flat tire. Adrian, follow the Littleton's home. Let's make sure there won't be a second attempt."

"Let me have the flashlight." Adrian dropped to one knee, flashing the beam across the inner side of the tire. When he stood, he said, "Wanted to see if we could recover the bullets. We can't."

As he stalked toward the front door, Scott pushed back on the rage. Once inside, he had to project a calm, unconcerned demeanor.

When he walked in, the Littleton's and his agents were grouped in front of a painting. Frank's bodyguard was missing.

Sensing his presence, Nicki twisted her head, looking toward the door. At the anxious look in her eyes, he nodded, reassuring her everything was okay.

Scott strolled to the restrooms located at the back of the building. As he walked past the door to the kitchen, he glanced inside. Seated at the table with empty plates in front of them, the two bodyguards carried on a conversation. Disgusted, he stepped inside the restroom to wash his hands. When he passed the kitchen door a second time, the driver was gone, and the other officer was back in the chair.

He stopped alongside the Littleton's. "Now, there is another interesting painting." He looked at the title, *Evening Sunset*. Scott would swear it looked just like the one across the room labeled *Morning Sunrise*.

With a delightful laugh, Amelia turned to face Scott. "I've been trying, without success, I might add, to convince Frank this is what he needs to spruce up his office."

Frank leaned over, his lips brushed her cheek before saying, "And, I've been telling you, without success, I might add, I'm quite happy with my office the way it is."

Amelia turned to Savvi. "My dear, what do you think?"

Out of the corner of his eye, Scott spotted the driver rushing inside. He stopped in front of the other guard. Straightening, the man listened, then nodded before striding toward the Littleton's.

Recognizing a loaded question, Savvi hedged. "It's unusual ..."

The guard interrupted, "Mr. Chairman."

Frank turned. "Yes, Wilson."

"The car has a flat tire. A replacement vehicle will be here shortly." He turned and headed outside.

"A flat tire, how odd," Amelia said. "I wonder how it happened?"

His eyes troubled, Frank looked at Scott over Amelia's shoulder. He'd seen Scott leave.

With a slight shrug, Scott said, "Could be something as simple as a nail in the parking lot."

"Well, I suppose so," Amelia said. "Nicki, tell Scott about the picture you bought."

Following Scott's lead to keep a casual conversation going, Nicki spent the next several minutes elaborating over the turmoil of should she or shouldn't she buy it. Finally winding down, she added, "It will be delivered to the office this week."

"Not your home?" Scott said.

"Nope. This one needs to be in the office."

With a wary look, he glanced around the walls. "Which one is it?"

A sparkle of almost malicious humor flashed in her eyes, adding to his uneasiness. "You'll just have to wait to find out."

Adrian's voice echoed in his ear. "Limo pulled in."

When the bodyguard walked up and said the car had arrived, Scott looked at Frank, then nodded his head toward the door.

"Well, my dear, are you ready to leave?"

She quipped, "I guess this means I lost the battle."

As they ambled their way through the people who still milled around, Scott leaned toward Nicki as if to say something. Instead, he whispered into his mic. "Savvi, call when you get to the house. Need to talk to you and Frank alone. Nicki head to the office."

Outside, he waited for the limousine to pull away from the curb before walking to his car. Despite his casual demeanor, tension clenched deep inside him. This time, they'd dodged a bullet. Could they do it again?

CHAPTER
20

WHEN SCOTT WALKED into the office, he heard Blake's voice. He stopped in the doorway and waited for him to finish his call.

As he hung up, Blake said, "That was Adrian. He's on his way in." His hand scrubbed his face. "Christ, what a hell of a night! I handed off the C-4 to a friend of mine in the bomb disposal unit. Told him it was classified, not to log it into the system. I've got the phone, but don't think it's going to be of any help. It's a run-of-the-mill burner."

Scott nodded. "I might as well make a pot of coffee. We'll be here for a while."

Still wired, adding caffeine probably wasn't the smartest idea, then Blake muttered, "What the hell," and followed his boss.

In the breakroom, Scott punched the button on the machine. He leaned against the counter to wait for it to brew. His mind raced over the evening's events, cataloging details and impressions. He wasn't sure which surprised him more, the encounter with the agent or the bomb, another amateurish attempt like the shooting in the garage. Someone was nervous, that's when mistakes happened. He just hoped he could find them in time.

Blake walked in and grabbed a cup.

Scott filled his, then stepped aside. Taking a sip, he said, "Once everyone is here, we'll set up a conference call with Savvi."

"Thank god, we took precautions. I can't get the image of the car exploding with everyone inside it out of my head."

"From the sounds of it, someone else was taking the same precautions. Blake, was the shooter Jaimie?"

"I think so. Knowing her, she wouldn't assume he was protected. She'd be right there to be sure."

"Hey, where is everyone?"

Scott shouted, "Breakroom, Nicki."

She walked in, followed by Adrian. She'd changed into her typical attire, jeans and a t-shirt.

"What the hell happened tonight? Savvi and I are both about to bust a gut to find out. Why was your French agent there?" she said, heading toward the collection of cups on the counter.

"You'll have to contain your curiosity for a few more minutes." He grinned when her eyes sparked with annoyance over the brim of her cup. "Let's take this to the conference room. We've got a lot to hash over."

As they settled in the chairs, Adrian said, "After we left the gallery, I spotted a van turning onto a side street. Might have been the same one, but I couldn't tell."

His voice harsh, Scott said, "I bet the bastards were waiting for the car to leave so they could set off the explosion. I wonder when they discovered it was a different limousine?"

Blake said, "As soon as they tried to dial the number. The phone went off on my way to the disposal unit."

With an expression of horror, Nicki said, "There was a bomb!"

"Yeah, there was," Scott told her.

Blake said, "I'm surprised they'd try to plant it at the gallery. Anyone could have been wandering around that parking lot. The valets, people coming and going who attended the reception. In my opinion, it was damn risky."

"I can tell you why," Scott said. "One of the changes Savvi made to the procedures for Frank's protection was checking for an explosive device before the limousine left the garage. It also raises a question about Hayes being involved. Would he condone killing two of his men?"

Adrian said, "Damn good question. If he did, there is a lot more at stake than what we know."

"Nicki, get Savvi on the phone."

When Savvi answered, Nicki said, "Hold on." She switched to the speakerphone before laying it on the table.

Scott asked, "Savvi, where are you?"

"Frank's office."

"Who else is there?"

"Just Frank. Putting you on the speakerphone."

Frank's voice, tense with urgency, echoed, "Scott, what happened tonight? I know it wasn't a damn nail."

"No, sir, it wasn't." He went on to detail the events outside the gallery.

Savvi's "my god" was echoed by Frank, who added, "Thank you for keeping Amelia out of this. If she knew, I'd never get out of the house, even if she had to chain me to a chair. Do you have any idea who is behind this?"

"Still working on it. Frank, other than my team and the shooter, no one knows what happened tonight. It's the way I want to keep it for now. I'd appreciate it if you didn't mention it to the President or Vance."

"Fair enough. I don't like the bit about the driver leaving his post, but I guess it will have to be addressed later."

"Something else, for both of you. If anyone seems unusually interested in your visit to the gallery, I want to know it. Frank, how well do you know Senator Halston?" Scott asked.

"Quite well. He chairs a subcommittee of the Senate Banking Committee. Is he involved?"

"I'm not certain. Have you had any issues with him?"

"No more so than any other elected official. Charles is an ambitious man. Has his eyes set on the top of the political ladder."

"There was another man with him. Do you know him?"

"Remy Chabot. I've met him a couple of times. He's the CEO of a French firm, Frankfort Wealth Management. He seemed to be most taken with Savvi." Frank laughed at hearing Savvi's groan. "Even Amelia noticed, declaring Savvi had a new conquest."

Nicki interjected, "It's true. The man couldn't take his eyes off her."

"Savvi, you may get a phone call from him, wanting to meet. If it happens, I want you to accept."

"Any idea why?" Savvi asked.

"Nothing I can share, but he certainly seems to have gone out of his way to set the stage he's interested in you. Let's see how it plays out."

Frank asked, "Why are you interested in him, Scott?"

"He's an Interpol agent, a detail you can't discuss with anyone other than Savvi."

"Interpol! Is it why you asked about covert bank investigations? What do they have to do with all of this?"

"I don't know ... yet."

After disconnecting, he leaned back, picked up his pen, and tapped. The agents waited. After a few seconds, he glanced at Adrian. "Could the shooter have been a woman?"

Adrian added, "Yeah, it's possible."

Nicki asked, "Was it Jaimie?"

Scott glanced at Blake, who nodded. "Yes, Blake and I both believe it was."

Adrian asked, "How would she know the Chairman would be at the reception?"

"Jaimie is undercover in the Federal Reserve. It's the only logical explanation for the bank stress reports she sent to Blake, knowing someone on the inside was involved, and having access to the Chairman's schedule. It means Interpol is running an investigation inside the Federal Reserve, and it will get messy."

"Damn!" Nicki exclaimed. "You said Chabot had lost contact with Jaimie when her handler was killed. It's why you believe he'll contact Savvi, use her to link up with Jaimie."

"Yeah, it's exactly what I think will happen."

"Here's another interesting tidbit to add to the mix, Chabot's comment on the alley," Nicki said. "Two men were found dead from gunshot wounds in an alley in Georgetown. So far, the police haven't been able to identify them or the shooter."

Blake exclaimed, "What if Jaimie killed those men? It means someone discovered her identity. She's in danger."

"Nicki, when you ran the personnel at the Federal Reserve, did you find any anomalies with any of the female employees?" Scott asked.

"No, nothing, which tells me her new identity is damn good."

"Then, the situation may not be as dire as you believe, Blake. But we can't do anything until we find her. I'm hoping Chabot will lead us to her. The next target window is the meeting in Wyoming. Blake, where do you stand on your arrangements?"

"I've got a room at the lodge."

Scott thought, then said, "Get another reservation. Depending on how this rolls out, I may go with you. Nicki, add Chabot to your list. I want to know more about the man. Unless there is something else, let's call it a night."

After grabbing the last of the coffee, Scott settled into his office chair. With his feet propped on the desk, he leaned back and sipped.

Thoughts circled around the links connecting bits and pieces of information. Setting aside his empty cup, his hand reached for his pen—tap, tap, tap.

From her office, Nicki heard the sound. With a grim smile, she entered the data to start another round of research. Her boss was in what she termed his brooding mode.

After accepting a position with the Trackers, it hadn't taken long to realize Scott had an unusual ability. Where others saw chaos and confusion, he saw patterns. More than once, he pulled the proverbial rabbit out of the hat and came up with answers.

The instigators in the assassination plot had no idea who they were up against. The individual they should be targeting was Scott, not Savvi. He was the person who could bring down their house of cards. Her only fear … would it be in time to save the Chairman's life?

CHAPTER
21

THE NEXT MORNING, Savvi strode along the hallway. The events of the previous evening rolled in her mind. The horrifying image of a car exploding seemed to be indelibly imprinted in her brain. Damn, she had to stop obsessing over what didn't happen.

In her office, she set the bag and briefcase next to her desk, then pulled out the chair. Her thoughts shifted to the puzzle she had yet to solve. After typing in her password, she accessed the program for the bank stress tests. When it opened, three categories appeared on her screen, Approved, Pending Approval, and Receipt.

Savvi had already examined several reports in the approved file. Each contained statements detailing the specifics of the bank's financial operation, such as income, balance sheets, assets, liabilities, liquidity, cash flow, and capital plans. Intrigued by the concept of the stress test, she had thoroughly studied the individual components. So far, her analysis hadn't uncovered any discrepancies. The banks easily passed the Fed's criteria.

A new report, Butler Bank and Trust, had been added to the approved file. She opened it. Her gaze slowly perused the numbers as she tabbed from one statement to the next.

As a child, she could easily add, subtract, or multiply numbers in her head. It wasn't until she entered the realm of formulas that she discovered her ability extended beyond simple calculations. While others struggled with a calculator, Savvi could run complex computations in her mind. The ridicule from fellow students soon stopped her from volunteering the answers. Even after joining the FBI, it wasn't a topic she shared with her fellow agents, though she suspected Scott knew. Not much escaped the man.

As she studied the report, Savvi's photographic memory allowed her to compare totals of percentages, ratios, and dollars from multiple columns.

Suddenly, she stopped to stare at a profit and loss statement on her screen. "That can't be right," she muttered. A click on the keyboard brought up the derivatives statement she'd just examined. She studied it for a few seconds, then clicked back to the profit and loss statement. They didn't jive. A decimal point was in the wrong place in the asset column. Toggling between the pages, she worked her way through the rest of the document. From statement to statement, the mistake became self-compounding. By the time she reached the end of the report, the error had amounted to 100 billion dollars of additional assets the bank didn't have.

With her gaze locked on the computer screen, Savvi leaned back in her chair. It was what she called funny money, moving money that didn't exist, a commonly used technique in bank fraud schemes. It was as fancy of a 'watch my hand caper' as she'd ever seen. While you're watching one hand, the other was busy stealing your wallet. Once the money in one account was reported, it was moved to another account, then again to another.

But it didn't make sense. When the report went public, any eagle-eyed conspiracy nut who liked to expose frauds would find it a gold mine of opportunities. So, why? The bank would have passed the stress test without adding additional assets. From her briefcase, she grabbed a flash drive. Once inserted, she copied the file.

Then she moved to the next set of reports, Caldwell Fidelity. This time it only took a few minutes. She'd found the match to the documents Blake received. Like Butler Bank and Trust, Caldwell

Fidelity reported 100 billion dollars in fraudulent assets. Two banks, how many more were there? She sent a copy of the file to the flash drive. When she started to close it, a name at the bottom of the review form caught her attention. She'd seen the same name on the form for Butler Bank and Trust—reviewed by Lois Barnett and approved by Ed Deegan. Bingo. She'd bet her last dollar, she'd found Jaimie.

The ring of the landline phone on her desk was an unwelcome interruption. When she answered, a low voice, with a sensual French accent, said, "Agent Roth. Remy Chabot. We met last night at the reception. I hope I haven't interrupted anything important."

Her irritation shifted to a tingle of anticipation. "Nothing that I can't spare a few minutes. What can I do for you, Mr. Chabot?"

· A chuckle erupted. "Oh, no, no. It's Remy. Ach! Titles are so very formal, don't you think?"

"All right, Remy. What can I do for you?" she repeated.

"My name on your lips, such a delightful sound. But, mademoiselle, this is more of what I am hoping I can do for you. There is an enchanting courtyard café I would love to share with you. The atmosphere, exquisite. It is only a few blocks from your building."

She'd recognized him when she met him at the gallery. He was the man she saw at the BroadBank Club, then again by his car when she left. When Halston introduced him, she'd been charmed by the undeniable spark of admiration in his gaze and worldly air. Impeccably dressed in a steel grey suit, which set off his rugged good looks, Savvi couldn't deny the flutter of interest she'd felt. Knowing he was an Interpol agent added to her fascination. She wondered how long he would play this game. "Hmm … I think I can squeeze in lunch."

"Wonderful. I'll pick you up at let's say, eleven-thirty."

"No, I'll meet you there, though I do need directions. I'm new to

Washington and haven't had much of an opportunity to learn my way around."

"Perhaps, I could be of assistance."

"We'll have to see, won't we?"

"So, for now, I must be content with lunch." After giving her the address, he said, "Au revoir."

For a few seconds, she pondered the conference call last night after the reception and Scott's instructions. With a few quick taps, she brought up the information on Frankfort Wealth Management. Headquartered in Canada, the multimillion-dollar corporation had locations in Paris, Frankfort, London, and Washington, D.C. It was privately owned by the Chabot Trust with Remy Chabot as the President and CEO.

As she read the extensive holdings of the corporation, the portfolio of clients, her puzzlement and interest grew. Where did Interpol fit into all of this? It didn't make sense, any more than the head of the company doubling as an agent.

A knock on her door sounded. With a quick tap on the keyboard, she shut down the computer, removed the flash drive, sliding it into her pocket.

"Come in."

Director Sutter opened the door. His eyes flicked around the office and desk as he strolled in. "I hope I'm not interrupting."

"Not at all. I'm leaving for lunch."

"If you are going to the cafeteria and wouldn't mind the company ..." his voice trailed off.

"Thank you, but I have other plans today."

"Oh? Then, I'll make this brief. I wanted to see if you had any questions."

"None so far."

"What are you working on?"

"Primarily the computer programs, still exploring." She nervously laughed. "More complex than I expected."

If she hadn't been watching his face, she would have missed the flash of derision in his eyes. Satisfied with the impression she'd left, she rose.

"One other issue before you leave. In the staff meeting this morning, Captain Hayes mentioned an issue with the limousine last night. I hope it didn't create a problem."

"There's not much you can do about a flat tire."

"I got the distinct impression it was more."

"Perhaps Captain Hayes referred to the delay in leaving, not liking the Chairman had been inconvenienced. We did have to wait for another car to arrive."

"Maybe so. I'll let you get on your way. Don't hesitate to ask for help if you need it," he said.

After he left, she stepped to the door and closed it. Uneasy over Sutter's questions, she pondered her briefcase. Not wanting to lug it with her, she laid it on the desk, pulled out the small laptop, then shoved it into her tote bag. If someone stole the case, at least they wouldn't get her computer. She spun the combination lock, then set the case on the floor underneath her desk.

Outside, she flagged a cab. After giving the driver the address, she settled back. Nerves tingled with keenness as her thoughts drifted to the upcoming meeting. When the cab pulled in front, she handed a bill across the seat, saying, "Keep the change."

Inside, the maître d' greeted her. After explaining she was meeting someone, he flicked a finger toward a waiter, telling him to escort the lady to a table in the courtyard.

How odd. *He didn't ask who*, Savvi thought.

At a table tucked into an alcove with overhanging flower baskets, Remy Chabot lounged in a chair. Spotting her, he stood. Even in the somber clothing dictated by the FBI, the glorious mass of curls neatly contained in a braid coiled around her head, the woman was stunning.

Remy still hadn't decided how to handle the encounter. Despite the sharp thrust of interest when he saw her at the BroadBank Club, he didn't plan to contact her. Since her assignment to the Federal Reserve didn't affect his agenda, it wasn't a risk he was willing to take.

That changed when he saw her with the Littleton's. Considering Scott Fleming's warning, he had to wonder if she was there to protect the Chairman. If so, he desperately needed a contact inside the Federal Reserve. Could he trust her?

On the far side of the tables under the pergola canopy, Savvi caught sight of him. The evening before his attire bespoke wealth and authority. Today, he looked downright dangerous. Black jeans molded powerful legs, and a black leather jacket covered a grey turtleneck sweater. Coal-black hair brushed the jacket collar. Dark eyes glinted under the strong brows that slashed across a high forehead as he watched her approach.

When she extended her hand, instead of shaking it, he lifted it. His full lips lightly brushed the back, while his eyes, alight with admiration, gazed at her.

At the touch, a disturbing flutter of awareness sent shivers racing down her back, and she quickly pulled her hand away.

The mocking half-smile reappeared, as if aware of her reaction. "Bonjour, mademoiselle. How delightful to see you again."

After sitting in the chair he pulled out, her lips tilted upward in a playful smile. "Mr. Chabot. What a very gracious greeting."

"Simply a tribute to a beautiful woman. Ach! We did agree, titles are so limiting. Please, call me, Remy."

"Since you insist, then it's Savvi."

His eyes twinkled. "An unusual abbreviation, it hints of shrewd-ness and good judgment. Dare I hope it's why you agreed to have lunch."

"Meeting new people is always a pleasure."

"I'm crushed. I have been lumped into a crowd. Now, how am I to extricate myself from the masses?"

The playful smile flashed. In a wry tone, Savvi said, "Somehow, I don't believe you'll have any difficulty resolving your dilemma."

His fingers touched his lips in a kissing motion. "My ego is re-stored."

She glanced around and took a deep breath, enjoying the aroma of flowers blooming in myriad containers hanging overhead and scattered around the patio. Most of the tables were occupied.

"Your description of the restaurant exceeds my expectations. Difficult to believe we are actually in the middle of Washington, D.C., with its rush of people and cars."

"Excellent. I am delighted it meets with your approval. A foun-dation on which I can build."

"I am curious, though."

A wary look flicked across his face before he smiled. "What has you curious?"

Was it possible Chabot was unaware she knew he was a French agent? She decided to let this play out, see where it went. Instead of the question she wanted to ask, she said, "How did the maître d' know who I was meeting?"

Relief flickered. "I told him a beautiful woman with hair the color of an evening sunset would grace his establishment and to please escort her to my table."

A chuckle arose. "I could almost believe you are Irish, with a touch of the blarney."

"No, mademoiselle, just an honest man."

Time will tell, she thought.

The waiter approached. He filled the water goblets, then handed each a menu.

"Would you care for a glass of wine?" Remy asked.

She shook her head. "No. I'd prefer iced tea."

Remy told the waiter the lady would have iced tea, and he'd have the same. With a slight bow, the man left.

The exchange was enlightening. By his demeanor, Remy Chabot was a man who liked to command and control. A trait she'd need to remember in her dealings with him.

After a quick perusal of the menu, she decided on the Cobb salad, then laid it aside. "What was your opinion of the reception last night?"

"In the light of honesty—boring, the paintings mundane. I'd seen another showing of the artist's works."

"I'm surprised you decided to attend." *And, yes, Mr. agent man, why were you there?* she thought.

The waiter walked up with their glasses of tea. After placing them on the table, he picked up the menus. At his questioning look, Remy waved him away.

"I hope that met your approval. Meals in my country are not a hurried affair, especially when a desirable woman is present."

Since she planned to delve deeper into the mystery seated across from her, she ignored the sexual provocation. "I'm in no rush," then took a sip of tea.

"Where were we? Oh, yes, why did I go? A social event, to see, to be seen. Unexceptional until an unforeseen incident happened."

With interest, she leaned forward. "And ... what was it?" wondering if he'd learned what happened in the parking lot.

"An introduction that captured my attention."

Laughter erupted. "Oh, yes, definitely, Irish." It was time to steer the conversation in another direction. "I understand you own a wealth management company, headquartered in Toronto. Are you here on business?"

"Better and better. Your interest in new people led you to research me."

She lifted her glass and took a sip. Over the rim, her eyes challenged him. "Goes with the territory, you might say," she said, and set the glass down.

"Ah, yes, ever the FBI agent. Is that why you and the lovely Agent Allison accompanied the Chairman and his wife?"

"Merely family friends. Nicki and I were in the academy together."

"I see. The estimable Scott Fleming was also there, though I did note he left for a short period. I hope nothing was wrong."

With an unconcerned expression, she shrugged her shoulders. Was there a purpose to his questions? Scott had informed him of the threat to the Chairman. Why the dance, the innuendos?

He flicked a finger toward the waiter who stood near the door. "Shall we order?"

After the waiter left, it was time to give the dance another spin, this time in her direction. Her finger traced a line in the condensation on the side of the glass before she looked up at him. "One of the articles I read labeled you as a monetarist, a rising moneyman guru in the financial world. Another described you as a hired gun to troubleshoot ailing companies."

"Hmm ... you *have* done your homework. I've had some success with the companies I represent."

"From what I read, it sounds more than some success."

He smiled. "Modesty forbids me to express it in any other terms."

"Monetarist, an unusual, intriguing description. A person who believes the supply of money ... physical currency, deposits, credits ... not the value controls the economy."

"It's an approach I've utilized in my business dealings."

"During my college years, the monetarist economic theory was one of the more thought-provoking subjects," Savvi told him.

"Harvard, dual degrees, very impressive," he said. This time his eyes challenged her as they gleamed with an intense look.

She motioned with her raised glass, acknowledging the hit. "I'm not the only one doing research."

"After our meeting last night, I was compelled to discover more about this fascinating woman I'd just met."

The waiter walked up, carrying a pitcher of tea and a basket of rolls. Another waiter followed with a large tray balanced on his arm. After supervising the placement of the plates on the table, then refilling the glasses, he asked, "Will there be anything else, sir?"

"Leave the pitcher of tea."

Savvi eyed the backs of the two waiters as they walked away. "Do you usually receive this level of service?"

Cutting a piece of grilled chicken, his mocking voice said, "I've found a judicious enticement works well."

She laughed. "In other words, you bribed the maître d'."

With a nonchalant shrug of his shoulders, he said, "Whatever works," then slid a piece of chicken into his mouth.

"The gallery isn't the first time we've seen each other." She munched on a bite of the salad. At his questioning look, she swallowed. "The BroadBank Club. You were with Senator Halston and again last night. A client?"

"Ah, very astute. You do live up to your name. Merely a business acquaintance." He speared a clump of green beans, chewed, then washed it down with tea before he asked, "What prompted the move from New York?"

Poking the salad with her fork, she wondered how much she should tell him. Best to keep it brief. "I was reassigned as a liaison to the Federal Reserve. It's a temporary assignment, a precaution with the upcoming implementation of the new currency."

As he lifted the fork with another chunk of chicken, he said, "I heard you had interviewed for a position in the Tracker Unit." With a watchful gaze, he chewed.

Her eyes, brimming with a cool look, met his. "Where did you hear it?"

"You know how the gossip mill runs. You pick up bits, pieces, here and there. Any truth to the rumor?"

Taking another bite of the salad gave her a few seconds to think of an answer. At the time, it wasn't a secret among her fellow agents Scott was in town to interview her. She could hardly deny it.

"It's true. I did interview for a position. Instead, I was transferred to the Director's office." Since she wanted to find out more about Halston, she asked, "How long have you known Senator Halston?"

"A few months."

"Strange that he's one of the few politicians supporting the Fed's new currency."

Remy said, "There's been a great deal of rhetoric, pros, and cons for the implementation of a parallel gold-backed currency system. Some believe it is the savior for a faltering economy. Others fear it will spiral the country into another depression to rival the one in the 1930s."

"Which side of the fence do you fall?"

Remy's gaze met hers. "I happen to believe whoever controls the *flow* of the money supply, irrespective of whether it's fiat or gold currency, is the one to fear."

The implications of his statement stunned her. Was it possible?

Chapter 22

SATISFIED BY THE dawning awareness in her eyes, he shifted closer to the table. In a low tone, he asked, "How deep are you in Scott's operation?"

Startled, she laid her fork down. Her voice soft, she answered, "Enough to know you're an Interpol agent."

Pushing his plate aside, he said, "Even better. I must assume then the reason for your presence in the Federal Reserve is to protect the Chairman."

"Yes," she said.

"I need your help."

"For what?" she asked, though she was sure she knew the answer.

"I need to contact someone inside the Federal Reserve."

Her lips twisted in a sardonic smile. "Navy Lieutenant Jaimie Marston, I would imagine," and shoved her plate away.

With a toss of his head, he laughed. "Ah, chérie. I am not so easy to surprise, but you and Scott have managed it more than once."

"Why can't you contact her?"

His voice turned serious. "Jaimie's contact was killed. Her cellphone is offline. I suspect she destroyed it. Jaimie doesn't know me. At the onset, Louie Bisset, head of Interpol, decided for her safety and the mission, she would be unaware of my activities. Which, under the circumstances, was a bit shortsighted on our part. I can't take a chance on an open contact, too risky. Can you convey a message?"

"If sending a message is all you want, why have we spent all this time tap-dancing around the issue?"

A hand patted the area of his chest over his heart. "Chérie, I am wounded. How could you believe I wouldn't cherish an hour spent in the presence of a beautiful, captivating woman." Eyes danced with humor as he looked at her.

The man was entirely too smooth. With a self-satisfied smirk, she said, "I'll make sure Lois Barnett gets it. That is the name she's using, isn't it?"

The look of disbelief on his face was exceedingly pleasant.

Footsteps approached. "Would you like me to remove the dishes?"

Remy glared at the waiter who quickly gathered up the plates, and before leaving, asked whether they wanted coffee.

With an impatient wave of his hand, Remy declined.

As soon as the waiter was out of earshot, he leaned forward. "How long have you known? Who else knows?"

Despite the harsh tone, Savvi sensed an underlying fear. Taking pity on him, she said, "I discovered her identity this morning, right before you called. Don't worry, Remy. Her secret is safe with me."

He took a deep breath and eased back. "I apologize. I did not mean otherwise. When her contact, Rick, was murdered, we were afraid her identity had been discovered. How did you find out?"

"The bank stress tests."

"What tests?"

She realized he didn't know about the packet. "Another agent in the Tracker Unit received a package. We believe it was sent by Jaimie."

His eyes narrowed. "What was in it?"

"A flash drive with bank documents and a coded message."

"We knew Jaimie planned to send another dispatch. Get me a copy of the message. I can decode it."

"We already have."

The soft tone of his voice intensified his protest in French before he added, "Impossible!"

"No. I'm afraid not."

"It would seem I have underestimated the ingenuity of Scott Fleming. How did he break it?"

"I don't have all the details. You'll need to ask Scott. What I do know is the message said the bank stress tests are compromised, and the assassination of the Chairman imminent."

Shaking his head in amazement, he said, "Tell me about the stress tests."

Savvi quickly reiterated what she knew. When she mentioned the money, he whistled in amazement.

"One-hundred billion in surplus assets they don't have. How the hell does it benefit them?"

"I don't know yet. It was those reports, though, where I learned Jaimie's identity," and added the details.

"What are the banks?"

"Caldwell Fidelity, Butler Bank and Trust."

"Ah, so," he muttered under his breath.

"Do they mean something to you?"

"Possibly."

"What do I tell Jaimie?"

Remy pulled a small notebook from an inner pocket, tore out a page, then wrote on it. He handed it to her. "Use Navajo to identify yourself. How soon can you deliver it?"

"Hopefully, today," she said as she memorized the phone number. An idea occurred to her. "Can you meet me at Nicki's apartment tonight?"

"Yes. What time?"

"Give me your pen." After writing the address and a phone number on the paper, she handed it back to Remy. "Make it around eight." She glanced at her watch. "I need to go."

As they walked inside, the waiter nodded his head.

Savvi laughed. "I assume you have already paid the bill."

"Oh, yes, before you even arrived."

"Don't you think it was rather presumptuous? I might have decided not to show up."

His tone confident, he said, "No, I knew you would come."

"Why?" she asked as they passed the maître d', who also nodded to them.

"I relied on your sense of curiosity." With a smug smile, he added, "I was right."

She wondered whether to tell him that Scott had anticipated the invitation and told her to accept it. Then decided, why burst the man's bubble. She'd save it for another day.

Outside, he flagged down a cab. Opening the door, she slid inside. "Thank you, Remy. It was an enjoyable lunch."

"We must do it again," he said as he closed the door.

As the car pulled away from the curb, his eyes turned cold. Caldwell Fidelity and Butler Bank and Trust, two banks of which he was already familiar.

★★★

Savvi wandered into the lobby. With her thoughts focused on what she'd learned, she had to call Scott before she got to her office. She stepped close to a front window, far enough away from the security guards to keep them from hearing her conversation.

Tapping the number for Nicki, she waited.

On answering, Nicki asked, "What's up?"

"I had lunch with Chabot. Very enlightening," she said, her voice low.

"Uh, oh. Are you in a bad spot to talk?"

"Sort of. Are you in the office?"

"Yeah, what do you need?"

"If Scott is there, he needs to hear this."

"Hold on, I'm headed to his office."

In the background, Nicki said, "Got Savvi on the phone, wants you to listen in, she had lunch with Chabot."

Then, her voice louder, she said, "Okay, we're both here."

"Scott, Jaimie Marston is working undercover in the Federal Reserve as Lois Barnett," then relayed Chabot's request.

"Did he tell you anything else?"

Savvi hesitated and glanced around. The guards hadn't moved, though one eyed her with suspicion. "No. I told him about the message and stress tests. I found the bank that matches the reports Blake received, Caldwell Fidelity. I also found a second one, Butler Bank and Trust. I'll have to explain later what I discovered. But when I mentioned the two banks, they seemed to mean something to him, but he wouldn't say what. I told him to meet me at Nicki's apartment tonight around eight."

"Good. I have a few questions for him as well."

The guard started toward her. "I've got to go." As the man approached, she rolled her eyes, saying, "Yes, mom. I know how difficult it is, but I won't forget."

The man stopped to listen.

"Mom, I promise. Okay, love you too."

Scott said, "See you tonight," and disconnected.

With a rueful look at the guard, Savvi slid the phone in her tote bag. "Mothers!"

"Do you work here?" he asked.

She pulled her badge case from her pocket and flipped it open. "FBI Agent Savannah Roth." He studied it for a second before turning and walking back to the desk. Savvi headed to the elevator.

Inside her office, she closed the door behind her. After dropping her tote bag on the chair, she stepped behind the desk. Bent over, she studied the briefcase. It had been moved. Laying it on the desk, she looked at the combination lock. It was set on a different number. Unlocking it, Savvi opened the lid and examined the papers inside. She'd left a couple of traps, but it appeared the attempt to gain access had been unsuccessful. Relocking it, she put it back under the desk.

She logged onto the computer. The personnel directory listed seven people, including Lois Barnett, who worked for Ed Deegan. Their offices were located on the opposite side of the building, a section she had yet to visit. She logged off. As she considered how to approach Jaimie, she checked the drawers. A box of index cards was in the bottom one. Perfect.

After several seconds of deliberation, Savvi wrote on several of them. Stuffing them into her pocket, she headed to the door, then stopped to eye the tote bag. Damn, she hated to carry it along, but since the office had been searched, she didn't have a choice. Grabbing it, she walked out.

Ed Deegan's office was opposite the elevator. The door was open. She knocked on the doorjamb to get his attention. When he motioned toward her, she stepped inside.

"Mr. Deegan, I'm Agent Savannah Roth. You may have heard I've been assigned to the Federal Reserve. I'm working my way around the offices to introduce myself to the staff. I hope I'm not interrupting. If I have, I'll be glad to come back."

"No, not at all. I heard you were here. Please, have a seat. What can I do for you?"

"Nothing more than a few minutes of your time to answer some questions. What does your department do?"

"I'm responsible for the intake, review, and ultimate approval of the bank stress tests. I take it you are familiar with them?"

"Yes, I am. It's an interesting concept, testing the financial health of banks. From what little I've learned, this year's disaster scenario is extreme."

"More so than it has been the last couple of years. But many of us," Deegan leaned back with a smug look, "believed it was important to push the structure of the test to a worst-case scenario, especially in light of the upcoming launch of a new currency."

"I can understand why. There is a great deal of dissension over the sustainability of running dual currency systems. Many believe it will tank the economy."

"If it happens, banks are going to take a hit. Can they survive, which is what the tests are structured to identify."

"How are the banks doing?"

He chuckled. "So far, not one failure. We should be finishing up the reviews within the next couple of days."

"I thought the process would take several weeks to complete."

"No, not this year."

With a ripple of self-effacing laughter, she said, "I'm probably mistaken. I've had a lot of dates and figures tossed my way since I arrived."

"It's always difficult to get acclimated to a new position. Are there any other questions?"

She stood. "No, but thank you for your time. Will I create a problem if I visit with your employees for a few minutes?"

He rose, saying, "Not at all. Please stop back if I can be of any further help."

She nodded, then walked out. Since Jaimie was in the last office, Savvi planned to visit the other employees first. She didn't rush. After introducing herself, Savvi spent several minutes discussing details of the work they did for the Federal Reserve.

As she stepped out of the fifth office, she spotted Deegan looking out his door. Savvi gave him a friendly wave before walking into the next one. *So, he's keeping an eye on me,* she thought.

When she left, Savvi glanced back along the hallway. Deegan's door was closed.

When Savvi stepped into the open doorway, the woman typing on a computer looked up. With a wave of her hand, she said, "Please, come in."

Once inside, Savvi closed the door as she had in the other six offices. She quickly scanned the walls and ceiling. While she couldn't rule out a camera, she didn't see any likely locations for one. But a listening device was a real possibility.

"Hello, I'm FBI Agent Savannah Roth."

A wary expression crossed Jaimie's face as she stood. Makeup didn't conceal the dark circles underneath her eyes. She leaned across the desk to shake hands with Savvi. "I'm Lois Barnett. Have a seat. How may I help you?"

Savvi went into the spiel she given to the other employees.

Jaimie said, "I'll be glad to answer any questions you have. I've been expecting you."

Tension tightened Savvi's shoulders at the thought Jaimie might say something about her real identity. "You have?"

"Everyone seems to be talking about the FBI agent. You've garnered a lot of attention with your interest in meeting the employees. What do you think of the place so far?"

Relieved, Savvi said, "Actually, I am rather fascinated by the entire process." She reached into her pocket and pulled out the index cards. "It's a far cry from what I normally do. Until now, I worked in the New York office, the Financial Crimes Unit. This is a pleasant break."

She selected one and held it up. On it, she'd written—JAIMIE MARSTON NAVAJO.

At the sight of the card, the woman froze, then her eyes darted up. Savvi lifted a finger to her lips.

"Mr. Deegan said his unit is responsible for the review of the bank stress tests. What do you do?" Savvi asked, then held up the next card—KEEP TALKING.

"After the banks upload their reports into the system, Mr. Deegan assigns a bank report to one of us to review."

Savvi changed cards—CALL, followed by the number.

After looking at it for a few seconds, Jaimie nodded.

"From talking to your associates, they said the process to review is time-consuming."

"It is. Even though the computer runs a series of checks designed to spot any discrepancies or errors, we double-check everything."

Savvi's last card read—TOMORROW, 10, BREAKROOM.

Jaimie nodded again. "I'm the new kid on the block, but others in the group have said this year's test is more difficult."

"When I spoke with him, Mr. Deegan mentioned the same issue, the severity of this year's test."

"I've been told the banks are under a lot of pressure to finalize their tests and get them approved before the new gold currency goes online. Probably the reason we're staying late to get them done."

That's interesting, no one else mentioned overtime. Savvi tucked the cards into her pocket. "Mr. Deegan did tell me that he was responsible for the ultimate approval of the test results?"

"Yes. We do the reviews, but Mr. Deegan must approve our reports before the bank's test results are sent to the approved file."

"How do you like working for the Federal Reserve?"

"It's a challenging job, but I like it."

Savvi rose. "I tend to agree with you, though sadly, mine is a temporary assignment. I don't want to take up any more of your time. Thank you. It was a pleasure to meet you."

"You're more than welcome. If I can help with anything else, please let me know."

Savvi walked out, closing the door behind her. As she

approached Deegan's door, it opened, and he stepped out. His gaze swept over her empty hands, then the tote bag swung over her shoulder.

"Did you get a chance to speak to everyone?" he asked.

"Yes. Thank you again for allowing me the opportunity."

"Glad to be of help," he said, before walking back into his office.

How did he know I was about to walk past his office? The answer sent a tingle of foreboding rippling through her.

CHAPTER 23

SAVVI PRESSED THE doorbell.

When the door opened, Nicki pulled her inside, giving her an enthusiastic hug. "Sounds as if you've had a crazy day."

With a huff of frustration, Savvi exclaimed, "Dang, that's an understatement!"

Nicki told her, "I'll hold all my questions until Scott and Remy get here. What would you like to drink, wine, soda, tea? I've even got orange juice."

Inhaling the aroma of pepperoni, she felt her stomach rumble. "Pizza! And yes, to the tea." She eyed the large pizza box alongside a stack of paper plates and napkins on the coffee table as she dropped onto the couch.

"It's fast and easy," Nicki said as she walked out of her small kitchen and handed Savvi a glass.

The doorbell chimed. When Nicki opened the door, and Scott stepped in, her face beamed. "Did you manage to sneak in without anyone seeing you?" she asked.

His eyes sparkled with merriment as he said, "All clear." At the sight of the glass in her hand, he asked, "Have you got any more?"

"You can have this one. I'll get another. Don't you dare ask Savvi any questions until I get back."

He grinned. "Yes, ma'am," and turned to greet Savvi.

Studying him, Savvi drank the tea and decided she liked the

casual look. Jeans, a polo shirt, and a lightweight jacket made him seem more approachable.

When the doorbell chimed again, Savvi hollered, "I'll get it." Opening it, Remy's dark eyes skimmed over her. Lips curved upward in that mocking half-smile. Annoyed by the trickle of excitement racing along her spine, she took a step back. With a cool note in her voice, she said, "Right on time."

His gaze swept the room as he stepped inside, before settling on Scott. In his typical mocking tone, he said, "I expected you'd be here," as they shook hands.

Nicki walked in and set the glass of tea on a small table next to the couch. "Hello. Nice to see you again. I'm Nicki. We met at the gallery. Have a seat. Did you enjoy the reception?"

With a laugh, Savvi piped up. "When I asked, he said boring and mundane."

"Well, I'd tend to agree, though I did buy one of the paintings."

Scott grumbled, "She plans to put the damn thing in our office. Savvi, do you know what she bought?"

Throwing her hands in the air, Savvi said, "Don't drag me into the middle of this."

Nicki chortled. "Don't worry, Scott. You're going to like it. Remy, what would you like to drink?" and went over the choices. "Help yourself to the pizza. I've got another one warming in the oven."

Slightly bemused by the byplay, he sat, saying, "Iced tea would be good. I did not expect such hospitality."

With an amused look, Scott said, "What! Did you think we'd string you up on a rack for an interrogation?"

Laughter erupted. "No, maybe not quite that far."

Once everyone was seated, Savvi opened her briefcase, removed a stack of papers, then handed out the copies. "Bank stress reports. Jaimie was right, the reports have been falsified. Two I found earlier today. The third before I left. Caldwell Fidelity, Butler Bank and Trust, and Ohio Mutual Funds reported assets they don't have, to the tune of 100 billion dollars each. What Blake received is Caldwell Fidelity's report. I've highlighted the sections that caught my attention."

Nicki interjected, "Ohio Mutual Funds is owned by the Halston Trust."

As they perused the documents, Savvi slid a piece of pizza on a plate and bit into it. By the time she swallowed the last bite, everyone had finished reading and were dishing up slices.

Looking down at the reports, Scott said, "Three hundred billion dollars isn't a small error. It doesn't make sense. Why would banks report non-existent assets? It also raises the question of how the reports were falsified. It doesn't seem logical that personnel at each bank could be involved in the scheme."

Savvi said, "At first, I thought it was an attempt to hide their losses. If a bank fails the stress test, there are harsh penalties. But these banks would have passed without the additional assets. But now, I am wondering if there's more to it."

Intrigued, Scott's eyebrows raised. "How so?"

"A comment Remy made during lunch."

At the mention of his name, he glanced at her. "Ah, you refer to our discussion over my modified definition of the monetarist theory. It's not just the control of the money supply that regulates the economy. Of greater concern is *who* controls it. The type of currency or value is irrelevant."

Stunned, Scott wiped his fingers on a napkin, then picked up the reports and shuffled through them. "Control the flow of money," he muttered.

Her voice grim, Savvi said, "I had the same thought. It's an inconceivable idea. Impossible to pull off. Yet, for some reason, I can't get the thought out of my head. But if it's a possibility, how do the stress tests play into it?"

Scott looked at Remy. "We need to get all the cards on the table. Why is Interpol running an undercover operation? What's your role?"

Remy swallowed his last bite of pizza before saying, "I'm sure you know by now I handle asset acquisitions. I was approached by Lionel Kinder, CEO of Butler Bank and Trust. In this case, the acquisition was gold, a multibillion-dollar purchase. The hefty commission was for, what Kinder termed, a discreet arrangement. When I questioned him, he claimed to be fronting a consortium of independent investors interested in purchasing gold bullion—anonymously. I began to get, how do you say, twitchy feelings."

Picking up his glass, he took a swallow, then continued, "I told him I would consider his offer and get back to him. I already had a meeting scheduled with the head of Interpol, Louie Bisset, on an unrelated issue. Without going into detail, let's just say, Louie and I have somewhat of a working relationship."

Scott grinned as he listened. In cop-speak, it meant Chabot had done other jobs for Interpol.

"When I mentioned my meeting with Kinder, Louie said they were already looking into the activities of his bank, along with Ohio Mutual Funds. They'd come under scrutiny in another case. His agents had intercepted several phone calls. References to the movement of gold bullion stepped up their scrutiny. Since the agents hadn't been able to identify the individuals on the calls, it was agreed I should accept Kinder's proposal."

He took another swallow before setting the glass down. "I set up the meeting with Kinder, and that's when I met Halston. He's the one running the consortium, though, at the time, he was represented as an interested party. During our meetings to discuss the technicalities of purchasing and shipping gold bullion, I started to drop subtle hints about the availability of certain offshore accounts, offering total anonymity. It didn't take long to get Halston's attention. He approached me with another proposition to set up the offshore accounts for the investors. By that time, I had discovered a link to the Federal Reserve."

Scott interrupted, saying, "How'd you find it?"

Remy laughed. "A late-night visit to his office. I'm sad to say the Senator wasn't present at the time. Over the last year, he penciled in numerous meetings with Ben Sutter in his appointment book. I couldn't find any plausible reason for meetings with a Director of the Federal Reserve."

Savvi and Nicki had stopped any pretense of eating as they listened with avid interest.

"Louie decided to insert an agent in Halston's bank and contacted Jaimie. She'd gained a reputation with her activities in Naval Intelligence and the military in Iraq. Interpol had experienced problems with their agents' dispatches and needed a secure method to transmit information. The Code Talkers' code provided it. Using Jaimie had an added advantage, her financial background. Thus, Operation Navajo was born. After I discovered the connection to the Federal Reserve, Louie changed her assignment."

"What about Jaimie? Did she call the number I gave her? Where's she at in all of this?" Savvi asked.

"Yes, she did. To say she was desperate would be a mild description. As you know, our agent, her contact, was killed. What the news reports didn't say is Rick had been tortured before he was shot. Though he didn't know her identity or have a way to contact Jaimie, he knew the location where they met, a leased apartment in Georgetown. When Jaimie had a packet to deliver, she'd set up the meet. The last drop was the stress reports, but Rick didn't show. When she left the apartment, she was followed. Two men tried to kill her, but she turned the tables on them. They were found dead in an alley. I still don't know how they discovered Rick, though Halston's security force is a collection of thugs."

Savvi spoke up. "Remy, I think her office is bugged," and relayed what happened after talking to Jaimie. "It's too coincidental Deegan stepped into the hallway as I was leaving her office. Here's something else. She made a comment about the computer's diagnostic review of the reports. If we caught the mistakes, why didn't the computer?"

Remy said, "Your question is very intuitive. What Jaimie couldn't tell you is she believes the computer program has been altered. The internal review protocols are designed to catch errors. She said the program is not flagging the false reports. She doesn't know why."

"Why is a damn good question," Scott said. "Nicki?"

"I need access to the system to find out."

"Can you get in without anyone knowing?" Savvi asked.

Remy said, "Wait a minute! Back up. Are you talking about hacking into the Federal Reserve computer system?"

At his expression of disbelief, Nicki shot him a disdainful look. "Yes. It's iffy. The Fed's computer system is reputed to have impenetrable firewalls, stronger than any agency within the government. I can do it, but it will take time, more than we may have."

"She's right," Savvi said. "Jaimie mentioned the unit was working overtime to finish the review of the stress reports. I haven't had a chance yet to query Frank on the timeframes or who changed them. It's not a discussion I wanted to have in the car."

Remy set his empty glass on the table. "This tracks with what I found out today. The consortium had a meeting. When I arrived, they were discussing the new deadline. Halston wanted to be certain all their reports had been submitted. They are still wary of me, so I didn't get a chance to learn the reason for the change."

"Who is in the consortium?" Scott asked.

Remy said, "The CEOs of Bank of New York, Caldwell Fidelity, Butler Bank and Trust, Risson Nat'l Bank, and of course Halston's bank, Ohio Mutual Funds."

Savvi interjected, "Tomorrow, I'll pull the reports for the other two banks."

Scott nodded in agreement. "I expect you'll find the reports have also been falsified. We may need Jaimie's help. Remy, if it's necessary, can you contact her?"

"I have become her Aunt Fanny. At least as far as caller ID. I can reach her anytime."

Relieved they had a communication link with Jaimie, Scott uttered, "Excellent! We'll start working on a plan. Do you know how Jaimie discovered the assassination plot?"

"She told me she'd been searching the offices at night. She didn't discover anything until she was assigned to the PGS project. One night it was Sutter's office. When she left his office, she heard voices in a small conference room. She stopped to listen. Someone was talking about finalizing the stress tests. Then a second person said everything was in place, the chairman could be removed. When she heard the hum of the elevator, she had to leave. She wasn't able to identify the voices."

"Umm ... so, far we've had two attacks, both in my opinion hastily conceived and carried out. Two men tried to kill Savvi and Nicki in the parking garage, then the bombing attempt at the gallery."

With a soulful expression, Remy looked at Savvi, "Chérie, you did not mention this?" Then he turned to Scott. "Why the attack on your agents?"

"We think Savvi was the target. She's making someone nervous."

Remy said, "Jaimie mentioned the second one. She said she shot the tire to disable the vehicle."

"We suspected Jaimie was the shooter," Scott told him. "Let her know we are taking all possible steps to protect Frank. My agents were in place last night, including Blake Kenner. She'll understand."

"I will. Now, I have a question for you. How the hell did you decode the message?"

After listening to Scott's explanation, he said, "Our plans didn't take into account Agent Kenner's involvement."

"It's getting late," Scott said after a glance at his watch.

Remy said, "I'll go first. I would like to be clear of the building before the two of you leave."

After expressing his thanks, and sending a pointed look at Savvi, he headed out the door.

Scott watched him with a thoughtful expression. While Remy had added several more pieces to the pattern, he still didn't know the why.

CHAPTER
24

ONCE THE DOOR closed, Scott turned to Nicki. "Tomorrow, run a search for vehicles registered to Halston. You might find the vehicle from the shooting in the garage. Add his security force to your list of background checks."

"Will do, boss man." She got up, stretching to work the kinks out of her neck. "Got a bad feeling on this one." She looked at their empty glasses. "Anyone want more tea?"

Savvi said, "I do, unless you are ready to leave, Scott."

"No, we have a few details to discuss." When Nicki glanced at him, he said, "I'll have another glass."

"Be right back," Nicki declared.

While he waited, lacking a pen, his fingers drummed his knee. Gaining access to the Federal Reserve computer was crucial. Protecting his agents even more so. Could they use the Chairman? No, better to leave him out of it.

Nicki refilled the glasses, then set the pitcher on the table. "How are we going to pull this off?"

"I've been considering the same damn question. Nicki, you mentioned the firewall system Holcomb designed. Do you believe he's upgraded the Fed's system?"

"I'm certain he has."

"Can you get past them?"

The fierce look of determination on her face was an expression he'd never seen. "Scott, I can beat him. Don't worry. I've got this!"

Savvi interrupted, "Someone care to clue me in on the discussion?"

"Sorry, Savvi. I forgot you didn't know about Holcomb." Nicki gave her a rundown of the man and his background.

Astonished, Savvi said, "The nerdy twerp who came to my office to give me a passcode is the guy you talked about in the academy? The computer genius?"

Nicki nodded. "Yeah, he's the one. Small world, isn't it?" What she didn't tell them was one night while still at MIT, and bored with studying, she decided to hack into Holcomb's highly touted, hack-proof system. Nicki never told anyone she'd successfully broke through his intricate firewalls. She wasn't looking for recognition. It was a lark to see if she could do it.

"Nicki, can you use Savvi's office computer, or do you need direct access to the mainframe?"

Knowing the hack was a go, she sipped her tea as she thought. "I could, but it would be better if it's the one connected to the mainframe. I'd bet Holcomb is tracking computer activity. Savvi is already under suspicion."

Savvi said, "You're right." She told them her office had been searched. "I'd been reviewing the bank stress reports."

"If I use the computer connected to the mainframe, I can erase the tracks. Something I'm not able to do from Savvi's computer. Plus, it will be a lot faster."

"Savvi, can you get Nicki inside the building?"

"It shouldn't be a problem. Though we need a good cover story to explain why we are there."

Nicki asked, "Do you know where the cameras are located?"

"The only ones I've spotted are in the lobby and the doors to the building. I'll ask Frank. Are we going to mention this little foray?"

Scott shook his head. "No, not unless something goes wrong. Fill him in on the stress tests, though."

Guards were Nicki's next question.

"The only ones I've seen are in the lobby. There are always two. It may be different at night. I'll find out."

"When are we going to do this?" Nicki asked.

"I think it should be tomorrow night. Jaimie said she'd be working overtime," Savvi told her.

"I agree," Scott said. He glanced at Nicki. "Can you be ready?"

She nodded.

While they talked, Savvi had been thinking of a reason to be there at night. "Nicki, dress casual. I'll do the same. Let's create an appearance we're out on the town, and you want to see the inside of the building. We'll be able to bypass the screening with our badges."

"Good. I'm not certain what gadgets I'll need."

They ironed out a few more details before Scott and Savvi were ready to leave.

★★★

During the drive to Frank's house, Savvi went back over the day and her impressions of Jaimie Marston. The woman had to be frantic with worry, not knowing who she could trust, yet she projected a stoic demeanor.

Pulling into Frank's driveway, lights flashed as Scott drove by. She grinned, thinking how protective he was of his agents. The porch lights came on, and Amelia stood in the open doorway. Despite the surreal feeling of her situation, living in the home of the Federal Reserve Chairman, she felt a sense of coming home.

As she locked the car, Amelia called out. "We were hoping you'd be home before we went to bed. How'd your evening go with Nicki? What a delightful young woman. I was most taken with her. Have you had dinner, dear?"

Savvi smiled as she followed her inside, assuring Amelia she'd stuffed herself on pizza.

"Frank is still in the library. He won't say so, but I know he's been a bit worried. Would you like any refreshments? Cook made an excellent chocolate fudge cake."

A tinkle of laughter erupted. "How can any self-respecting woman say no to chocolate fudge cake? I'd love a piece."

Amelia glowed with delight. "Go on into the library, and I'll bring you a tray."

When Savvi stepped into the doorway, Frank looked up from a document he was reading. A wide smile crossed his face as he laid it to one side. "Savvi. Come in, come in. Have a seat. We were wondering how your evening went."

Savvi looked over her shoulder to ensure Amelia couldn't hear. "It was more business than pleasure," she said as she set her briefcase and tote bag on the floor alongside a chair. Settling, she took a few seconds to relax while Frank watched with a sympathetic gaze.

"I have many days where, for a few minutes, I need to shut it all down."

A rueful look crossed her face. "I can't begin to imagine how terribly difficult your job must be with the responsibilities you carry every single day."

He shrugged his shoulders. "You get accustomed to it. Here's my sweetheart. I see she talked you into trying the cake. But there's only one piece. I don't get any?"

"Frank, don't give me your mournful, hound dog look. You know very well you had a large piece after dinner and don't need to eat another this close to bed," she quipped as she set a tray on the table next to Savvi's chair. "I'll leave you to your discussions. Don't let him talk you into sharing, my dear. He's had more than enough tonight."

Once the door was shut, a grim look crossed Frank's face. "I had a disturbing call from your boss. He filled me in on the Interpol investigation and the young woman who is an agent. He told me she left the warning in my coat."

"Yes, Naval Lieutenant Jaimie Marston, though her assumed name is Lois Barnett. She's working for Ed Deegan." Taking a bite of the cake, she almost groaned from the rich taste.

"To get past the background check for the Federal Reserve, someone did a first-rate job on her credentials. I hope to meet her once this is over. Scott mentioned the stress tests."

"Umm ..." She swallowed. Setting the plate on the table, she picked up the briefcase, opened it, removing a stapled set of documents. "This is a copy of the reports for three banks. All have erroneous data."

He stood and walked around the desk. When she handed them to him, he paced and slowly read each page. Savvi watched as she consumed the rest of the cake and noted the extra time he spent on the highlighted pages. Scooping the last bit of icing from the plate, she heard him mutter, "This isn't possible."

"I'm afraid it is. The reports for Caldwell Fidelity are what Jaimie smuggled out. I found the other two."

He stood in the middle of the room. His hands flapped the papers. "I don't understand. The computer program is specifically designed to catch any discrepancies or errors. How could the system have failed to catch errors totaling 300 billion dollars?" Awareness dawned in his eyes. "Someone altered the program. It's the only logical answer."

"It's what we believe. There may be at least two more banks."

"My god, if the same error rate exists, it pushes the total to 500 billion. For what reason? It doesn't make sense. I'll start an investigation as soon as I get into the office in the morning."

"No, not yet. This must be kept confidential."

"Ah, that's what Scott meant when he told me to listen but do nothing."

"Either Scott or I will keep you updated, but for right now, you need to continue your daily routine as if nothing unusual has occurred. Did anyone question you about the reception last night?"

"Ben Sutter stopped by my office. He'd said Hayes mentioned the incident to him. I assured him a flat tire couldn't be predicted, and it didn't take long for a replacement vehicle to arrive."

Since Sutter had steadily climbed her lists of suspects, Savvi wasn't surprised by Frank's answer.

He looked at the reports again. "Three banks. One of them owned by the Halston family. I assume they are under investigation?"

She nodded.

"Who are the other two?"

"We suspect Bank of New York and Risson Nat'l Bank. I plan on pulling their reports tomorrow."

He sighed. "I know the CEOs, along with many of the personnel at each of those banks. Hard to believe any of them would be involved in a plot to defraud the Federal Reserve."

In a soft tone, Savvi said, "And to assassinate its Chairman."

His head bowed as he said, "I hadn't forgotten."

"I haven't had a chance to check the security setup for the building yet. Are there any cameras other than in the lobby and exit doors?"

"Two more in the garage. There's never been a reason to extend the system any further into the building."

"How many guards work inside?"

"Two in the lobby and a third in the security office."

"And at night?"

He eyed her with suspicion. "It almost sounds as if you're casing the building. Is something else happening that you'd care to share?"

A twinkle glinted as she said, "No, sir. All part of getting a feel for the place."

"Humph. I'm not buying it, but to answer your question, two guards are on duty at night, one in the office, one in the lobby."

"A couple of other non-related issues. The computer technicians. Do they stay late, run any programs at night?"

The glimmer of suspicion deepened. "Young lady, your wide-eyed look of innocence doesn't fool me one iota, but I won't ask. To the best of my knowledge, they go home at the same time as the rest of the personnel." He sighed. "What's the other question?"

"Did you authorize a change in the deadline to finalize the reviews on the stress tests?"

"No, I didn't, but then Director Sutter is in charge of the review process."

"Would there be a reason to shorten the deadline?"

He paused, stared down at the papers clutched in his hands, then looked back up. "None, absolutely none."

She stood, reaching to pick up the tray to return it to the kitchen. "Leave it. I'll take care of it."

"Thanks. I'm calling it a night then," she told him as she gathered up her briefcase and tote bag.

His voice stopped her at the door.

"Tomorrow morning stop by my office. I have a key and passcode you might need," Frank said and winked.

CHAPTER
25

SCOTT OPENED THE door to the sounds of hard rock booming over the sound system. With a grin, he walked to Nicki's office. Oblivious to his presence, her body rocked and gyrated in the chair. The long braid of black hair swayed. Fingers flew over the keyboard as she manipulated the program on the wall monitor. Occasionally, a hand would raise, and she'd click her fingers in time with a drum roll.

Chuckling, he walked up alongside her.

Her head angled as she looked up. An impish grin lit up her face. With one keystroke, the music died. "Morning, boss man."

"How the devil can you even think with that music blasting your eardrums?" he grumbled.

"Superior concentration," she quipped. "Besides, it's energizing, a musical shot of caffeine."

A look of skepticism crossed his face. "Since it works, who am I to complain. What are you working on?"

"Halston and his merry band of rogues. The head guy, Max Roman, has been with the family since Halston turned twenty-one. Before then, he had a couple of assault charges. He liked to get into bar fights. Since being hired as Halston's bodyguard, he's kept his nose clean. When Halston ran for office, Roman took over his security and hired a few men, ex-military with less than distinguished records. A couple received dishonorable discharges."

Scott stared at the monitor as the data rolled across it. "Strange lot for a senator."

"No, kidding. One was a bomb disposal technician in the Army. Thought it would interest you."

"It does. Anything on the car?"

"Yep. It's the morning's breaking news from the desk of Nicki Allison. Halston rents his vehicles. Roman filed a stolen vehicle report on a black SUV. The last two numbers on the plate are 06. It was found, burned, in a field about a hundred miles from here."

"An enlightening dead-end, and one that wasn't very smart."

Voices sounded in the outer room. Adrian and Blake had arrived. Scott headed for the door, saying, "Conference room in ten."

After dropping his briefcase in his office, he checked his emails, then headed to the meeting. A cup of coffee was on the table in front of his chair. He shot a grateful look toward Nicki before he greeted the other two agents.

"New developments. Blake, we confirmed Jaimie is working undercover as Lois Barnett at the Federal Reserve building."

When Blake leaned forward, his eyes clouded with worry, Scott added, "Blake, she's fine. Savvi contacted her and plans to meet her again this morning. But I'm getting ahead of myself." He went over the details he learned the night before from Savvi and Chabot.

When Scott paused to take a sip of coffee, Adrian asked, "Where does it leave us?"

With a smirk, he said, "Helping Nicki hack the Federal Reserve computer network."

A burst of laughter erupted from Adrian. "You're going to hack a system that has a reputation of invincibility? Good lord, woman. Is there no end to your abilities?"

With a tongue in cheek look, she said, "If there are, I haven't found them."

"Here's the plan," Scott said, getting their attention back on the topic under discussion. "Nicki and Savvi will be wired with ear mics. The three of us will be outside watching for any unexpected visitors. I haven't heard from Savvi yet on the location of the cameras in the building."

Nicki flicked up her fingers to stop him. "I didn't get a chance to tell you, but Savvi called last night. According to Frank, cameras are in the lobby, the other doors to the building, and two in the garage. At night, there are only two guards on duty, one in the lobby, the other in the security office watching the cameras. But … wait for it." With a look of excitement, her fingers drum rolled the air. "Savvi will have a key to the computer room and the passcode to the computer, courtesy of Frank Littleton."

"How'd she pull it off?" Blake asked.

"She said the Chairman guessed what she was up too even though she denied it."

With a sense of relief, Scott asked, "Nicki, any idea how long this might take?"

"No. With the passcode, it makes it a hell of a lot easier to get in, but I've got to be super cautious not to leave a footprint. It will slow me down. Once I've accessed the program, I'll download everything to an external hard drive. We can review it later."

"I've got blueprints of the building. Take five." When he walked back in, he brought up a blueprint on the wall monitor.

Blake had followed with a steaming cup of coffee and walked toward the screen. "Do you know where Savvi's office is?" he asked.

Nicki stepped alongside him, studying the hallways. Picking up the laser pointer, she aimed it toward a set of offices near the elevator on the second floor. "Here. Savvi said she was across from the elevator and down a couple of doors."

Scott plucked the pointer out of her hand. He pointed to a room on the ground floor at the back of the building. "This houses the heating and air-conditioning equipment. Next to it is the computer room."

"Hmm ...," Nicki mused. "The guard needs to see the elevator going to the second floor." Holding out her hand for the laser, she added, "Once there, I can take this set of stairs, and haul ass back down to the ground floor. Uh, oh. Here's a problem."

She pointed to the stairwell doorway. "To reach the computer room, I've got to go out this door, turn and walk back along this hallway. If the lobby guard happens to be looking toward the stairwell, he'll see me. I'll have the same problem coming back."

"We'll have to create a distraction," Scott said. "Anyone have any ideas?"

★★★

Mid-morning, Savvi strolled into the cafeteria. Except for an attendant stacking wrapped sandwiches onto a platter, the place was empty. The woman flashed a look of disinterest her way before walking into the kitchen.

Caught between the breakfast and lunch crowd, the food choices were limited. Since she'd already had breakfast, selecting an item was just for show. She slid a cinnamon roll onto a plate, then walked to the large coffee urn. Behind her, Savvi heard a voice.

"Well, hello again."

Turning, she saw Jaimie. "Hello to you. I missed breakfast and decided to get a quick snack. Have you got time to join me?"

"I'd love to," Jaimie said, eyeing the cinnamon roll. "It looks sinfully good."

Savvi laughed. "It does, though I probably don't need the calories."

Jaimie's eyes flicked over Savvi's slim form. "Somehow, I don't see it as a problem."

After filling a cup, and balancing a napkin and fork under the plate, Savvi walked to a table in the corner of the room. From there, she had a clear view of the doorway. She set the items on the table and slid into a chair. While she waited, she studied the young woman at the coffee bar. Yesterday, her impression had been one of a self-controlled but worried woman. Today, she seemed more relaxed, though her eyes still held a wary look. Conservatively dressed, the dark brown pants suit, hair pulled in a bun, and wire-rim glasses all enhanced her studious, quiet image. No one would give her a second glance, which Savvi figured was deliberate. Undercover agents needed to blend in, not stand out.

Once she was settled into the chair, Jaimie shot a quick glance toward the doorway before saying in a low tone, "We may not have long. Deegan's watching me."

Savvi pulled a folded piece of paper from her pocket. "Emergency contact number."

Jaimie quickly shoved it in her pocket.

"Are you working tonight?" Savvi asked.

"Yes. I'm supposed to finish the reviews for Bank of New York and Risson Nat'l Bank. Just like the others, they've been falsified. Something is wrong with the program. It's not catching the errors," she said, cutting into the roll with her fork.

"We figured it out."

"Who is we?"

"The FBI unit I'm in, Blake's unit. I'll be here tonight with another agent, Nicki Allison. We plan to access the computer system."

Shocked, Jaimie's eyes darted upward before she quickly suppressed the emotion. "How?"

"From the computer room. Nicki is considered the best in the bureau. If anyone can get in, she can. Your office may be bugged." The ding of the elevator sounded.

Savvi leaned back and laughed. In a normal tone of voice, she said, "I can't believe someone would fall for such a ridiculous pickup line." From the corner of her eye, she saw a guard stroll into the room. "Some men have absolutely no common sense. But what a funny story," then took a bite of the roll.

Jaimie reacted with laughter. "This guy was a lawyer. I basically told him to take his what-ifs and wherefores somewhere else. I wasn't interested. Even then, he didn't want to give up. I thought about not going back, but I really like the club's atmosphere, good jazz." She forked up another piece of the roll and chewed.

"Being new to the area, I haven't had an opportunity to do much sightseeing."

"Some night, I'd be happy to show you a few of the hot spots. My god, this is incredibly delicious," she said, waving her fork at her plate. "I hadn't tried one before, but I may have to make this a regular item on my menu. I tend to get lost in my work and forget to eat."

The guard had slowly worked his way along the counter, getting closer to their table. Savvi never looked at him. Jaimie didn't either, though, from the glint in Jaimie's eyes, Savvi knew she was aware the man was listening.

Savvi chuckled. "It's something we have in common. I do the same thing. I get so engrossed that I forget the time. Speaking of which," she glanced at her watch, "I'd better get back to my office." She popped the last piece of the roll in her mouth.

"Oh, my gosh, I'd better too. I'm on a deadline to get a report finished. I planned to get a cup of coffee and scurry back. But the break was fun."

Jaimie stood and picked up the plate and fork, placing them on a conveyor belt for the dirty dishes. Savvi did the same.

The guard walked to the coffee urn, filled a paper cup, then stepped to one side. His cold gaze raked the two women.

"I'm going to get a cup to take with me. The caffeine will help relieve the tedious task of looking at numbers," Jaimie said. While she filled a paper cup, Jaimie ignored him. She capped it with a lid, then turned toward Savvi.

"You know where my cubbyhole is."

"Thanks, Lois. Once I get settled into an apartment, I'm going to take you up on the offer to check out some of the nightlife."

Jaimie nodded and walked out. The guard stopped in the doorway, seemingly to adjust the lid on his cup as he watched Jaimie. Savvi took her time filling a cup, then put on a cover. When she turned to walk out the door, the guard stood in the hallway. She punched the button for the elevator, and when it arrived, she stepped inside. When the guard didn't follow, she looked out, glancing at his name tag. "Going up, Officer Garnett?"

"No," he said and walked away.

Her heart raced with fear as thoughts tumbled. Her instincts told her Jaimie was in danger, but why? Did they know she was an undercover agent? If so, her life wouldn't be worth a plug nickel. In two days, Savvi was headed to Wyoming with Frank. There wouldn't be anyone inside who could help.

★★★

Feet propped on the desk, Scott's fingers idly tapped his pen. Details, some important, others seemingly irrelevant, raced in his head. Most of the puzzle was in place, but he still didn't have the full picture. How would anyone benefit?

His phone chirped. Glancing at the screen, he picked it up, answering he said, "Hi Paul."

"Anything new on your end?"

Scott said, "Not yet. The pieces are still coming together."

A grim chuckle sounded. "I hope you get it assembled soon. In two days, the Chairman leaves for Wyoming, and Vance is worried. He's not certain we can protect him up there. He's already asked Frank to cancel the trip. Frank refused."

Scott said, "It's not surprising. I knew he would."

Paul sighed. "What do I tell Vance then, to keep him from calling out the troops?"

"We've got it under control. If anyone goes storming in to protect Frank, our chance of finding who is behind this is gone. All we'll have accomplished is to drive them underground, and who knows where they'll surface next?"

"Okay, I get your point. I hope I can convince Vance. Something else happened. I got a call from Senator Halston's executive assistant. Halston has arranged for Savvi to receive a commendation from Congress. The award ceremony is scheduled the day after the Chairman leaves for Wyoming. I was informed the Senator expects her to be present."

Scott's feet hit the floor. "What did you tell him?"

"I said she was unavailable for at least another week. I fully expect another call, this time from the Senator. I've already given Vance a heads-up in case he gets a call."

Ignoring the urge to chuckle with satisfaction, he said, "They are getting nervous and making mistakes. This is a big one."

"Does this mean you suspect Halston?"

"He's at the head of the list, but that's all I can say for right now."

"Scott, I don't need to tell you how much is riding on your decisions. I'll do my best to keep Vance at bay. But you know as well as I do when Vance is nervous it means the President is nervous. I'm surprised he hasn't asked for a meeting."

"Head it off if you can. I don't need to be seen walking into the White House. It would be a good way for someone to chop off this limb I'm standing on."

"I'll try. Who are you sending to Wyoming?"

"Blake and Adrian. I had originally planned to go, but I need to be here."

"I won't ask why." The line went dead.

As he laid the phone on the desk, Blake walked in, closing the door behind him. Dropping into a chair, he said, "I've got a bad feeling about Jaimie, one I can't ignore. One Interpol agent has been killed. Once Savvi leaves, there's no one inside to help her."

"I know, Blake. I also know you'd like to stay here, but you've got to be in Wyoming."

With a spark of anger, Blake said, "Dammit, I know it. I'm not asking for a change in plans. But we both know she's in danger. How the hell are we going to protect her?"

"Instead of going with you, I'm sending Adrian, though he doesn't know it yet. The reason I'm staying is because of Jaimie. Chabot and I will be in constant communication. Savvi arranged a meeting with her this morning. I gave her a phone number to pass on. If Jaimie can't reach Chabot, she's got another number to call."

Some of the tension in Blake's body faded. "Do you want me to pass on the good news to Adrian?" he asked with a wry smile.

"No, let's get him in here, and we'll discuss it."

When Adrian walked in, a wary look crossed his face. "You two ganging up over something?"

Scott chuckled. "Wyoming. You have a chance to experience the fresh odor of pine-scented air."

"I've been expecting it. You're staying here, and I'm going in your place. What's the game plan?"

"I'll change my reservation to your name. I've chartered a plane under Blake's name. Keep a low profile on being agents. You are a couple of businessmen taking a fishing trip. If you need fishing gear, buy it. Hopefully, you can make it look used."

Blake spoke up. "If Adrian doesn't have any, I've got an extra rod, lures, and other items he'll need."

Adrian's head swiveled toward him. "Fishing? You actually fish?"

"Yeah, why wouldn't I?"

Adrian's gaze took in the gleaming wingtip shoes, pants with a crease so sharp there was nary a wrinkle, the white shirt, tie, and black coat. "Somehow … you dressed in waist-high waders with suspenders, standing knee-deep in water with a fishing rod in your hands doesn't compute. Nah, you've got to be putting us on."

Shooting him a look of irritation, Blake said, "Come by the apartment tonight. I'll have your gear ready." A smirk crossed his face. "Do you need a lesson on how to cast?"

"Not necessary. Been on a few trips, and I do have some gear. But thanks for the offer."

"Okay," Scott intervened. "Now that we've got all that settled, when this first came up, I considered a sniper was the most probable method. After the incident at the reception, I'm not so sure. If the assassination is to create turmoil, what better way than an explosion. Nicki also discovered one of Halston's thugs is a demolition expert."

Blake said, "The same thought occurred to me."

"Since you'll be there ahead of the conference, you'll be able to assess the security procedures."

As he walked out of Scott's office, Blake's gut instincts told him whatever security precautions were in place wouldn't matter. There'd be a bomb. But could he find it in time?

CHAPTER
26

SAVVI AND NICKI hopped out of the cab. As they swaggered into the lobby of the Federal Reserve, Nicki laughed, pointing her finger at Savvi. "Okay, since I paid for the cab, you get to buy the first round of drinks."

"Not fair," Savvi protested. "Drinks are a lot higher than a puny cab fare."

Seated behind a desk, the guard's boredom vanished. Young and impressionable, he wasn't immune to the surge of deep lust at the sight of the tight jeans encasing the women's slim legs and three-inch stiletto heels. A sliver of flesh around the waist flashed as the loose tops floated as they strode toward him. On one, a mass of red hair tumbled down her back. The other, thick straight hair, black as coal, hung to her waist. He gulped, forcing himself to remember why he was behind the desk.

The redhead laid her arm on the counter, then leaned forward. Her lips, full and bright red, curved upward. "I haven't met you before. Are you new?" she asked.

A flowery scent tickled his nose. Her soft voice sent shivers scrambling down his back.

"Uh, no. This building is closed. Only authorized personnel can enter."

Savvi leaned further over the counter, letting the shirt gape open. His eyes darted to the swell of her breasts. Checking his name badge, she said, "Roger ... I know. I'm Special Agent Savannah Roth. I work here."

"Uh ... uh ... I need to see your identification," he stammered.

She reached inside the tote bag draped over her shoulder, pulled out a case, and flipped it open. Light glinted on her FBI badge.

He gulped again when the other woman leaned on the desk, an open case in her hands. "I'm Special Agent Nicole Allison, but my friends call me Nicki," she cooed.

"Oh, yes, ma'am. Can I help you?" In all his years, he'd never prayed harder than he did at that moment for one of them to say yes.

"Oh, I wish you could," Savvi exclaimed, leaning even closer. "But I know you're stuck behind the desk. Nicki loves historic buildings and has never had a chance to be inside this one. I promised her a tour before we headed out on the town."

"Uh, okay. I'll be right here if you have any questions. I'm pretty familiar with the building," he rushed to tell them.

"Roger, I bet you are," Nicki said. "I'll be sure to ask *you* if I do."

A red blush stained his cheeks as he grinned.

Before they headed to the elevator, Nicki strolled around the lobby, gazing in awe at the ceiling, oohing and aahing, as she exclaimed over the dual staircases. The guard's eyes followed them with a worshipful gaze. Once they'd adequately waxed over the downstairs, with hips swinging, they strode toward the elevator.

Once the doors closed, their laughter had them holding their sides.

Gasping for breath, Nicki said, "My god, I thought the poor kid's jaw would hit the desk when you bent over."

"Well, we got his attention. Anyone who questions him won't have a hard time believing why we're here."

As they stepped out of the elevator, Nicki's voice turned serious as she said, "Showtime. Your mic hot?"

"Yeah, testing. Anyone out there?"

Adrian's voice echoed back. Positioned in a dark alley across the street with a set of binoculars, he had an unobstructed view of the lobby. "Hell of a performance. The poor schmuck may never recover."

Blake, who was in the garage, said, "While I didn't get to see it, the sounds were enough to set a man's blood boiling."

Short, impatient taps on the mic sounded. "Yes, yes, Scott," Nicki said. "I'll stop dithering. I'm on my way. Time for operation flowers."

Shaking her head as she walked to her office, Savvi wondered at the mind link that seemed to exist between Scott and Nicki. At times, it was downright uncanny.

Downstairs, Adrian, who had acquired a florist's delivery jacket, walked in, holding a huge vase of tall flowers in front of his face. While Adrian argued with the guard, insisting he had to leave the flowers, Nicki ran down the stairs, slipped out the stairwell door, and into the hallway.

Savvi flipped on the lights and settled in her chair. Unless Nicki needed help, it was her job to fob off anyone who came looking for them and to contact Jaimie. Over the mic, she heard Adrian declare operation flowers a success, which meant Nicki had made it to the computer room.

From her desk drawer, she grabbed an index card. As she started to write, a shadow crossed the light spilling into the hallway. Her hand crept toward the gun inside the bag.

When Jaimie eased into the doorway, she breathed a sigh of relief. Before she could say anything, Jaimie's finger crossed her lips. She held up a card with large block letters, BATHROOM, then turned, gliding out of sight.

Savvi stood, alert for any sounds before stuffing the index card in her tote bag. Slinging it over her shoulder, she eased her way into the hallway. Jaimie had disappeared, but the bathroom was around the corner. She paused, listening, then worked her way along the hall. Pushing the door open, she stepped into a dark room.

Once the door shut behind her, she whispered, "Hey."

Jaimie's soft voice answered, "Here. I didn't want someone to see a light under the door and get curious. Deegan is pushing hard to get the last two bank reports finished. I haven't been able to find out why the urgency. Where is the other agent?"

In her ear, she heard Blake's voice, a faint whisper as if talking to himself. "Jaimie, my Jaimie."

"Nicki is working on the problem we discussed earlier. My boss is concerned about your safety and wants to pull you out. He plans to talk to Chabot about it."

Her voice vibrated with anger. "No! Not yet. Deegan is in this up to his neck, and I suspect so is his boss, Director Sutter. I need hard evidence to prove it. I can't quit until I do. I've been searching the offices. If I can keep going, I'll find the evidence. Someone killed my partner. They are not going to get away with it."

When Scott broached the subject earlier, Savvi told him she'd be wasting her breath. If she were in Jaimie's position, she'd be doing the same thing.

"Okay, then we've got you some protection. I want to trade watches with you." She reached inside the tote bag and pulled out a small watch with a worn leather band from a side pocket. "I need to turn on the light, just for a couple of minutes."

"No, wait." A small beam lit up the room.

At the look of surprise on Savvi's face, Jaimie grinned. "Pocket flashlight, standard operating equipment for any decent under-cover agent," she quipped.

With a light chuckle, Savvi said, "The watch has a tracking device. To activate it, push the knob on the side all the way in. To deactivate, pull it out. If anyone checks, it does work. Turning the knob, turns the hands on the dial. Give me yours."

With the small flashlight between her teeth, Jaimie slipped off her watch and handed it to Savvi. She buckled the new one around her wrist, then reached for the light, turning it off.

"I've got to go. Deegan left to get something to eat. I don't want him to find me gone when he gets back. I'm the only one working. When he first mentioned the overtime, he made it sound as if it was the entire team. When I asked, he said everyone else had finished their reviews, but it's not true. There are still bank reports waiting to be assigned to a reviewer."

A sharp thrust of anxiety struck Savvi's gut. "How many banks have you reviewed?"

"If you add these last two, it's eight. The first three I reviewed were correct."

Her anxiety deepened at the thought Jaimie had been assigned all the reports for the consortium. "Are you working tomorrow night?"

Jaimie's light flashed as she stepped toward the door. "Yes. I'll stall on sending the last two reports to Deegan. I want to search Sutter's office again."

Savvi said, "I don't think it's a good idea for you to be here alone. I'm certain you can't get a gun by the guard. There's a reason why you were assigned the false reports."

Her tone somber, she said, "I should have thought of it. Don't worry, I'll be careful. I have to go."

An idea, one that had been nibbling at the back of her mind, took root. "Jaimie, wait. How soon are you leaving?"

"An hour or so. Just long enough to make it look like I've been working. Why?"

"I'm wired. Blake's listening. I know you can't make contact, but he'll follow you home."

Blake's voice echoed in her ear, "Damn right, I will!"

Jaimie asked, "Blake, he … he can hear me?"

"Yes."

She whispered, "Blake, I love you. I'm so sorry for the pain I caused." Shoving the door open, she was gone.

Savvi had to push back the tears that formed before she could ask, "Nicki, status?"

"I'm in, no problems, so far."

Inside her office, she couldn't sit still. She paced. The minutes crawled by. Every instinct screamed Jaimie was in danger, but there was nothing she could do.

"I'm finished," Nicki said.

Time for act two. Savvi turned off her office light and strode toward the elevator. When she stepped out, she meandered her way over to the guard's desk, making sure he was watching.

Perking up at the sight of her, he smiled, then looked behind her. A frown crossed his face. As she reached his desk, he asked, "Where's the other agent?"

"Oh, she wanted to make a pit stop before we left. She'll be down in a minute." Savvi stepped around the end of the desk toward the window to look outside.

To watch her, the guard had swiveled his chair. His back was to the stairwell door.

Savvi turned to look at him. "How long have you worked here? I would think being a guard in the Federal Reserve would be challenging." Though her eyes never shifted from his face, she saw Nicki slip into the stairwell.

Flattered by her admiration, he said, "A little over six months. But this is temporary. After a year, I can take the exam for a promotion."

"Good for you. I can't imagine you'll have any difficulty." Seeing the elevator was on the way down, she added, "Here comes my friend now," stepping away from the desk. She wanted to make sure he saw Nicki get off the elevator.

When the doors opened, Nicki rushed out. "Why is it, I am always late?"

Laughing, Savvi said, "Woman, I bet you were born late."

"Well, if we don't get going, we'll miss our reservations."

Nicki waggled her fingers at the guard before walking toward the door.

Savvi gave a last smile to the guard, then cried out, "Hold up, or you'll be leaving me behind."

Outside, they stopped. Seeing a cab, Nicki stepped off the curb, flailing her arms.

"You, idiot! Get out of the street," Savvi laughingly protested as it screeched to a halt.

Nicki gave the cabbie the address for a restaurant where they planned to switch cabs, then go back to Nicki's apartment. The rest of the team would be waiting to debrief.

CHAPTER
27

BEFORE LEAVING THE office, she'd given a key to Scott. When they got to the apartment and walked in, Scott and Adrian were sprawled across the couch. Each held a bottle of beer. The men raised them in a toast along with a rousing cheer.

Scott said, "A brilliant performance. If either of you decides to change careers, I'd seriously give acting a strong consideration."

"Hear, hear!" Adrian added.

"Have you heard from Blake?" Savvi asked.

Scott told her, "He's on his way. Right after you left, Jaimie walked out."

The doorbell chimed. Nicki opened it, and Blake walked in.

When he looked at Savvi, he mouthed—thank you.

Once they were seated, Scott asked, "Did you get anything?"

Nicki shot him one of her wounded, indignant looks. "Boss man, ye of little faith. I got it all."

He smirked. "I knew you would," and took a sip of beer.

Knowing she'd been had, she glared back.

Blake said, "When did you decide on the watch deal?"

Scott answered, "Late this afternoon. I called Paul, told him what I needed. It was delivered right before I left. I didn't want to say anything in case it didn't work out."

Blake seriously doubted there was much his boss couldn't accomplish when he set his mind to it. "I feel better knowing she's got it. If …" he choked, then started again. "If she has to activate it, who gets the signal?"

"It's linked to my phone, Nicki's computer, and Chabot's phone."

"Does Chabot know?" Savvi asked.

"No, I haven't had a chance to talk with him. I'll call once Nicki and I get back to the office."

With a smug look, Nicki said, "I figured we'd be working late tonight."

"I want to find out what's on your hard drive. Blake, you and Adrian head home. You've got an early start in the morning. Anything before you leave?"

Both men shook their heads. Then Scott gave Savvi a questioning look.

"No, though, I am bothered by what Jaimie told us tonight."

Scott said, "Something else is going on we haven't figured out. It could also involve you. So, watch your step. Halston's office contacted Paul today on a commendation from the Senate. The award ceremony is the day after you leave for Wyoming. Halston insisted that you be there."

"Still trying to get me out of the picture."

"Maybe it's because you are glued to Frank. Paul turned down the request, told the caller you wouldn't be available for at least a week. They may try again. Just in case." He reached inside his jacket pocket and pulled out a watch. "I got one for you. I've linked it to Adrian, Blake and my phone and Nicki's computer." As he handed it to her, he said, "Don't get into a situation where you're by yourself."

"Good thought. I won't. That reminds me." Rising, she walked to the tote bag and pulled out the watch Jaimie gave her. Stepping back to the couch, she handed it to Blake. "I think you need to hang onto this until you can return it to Jaimie."

The watch lay across his palm. His fingers closed tight around it. He held it for a few seconds, cleared his throat, and shoved it in his pocket.

Savvi said, "I need to get back to Littleton's house."

Adrian rose. "I drew the short straw, so I'm following you tonight."

Hugging Nicki, she said, "When this is all over, we're going to do it for real, our night on the town," then followed Adrian out the door.

On his way out, Blake said, "As soon as we get settled tomorrow, I'll contact you."

"Let's go." Nicki grabbed her backpack. "I want to find out what the hell these guys are up too."

★★★

Nicki followed Scott inside and headed to her office. "I suspect it will be a long night. Rocket fuel, extra-strong. It's what we need."

Laughing, Scott said, "You start on the research. I'll start the coffee."

After punching the start button, he leaned against the counter. His mind hummed as he considered the men involved. Which one was the kingpin, the mind that conceived the elaborate plot, starting with the assassination of the Chairman? Was it Halston, the power-mad politician, Sutter, a brilliant economist playing second fiddle or Holcomb, a computer genius who liked to live on the edge?

All he needed was the final layer—the why— that had eluded him from the start. The reports were the crux of the plot, the missing piece of the puzzle.

When the machine beeped, he filled two cups. He stopped in the doorway of Nicki's office. Eyes focused on figures flashing across the wall-monitor, her fingers danced on the keyboard. Stopping alongside her, he set a cup down within easy reach. A quick flick of the eyes was the only acknowledgment. She was in the zone.

In his office, he dropped into the chair, propped his feet, and sipped. His thoughts returned to his earlier dilemma. What would they gain by altering the stress bank tests to report assets they didn't have? Yes, it would prevent the sanctions when a bank failed the test, but according to what they'd already discovered, the banks wouldn't have failed. There was no reason to falsify the assets. All he could hope was the answers were on Nicki's hard drive.

His feet hit the floor, his chair spun. Setting the cup on the desk, he pulled out his cell phone, tapping the number for Chabot.

A mocking voice said, "Ah, my American counterpart. Looking for an update?"

"You could say that, though I have one for you as well. Have you heard from Jaimie?"

In a more serious tone, Remy said, "I have. She mentioned the watch. Who gets the alert?"

"My phone, Nicki's computer, and your phone."

"Excellent. I was concerned I would be, how do you say, kept in the dark?"

"Once we suspected her office was bugged, adding another level of protection seemed to be a wise precaution."

"She also mentioned you wanted to bring her in. I find it disconcerting you presumed to interfere with an Interpol agent." The mocking tone had disappeared, replaced by one of anger.

"Remy, your investigation is taking place on U.S. soil. Need I remind you, an investigation which hasn't been cleared by any U.S. agency."

"With good reason, considering who is involved," he snapped back. Then said, "Ach! A futile argument. What's done is done."

Scott could imagine the shrug of the man's shoulders as he dismissed Scott's comment.

"Did the incomparable Nicki gain access to the computer system?"

"She did and is going over the data as we speak."

In a somewhat malicious tone, he said, "I must recommend to Bisset that he consider recruiting the very talented, beautiful Nicole Allison."

Despite a prick of uneasiness at the thought, Scott chuckled. "I don't believe you'd have any success."

"Ah, my friend. One never knows. Interpol broadens the horizon to worldwide opportunities."

The unease deepened. Could they entice her away? Pushing it aside as a distraction he couldn't afford, he said, "Did you meet with Halston today?"

"Oui, most interesting meeting. He wanted to ensure I had all the offshore accounts in place. I gave him a list of the account numbers. When I asked how soon I would receive my fee, he said in two to three days. In an earlier conversation, he told me I'd get paid when the transfer hit the offshore accounts."

"It's getting ready to go down. Did you discover where the money was coming from?"

"He wouldn't say. What are you doing to protect the Chairman?"

"Blake and Adrian are flying to Wyoming tomorrow morning. Of course, Savvi will be with the Chairman."

"Halston also mentioned Agent Roth. He was most displeased the Director refused to allow her to attend some award ceremony."

"Did you get any inkling they'd make another attempt at removing her?"

"There was some talk. Halston does not like her involvement with the Chairman, and as he put it, in a position to upset his apple cart."

"What do you know about Halston's security force?"

"The head man is Max Roman, who likes to hire ex-military with shady backgrounds. Why?"

"We linked the car used in the attack on Savvi and Nicki in the garage back to Halston's goon squad. Savvi caught the last two numbers of the license plate. A rental car that Roman reported stolen matched the description. The license plate had the same last two numbers. It was later discovered in a field, burned."

"How very convenient."

His tone dry, Scott said, "Yeah, wasn't it?"

There was a short silence before Chabot said, "I think, my friend, your Agent Roth is still very much in danger." The line went dead.

With an air of thoughtfulness, he laid the phone on the desk. What could he do? Lacking evidence of any crime, the disturbing answer was nothing. Frank would never agree to cancel his trip.

As the night progressed, Scott researched the banks and people he'd identified. He went over Nicki's reports on all the background checks, sifting through the information, matching up even the most minor of details. Searching for a wedge to crack open the dam.

During his breaks, he checked on Nicki. Engrossed in analyzing the data she obtained, she wasn't aware of his presence or that he kept her coffee cup replenished. He glanced at his watch. Time to shut it down as his hands rubbed his eyes, burning from staring at a computer screen. Nicki's would be the same. They needed to get a few hours rest, then come back at it.

"Hey, boss man." Her face tired, she leaned against the doorjamb. "The algorithms used to analyze the stress reports were changed. The computer was re-programmed to ignore the errors. I also discovered another file with five bank stress reports—the same five banks. I haven't had a chance to compare them. I'd bet these are the original reports, which means they were altered after they were loaded into the fed's system."

Scott said, "It makes more sense than personnel within five banks falsifying a report."

"I also encountered an unusual number of firewalls isolating certain sections of the program. It has Darren Holcomb's touch all over it."

At the questioning look on Scott's face, she added, "I don't know

why yet. I've got another program running. It will give me a timeline of when changes were made in the system. It will take a few
hours to complete."

He nodded. "Good. I'm ready to shut this down."

"I'll stay and ..."

Scott interrupted. "No! You won't. We're not spending the night
here. We both need to get a few hours of sleep. Grab your gear and
let's go."

Too weary to argue, Nicki headed to her office. She took one last
look at the goblin racing across the screen. Accessing the Federal
Reserve computer system had been unusually stressful. As soon as
she logged in, she knew it would test all her skills. Holcomb had
refined his programs. It meant each step had to be carefully analyzed, searching for the subtle traps he'd built into the program.
This time, it wasn't a lark, it was for real.

Not that anything would have happened to her since technically
they had the Chairman's permission. After all, he gave Savvi a key
to the computer room along with the password. Still, had she been
caught, it could have blown the whole operation, even had deadly
consequences.

A strange mixture of fear and exhilaration had heightened her
senses. A feeling she'd never experienced. All the while she was on
the computer, she kept looking over her shoulder, expecting a
guard to come rushing in.

Her entire career with the Bureau had been behind a keyboard.
As she picked up her backpack, she glanced around her office.
Computers were her comfort zone, had been since she was a kid.
Her mind could take flight and reach anywhere in the world.

Tonight, she stepped out of her cocoon, her first field operation,
if it could be called such. She'd discovered something about herself
that was disturbing. She liked it.

CHAPTER
28

U NABLE TO SLEEP, Scott decided he might as well be in the office. He could be just as uncomfortable there as he was in bed. Welcoming the jolt of caffeine as he sipped his first cup of the day, he stared at the street bustling with vehicles, people already rushing to work. Over the horizon, the sun was barely visible.

The fear he was running out of time pushed at his mind. In less than twenty-four hours, the Chairman would be on his way to Wyoming. He still didn't have the answers. When a chirpy voice rang out, relieved, he turned. Her voice had a way of dispelling the darkness, bringing in light.

"Hah, you did beat me in. I could smell the coffee before I even opened the door."

"And good morning to you," he quipped.

Mischief glinted in her eyes. "Now, don't be thinking I'm not grateful the coffee is ready and waiting." Her hand, hidden behind her back, produced a sack that she waived in the air. "I stopped at the bakery. Ham and egg croissants and chocolate glazed donuts."

He kissed his fingers at her. "You are a goddess among women. How many did you buy?"

"Finally, I'm getting some recognition around here. Don't worry. There's enough to satisfy a manly appetite. I'm getting a cup of coffee."

Following her to the breakroom, he grabbed two paper plates

from the cupboard. From inside the bag, he slid two croissants on each plate.

After filling a cup, Nicki glanced at the plates. "No, I only want one. I got three for you."

Grinning, he picked up one from her plate and took a large bite.

"Did Adrian and Blake get off, okay?" she asked.

After swallowing, he said, "Yep." He looked at his watch. "Been in the air for over two hours. It's a five-hour flight." He took another bite.

She grabbed her plate. "I'm going to check my program."

When she walked in, the goblin had stopped. She set the plate and cup to the side, then sat and tapped the keyboard.

Numbers scrolled across the wall monitor. Picking up the sandwich, she bit into it as she studied the figures. This was going to take time, she realized and leaned back. While she munched, sipped, and analyzed, she searched for answers.

On his way back, Scott paused in her doorway. For several minutes, he watched the quick movements, the way her head tipped to one side. Though he couldn't see her face, when her shoulder slightly hunched, he knew something had caught her attention.

Her program was the only lead they had. In less than twenty-four hours, Frank Littleton would be putting his life on the line. A thought he couldn't unstick in his head.

WYOMING

Air turbulence rocked the plane. The laptop on the small desk in front of Adrian slid toward the floor. A quick grab, and he closed it, then stuffed it into his backpack. A snore overrode the sound of the engines. For the last two hours, Blake had snored. How the hell could he sleep when the plane bounced around like a yoyo?

"Hey, buddy. Wake up." Adrian reached across the aisle and shook Blake's shoulder.

His eyes slowly opened. With a stretch of his arms, he yawned, then gazed out the window.

"How can you sleep? This isn't the smoothest ride I've ever been on."

"Try riding in a military helicopter. How far out are we?"

"Pilot announced we'd be landing in fifteen minutes. I still can't get my head around the idea of an international bank conference at a remote resort in Wyoming. The only explanation I've found is a former Federal Reserve Chairman liked to fly fish. Guess it's as good a reason as any."

Blake said, "It makes even less sense to pick this place to assassinate someone. The fact it's remote provides an intrinsic level of security for the conference. Fifteen miles out of town, one road in and out. A small community where everyone knows everyone else. The employees live here year-round. While the resort doesn't make an overt display of security, a cop with a bomb dog routinely checks the place. When Frank arrives, he goes straight from the car into the resort. He's surrounded by his guards and staff who came with him. His suite of rooms is inside the lodge, not one of the cabins, and he never leaves. A sniper is limited to two chances."

The thud of landing gear locking into place jolted the plane. The pilot banked in a slow turn then started his descent. The book Blake brought but never opened went back inside his pack. His hand patted a zippered pocket in his vest. Inside was Jaimie's watch.

The fear he'd been living with since learning she was alive and working undercover, rose in his gullet. Every instinct told him she was in danger, but he was helpless.

Once the engines stopped, they unsnapped their seatbelts and waited for the co-pilot to open the cabin door. As Blake walked down the steps, the sight of mountains, topped with snow, and crisp, cool air with a hint of pine stimulated his tired senses. With a renewed purpose, he slid on the sunglasses, muting the bright glare, and strode across the tarmac toward the Executive Terminal.

Near the back of the lounge, a young man eyed them from behind a counter.

Adrian said, "I'll get the car while you round up our bags."

After identifying himself, Adrian signed the rental papers and was handed a set of keys. He looked for Blake, who stood by an outer door along with a small cart loaded with their gear.

The advantage of a private plane was the weapons they could carry. In addition to their suitcases, one bag contained vests, night goggles, ammunition, and other tactical equipment. Another held fishing equipment, which was for show. Each of the two large locked metal cases contained a Remington 700 sniper rifle. They'd even added a fishing rod to each one.

After loading everything into the back of the SUV, Adrian got behind the wheel. As he drove, they used the time to study the rugged terrain. When he reached the entrance to the lodge, he pulled into a small roadside park.

Exiting, the two men surveyed the dense brush and timber around the lodge. Adrian said, "I believe a nature hike would be in order after we get checked in."

"Good idea," Blake said, slowly turning, looking for gaps where a sniper could set up.

"Let's see what we're faced with inside," Adrian said.

A valet pulling a luggage cart stepped out as Adrian parked in front. When they exited, he said, "Welcome to Grand Mountain Resort. Is this your first visit?"

"Yes, it is," Blake told him.

"I'm sure you'll enjoy your stay. We pride ourselves on providing our guests with an unforgettable vacation."

With an ironic expression, Blake said, "I'm sure our visit will be more than memorable."

Adrian shot Blake an amused glance and grunted.

As the valet helped Adrian place a metal case on the cart, he said, "Very nice cases."

"A good way to transport fishing rods," Adrian told the man.

"If you like, I'll park your vehicle, or you can park in the lot across the driveway."

Not wanting to relinquish the keys, Adrian declined his offer.

Inside, the two agents paused as they stared in amazement.

"I never expected this in the middle of a national forest," Blake commented.

The lobby extended into a large room filled with sofas, chairs, and tables. A sign, the words Great Room burned onto it, separated the two rooms. Across the back wall, windows at least forty feet high framed the magnificent Teton mountains. The wide-planked wood floor gleamed. Chandeliers sparkled under the sunlight streaming into the room.

Noticing the direction of their gaze, the valet said, "It's where the lodge gets its name." Leaving the cart near the bell captain's desk, he led them to the reception counter. "This is Missy. She'll get you checked in."

Adrian extended his hand. With a quick grip, the bill he held slid into the man's hand.

Blake said, "Blake Kenner and Adrian Dillard. We have reservations."

After greeting them, she slid a registration form toward him. Under interests, Blake checked the box for fly-fishing.

Missy's gaze quickly scanned it. "Mr. Kenner, your reservations are all set and paid for. Your room is on the second floor. Behind the staircase is an elevator."

She motioned toward a nearby attendant. "Would you like to

schedule a fly-fishing tour?" she asked as she handed the man the keys.

He smiled. "Maybe later." Turning, Blake saw a deputy sheriff walk around the luggage cart while the dog he led on a leash sniffed their cases.

Once the attendant had carried the gear into the room, another bill exchanged hands.

"The Bureau sure didn't scrimp on this one." Blake's gaze skimmed the small living room, kitchenette, with a bedroom on each side.

Adrian studied the luxurious room. "Certainly adds to our persona of wealthy executives. Which bedroom do you want?"

"Doesn't matter. Did you notice the pass with the dog?"

"Yeah. Good to know the luggage is screened."

"I'd better call Scott." Pulling his cellphone, he tapped the speed dial, then the speakerphone so Adrian could hear.

"Any problems with the flight?" Scott asked.

"Other than a few bumps, it was uneventful."

When Adrian grunted, Blake grinned, before adding, "This place is certainly a showcase."

"Don't get too comfortable."

Blake laughed. "Somehow, I don't see it happening. Anything new?"

"Yes. Frank will arrive mid to late morning instead of the afternoon. Chabot passed on a warning. Savvi could still be in danger."

"Any idea why?"

"If we could figure it out, we'd be a lot closer to knowing their plans. Nicki's still picking apart the data from the Feds computer system. I'll be in touch."

With a grim expression, Adrian hauled his cases into a bedroom. "Time to start exploring."

As they walked down the stairs, the sliding glass doors slid open. The deputy sheriff and dog walked in. The deputy gave them a suspicious look as he headed to the reception desk.

At the small, free-standing bar, the bartender walked over as they slid onto stools. After setting the bottles of beer they ordered in front of them, he moved to the other end.

In a low voice, Blake said, "The deputy's talking to the desk clerk. He's keeping an eye on us."

"I noticed. Wonder if he's doing the same with the other guests?" Adrian twisted on the stool. His elbows propped on the bar and the bottle in his hand, he studied the people seated in clusters around the room. "The bigwigs don't start arriving until tomorrow. From the schedule I saw, the Chairman makes his speech day after tomorrow at nine in the morning."

He took a swig then choked. Coughing, he said, "I'll be damned."

"What?"

His head tipped toward the lobby door. "Look who walked in. Know him?"

Blake swiveled his stool to look. A tall, slim man conservatively dressed in slacks, a polo shirt, and a light jacket, stood by the sliding glass doors. Dark hair, streaked with white, glasses, and a narrow face, added up to a scholarly appearance.

"Never seen him before."

"Todd Bracken. Ring a bell?"

"The Texas Gold Depository ... Director Todd Bracken?"

"Yeah, that's him."

"What's he doing here?"

"I don't know, but we're screwed. He knows who I am. We met after the foiled heist of the gold shipment in Texas."

They watched Bracken's gaze idly skim over them as he strode across the room, then flick back with a look of puzzlement as he stared at Adrian. The moment recognition dawned, he changed course, heading straight to them.

Out of the corner of his eye, Adrian saw the bartender wiping the bar as he slowly came closer. "Our cover is about to be blown."

Blake set the bottle on the bar and slid off the stool. Before Bracken could say a word, he extended his hand. In a voice infused with enthusiasm, he said, "Adrian just told me you're Todd Bracken, head of the new gold depository down in Texas. I'm Blake Kenner. What a pleasure to meet you." Sounding like an idiot, he chuckled and pumped Bracken's hand. "I've always heard everything's bigger in Texas, even your version of Ft. Knox."

Curiosity sparked in Bracken's eyes.

With a step backward, Blake sat down. "Ever since you made the presentation to Adrian's company, he's been trying to get me to contact you."

Adrian's hand reached out. "Todd, what a small world. Didn't expect to run into you up here."

"The surprise is mutual," he said as they shook hands.

"Can I buy you a drink?" Blake asked.

"Thanks. I'll have what you're drinking."

Blake nodded to the bartender, who'd been listening to the by-play. "Another bottle, please."

Adrian glanced around the room and spotted several chairs in a secluded corner surrounded by potted trees. "Why don't we get comfortable," he said, motioning with his hand.

With a light laugh, Bracken said, "Good idea. It'll give me another chance to convince you my proposal is the right one for your company." When the bartender handed him the bottle, he headed to the chairs. After dropping several bills on the bar, Blake followed.

As they sat, Adrian looked around. A good spot with no one nearby who could hear their conversation.

Todd leaned forward to set his bottle on the table. His voice low, he said, "My, my. I must presume ... *you* don't want anyone to know who you are."

Blake said, "Our apologies. We didn't have much time to come up with a plan once Adrian spotted you."

"Oh! No apologies are necessary. One day in the future, I expect this will make a damn good story."

"We appreciate your fast uptake."

"Hmm, I don't suppose you will tell me why you're here?"

With a wry look, Adrian said, "Let's just say we plan to engage in a bit of fly-fishing."

A laugh erupted. "Why does it make me think you're fishing for something bigger than trout?"

Adrian laughed along with him. "Well, sir, you never know what you might catch."

"It's Todd since my tiny role in this conspiracy is to keep quiet," and chuckled again.

"Why are you here?" Blake asked.

After taking a swig of the beer, he said, "I'm drumming up business. I'm giving a presentation on the benefits of storing gold in the Texas Gold Depository. Foreign central banks and other worldwide financial entities are increasing their gold reserves and need a place to store it. The top officials will be at this conference. It's a timely topic this year since the Federal Reserve is getting ready to implement a gold currency system."

"Is this your first time here?"

"Yes. What a magnificent area of the country. I've already decided to make another trip and bring my family."

They talked for a few more minutes. Adrian was quite interested in the progress of the depository. With a note of pride, Todd informed them the depository's security force had been upgraded by the Texas legislature to commissioned peace officers. "It puts us on par with the U.S. Mint Storage facility at Ft. Knox and the Federal Reserve storage vault in New York City."

Blake laughed. "Didn't I say everything was bigger in Texas?"

When they stood, ready to leave, Todd shook each of the men's hands, saying, "If I can be of any help, let me know. If either of you gets to Austin, be sure to stop by."

Adrian watched him walk away before saying, "I'll be outside."

"I'll meet you back in the room later this evening. I'm going to wander, check the exits, listen to people talk. Never know what I might hear."

CHAPTER
29

WASHINGTON D.C.

WHEN **HAYES STEPPED** into his office, Sutter held up a finger as he finished a phone call. "Yes, I will check into it. If I find anything significant, I'll call you." Hanging up the receiver, he pointed to the door.

Hayes closed it behind him. "We may have a problem," he said, dropping into a chair.

Sutter raised an eyebrow.

"Roth was in the building last night, along with another agent."

"What the hell was she doing here?"

"According to the night guard, giving her friend a tour of the building."

"Damn! Where did they go?"

"I watched the tapes. All I know is they wandered around the lobby, then got on the elevator. It stopped on the second floor, and never moved."

"How long were they in the building?"

"According to the entry log, around an hour."

"An hour to show someone the damn building?"

"I don't like it either."

"Anything else happen?"

"A minor disagreement over a delivery of flowers. The guard told the delivery man he'd have to come back."

"Did he?"

"Did he what?"

Suppressing his irritation, Sutter said, "Did the man come back?"

"Uh, I don't know."

"Find out. What happened when the agents left?"

"Nothing. Roth was by herself, told the guard the other woman stopped in the bathroom. A few minutes later, she got out of the elevator."

"Where was Barnett?"

"Deegan said she was in her office."

"Did you pick up anything from your surveillance?"

"She never made a call or spoke to anyone other than Deegan. You already know about Roth's earlier visit. Yesterday, my man followed Barnett into the cafeteria. Roth was there. He all they talked about was some bar."

Sutter fumed, staring at Hayes with narrowed eyes. Ever since Deegan alerted him to Barnett's undue interest in two of the stress reports, he'd been edgy. Transferring her to Deegan's group had seemed a good idea. A new hire, he figured Barnett could easily be manipulated. Now, it appeared to be a mistake. One he planned to rectify.

Then Roth showed up, another unexpected complication. Despite Halston's assurance he could take care of the problem, the attempt to eliminate the woman had been a dismal failure. It was why he moved up the timetable on Frank. Since she'd insisted the car be checked for explosives before leaving the garage, his only option was at the reception. Sutter still didn't know what went wrong. Halston's man swore he planted the bomb. Then there was the highly suspect flat tire, and no explosive device when he checked the car. Now, this. He didn't like the feeling that events were spinning out of his control.

"Who was the other agent?"

"Nicole Allison."

"For god sakes, don't you know who she is?"

With a mulish look, Hayes said, "Yeah, I do. She's buddy-buddy with Roth and works for Scott Fleming."

Under his breath, Sutter swore. He couldn't afford to alienate him. He'd already had to deal with the man's objections to the car bomb. While he finally convinced him that losing two men would deflect any suspicions away from him, he suspected it was the hefty bonus he promised that changed Hayes' attitude. "She also happens to be the number one computer expert in the Bureau."

"You think she did something to our computers? How could she get inside the room? It's never left unlocked."

If you think a locked door will slow down one of Fleming's agents, you're a bigger idiot than even I realized, he thought. Shoving back his chair, Sutter rose. "I want to see the camera tapes." With an angry stride, he threw open the door and walked out.

When he stepped into the security office, the guard who had been lounging in the chair, straightened to attention.

"Take a break. Come back in fifteen minutes," Sutter told him.

"Yes, sir." The man jumped up and rushed out of the room.

Sutter looked at Hayes. "Bring up the tapes from last night."

Hayes sat and tapped the keyboard. The live feed stopped, then another tape with the previous date appeared. Hayes advanced the film to when the two women walked in.

Sutter watched as they flirted with the guard, before walking around the lobby. As Hayes had said, the camera angle showed the elevator stopping on the second floor.

As the tape continued to roll, a man walked in, his face hidden behind a large vase filled with tall stems of foliage and flowers.

Muttering under his breath, Sutter watched the interplay at the security desk. Not once did the camera get a picture of his face.

"Back it up to when he walks in." This time, he looked at the elevator. It didn't move from the second floor. With a sinking feeling, Sutter realized the stairwell door was out of the range of the camera.

"Fast forward to when the women leave."

A quick tap on the keyboard brought up the image of Roth walking out of the elevator. She stopped at the desk, then stepped to the window. The camera picked up the movement of the guard's eyes to watch her. In the background, Sutter saw the closed elevator start back up, then stop on the second floor, before returning to the lobby. Allison strolled out as if she didn't have a care in the world.

Cursing, he stomped out of the room. Outside, he waited for Hayes. His eyes blazed with anger. "Find out if Allison tampered with the program."

When Hayes stared at him, he barked. "Damnit, man, don't just stand there. Talk to Holcomb."

Fear raced over him as Sutter headed back to his office. Was it paranoia, or as slick of an operation as he'd ever seen? If two years of work just went down the drain, his life was over. He couldn't run far enough or fast enough.

Nerves raw, he waited. When his secretary buzzed to tell him a supplier was on the phone, he snapped back. "Take a message."

When a rap sounded, his heart thudded. "Come in."

Hayes walked in, followed by Holcomb, who closed the door behind him.

"Well?" Sutter demanded in a loud tone.

"I can't find any evidence of an intrusion in the system," Holcomb said.

"Are you absolutely sure?"

"I set up the firewalls myself. I'm telling you no one could get around them without leaving a footprint. There is no trace, and nothing in the program has been altered."

Darren Holcomb was considered one of the top computer

experts in the country, which is why Sutter hired him two years ago. While his tension eased, he still wasn't completely satisfied. "Do you know Agent Nicole Allison?"

"I know the name, but never met her. Supposed to be the big shot with computers in the FBI. She was a few years behind me at MIT."

Amazed, Sutter stared, then his anger erupted. "MIT! She graduated from MIT?"

"Yeah, what of it? Lots of people graduate from there."

"But they don't go on to gain the reputation she has or become the top computer expert in the FBI. Can she get around your firewalls?"

An expression of disdain crossed Holcomb's face. Sutter might be a financial wizard, but he seemed to forget who was driving this bus. For all their fancy plans, they were dead in the water without him. He snorted in disgust, then said, "She couldn't even get close. No one's ever hacked one of my systems. Now, if you don't have something important to discuss, I need to get back to my office."

Holcomb shot Sutter a derisive look, then turned to walk out of the room. The door slammed behind him.

Swearing under his breath, Sutter struggled to maintain his composure. Patience, he reminded himself. Losing his temper solved nothing. He looked at Hayes, who stood by the door. "Sit down. We need to talk about Roth."

★★★

Savvi pecked away on the keyboard, examining documents about the bank stress tests and the gold currency. The new currency was scheduled to go live in a little over six weeks. She wondered if she'd still be assigned to the Federal Reserve to watch it happen.

When a tap sounded on the door, she shut down the computer. "Come in," she called out.

Captain Hayes stepped through the doorway. "Am I interrupting?"

"No, reading articles on the new currency."

"I understand you plan to travel with the Chairman to Wyoming."

"I'll be leaving with him in the morning."

"I thought your job was to oversee the implementation of the new currency system. Why are you going with him?"

"Is it a problem?" she asked.

"Yes, it is. The Chairman's bodyguards are police officers who are fully qualified to protect him. Since ensuring his safety is my primary concern, adding another person to his itinerary isn't in his best interest. You're an unnecessary complication."

Savvi's smile never reached her eyes. Her tone flat, she said, "Your concern, Captain Hayes, is noted, but must I remind you, I am an FBI agent. My presence won't interfere with the activities of your guards. In fact, it will augment your security procedures for the Chairman."

"Since you persist in your uncooperative attitude, I'll have to re-fer the issue to Director Sutter. He's in charge of the Chairman's itinerary."

"No! I suggest you take it up with the Chairman since he's the one who requested my presence as you so aptly termed it."

An angry blush stained his face as he huffed. "It still doesn't change my mind. Your traveling with the Chairman is an unwar-ranted risk."

Furious, she watched him walk out. They wanted to make sure she didn't get in the way of their plans to kill the Chairman. Her phone rang. Still scowling at the door, she answered, "Roth!"

"Whoa. Something's happened. Can you talk?" Nicki asked.

"No."

"Okay, tell me later. Got a question for you. You can answer yes or no. Did Jaimie say Deegan approved her reports?"

"Yes."

"Is his approval required?"

"Yes. I think you are right."

"Can you confirm? It's important."

"I'll find out."

"Call me as soon as you know," Nicki told her.

Disconnecting, she slid the phone into her pocket. How was she going to find out? Frank had back-to-back meetings. If she interrupted, questions would be asked. She'd have to contact Jaimie. But how? Chabot!

Since she'd already programmed his number on her speed dial, a quick tap and his voice echoed on the other end.

"Remy, are we still on for lunch today?"

"Music to my ears. Chérie, where do you want to meet?"

"Since it's close to the office, can we go back to the same café?"

"I can be there in fifteen to twenty minutes."

"Good. See you there."

She locked her briefcase, stuffed it back into the same spot under her desk, then headed out the door.

When she walked into the restaurant, the maître d' recognized her. "So delighted to welcome you back. Your table is ready," and waved a hand toward the waiter who led her across the deserted patio.

Remy had already arrived. At the sight of him, a tingle of eagerness caught her by surprise. He rose to pull out her chair. After being informed they only wanted coffee, the waiter left.

"I don't have much time. Can you call Jaimie for me?"

His eyes gleamed with suppressed humor. "Oui, chérie, and here I believed you were pining away. Wanting to see me one more time before you left. I am desolate. You only need me to make a phone call."

Even as he spoke, he pulled his phone from his pocket and tapped the dial. The teasing voice gone, he said, "Agent Roth wants to speak to you. All right." Laying the phone down, he said, "She's going to call back. Why do you need to talk to her?"

"It's about the stress test results."

The phone rang. Remy picked it up, answered, then handed it to Savvi.

"Jaimie, where are you?"

"Bathroom. I don't figure a bug's been planted in here. What do you need?"

"To confirm that Deegan is required to sign off on your review."

"Yes. He's required to approve all the reviews before they get transferred to the approved file. Why?"

"Nicki is asking, though, I don't know the reason. What about the last two reviews? Are they done?"

"Yes. I sent Bank of New York's review to Deegan. I am holding off on Risson's review until tonight. It's my excuse to work late. I need to get back to work. Call you later." The line went dead.

She handed the phone to Remy. "Let me make one more call, and I'll tell you what's going on."

She pulled out her phone and tapped Nicki's number.

Nicki answered, "What did you find out?"

"Deegan's approval is required. Why the question?"

"Bad answer coming up. Here's what I've discovered about the process. The reviewer sends the report to Deegan, he signs off, then transfers the test results along with the approval form to the approved file. Since his authorization is required, here's the bad. Deegan approved Jaimie's first three reviews. On the next three, which are the false reports, Deegan's name is missing. The individual who approved them is Lois Barnett. Someone has made it look like she approved the reports, bypassed Deegan, and sent them to the approved file."

Savvi vehemently protested. "Wait a minute, I saw Deegan's

name on the first two reports I found, Butler Bank and Trust and Caldwell Fidelity. He approved the reports."

"Not anymore. His name is missing. The fact he approved three of Jaimie's reports paints an ugly picture. It could be used to show that when she approved the reports and bypassed Deegan, it wasn't a mistake but a deliberate act. I'd bet my last dollar, if she has sent the last two reports to Deegan, when they hit the approved file, they'll be the same. She approved them, not Deegan."

"One has already been sent to him, Bank of New York. She's holding off on the second until tonight."

"By the way, how did you contact her?"

"Remy's phone."

"Oh, yeah!"

"I've got to go."

"*We* will talk about this later." The phone went dead.

Remy asked, "Savvi, what happened?" The mocking look was gone, and faint lines of worry puckered his eyes.

"Nicki found something from last night's download." After explaining the two conversations, she added, "It's likely when those hit the approved file, they'll show the same, Lois Barnett as the approver."

At the approach of the waiter, his hand lifted to warn her. After setting a carafe and two cups on the table, he asked, "Will there be anything else?"

Remy told him no. While he waited for him to get out of earshot, he picked up the carafe and filled the cups, then said, "Go on."

"I know Deegan approved two of those reports. There's only one reason it's been changed, set up Jaimie as the fall guy. Nicki brought up a valid point. With three other reviews in the system that Deegan did approve, it does establish the act was deliberate, not a mistake."

"I am beginning to agree with your estimable boss. It's time to pull her out. Yesterday, I met with Halston to let him know I had the offshore accounts set up. He's expecting to transfer the money within a few days. Have you figured out how it ties into the stress tests?"

"Not yet."

"You also came up in the discussion."

"I did?"

"Hmm … yes. He was livid because you wouldn't be attending his award ceremony." With a mocking tone of amusement, he added, "I don't think you will get your award after all."

She had to laugh. "Like I really care," and drank the coffee.

"Chérie … he's got a reason for wanting you out of the way."

"Someone else may have the same reason."

An eyebrow quirked upward as he lifted the cup to his mouth.

"Captain Hayes. The man's not happy about my trip to Wyoming." Anger resonated in her voice. "He claims I'll jeopardize the Chairman's safety and wants me to stay behind. Can they really believe I'm that stupid? That I don't know what's going on?"

Setting down his cup, Remy leaned forward. A finger lightly stroked the back of her hand.

Despite the rage she felt, unexpected tingles curled over her shoulders from his touch.

"Last night, I spoke with Scott. I told him you were still in danger, and this only deepens my concern. You must take every precaution."

"Don't worry. I will. Once I get to Wyoming, Blake and Adrian will be there. What are you going to do about Jaimie?"

"I'll call her. She won't be going back tomorrow."

She glanced at her new watch. "I have to go."

"You have my number. Call if you need anything." The mocking tone gone, an intense gleam darkened his eyes. "I will see you when you return."

Not sure how to respond, she nodded and rose.

Remy tossed a few bills on the table and followed her out the door. A wave of his arm and a cab pulled to a halt in front of them. He opened the door. Once she settled on the seat, he leaned in. "Be very, very careful, chérie." He closed the door and stepped back.

Taking a deep breath, she let it out slowly. Well, dang, what the hell was she going to do about Remy? Did she want to do something?

NICKI LAID THE phone aside. Savvi's information added to her conviction Jaimie had become a patsy. But for what reason? A question Scott wasn't going to like.

At the sound of the tap, tap, tap, she stopped in the doorway. In his thinking position, feet propped on the desk, eyes closed, he leaned back in his chair. The pen, lightly held in one hand, tapped the desk.

"Boss man, I sure hope all that thinking is doing us some good."

With a slight shift of his head, he opened one eye. "It might if my guru gave me something to work with," he quipped.

She plunked into a chair, leaned back, and mimicked his position. Feet dropped on the desk with a thud. She groaned. "I've studied those damn program files to the point I could recite them in my sleep."

When he didn't respond, she looked over. His eyes had closed.

A bit irked, she said, "But, it's not all bad news. Savvi confirmed something I found."

His eyes popped open.

That got your attention, she thought.

"What?"

After listening to Nicki's explanation, his feet slid off the desk. His body tensed as a worried look crossed his face.

"Something's clicked," she said.

"Yeah, it has. Is there a track in the system to show Jaimie sent the reports to Deegan?"

"No. Another small detail that adds to Jaimie's role as the fall guy."

"You're right. If someone inadvertently discovered the falsified reports, Jaimie would get the blame."

"All the evidence would be against her," Nicki added.

As he gathered his thoughts, his apprehension intensified. With a grim tone, Scott said, "Especially if she isn't around to defend herself. Do you know if she's finished the last two reports?"

"According to Savvi, she has. One was transferred today. She's holding off on sending the last one until this evening."

"Once they have it, they have no further use for her. How did Savvi contact her?"

"Through Remy."

He grabbed his phone. Tapping a number, he waited for Remy to answer. It rang until it rolled to voice mail. "Damn," he muttered. "He's got to get her out of there." A comment Remy made popped into his mind.

"Last night, Remy told me Halston wanted to be sure the offshore accounts were ready. He gave Halston the account numbers. I wonder?"

Following his thought process, she said, "They plan to do the same to him."

Another trait he liked. With Nicki, he never had to explain. "Makes sense if whoever's in charge is trying to cover his tracks. Jaimie takes the fall at the Federal Reserve. Remy takes it for setting up the accounts," Scott said. "Remy's in as much danger as Jaimie."

He tried the number again. No answer. "Call Savvi."

Nicki placed the call, then handed the phone to Scott. When Savvi answered, he tapped the speakerphone.

"Hi, Nicki," she said.

"Savvi, it's Scott. Are you where you can talk?"

"Not really."

"Okay, Jaimie's in danger," he told her, then explained why. "Do you know where Remy might have gone? He's not answering his phone."

"No."

"Can you get word to her to leave?"

"I'll try."

"Let me know." His face grim, he disconnected and handed the phone back. As Nicki walked out, he tapped Remy's number on his phone. Still no answer.

★★★

She slid the phone in her pocket. How could she contact Jaimie without alerting Deegan? There was only one way. From the bottom drawer, she grabbed an index card. In large block letters, she printed—DANGER—GET OUT NOW.

Slipping it into the pocket of her jacket, she picked up her tote bag and strode out the door. As she exited the elevator, Deegan's door was closed. With quick but quiet steps, she walked to Jaimie's open doorway, where she stopped. Jaimie looked up, and Savvi held up the card.

After a brief glance, Jaimie nodded, then turned to her computer.

The elevator dinged just as she reached Deegan's office. She spun and rapped on his door.

Behind her, Deegan's voice said, "Agent Roth, can I help you?"

She turned to face him. "Hello again. I was hoping you hadn't left for the day."

Deegan walked past her and unlocked his door. As it opened, he motioned for her to step inside, then followed, closing it behind him. "Please, have a seat," he told her, stepping behind his desk.

"Thank you, but I won't take but a minute or two of your time. I had a question on the review process for the bank stress reports."

"Oh." A momentary look of apprehension flashed across his face before he settled into his chair. "What can I answer for you?"

"Once the stress reports have been transferred to the Approved file, are they subjected to any further action?"

"If the bank has passed the stress tests, it's the end of the process. Of course, the banks receive notification of the results. If a bank fails the test, the reports are forwarded to the sanctions committee for action."

"How often do you have a bank fail the test?"

"Since I've been assigned to the review process, there's only been one, and it was a few years back. I know you've been reviewing the stress tests. Is there a reason for your questions?"

She wondered how he knew she'd been looking at them. "Not really. Since I'm not familiar with the reports, I'm still trying to understand the dynamics of the process."

With a smirk, he said, "Yes, it's a complicated process for many people to understand."

She smiled, satisfied the smug bastard didn't have a clue. "You could be right. Thank you for your time. Have a good evening."

As she walked out the door, Savvi glanced over her shoulder. He was already tapping a number on his phone. Hayes or Sutter, she wondered.

Back in her office, she gathered up the files she planned to take with her to study on the plane. Stuffing them into her briefcase, she glanced around, making sure she didn't leave anything of interest to anyone.

In the lobby, she stepped toward the windows where the guards couldn't hear, then called Nicki. When she answered, Savvi told her she'd contacted Jaimie, and passed on the warning.

Next, she called Frank. When he answered, she told him she was staying in town and would grab a cab. Even though Frank hung up, she continued to act as if she was talking to someone while she kept an eye on the elevator.

A continual stream of employees exited, but Jaimie wasn't one of them. As tension built, she wondered if something had happened. Another ding sounded.

This time, Jaimie was the second person to step out. When she looked around, she made eye contact with Savvi but continued to walk toward the door. Savvi turned away, pocketed the phone, and strode toward the front doors.

Outside, Jaimie had flagged down a cab. As Savvi stepped out, she shouted, making sure the guard could hear. "Lois," and waved her hand in the air to get her attention. When Jaimie turned, she hollered, "Do you mind if I share your cab?"

"Not at all," Jaimie shouted back.

Savvi rushed over and slid onto the backseat, setting her briefcase on the floor. She huffed as if out of breath, "Thank you. Cabs are so hard to find today."

The driver looked over the seat. "Okay, ladies, where are you going?"

Savvi said, "You first."

Jaimie gave him an address. Then he looked at Savvi.

"I'm not certain yet. While I decide, drop my friend off." Savvi turned her head to look at Jaimie. "I'm headed to Wyoming tomorrow and need boots."

During the ride to an apartment complex, several miles away, they kept the conversation light, work, shopping. When the driver pulled up in front of the apartments, Jaimie asked how much, then passed him the money.

As she exited, she looked at Savvi. "Have a safe trip. When you get back, I'd love to have lunch with you."

Savvi said, "It's a date. I'll come to your office. We'll set up something." As the cab pulled away, she looked over her shoulder as Jaimie walked inside the building.

"What'd you decide?" the cabbie asked.

"A couple of miles back, we passed a shopping center. Drop me there." She'd switch cabs before heading to Frank's house. If someone decided to question the driver, she'd covered her tracks.

★★★

Scott paced. He was close, so close to the why in all of this that it teased him, hovering just beyond his comprehension. He walked past Nicki's door. Deep in her research, she hunched over her keyboard.

Not wanting to break her concentration, Scott headed to the breakroom. He had to do something. The only option was the damn coffee pot. While he didn't need another cup, he punched the button anyway.

When his phone rang, he almost ripped his pocket in his haste to get it.

"Remy, you're a hard man to reach."

"Ach! It does my heart good to know I am needed. Unfortunately, there was a slight mishap to keep me from answering the phone."

Even though his voice held the same mocking amusement, Scott heard an underlying tone of anger. "What happened?"

"Americans, so hasty to take offense at the driving habits of others. Some minor damage to my car, which includes two bullet holes."

"Any idea who it was?"

"A dark van, two men, the license plate covered by what appeared to be mud. I gave chase but lost them once they got on the freeway. So, your reason for the multitude of missed calls?"

"To warn you that you might be in danger."

"Your concern for my well-being is most gratifying. When did you learn of this danger?"

Scott detected a faint snit in his voice. "Maybe ten minutes before I started calling."

Remy's voice warmed as he said, "Then, my thanks. What prompted them?"

Scott explained. A couple of times during his comments, he heard a muttered oath. When he finished, Scott added, "Savvi was able to get a warning to Jaimie. I was trying to reach you."

"Events proved you were right. I must check on Jaimie." He disconnected.

Scott slipped the phone in his pocket, then filled two cups. In Nicki's office, he set one on her desk.

When she looked up, he said, "Remy called." Scott dropped into a chair, took a swallow of the hot brew, and then told her about the attack.

"Jeez, boss man, you nailed it."

A phone vibrated. It was the burner phone.

When he answered, a harsh voice greeted him.

"Scott, I had a disquieting conversation with Director Ben Sutter this afternoon."

"Where are you?"

"At home. I didn't want to discuss this at the office or say anything to Savvi until I spoke to you."

"What happened?"

Anger vibrated in Frank's voice as he explained. "Ben Sutter filed charges against Savvi with Captain Hayes for tampering with government documents. He also mentioned another woman, Lois Barnett, who works in the review section, is implicated as well. Ben said Savvi and Barnett altered the stress test reports, and he has proof. Since Savvi is under investigation, he demanded to have her removed from her position at the Federal Reserve. To ensure there was no appearance of improprieties, I should have no further contact with her. When I asked why I had not been informed before he contacted Captain Hayes, he said he didn't want to compromise my position. I didn't contradict him, even though I know Barnett's real identity."

As Scott listened, anger overwhelmed him, choking the breath from his lungs. For a second, he couldn't speak, but when he did, he couldn't control the harshness in his voice. "Sutter is in this up to his neck, along with Hayes and Holcomb. Since you had to interact with your staff, I didn't want to put you in an untenable position. There has already been one attempt to kill Savvi and Nicki."

"When!"

"The night before the gallery reception. There have been other attempts, not quite so deadly, to get her out of the way. Savvi's not out of danger along with Jaimie Marston."

"What does Ben hope to gain by filing these charges?" Frank asked. "Surely, he has to know it would all come out."

"To keep Savvi from getting on the plane tomorrow."

"It still doesn't make sense. There would be an investigation."

"Not if you were dead."

"Dear God in heaven," he whispered.

"The only way Sutter plans on you returning from Wyoming is in a coffin. And those charges would have mysteriously disappeared. Who else knows?"

"Right now, only Hayes. I ordered Ben not to do anything until I had an opportunity to examine the evidence. After Ben left, I called Captain Hayes. Since he's a law enforcement officer, I have no authority over him, but I did advise it would be prudent for him to hold off on the charges. I told him if he didn't agree, I would contact the police chief."

"I can assure you they don't want you to contact his boss. In the morning, when you leave, you might encounter some resistance."

"No, I won't! Savvi will be on the plane."

"Where is she?"

"I'm not sure. I received a call to tell me she'd take a cab."

"When she gets there, fill her in, then ask her to call me."

"Scott, what's the status on Jaimie Marston? You said she was in danger."

"We're taking steps to protect her. It's all I can say right now."

"When you can discuss it, I'd appreciate your letting me know."

"I will." The line disconnected.

"My god, boss man, what was that all about?" Nicki exclaimed.

Scott went over the details she hadn't been able to hear.

"To pull a stunt like this, they must believe their plan will work," Nicki said.

"That's what has me worried," Scott growled.

His next call was from Remy.

"Jaimie's home. I told her what you had discovered on the reviews. She said she forwarded them to Deegan, and the proof is on her computer. I tried to dissuade her, but she's determined to get copies of the emails. Tomorrow morning, she's going to her office. I'll be waiting to pick her up."

"Do you want me to assign an agent to keep an eye on her tonight?"

"No, I'll be watching."

Scott went on to explain Sutter's fake charges, which prompted a lengthy tirade from Remy, all in French.

Once he wound down, Scott said, "I'm not sure what you said, but from the tone, I'd probably agree. I need the numbers to the offshore accounts."

"Wait a minute, I'll get them."

Scott tapped the speakerphone. When Remy came back on the line and read off the numbers, Nicki copied them down.

"How did you get them set up?"

"I didn't. Louie Bisset handled it. On the surface, the accounts appear legitimate, but they aren't."

Scott asked, "Once the money is in the accounts Interpol set up, can it be transferred to another account?"

"Yes, but if that happens, we'll be tracking it. We want to find every viper in this nest."

"I'll be in touch." He disconnected

"If Interpol set these up, it doesn't matter if they link back to Remy. Any reason I need to look at them?" Nicki asked.

"Yeah, go ahead. You never know. I'll be in my office." The sense of something lurking in the shadows of his mind had grown stronger. As he walked out the door, Nicki's phone rang. "It's Savvi."

She tapped the speakerphone as she answered, "Savvi, Frank called … "

Interrupting, Savvi said, "Can you believe what that sorry-assed bastard tried to pull? It wasn't the only stunt they pulled today."

"Hold on. Here's Scott." She looked at her boss. "Boy, is she pissed."

"I heard that, and you're damned right, I'm pissed. I hope I get to slap the cuffs on the bastard."

Scott asked, "What else happened today?"

She relayed the details of Hayes' visit. Still fuming, she said, "When it didn't work, they cooked up another scheme."

"Fill me in on Jaimie."

A bit calmer, she explained the use of the index card to get a message to Jaimie. "Deegan almost caught me after I left her office. I fobbed him off with a couple of questions about the stress test reviews. He mentioned that he knew I was studying the reports, which I found interesting. How would he know unless they are monitoring the computer activity? Anyway, I waited in the lobby for Jaimie to leave, then snagged a ride in the same cab with her, making sure she got home."

"When you met Jaimie in the cafeteria, you mentioned a guard. Was he one of Frank's bodyguards?"

"No, one of the lobby guards. I'd like to keep his bodyguards off the plane, but I know we can't. By the way, it's a toss-up who is more pissed, Frank or me. When I got here, he was highly agitated, even barked at Amelia. He insisted on knowing about the shooting incident. I didn't tell him you'd linked the car to Halston."

Scott said, "Something else you need to know. Someone tried to take out Remy tonight."

"Is he all right?"

"Yes, but his car isn't. Nicki and I figure they planned to pull the same stunt on Remy as they did on Jaimie."

"Did he pull her out?"

"Yes. Jaimie has proof she sent the reports to Deegan. She's going to her office in the morning to pick it up. Remy will be waiting for her."

"Good. She needs to get the hell out of there. There's nothing else she can do. Once we land tomorrow, I'll call."

Scott told her, "I'll call Blake and Adrian, bring them up to speed on what's happened."

After disconnecting, Scott called Blake. When he answered, in the background, he could hear music.

"Where are you?"

Blake laughed. "In what is referred to as the Great Room where a couple of locals with guitars are entertaining the guests. They've got a good sound. I'll call you back as soon as we get to our room."

While Scott waited, he wandered into the breakroom. Earlier, Nicki had ordered sandwiches from a local deli. He grabbed one from the fridge, along with a can of diet soda, then plopped on the couch. He'd just popped the lid when the phone rang.

"We expected you'd be calling," Blake said. "Adrian's listening."

"What's the situation up there?"

"Even though many of the guests aren't part of the conference, security is still tight. I've seen a few who I suspect are security types, maybe fronting for one of the conference attendees. Most will arrive tomorrow. Deputies take turns with the dog, scoping out the public areas, inside and out. Be difficult for someone to plant a bomb since they check the luggage. We're back to the sniper theory."

Adrian said, "I hiked the terrain in front of the lodge. It's rugged, lots of trees and underbrush. For someone to have a shot, the Chairman would have to be out front. Call Savvi, let her know to be careful when they arrive. She'll have to keep him inside, no walking around the grounds. But as isolated as this place is, only one road in and out, I don't know how they could pull it off."

Scott said, "It's not an *if* anymore. I fully expect they will make a try for the Chairman." He started by telling Blake that Chabot was pulling Jaimie out.

Blake's sense of relief at hearing the news was short-lived. After listening to Scott's explanation of why, he erupted with anger. "Damn! Are you sure she's safe? If they'd make a try for Chabot, you've got to know Jaimie's on their hit list."

Scott said, "Remy's playing bodyguard and will pick her up tomorrow when she leaves the building." Then he told them of the latest stunt to get rid of Savvi.

Adrian said, "Damn, they sure are determined to get her out of the way. If Nicki has pictures of Halston's security force and Frank's security team, send them."

"I'm sure she does. Here's the problem. The threat may not be coming from the outside but from the Chairman's team."

"His bodyguards," Blake muttered.

CHAPTER
31

SINCE THEY WERE leaving at the crack of dawn, Savvi had set the alarm to allow plenty of time to finish packing. Despite her protests, Amelia told her breakfast would be waiting.

As she showered and dressed, the anger from yesterday resurfaced, not for herself but for the Chairman. She'd received a call from Scott. He passed on Blake's warning. There was no doubt in her mind someone intended to kill Frank.

A grim determination built, flushing away the anger. None of them had any idea the Trackers were hard on their heels, about to expose their plot for what it was, greed and power. She'd make sure Frank Littleton had a ringside seat to watch it go down.

Carrying her bags and a backpack instead of the tote bag, the heady aroma of food cooking led her into the kitchen. The cook was flipping pancakes. Frank was already seated at the table they used for informal dining, a cup of steaming coffee in front of him.

Amelia bustled, placing glasses of juice on the table. "My dear, you certainly look chipper for so early in the morning."

"I'm looking forward to the trip. From what I've read, and Frank's told me, I am in for a rare treat."

"Oh, you are. The Teton mountains are indescribable. You stand and look at them in awe. Blueberry pancakes coming up. Frank, how soon is the car going to be here?"

Savvi smiled at the constant jumps in Amelia's conversation.

It wasn't long until they stood in the mudroom attached to the garage. The limousine had pulled into the driveway.

Frank stepped back into the house to retrieve a file he'd left on his desk.

Amelia placed her hand on Savvi's arm. In a tone Savvi hadn't heard, she said, "I know more than Frank realizes. Keep him safe. Please keep him safe." Tears welled in her eyes.

Savvi slid her arm around the small woman's shoulders and squeezed. Hearing Frank's footsteps, she whispered, "It's what I plan to do. I'm not alone. Scott sent two other agents to Wyoming."

The car stopped in front of the open garage door. The driver and two men exited. One she recognized. It was the guard from the cafeteria. He stared at her with a hard, cold look. The other she didn't know and was probably the person Frank said would return the car.

Frank exclaimed, "Ted, where is Wilson?"

Ted said, "He's not feeling well. Captain Hayes told him to stay home." He motioned to the two men. "Officers Headley and Garnett will accompany you. I was told to return the car."

Scowling, Frank said, "Why wasn't ..." then stopped when he saw the look of concern on Amelia's face. Instead, he said, "I hope it isn't anything serious."

Ted, picking up bags to stow in the back, said, "No, sir. Just one of those twenty-four-hour bugs."

Savvi smiled as if unconcerned over the change. Once the bags were loaded, Frank gave Amelia a last hug, telling her he'd call as soon as he arrived in Wyoming.

Traffic was light, and they arrived early at the airport. As the driver pulled alongside the large jet aircraft, an attendant ran down the metal steps.

Savvi stepped out, followed by Frank. The attendant said, "Mr.

Chairman. The pilot is doing his final checklist. Once he's finished, we'll be ready to take off."

As they walked up the steps, Savvi stayed close behind Frank. Ted and an attendant unloaded the bags, transferring them to the cargo hold. The bodyguards watched.

Inside, two men and a woman rose when Frank entered, staff members that Frank introduced to Savvi. The attendant, hovering nearby, told them once they were in the air, coffee, juice, and various breakfast items would be ready.

As Savvi settled into a chair, her backpack stowed under the seat, she gazed at the luxurious accommodations. Spacious seats and conveniently spaced worktables filled the interior. It should prove to be an enjoyable trip until she glanced toward the rear of the plane. The bodyguards had been the last to enter. Seated side-by-side, their heads together, they talked. She felt the same jolt of trepidation she felt when she saw them step out of the car.

The fasten your seat belt sign flashed on. As the plane rolled and then lifted into the air, Savvi pondered the reason for the change in guards. How did it play into what was planned?

Once the plane reached cruising altitude, the seat belt sign was turned off. The attendant stopped at her chair to ask what she'd like. "Coffee, black," she told him. Unzipping the backpack, she pulled out the file folders containing the bank stress reports and laid them on the small table in front of her.

The attendant pushed a button on the table, ejecting a cup holder. The earthy aroma of freshly brewed coffee wafted from the thick-handled cup he set in the holder.

She settled into the chair and picked up the first report, Halston's bank. While her eyes skimmed the figures, mentally, she verified the calculations. The results didn't change. The bank reported assets they didn't have. It was the same for the other four banks.

After the second run-through, she laid the reports on the table, resting her head against the seat. The answer had to be there, why couldn't she find it? This was like her bank increasing the balance in her checking account even though she hadn't made any deposits. Except, in her case, she could withdraw the money.

A light started to spark. This year's stress test added a new criterion, the bank's baseline of assets. Savvi's thoughts raced, examining it from every side, and knew she had it.

She looked across the aisle to where Frank was seated. Since take-off, he'd worked with his staff on his presentation to the conference. Sensing Savvi's gaze, a smile crossed his face when he looked at her.

The fasten seat belt sign flashed. Engrossed in the reports, she'd lost track of time. They were ready to land.

At the airport, people milled around parked cars near where the plane had stopped. As they exited the plane, Savvi stayed in front of Frank. Taking deep breaths of the clean mountain air, she stared in awe at the mountains. Amelia was right.

At the base of the stairs, one of Frank's security officers waited. When Frank stepped onto the tarmac, he said, "This way, Mr. Chairman," motioning to a nearby car.

Before Savvi could step alongside Frank, the second officer blocked her. "You'll be riding in the second vehicle."

Her eyes flashed with anger. "No, I won't, Officer Garnett! I'm riding with the Chairman," and stepped around him. He reached to grab her, then pulled his arm back. "A wise move," she said.

As she slid beside Frank, he asked, "Everything all right?"

Suppressing the anger, she dropped the backpack at her feet. "A bit of confusion over the seating arrangements. I got it squared away."

Garnett slid behind the wheel. Headley was in the front seat. As they pulled out of the airport, Savvi could see Garnett in the rearview mirror. Despite his concentration on the traffic, a look of rage had settled over his face.

Frank provided a running dialogue as they headed north. This was his third trip, one had been a vacation with Amelia. When they pulled in front of the lodge, a valet rushed outside. Savvi didn't wait for the guard. She opened the door, stepped out and quickly glanced around. With the backpack slung over her back, she moved just far enough away to let Frank exit, then stepped behind him.

The valet reached to shake Frank's hand. "I'm delighted to see you again, Mr. Chairman. Your suite is ready for you." He escorted Frank into the lobby, motioning to another valet to help with the luggage. Inside, Savvi could only gaze in wonder at the view of the mountains through the large windows at the back as she followed Frank and his entourage. It wasn't until they reached his room, did she notice the bodyguards were missing.

When the valet unlocked the door, Savvi stepped forward, entering the room first. Holding up her hand to stop Frank, she walked through the suite of rooms, checking closets, beds, bathrooms, cupboards, and anywhere else an explosive device could be hidden. Anger built. His bodyguards should have been here, checking everything. Only when she was satisfied, did she motion him in.

He smiled, though, she knew from the glint in his eyes, he approved her thoroughness. "Satisfied that I'm safe and sound here?"

"Now, I am. I know you mentioned you didn't plan on leaving until later this evening. Would you give me a call before you do?"

She'd been watching the valet unload the luggage. When he reached for her bags, Savvi stopped him, saying she'd pick them up in the lobby.

Walking to the reception desk, she gazed around and spotted Blake at a nearby table littered with coffee cups and plates.

A young woman greeted her. Savvi identified herself as Savannah Roth.

"Oh, yes. You are with Chairman Littleton's party. You're already checked in." She slid a diagram of the resort toward Savvi, then picked up a set of keys, laying them on the counter. She circled a cabin. "You will be in cabin four. To reach it, follow this path." Her pen traced a line from the lobby to the cabin.

Savvi looked at the woman's name tag. "Missy, I believe there is a mistake. My room was to be adjacent to Chairman Littleton's suite."

"Oh, no, Ms. Roth, your reservations stated you wanted a cabin."

"Please recheck your records. I did not request a cabin."

Flustered, the woman picked up a phone. "Mr. Greenstone, can you come to the reception desk?" After hanging up the receiver, she explained, "Mr. Greenstone is the manager."

A door opened near the reception desk, and a man stepped out. Fiftyish with a jovial face, he said, "I'm Harmon Greenstone. How may I help you?"

Savvi's explanation prompted a protest from Mr. Greenstone. "There is no mistake, a cabin was requested. I talked to the person myself."

"When and who?" Savvi demanded to know.

"This morning. The man said he was Chairman Littleton's administrative secretary, and requested the change, Ms. Roth."

Savvi pulled her badge case from her pocket and flipped it open. "FBI Special Agent Savannah Roth and I'm part of the Chairman's protection detail. I'm not sure what happened, but I did not authorize a change in my accommodations."

Missy and Mr. Greenstone stared at her badge. "Oh, my," Missy said.

Mr. Greenstone shifted the monitor on the desk to face him. He

tapped the keyboard. "Missy, change Agent Roth's room to 108."
He looked at Savvi, saying, "This room is across the hall from the
Chairman's suite. Will it be acceptable?"

Savvi nodded. "Yes, thank you."

"Your luggage?"

She looked around, spotting the cart with her bags. She motioned toward it.

Mr. Greenstone snapped his fingers, and an attendant appeared.
Handing him the key, he said, "Please escort Agent Roth to her
room. Her luggage is on the cart." Then he turned to Savvi. "Please
accept our apologies for any inconvenience."

"It wasn't your fault. I do appreciate your quick response to rectify the situation. One more question. What is the room number for
Officers Headley and Garnett?"

Greenstone looked back at the computer screen. "Room 112."

Savvi nodded her thanks, then followed the valet. Once he'd set
her luggage in the room, she closed and locked the door.

Damn, she needed to talk to Blake and Adrian. First, though,
was a call to Scott. The phone rang, then shifted to voice mail. She
left a message, then tried Nicki's phone. Same thing. Where were
they?

CHAPTER
32

JAIMIE STEPPED OUT of the cab. Her gaze swept the Federal Reserve building. Her last trip inside. She took a deep breath, pushing down the trepidation gnawing at her gut. She was all too aware of the risk of one more trek. But she had to get a copy of those emails. It should take thirty, maybe forty-five minutes, top. Besides, it was daylight, the building wasn't deserted, what could happen?

She made a quick call to let Remy know she was headed inside. He told her he was parked down the block, ready to pick her up when she left.

Inside, she dropped her backpack on the conveyor belt, then walked through the screening device. A new guard was in place, one she hadn't seen before. Upstairs, she opened her office door. Stepping inside, she quickly scanned the area, looking for any disturbance in the small traps she left, before walking toward her desk.

Behind her, the door closed. When she turned, something struck the side of her head. Her last thought as she collapsed into the dark mist—*she'd been wrong.*

★★★

Nervous that events would soon spiral out of his control, Scott arrived at the office before sunrise. After clearing out a few emails, he glanced at his watch. It was too early to call Wyoming. Instead, he pulled up the bank stress tests. Engrossed in the myriad details, he was unaware of the passage of time. The only interruption was Nicki's arrival. When she slid a cup of coffee under his nose, he just nodded in thanks.

The endless repetition of the same question echoed in his head. What did the banks have to gain by falsifying their assets? The answer had to be in the damn reports.

A buzzing noise worked its way into his thoughts. His head shot up. An alert on his phone. Jaimie!

Nicki rushed in. "Did you get it?"

His voice harsh, he said, "Start tracking the signal."

"I already have. I'd programmed the computer to start the track as soon as a signal was received."

They ran to her office. On the monitor, a small triangle moved along a freeway on the large map. It was already outside the city limits, moving north.

His phone rang. Scott said, "Remy, what happened?"

"Goddamn, I don't know. Jaimie called to tell me she was headed inside the building."

"How long ago?"

"Thirty-five minutes or so."

"We've got a track!" After giving him the location, he added, "Once I'm in my car, I'll call." Scott punched the disconnect button and shoved the phone in a pocket. He ran to his office and grabbed the keys lying on the desk.

When he reached the front door, Nicki appeared with a backpack slung over her shoulder.

"You're not going. I need you here, on the computer."

"I've got my computer, and I'm going. We're wasting time." Whipping past him, she pushed open the door and rushed out.

As soon as they were in the car, she booted her computer. Scott drove out of the garage and headed toward the freeway. When the map came up on her screen, she said, "Still on the same road, going north."

"Get Remy on the phone. Keep the line open." He swerved around traffic.

Once they were on the freeway, he floored the gas pedal. "Remy, where are you?"

Remy's voice echoed from the speakerphone with a mile marker number.

Nicki, her eyes focused on the computer screen, said, "Remy's two miles ahead of us."

"Any idea where they could be headed?"

"Not yet," Nicki replied as she typed.

"Remy, any possible location from your investigation?"

"None."

The vehicle they chased continued north for several miles before turning west on another road. While Scott had closed the gap with Remy, the two cars were still over twenty-five miles behind.

A cry of horror erupted. "I've lost the signal." Nicki frantically tapped the keyboard. Another agonizing cry. "It's gone."

A burst of angry French echoed over the phone line.

Scott's mind raced. "We'll keep going until we get to where we lost the signal. Nicki, start a search for possible locations."

Hunched over the laptop, Nicki's fingers flew across the keyboard. Linked to the mainframe in their office, she had access to data she'd already collected plus the law enforcement Fusion network. She set up a name search in the surrounding county tax rolls. Once she hit enter, the power of her computer took over, digging and searching.

Not long after heading west, she said, "Find a place to pull over. This is where we lost the signal."

"A convenience store ahead. I'll park on the side," Remy said.

When they reached the store, Scott pulled alongside Remy's vehicle. He hopped out and slid into the back of Scott's car.

"Anything?" he asked.

"Not yet," Nicki told him. The computer beeped. She stared at the screen.

"What is it?" Scott asked.

"That stolen car, the one torched. The field where it was found is about three miles from here."

"It's too much of a coincidence," Remy said. "We've got to be close."

Nicki narrowed her search perimeters to the county they were in. The goblin danced, then stopped. An address appeared.

"Sutter owns a place six miles from here." She typed in the address, bringing up a map with a pin stuck in the middle. She turned the screen to let Scott look at it. Remy leaned over the seat.

"Pull up an aerial," Scott said.

Two taps and the image popped up. A long driveway led to a house nestled between two hills. Behind the house were a patio and pool. Two outbuildings were nearby.

Nicki zoomed out for a view of the surrounding terrain.

"How do you want to play this?" Remy asked.

Scott studied the hilly landscape. A dense stand of trees bordered the road that ran in front of the property.

Pointing, he said, "If this is the right place, we'll park here. Their view will be blocked by the trees. We'll go in on foot on this side of the hill. We should be able to come in from behind. If we can, let's get her out without a ruckus. If it turns into a firefight, the whole operation could be blown."

His tone grim, Remy said, "You're assuming she's still alive."

"I'm betting on it. I think they want to find out what she knows. Remy, get what you need from your car. We'll leave it here."

He nodded and jumped out.

Scott looked at Nicki. "You drive. I want to make a pass by the place. We'll duck down. If someone is watching the roadway, all they'll see is a woman driving by."

As they swapped places, Remy opened the backdoor, tossed a backpack on the seat, then slid inside. Nicki backed out. Looking over the seat, Scott explained while he watched Remy pull a gun and magazines from the pack. After buckling a holster on his belt, Remy slid the gun inside, then shoved the extra magazines in a pocket.

Nicki turned onto the road leading to Sutter's place. Scott and Remy slid down.

At a steady but slow speed, she spotted the house ahead. "A black van is parked in front. A man walked into the barn." Then the house was out of sight. "Damn, that's all I got."

As he sat up, Scott said, "It's enough. When you can, pull over." Once Nicki had parked, he said, "Make sure your phones are on mute."

Climbing over a wood fence, they weaved around the trees. Keeping the low hill between them and the house, they trotted toward the back of the property.

Scott kept an eye on the lightning rod mounted on the roof of the house. As they drew near, the sound of angry voices grew louder. When they were even with the house, he stopped. Motioning for them to wait, Scott climbed the side of the hill. As he neared the top, he dropped to his belly and crawled the rest of the way.

The house appeared to be deserted, drapes drawn, and the pool empty. A van had backed into the driveway. An overhead door to the barn was open. A man walked out trailed by a second.

In a strident tone, the second man proclaimed, "Eddie, you're not listening. Damnit, you shouldn't have hit her again. I'm not taking the fall for this. No telling how long she'll be out. The boss is already pissed because the broad didn't show up at her office last night. He wants answers, and thanks to you, he ain't going to get them. I'm telling you, I ain't taking the rap for it."

Eddie stopped and spun to look at him. "Don't lay this on me when it's all your fault. You're the one who taped her hands in front. If you hadn't screwed up, she wouldn't have gotten loose. I wouldn't have had to coldcock her again. Hell, she almost got the damn door open."

"You shouldn't have hit her again. The boss ain't going to like it."

"Shut up! Just shut up. Let me think. What about ice? Go in the house, see if there's any."

"There's no electricity, so how the hell do you think there'd be any damn ice? You shouldn't have hit her. She might even die."

Eddie paced, staring at the barn, then the house. "Okay. Drive back to the convenience store and get a couple of bags." He looked at his watch. "We got time. It'll be another couple of hours before he gets here. I'll make sure she's ready to talk even if I have to shove her head in a bag of ice."

When the man didn't move, Eddie said, "Get your ass in gear! Remember, you're in this as deep as I am."

The man stomped to the van. Tires squealed as he peeled out of the driveway. Eddie watched until the vehicle was out of sight, then walked back inside the barn.

Scott slid down. In a whisper, he asked, "Could you hear?"

Remy and Nicki nodded.

"I figure twenty, twenty-five minutes is all we have before he gets back with the ice. Nicki, you're going to play decoy. Get back to the road, then come up the driveway. Start shouting, you need help. Use some kind of excuse, car trouble. Anything to get him away from the barn. Keep his attention on you, so Remy and I can get inside."

"Got it." She ran.

"And, my friend," Remy whispered. "What do we do once we're in the barn?"

"Damned if I know, improvise. Between the two of us, we can get the drop on him, but I'd like to do it in a way he doesn't see us."

Scott took the lead as they moved to the end of the hill. When it began to slope, the roof of the barn came into view. Scott crawled to the top. The back of the building was in front of him. The man was out of sight. He motioned for Remy to follow. Standing, he eased his way down, then sprinted to the back with Remy close on his heels.

Nicki's voice rang out. "Hello, anyone home? Hello!"

Scott peered around the corner. Stunned, he watched in amazement as Nicki sashayed up the driveway. Her attire had undergone an unbelievable transformation. She oozed sex. The t-shirt tied in a knot under her breasts exposed an impressive midriff. The ponytail was gone. Instead, long strands of coal-black hair clung to the swell of her breasts under the tightly drawn shirt. The jeans were unbuttoned.

Eddie walked out of the barn. "What the hell do you want?" he shouted.

She stopped. Her eyes gleamed as she slowly looked up and down his body. A simpering smile built. "Well, hello there. I've got a flat tire and could use some help."

"I can't. You need to leave."

"Ah, now, honey." She twirled a lock of hair. "You're a cutie," she cooed. "Why, look at those muscles. Someone as strong as you could change a little ole tire in no time at all."

The man walked toward her. "I'm not changing any damn tire. Call a tow truck."

"It takes money." Her lips pursed. "I'm kinda tapped out. If you'd help, I'd really be grateful." Her hands slid over her hips, pushing the jeans even lower as the zipper slid open. "I'd give you something for your time ... if you know what I mean."

Eddie moved even closer. By this time, he was halfway down the drive.

Scott slipped along the side, around the front, and into the building. Stepping quickly, he shifted to the side as Remy followed.

His gaze swept the inside. The breeze through the open doorway kicked up dust motes from the dirty, oil-stained concrete floor. Tools littered a long counter. Pool supplies were stacked in a corner, along with rakes, a lawnmower, and other pieces of yard equipment. On the opposite side, a woman, legs, and arms bound lay facedown on the floor.

Beside him, a low, angry voice muttered in French. Scott glanced at Remy's grim face and whispered, "Door."

While Scott dropped to his knee alongside Jaimie, Remy stepped back, crossing to the other side. Scott's fingers felt for a pulse in her neck. Relieved at the steady beat, he pulled out the knife clipped to the inside of his pants pocket. With a few strokes, he cut through the tape around her ankles and wrists. Then eased her onto her back.

He looked at Remy, who'd been shifting his gaze between Scott and the driveway. Scott gave him a thumbs up.

Outside, Nicki still argued with Eddie. "Well, I never. If you can't see fit to help a woman in distress, I'll find someone who can," she grumbled.

From the doorway, Remy motioned. Scott stood and moved to the other side. The man walked in and collapsed when Remy's fist struck him on the side of his face.

Scott looked out. Nicki slowly meandered her way down the driveway. He whistled. She turned. "Get the car," he shouted.

She sprinted out the end of the drive.

Remy had gone to Jaimie. His hands patted her body, checking for broken bones.

Scott said, "We need to get moving." He reached down, pulled off the remaining pieces of tape on Jaimie's body, and tossed them on the floor. On the counter, he rummaged among the tools and found a small box cutter. He dropped it among the pieces of scattered tape. "It's the best we can do. Hopefully, they'll think she came too and managed to escape."

A horn tooted. Remy picked her up, cradling her body in his arms. Scott grabbed the backpack lying next to her and dashed out. Nicki had backed the car and opened a rear door. While Scott and Nicki hopped inside, Remy laid Jaimie on the backseat, then climbed in.

"Turn right," Scott said. "We don't want to pass the other guy on his way back."

As they sped down the road, Scott watched out the back window until Nicki skidded around a curve, and they were out of sight.

"How is she?" Nicki asked, her eyes flicking to the rearview mirror.

"Alive and no apparent injuries, other than a good-sized knot on her head," Remy said.

"Where to, boss man?"

Relaxing, Scott took a deep breath as he considered their next step. "A place where they won't think to look."

A faint groan echoed.

Remy bent over her. "Jaimie, wake up. You're safe." His hand lightly patted her face. "Come on, chérie, wake up."

Scott leaned over the backseat.

Jaimie's eyes fluttered open. Unfocused, she stared upward, "Remy?"

"Yes, you are safe."

"Where am I?"

"In a car with friends."

Awareness built as her eyes shifted to look toward the sound of his voice. When she moved her head, another loud groan erupted. Her hand lifted, and Remy wrapped his fingers around it.

"Where do you hurt?" he asked.

For a few seconds, she thought, "My head, knee. I think I hit it."

"What do you remember?" Remy asked.

She struggled to sit up.

"Easy, let me help you." Sliding his arm around her shoulders, he raised her up. Her legs swung to the floor, and her head tapped the headrest, which prompted another groan of pain.

"Damn, what did they hit me with, a two by four?" The spark of humor was a welcome relief.

Scott said, "A doctor should look at her."

"No! No doctors," Jaimie protested.

Remy held up two fingers. "How many?"

"Two."

He switched to four. "Now, how many?"

"Four. And before you ask, I don't have blurred vision. All I've got is the mother of all headaches. No doctor."

Remy nodded. "Okay. Scott, she'll be safe in my apartment. No one knows of our connection."

Several seconds passed as Scott considered options. "It's true, but you're still on their radar. They could make another try at you."

"Umm ... a possibility. Still, I think my apartment is the best place. It's a gated community with a guard at the front entrance, and I have a top of the line alarm system."

Jaimie interjected, "Hello, I'm here, and part of this."

Scott grinned, before saying, "Sorry about that. I'm Scott Fleming, Blake's boss. The driver here is Nicki Allison, another Tracker agent."

Her eyes blinked in astonishment. "Does Blake know?"

"No. He's in Wyoming."

"With the Chairman. Nicki, you're the one with Savvi the other night. See, my memory is just fine." With a sigh, her eyes closed.

Remy asked, "What happened?"

"I walked into my office, and someone clobbered me over the head. When I woke up, I was in the back of a van." She stopped to let a wave of dizziness fade.

"Take your time," Remy said.

After a deep breath, she added, "The idiot taped my hands in front. With a few good tugs with my teeth, I got loose. I almost had the side door open when the guy in the front seat knocked me upside the head again."

Nicki asked, "Any idea how they might have got you out of the building? Did you see anything unusual?"

"Now that you mention it, there was a cleaning cart in the hallway. I remember thinking someone must have forgotten it."

Remy said, "I bet they stuffed you inside."

"How did you find me?" Then answered her own question. "The watch. I remember now. I activated it when I came to in the van." She looked down at her wrist. "It's broken. When did that happen?"

Scott said, "We were tracking you and lost the signal. I bet it broke when you tried to escape."

Puzzled, Jaimie tried to concentrate on his words, but the pain made it difficult. "Then how did you find me?"

Nicki laughed as she looked at Scott. "As the boss man would say, it's all about connecting the dots."

CHAPTER
33

Anxious To Let Scott know what she'd discovered, she tried calling again. The call went straight to voice mail. Concerned, she booted her computer. Maybe there was an email. The only one was addressed to Blake and copied to her. Nicki had sent pictures of Halston's so-called security guards along with Frank's security team. After a quick glance, she closed the computer.

She didn't want to waste time waiting for a call. A stroll inside, then around the grounds, was the next item on her agenda. In the deserted hallway, she stepped in front of the guards' room. Even with an ear close to the door, there wasn't a whisper of a sound. She wondered what they were up to.

When she wandered into the Great Room, Adrian had joined Blake. She stopped at the bar and asked if she could get a cup of coffee. With the cup in hand, she moved to a nearby table. She set it down along with her backpack and pulled out a chair. As she sipped the rich dark brew, her gaze skimmed a room filled with more people than when she checked in. They clustered in groups. Snippets of conversation, everything from currency rates to hiking, filtered in the air. No sign of the guards.

A voice slightly louder than before, said, "I'm telling you, Blake, we need to take a couple of extra days and do some climbing."

"I wish I could, but I've got a meeting I can't cancel. But it's a good reason to make another trip up here. Maybe spend a week or two." Blake glanced at his watch. "I'm going to the room. I need to make a couple of calls."

Once Blake was out of sight, her phone rang. The text message read, 212. She smiled and glanced toward Adrian. He rose, dropped a few bills on the table, then strolled toward the staircase.

She sipped her coffee and used the time to become familiar with the layout, more specifically, the location of doors. On one side of the Great Room was a wide entrance to the dining room. A double set of doors led to the patio for guests who preferred to eat outside. At the back, another door led to the kitchen. A short hallway ran alongside the dining room. It led to the kitchen and a door that opened onto the front of the building.

On the other side of the room, a hallway led to the conference rooms. A staircase rose to the second floor, and toward the front was the hallway leading to the ground floor suites. From the diagram the resort provided, she'd already learned each of the two hallways had exit doors at the end.

She'd kept an eye on the flow of people, looking for a familiar face. None raised a red flag, though she was astonished at the ones she did recognize, at least from news reports.

With the pack slung over her shoulder, she climbed the staircase to the second floor. Shops selling clothing, books, jewelry, and souvenirs lined the walls. With a casual pace, she browsed the shop windows, working her way to the hallway leading to the rooms. Occasionally, she paused to glance over the rail, looking for anyone overly interested in her. When she moved into the hall, she picked up her pace. One tap and the door swung open. Blake stepped back, and she darted inside. "Sure glad to see the two of you."

Blake motioned toward a chair. "Have you been able to reach Scott or Nicki?"

Alerted by the worry clouding his face, she said, "No. I was going to ask the same question. Do you think something is wrong?"

"Yeah. Jaimie planned to go to her office to pick up the proof she sent the reports to Deegan. We haven't heard a word."

Adrian added, "We've been calling all morning."

Blake's hand slammed the counter. "I know it. Something's happened, and I can't do a damn thing except wait."

"Surely, he would have called by now if something had gone wrong."

His bleak expression told her Blake wasn't buying her reassurance. "This isn't helping us," he said. "Any problems with your trip?"

Going with the change of subject, she said, "Big time," and proceeded to tell them of the substitution of bodyguards, then the problem with her reservation.

Adrian had his computer open. "Which ones?" he asked.

Savvi slipped into the chair next to him, eyeing the images on the screen. "Headley and Garnett."

"Here they are."

"Can you keep an eye on them?"

Blake answered, "We will. Scott mentioned his concerns on the guards last night."

"Did he also tell you what Hayes and Sutter did yesterday?"

Adrian said, "Yes. You sure lit a fire under them. Any idea why they are so hot to keep you away from the Chairman?"

"I haven't figured out what it is yet. Whatever they have planned, they don't want me to be able to stop it."

"Blake and I have spent a lot of hours discussing the same topic. We figured it would be an explosive device, but after watching the security around here, it would be difficult to plant a bomb. The passes with the bomb dog are random. If they can't get to him inside, then it has to be outside, and we're back to our sniper theory. I found some likely spots across the highway, though the Chairman would have to be on the driveway or parking lot. You've got to keep him inside. I was on the ridge this morning when you arrived."

"At the airport, Garnett tried to keep me from getting into the same car as Frank. For a few seconds, I thought he'd get physical, but as he reached to grab my arm, he decided against it. You don't think ..." Her voice trailed off.

A look of disquiet crossed Adrian's face. "You may have foiled an attempt. I saw how you had him covered from behind as soon as he stepped out of the car. If a sniper had been hiding on the ridge, he didn't have a shot without shooting you first. As fast as the Chairman walked, a second shot would have been dicey."

"Scott called this morning and passed on your warning. It's why I told Frank that as soon as we arrived, not to waste time getting inside. If your theory is right, then there is at least one more accomplice. Frank will be tied up with meetings. I've already told him not to wander around outside. There's only one more time he'd be exposed, when we leave for the airport. There must be a way for him to leave the building without having to walk out the front. I'll start looking."

Blake's phone was on the table. When it rang, he lunged to pick it up. "It's Scott," he told them. Answering, he said, "Is Jaimie all right?"

Scott answered, "Yes, she's safe."

His shoulders collapsed with relief, and he sunk in the chair. "I knew something had happened."

"It did. Where are you?"

"In my room, along with Adrian and Savvi. Putting you on the speakerphone."

After relaying the details of Jaimie's kidnapping and rescue, he added, "She's still somewhat disoriented. Other than the blows to her head and a banged-up knee, she's not hurt. Remy is going to keep her in his apartment until this is over."

"Thank god. Scott, I don't know how to ..."

Scott interrupted, saying, "Then don't, though, Nicki's quick-acting makes an interesting tale."

In the background, a growl of protest erupted. Nicki muttered, "The less said about it, the better."

Ignoring her, Scott added, "Tell you later. How do things stand up there?"

Adrian and Blake gave him a quick rundown, followed by Savvi.

"Damn!" Scott said. "They'll try again, and Savvi, you've become the thorn in their side. Be careful."

She said, "I've got two aces in the hole they don't even know about," and grinned at Blake and Adrian.

"But Scott, that's not all. On the way up here, I figured it out. I know what Halston and his consortium plan to do. It's so simple, we all missed it." As she explained, Adrian and Blake gazed at her in astonishment, tinged with a new level of respect.

"I'll be damned," Scott said.

"Nicki, look for a timing sequence in the program. If it's there, which I believe it is, we need to find a way to get you access to the mainframe again. It will be the only way to stop the program from cycling."

Nicki chuckled.

Scott said, "You can't see it, but Nicki's drum rolling with her fingers. She's about to astound us."

Her tone chirpy, she said, "Wait for it ... wait for it. I installed a back door to the system when I was there. I can get back in anytime I need too."

For several seconds, four people were silent, then Scott burst into laughter. The three agents in a room in Wyoming followed.

Once they'd calmed down, Scott said, "Now we know their plans, we'll work this on our end. Savvi, for right now, don't say anything to Frank. Unless you've got some other bombshell to drop on me, I need to call my boss. He's left a couple of pointed messages wanting to know why I haven't called."

Light-headed with relief, Blake disconnected. To counter it, he said, "Okay, what's the game plan?"

Savvi stood, grabbed her backpack, saying, "I'm going to explore. I also haven't seen hide nor hair of those two guards. I'd sure like to find out what they are up too."

"We'll help. Blake's been wandering around the hotel, and I'm keeping an eye on the outside."

Blake said, "I want to make another pass. I still haven't totally eliminated an explosive device."

As Savvi stepped to the door, Blake raised his hand. "Hold up. Let me check the hallway." Opening the door, he stepped out, then motioned.

Savvi slipped by him, then meandered her way to the elevator. Descending, she strolled out into the Great Room. The crowd had increased along with the sound level. With cameras balanced on shoulders and microphones stuck in front of faces, the news media had arrived in full force. Her gaze skimmed each one, searching for a match to any of the images Nicki had sent. On her way toward the lobby doors, she passed a man walking out of the hallway leading to the ground floor rooms.

The valet nodded to her as she walked outside. Pulling her phone, she called Blake. When he answered, she said, "One of Halston's men showed up. He's in the lobby. When I saw him, he was coming from the direction of the guards' room."

"Which one? Do you remember?"

Recalling the images Nicki had sent, she said, "Roland. Around five-ten, one-eighty, blond, jeans, and a canvas jacket."

"He shouldn't be hard to spot. We're headed to the lobby. Where are you?"

"Outside, looking around."

"Be careful."

The sun, slowly sliding behind snow-topped mountains, tinted the hazy white puffs of clouds in shades of red and gold. Clean, crisp air clung to her throat as deep breaths filled her lungs. While she sauntered, her eyes took in the rugged terrain and tall trees, and she understood why this was a hiker's paradise. A few people ambled along the paths, heading to and from the cabins.

She wandered over to the pool, empty now, though she'd seen several people enjoying it when she arrived. Changing course, she walked around the main building. On one end was a loading dock, and a truck was backed in. Two men unloaded what look like crates of lettuce and vegetables.

She'd found her exit route, a way to get Frank safely out of the building. Now, she had to make sure she kept him safe so he could use it. Turning to walk back to the front, she saw a man crossing the parking lot, headed toward the lodge. It was Garnett. What the devil was he doing out there this late?

She ducked into the dark shadows under the overhang of the roof. Engrossed in his thoughts, he stared straight ahead. When he stepped inside, she hurried to the front. He was headed to his room.

Walking back outside, she strolled across the parking lot, following his path. It brought her to the edge of the entrance to the resort. Puzzled, she stared at a deserted roadside park and roadway. Where the hell had he been?

A shiver rushed down her back, an itchy feeling someone watched. Slowly, she backed, then turned. With a steady pace, she headed to the lodge, though every instinct screamed for her to run. Savvi was never one to ignore her instincts, a second sense that saved her more than once. Never had it been this strong, as if a dot glowed on her back.

After the morning's debacle, he'd called Garnett to find out what the hell happened. He had to make sure the damn bodyguards didn't screw up again. Once the guard left, he'd pulled his rifle from the case, for one last check. With it tucked tight to his shoulder, he watched through the scope as Garnett walked inside. Then he spotted Roth at the end of the building, and her suspicions led her right to him.

An icy rage consumed him as he stared at the reason for another failure. If it hadn't been for her, this would be over, and he'd be on his way home. Ever since her arrival at the Federal Reserve, she'd caused problems. There'd been the incidents at the garage and gallery. His boss didn't tolerate mistakes and why he was the one lying behind a rifle under heavy brush. Roland was one of his best men, but he couldn't take the chance something else would go wrong. But it did. Garnett was supposed to make sure Roth wasn't in the car with Littleton. And, because of it, he didn't have a shot when Littleton arrived. To cap it all off, he got a call to let him know that Barnett had escaped. In his gut, he knew Roth was the reason.

The crosshairs settled on her forehead. With a slight shift, they slid down, caressing her face and body until they stopped over her heart.

His finger itched to pull the trigger, so easy, just a tug. While he was tempted, he had to wait. Her puzzlement as she stared at an empty road slowly changed. Fear blossomed in her eyes. She knew, and he felt a jolt of exhilaration before she turned away. Even then, she was his as the crosshairs centered on her back. He watched until the lobby doors closed behind her.

Only then did he move his finger off the trigger. Tomorrow, he promised himself. Littleton was a job. Roth was a gift to himself.

CHAPTER
34

NICKI HAD WORKED most of the night. For once, Scott didn't fuss at her for sleeping on the couch, since they'd taken turns. Savvi's discovery had triggered a new round of research. Nicki went back over the files she'd downloaded not once but twice. There was no timing sequence, and she was pissed. Throughout the night, muttered expletives resounded in her office.

He'd spent the night studying the bank stress reports, examining the figures, along with the documents Nicki had sent him about the stress tests. Savvi had nailed it. The simplicity is what everyone overlooked.

With another cup of the endless coffee he brewed, he wandered back to his office. He'd taken advantage of the lull and gone downstairs to the gym. After a shower and clean clothes, he felt more alert.

The sun edged over the horizon as he stood in front of the window. Whatever was to come, in a few hours would be over. Once again, as he had in the past, his role was to wait. Nothing more he could do.

Behind him, Nicki said, "I'm hungry. Any idea what you'd like for breakfast?"

Turning, he saw a weary woman standing in his doorway. "Tell you what. You go downstairs and take a long, hot shower. I'll go out and get the breakfast croissants, or would you rather have bagels?"

"Both and some orange juice to go with it."

When Scott returned, his hands filled with bags and two containers of orange juice, he heard her singing in the breakroom. Dropping the sacks on the conference table, he shouted, "Come and get it."

Waltzing in, her face chipper and alert, the shower didn't account for the changed attitude.

"What happened?"

"I found it, the timing sequence." She grabbed the sacks, pulled out the wrapped croissants and bagels, and stacked them on a plate. Opening a container, she took a swig of juice.

"All right, let's hear it."

Her eyes sparkled, and a smug smile crossed her face. "Holcomb reprogrammed the computer."

He unwrapped a sandwich. "I presume this means you hacked back into the system."

"Hell, I've been in it most of the night. Savvi was right. Smart woman, but I'm not going to tell her. She won't let me forget it. Anyway, when I couldn't find it, I kept checking the main system. While you were gone, I checked again, and a new program has been installed."

She grabbed a bagel and tore it apart. "Once the new software is activated, the program is designed to perform a series of system checks. It should take upwards to an hour to complete. Assuming none of the subsets error out, the new currency will be up and running. Though most people won't know it unless someone is on the system and notices the change." She popped a piece in her mouth.

Scott chewed as he thought. "I'll be damned. That's the reason for the assassination, to keep anyone from knowing what's happening in the computer system. If Frank is killed, it's a sure bet work will stop, at least for a short period. How long will the full process take?"

"Let's say an hour or so to run the system checks, then maybe another hour for the transfer. I don't expect they'll wait around once the currency is live. Here's another tidbit. Holcomb has hidden the activation program inside a set of firewalls. Until it's activated, no one can see it."

"Is the program set to automatically start, or does someone have to trigger it?"

"Have to enter a command." She stuffed another piece of bagel in her mouth.

He gulped down the rest of the orange juice, then said, "I need to talk to Frank and Remy. Can you shut it down?"

Nicki eyed him as she swallowed, then smiled. "You know I can."

Standing, he laughed, "Yeah, I do." When he reached the doorway, he stopped and looked over his shoulder. "Been meaning to tell you, you did good out there yesterday."

To his surprise, she blushed, something he'd never seen. Her tone serious, she said, "It was … I'm not certain how to describe it, other than it felt right. *I* felt right."

"You don't need to, I understand. Watch your program. If anything changes, I need to know it."

Pulling his phone, he tapped Remy's number as he strode to his office.

Chabot answered, "Did you even go to bed?"

"A couple of hours on the couch in the office. You?"

"A couple of hours on my couch."

"How's Jaimie?" he asked, dropping into his chair.

"Sound asleep. I made her stay awake for several hours to be sure she didn't have a concussion. Halston sent me a text message last night. Wants to meet this morning. Anything I need to know?"

"Yeah," and proceeded to bring him up to date.

After listening, Remy exclaimed, "My god, they plan to activate the gold currency system!"

"Nicki's confirmed it. The program to activate it was added this morning. I believe they are waiting on events in Wyoming."

"I didn't expect this. Can it be shut down?" Remy asked.

"Yes. Nicki can override the commands. But if we do, we lose our evidence."

"That nasty thought has already occurred to me. Have you told the Chairman yet?"

"He's my next call."

"I have to talk to Bisset. I'll be in touch." The line went dead.

He picked up his pen, tap, tap, tap. Thoughts rolled as he considered the options. It was a case of damned if he did and damned if he didn't. The pen tapped the speed dial.

Surprisingly, Frank answered on the second ring. "Yes."

"Frank, it's Scott."

"Hold on, let me turn on a light," he said. "Must be bad to be calling this early."

"Depends on your viewpoint. The plan is to activate the new currency system." *No point in sugar-coating it*, Scott thought.

"Impossible! The program's not ready to be implemented," Frank protested.

"This morning, your computer system was reprogrammed. Once the new program is activated, the software runs a series of tests. If there are no errors, the new currency goes live."

"I'm not going to ask how you know, but it's got to be stopped."

"It can be done, but here's the reason behind it." He explained what Savvi had discovered.

"Hell! It would work. What a diabolically, clever plan. It answers why the stress tests were rigged. Correct me if I'm wrong, but what I'm also hearing is if I stop it, there is no evidence against any of these people."

"At this point, with what we have, we can't charge anyone with a crime. Frank, what happens if we don't stop it?"

"Programming the international financial networks that process currency transactions is still underway. The damage to the international currency market would be disastrous."

"I was told when activated, it's only live in the Federal Reserve computer system. Other than the few who are involved, or unless someone is in the system, no one will know. Is it true?"

For several seconds, the only sound was Frank breathing. "Technically, it's correct. On the initial activation, the currency is only live in the computer system. The second phase is to connect the currency to the international networks. Son-of-a-gun! There's your answer. Stop the second activation. If you can ... you'll get your evidence."

"Then tell me this. It's my understanding that once someone owns the gold currency, it can be exchanged for gold. What would happen if the Federal Reserve got hit with a 500 billion-dollar exchange for gold?"

Silence on the other end. When Frank finally spoke, his tone flat, he said, "An economic disaster that would reverberate around the world. The exchange would hijack the new currency system and effectively render it useless. We'd have to pull the gold currency back until we could recoup. Considering the existing political climate, I doubt it would happen. Many of the dissenters would be pointing their fingers, proclaiming to the world why they were right. Its why safeguards were put into place to limit the number of fiat dollars that could be exchanged for the gold currency. Can you keep it from happening?"

"Frank, I don't want to make false promises. As soon as I know, I'll contact you. One more point, don't trust Headley or Garnett.

They're part of this. Two more of my agents are up there. Listen to them."

"I know about Blake and Adrian. Savvi pointed them out to me. You can fill me in later on my so-called bodyguards."

"I'll let you get back to sleep then."

"Somehow, I don't think it's going to happen."

Disconnecting, Scott headed to Nicki's office.

"We have a solution," he told her. After explaining, he asked, "Did you find another program, the second phase Frank referred to?"

"No, but now I know there could be a second one, I'll be watching to see if they add it."

"If it's not there, then I don't believe they will."

As he walked back to his office, he considered calling his agents, then decided against it. They had enough to handle, and the computer activation was square on his plate. Instead, he called Remy. When he answered, Scott said, "Set up a call with Bisset. I need to talk to him."

While he waited, he gathered up the papers strewn across his desk. When the phone rang, he shoved papers aside to grab it.

"Scott, Louie Bisset is on the line. Louie, this is Scott Fleming."

"Hate to meet like this, Scott, especially after what I've heard. Remy has filled me in on what is happening. How can I help?"

"Remy said you would be watching the offshore accounts."

"Yes. As soon as the money is transferred, we'll know it."

"If the money is transferred out of the accounts, will you be able to track it and recover it?"

"We should."

"I need to know with one-hundred percent certainty you can, and here is why." He explained what Frank had relayed. "If the money disappears, the consequences are unthinkable."

"My god, you're right. I cannot give you absolute assurance. The speed with which money can be moved presents problems if there are multiple transactions," Louie said. "There is always a chance something could go wrong."

"Do you have enough evidence to tie the offshore accounts to our list of suspects without the second transfer?"

"Yes, we do. Though, a transfer order provides a lock on the evidence."

"If a transfer order is placed, can you see the ultimate destination, then stop the transfer."

"Yes, we can. That's probably the best way to handle this. We might lose a few fish down the line, but we'll have the big ones."

"Louie, whatever happens, *do not* let that money leave those offshore accounts."

Scott's next call was to Frank.

CHAPTER
35

WYOMING

WITH A SHRUG of her shoulders, Savvi shifted the straps of the Kevlar vest under her shirt, then adjusted the holster clipped to her belt. After slipping on the jacket with FBI emblazoned on the front and back, she walked out. While it was still dark, she wanted to take advantage of the lack of people to look around.

For a few seconds, she paused in the Great Room, then wandered into the dining room. Waiters bustled, carrying stacks of plates, cups, and glasses as they set the tables for breakfast. From there, she headed to the conference room where the meeting would be held. She was surprised to see Blake near the podium.

"You're up early."

He turned. "So are you."

"Looks like we're doing the same thing."

"What are you two doing in here?" a man said, his voice harsh.

When they looked around, a deputy sheriff leading a dog on a leash walked toward them.

"Oh, you're the FBI agent with the Chairman's group."

Savvi extended her hand. "Savannah Roth." The dog sat, head tilted to look up at the agents.

"Kenny O'Leary," he said as they shook hands.

He looked at Blake. "I know why she's here. Why are you?"

Catching Savvi's eye, he shrugged. "No reason now, not too," then looked at the deputy. "Agent Blake Kenner."

"Let me see your identification. This time of year, we don't take any chances."

Blake pulled it out and handed it to the man, who studied it for several seconds before giving it back. "Didn't hear anything when you checked in about you being an agent."

"I'm part of Chairman Littleton's security detail."

"Surprised no one told us."

Blake picked up on the underlying tone of censure. "There was a reason, but it's not important now. We've got another one running around. He's outside. Nope, here he comes now. Agent Adrian Dillard, Deputy Kenny O'Leary."

Adrian greeted the man. "Guess we're out in the open now."

Blake looked down at the dog. Her tail lightly thumped the floor. "Is she going to be here all day?"

"Yes," He looked down. "Sadie, friends. Let her smell your hands. We'll be wandering in and out. There are two of us who are the handlers. We take turns and try not to have a set pattern."

In turn, the agents let Sadie sniff a hand. Blake ran his hand over her head. "We've noticed. It's the right way to run a search pattern."

"Sounds as if you've had some experience," O'Leary said.

"Um ... you might say that."

"Reckon, I'll see you around." They circled the room before walking out.

"Anything outside?" Savvi asked.

"No red flags."

"Last night, I saw Garnett walking across the parking lot. He was coming from the entrance to the highway. I walked over there but didn't see anything."

"What would he have been up too?" Blake asked.

"Whatever the reason, I don't like it. If you haven't noticed, they've been missing since we arrived. Frank had a dinner meeting in one of the private dining rooms last night, and they were nowhere to be seen."

Blake told her, "We've been looking for them. All we could figure is they were staying in their rooms."

"What about Roland?"

"By the time we got to the lobby, he was gone. I checked with the reservation desk, and no one is registered by that name. We'll be watching for him. Adrian will be outside since he's already familiar with the terrain. I'll be inside with you. While you stick close to the Chairman, I'll circulate."

He reached into a backpack lying on a table and pulled out a wireless radio set. Handing it to Savvi, she inserted the small earbud, then clipped the wireless mic to the collar on her jacket. Pushing a side button, she turned it on, tapping the surface. "Testing, one, two, testing."

Blake said, "Read you, loud and clear."

"Did you get the Chairman to agree to wear the vest?" Adrian asked.

"Not without a struggle. He didn't seem to think it was necessary as long as he was in the building."

"I'm going back outside. I'll keep an eye on our missing guards' room," Adrian told them.

"Let's walk. I still have a lot of places in this building to look at," Blake said. In the Great Room, he wandered behind the bar, then around the chairs and tables before striding into the dining room. They weaved their way around the tables, and then into the kitchen. It was a beehive of activity.

A shout of protest erupted as a man wearing the traditional chef's hat rushed toward them. "Guests aren't allowed in here." His hands fluttered in the air, shooing them away.

Savvi pulled out her badge case. "FBI agents. We'll be in and out all day."

Blake ignored him and started his slow prowl. When he finished, he nodded to the chef, who glared at them with a look of frustration.

They headed to the second floor. The shops wouldn't open for several hours, but Blake checked the benches positioned along the walkway for a guest's convenience.

Once they covered the public areas inside the building, Blake stopped. "Want a cup of coffee?"

Savvi, who had tagged along in silence, said, "Good idea."

After ordering coffee and a cinnamon roll in the deli, located near the reception desk, Savvi followed him into the deserted Great Room. Seated, she stared in wonder at the sight of the mountains through the windows as the rising sun kissed the snow-covered peaks. For a few seconds, she enjoyed the view before her mind shifted to the reason she was there. Picking up her fork, she glanced at Blake.

Lost in thought, he stared across the room. He knew she was curious, though she'd said nothing. But he could see it in her face. How to explain, and was it important she knew? Maybe today of all days, it was.

"I spent several years in the military, most in Iraq and Afghanistan. It's where I met Jaimie. I was assigned to an explosives unit. My team was responsible for finding IEDs before they killed our troops." Images flooded his mind, the ones they'd found, and the ones they didn't.

Sensing this was important, Savvi forked up a piece of the roll, letting him continue at his pace.

With a wry smile, he said, "I acquired a nickname, Kenner, the human bloodhound. I had a talent for finding IEDs, and no one understood how. It was something I didn't know about until I went through my first explosives school. The components emit an odor. It's how dogs find them. Just like a dog, I can smell them." He picked up his cup and drank.

"I'll be damned. How many lives you must have saved, and what a hell of an asset for an agent," Savvi said. "No wonder Scott recruited you. I've heard the Trackers have a reputation for being somewhat unusual. But, believe me, no one laughs when it comes to the results the team has achieved."

Surprised, he stared at her. "I never thought of it in that light. I guess you're right."

"I know I am." She glanced at her watch. "In another thirty minutes or so, the Chairman will be on the move. After he leaves his suite, I'll dog his every step. He has a breakfast meeting in the dining room, then a second one in a private room. Once it's finished, he goes to the conference room for the start of the symposium. He'll be there all day. At nine, he gives his presentation."

"Got it," Blake said. "I'll start another round."

As the morning progressed, Savvi kept Blake and Adrian appraised of the Chairman's movement. Still, no sign of the bodyguards.

When she followed the Chairman to the conference room, she was surprised to see Headley in the hallway near the door to the room. She gave him a sharp glance as she followed Frank inside.

Attendees clustered in small groups. The deputy and Sadie walked around the room. When they left, the deputy nodded but didn't stop. A man walked toward Frank and greeted him.

As they began to discuss the agenda, Savvi moved to the back of the room, leaning against the wall. Garnett, a backpack over his shoulder, walked in. When he looked around the room, he spotted her. An expression of animosity settled on his face as he strode toward her. When he stopped, he was almost nose to nose with her.

His tone vicious, he said, "This is my job, not yours. Leave."

The anger built. "Still trying to get rid of me? Not going to happen. Now get out of my face."

A muscle along his rigid jawline twitched. With a quick glance around, he saw Frank was watching. He nodded, turned, and walked out the door.

She pushed the button to keep the mic turned on. "Both guards are here."

Blake responded, "On my way. Where are they now?"

"Hallway."

A few minutes later, Blake said, "I don't see them."

Adrian said, "I'm headed to the ridge across the road."

Savvi tapped the mic to acknowledge but couldn't comment. People had taken their seats, and a man was at the podium ready to start the conference.

Troubled by Garnett's actions, the voices in the room flowed over her. The dog had left, Garnett had a backpack. What better way to bring in explosives, than someone in the Chairman's party. Was it the reason he wanted her out of the room, so he could plant a device?

She slipped out to find the hallway was deserted. Her voice low, she said, "Garnett has a backpack. May have explosives inside."

Blake responded, "Looking for him."

As minutes passed, Savvi resisted the urge to pace, though every nerve throbbed. Where was Garnett's next likely target? She thought about the agenda. After Frank's presentation, a short break was scheduled. Another meeting room next door had been set up with coffee and breakfast items.

"Blake, the room next to the conference room. They'll be taking a break soon."

Blake had already walked the public areas and was headed to the kitchen. "On my way," he said. He turned and ran. When he stepped into the room, he smelled it. A waiter fussed with a stack of cups on a long table. He said, "Another officer already checked the room. He just left."

Blake dropped to one knee and looked under the table. A block of C-4 and a denotator were attached to the underside. It was another simple device. With a couple of snips, he deactivated it and removed the cell phone.

Savvi had followed him into the room. He crawled from under the table. "It's been neutralized. I'm headed to the manager's office. Evacuate, no telling where else he's planted one."

Savvi spun and darted out the door. Frank was at the podium and broke off when she rushed into the room. She stepped alongside him and spoke into the microphone. "I'm FBI Agent Roth. Everyone, please, walk outside. We have received a threat and need to ensure the building is safe."

Voices raised with a shrill tone of fear. Men and women pushed back their chairs.

"Please, there is no need to panic. We will let you know as soon as it is safe to return."

Savvi grabbed Frank's arm as the attendees streamed toward the door and into the hallway.

"What's happening?" he asked.

She wrapped her arm around his and pulled him tight against her body. In a low voice, she explained as they shuffled into a hallway crammed with people. She looked toward the far end. Could she get to the exit door? Then a voice screamed the door was locked. People turned, pushing their way back toward her.

Savvi told him, "Don't let go of me. When we get to the Great Room, we're going out through the kitchen. Blake, where are you?"

Her eyes continually shifted. Where would the danger come from? Did anyone have a weapon? How could she protect him in this mass of people?

Blake's voice echoed in her ear. "Kitchen hallway."

A loud explosion ripped the air, then a second. Dense smoke flooded the hallway.

The evacuation turned into a panic-driven horde as people pushed and shoved to get out. A man rammed her shoulder as he forced his way past her.

"Blake?"

His voice echoed over the terrified screams. "Kitchen is out, so are the doors in the dining room. Have to go out the front. Adrian, you copy?"

Adrian said, "Yes. I'm looking for him."

When they stepped into the Great Room, flames and black smoke shot out from the dining room. People streamed down the staircase, pushing their way into the mass of guests and hotel staff already crowded inside the room. Chairs and tables toppled as they crawled over them.

Her earpiece crackled. "Where are you?" Blake asked.

Instead of moving further into the room, Savvi had pushed Frank toward the wall behind the staircase. While still crowded, the narrow space limited the number of people.

"Behind the stairs, near the elevator," she replied.

"Trying to get to you," Blake said.

As she clung to Frank, making sure they didn't get separated, anger overcame the surging fear. The bastards had cut off her escape routes. Like cattle, they were being herded to the front of the lodge, and she knew why.

Frank coughed as the smoke swirled around them, then stumbled when he was hit from behind. Her tight grip on his arm kept him on his feet. Shifting her arm, she wrapped it around his waist, while her other hand clutched his arm. She leaned close to his ear. "You okay?"

"Yes. Don't worry about me. We're going to make it out of here," Frank said, his voice husky from the dense smoke.

Blake said, "I can't get to you."

Through the windows, Savvi could see the surge of people as they ran outside. Others clustered on the parking lot. At least three men waited. Where were they?

The people crowding through the doors kept them open. As they got close to the open doorway, someone shoved her. Savvi tightened her hold on Frank, while her gaze skimmed the driveway. They had to get away from the building. But which direction? Then she spotted the car near the entrance. Could they reach it?

"Frank, there's a car."

He said, "I see it."

"As soon as we are outside, we're going to run to it. Stay behind me. When I tell you, get down, you drop to the ground!"

Once they cleared the entrance, she let go of him, stepping to get in front. Her hand reached for her gun.

Blake's voice screamed in her ear. "Look out!" A blow hit her in the back. She staggered, and a second blow pushed her to the ground. A shot rang out.

Fear, unlike any she'd ever known, ripped through her. Had Frank been shot?

Then she heard Garnett. "Mr. Chairman. Come with me. I'll help you."

Frank cried out, "Let go of me! Let go!"

She pushed herself up and saw Frank struggling with Garnett as the man tried to drag Frank away from the crowd. She ran, jerking her gun from her holster, and screamed, "Frank! Get down! On the ground! Get down!"

Frank broke free and started to turn. A man slammed into him just as another shot rang out. The two men fell, one on top of the other.

Seeing Savvi charging toward him, Garnett took off running. A shot cracked, and this time Garnett fell. Savvi threw herself over the two men, her body covering their heads. A crushing blow in the back flattened her. Excruciating pain whipped through her body. Her back felt as if it was on fire. Her heart lurched as her lungs clamped down. She couldn't breathe. Her vision faded. In a far distance, she heard Adrian's voice.

"Shooter down! Shooter down!"

"Where's Headley?" she wheezed, trying to push herself up.

Blake answered, "Dead. Where's the Chairman?"

"On the ground."

Adrian said, "I've got Roland."

Savvi crawled off the two men. How bad was she hurt? At least she could move as she pushed herself to her knees. Her body wobbled as she stared at a pool of blood, seeping into the cracks of the concrete. Was it hers? She looked down. Blood stained her clothes, but if she was bleeding, she couldn't feel it. As her mind slowly cleared, she realized the vest had stopped the bullet.

Her hand trembled as she reached to check the two men. The blood was coming from the man on top of Frank. He wasn't dead, but a long gash over his ear bled profusely. She couldn't get to Frank. All she could do was feel for a pulse. Despite the pain, relief flooded her senses. He was alive. Blood oozed between her fingers when she pushed down with her hands to stop the bleeding from the man's wound.

Blake ran up. When he saw the blood on the front of her clothes, he exclaimed, "What the hell! Are you hurt? What happened?"

She glanced up, eyeing his blackened face and singed clothing. "Blood's not mine. This guy knocked Frank down. Probably saved his life but got shot doing it."

Then Deputy O'Leary rushed up. "Ambulance on the way."

"Get me something! A towel, anything!" Savvi told him.

O'Leary shouted at another man.

"What's Frank's condition?" Blake asked.

"He's alive, that's all I know."

Savvi looked up and realized mass confusion reigned. A fire-truck had arrived. Firemen pulled out hoses, others rushed into the building. Guests and employees who had fled onto the parking lot began to press closer to the building. Cellphones flashed, and media cameras were filming.

When a man stepped toward them to take a picture, Blake stood, blocking his path. He shouted, "Everybody! Get back! Get back! I want this area cleared. Move!"

O'Leary rushed back and handed her a torn piece of a shirt. "Can I help?"

"Help Blake." She quickly folded the cloth, laid it on the wound, then pressed down.

She didn't want to move the man but didn't have a choice. Once Blake had left the crowd control to the park rangers, he, O'Leary, and a park ranger picked the man up by his feet and shoulders. Savvi cradled his head to keep it steady. They eased him off Frank and onto the ground. O'Leary kept the compression pad on the wound while Savvi examined Frank.

Still unconscious, the side of his face lay in a pool of blood.

Two medics rushed up. Savvi and Blake stepped away to give them room.

"Are you sure you're okay?" Blake asked. "You don't look so good."

"Yeah, I'm fine."

Each medic bent over the men, their hands moving to assess their injuries while Savvi told them what had happened. One looked up at O'Leary. "Get a couple of men to get the stretchers over here."

Adrian walked up. As they watched the medics, he said in a low tone, "Max Roman was the shooter. He's dead. Roland was his driver. He's been arrested. What happened to Headley?"

Blake said, "I shot him. He had a gun aimed at Savvi and Frank."

When the stretchers were brought up, the agents moved further away, and Adrian caught a glimpse of Savvi's back. He walked behind her. A curse rippled.

Blake stepped beside him. "Holy hell, Savvi!" he exclaimed as he looked at the hole in the back of her jacket. "You took a round in the back. Damn, we need to get you on a stretcher."

She shot them a glare of disdain. "Yeah, it hurts like hell, but the vest stopped it."

The medics began the preparations for transport and turned the man onto his back. Adrian and Blake both gasped.

Adrian said, "How the hell did he get involved?"

Blake explained.

"Well, now, if that don't beat all," Adrian said.

Savvi asked, "Do you know him?"

"Yeah, we do. Todd Bracken."

After cleaning her hands on a wipe the medic handed her, she stepped away and pulled her phone.

CHAPTER
36

NOTHING FROM WYOMING. His fingers itched to pick up the phone and call. He resisted the urge, knowing he had to let his agents do their job. Instead, he paced, wondering if it was possible to wear a hole in the carpet.

After meeting with Halston, Remy had called. His information intensified Scott's anxiety. Halston wanted an account number and told Remy to expect his payment by the end of the day. Remy gave him another offshore dummy account, set up by Interpol. One more piece of evidence to hang around the neck of the man.

Nicki had been watching the Federal Reserve's computer system. Nothing had changed.

When his phone rang, he dove toward his desk to pick it up. Nicki's footsteps pounded as she raced into his office.

Savvi's words were an instant source of relief. "Frank's been injured, but he'll live. It's over."

"Hold on. Nicki, get back on your computer. I need to know if there is any change. What happened, Savvi?"

He followed Nicki to her office as he listened. Nicki watched her monitor as algorithms scrolled across the screen, then shook her head no.

When Savvi reached the point of the second man, he exclaimed, "Todd Bracken, what the hell was he doing there?"

"I don't know, but he knocked Frank down. Instead of the bullet hitting Frank, it grazed Bracken's head. The ambulance is getting ready to transport. I need to go with them."

His thoughts buzzed as he grappled with details. Would it be enough? He feared it wasn't. "Savvi, when you get to the hospital, make sure both men are sequestered. Keep the hospital personnel to a minimum. Tell them under no circumstances are they to make any comment, a matter of national security. We need to make it appear as if Frank is in grave danger and may not make it. Call me as soon as you arrive."

"Okay. Call Amelia? There will be pictures hitting the internet."

"I'll take care of it. What's the status at the lodge?"

"I'll let Adrian fill you in. He's staying. Blake is going with me." She disconnected.

He told Nicki he'd be in his office making calls. The first was to Amelia. Her questions delayed him, but he didn't let his impatience show. Then he called Paul. An even longer conversation that didn't leave his boss happy. The final one was to Remy. Astonished, he said he'd contact Scott if he heard from Halston.

In the conference room, Scott turned on the wall-mounted TV to one of the major news channels. Once again, he waited and paced.

WYOMING

As she pocketed her phone, someone shouted, "Is that Chairman Frank Littleton?"

She ignored the question. Another shouted, "Is he dead?"

A woman shoved her way toward the front of the crowd, a microphone in her hand. Excitement glittered in her eyes as she proclaimed, "Agent Roth, I'm with the Washington Dispatch. I was told Chairman Littleton has been shot. What's his condition?" Behind her, a man stood with a camera hooked over his shoulder.

Savvi stepped away from the ambulance, where Frank's stretcher was being loaded. All eyes were on her. "I cannot comment on his condition." A tear slid down her cheek, which wasn't difficult as sharp pains jabbed her ribcage. She looked at the camera and said, "Any official announcements will be made later."

She turned to walk to the back of the ambulance, where the second stretcher was being loaded. A blood-stained towel covered Bracken's face.

She heard the reporter say, "Live from the Grand Mountain Resort, where Federal Reserve Chairman Frank Littleton has allegedly been shot. His personal bodyguard, Special Agent Roth, covered in blood and who was also shot, while refusing to comment on his condition, was visibly upset. Agent Roth stated an official announcement would be forthcoming, leaving us to speculate Federal Reserve Chairman Frank Littleton may have been killed in a heinous attack. Stay tuned as we continue to follow this heartbreaking tragedy." Once she signed off, the woman said, "It's a wrap. I hope you got a shot of the bullet hole in the back of her coat. We've got to get to the hospital."

In the back of the ambulance, the medic protested when Savvi and Blake squeezed their way in. "You can't ride with us. There's not enough room."

Blake closed the door. "I'm Agent Kenner, and this is Agent Roth. We're not leaving, now let's get the hell out of here."

Her face grim, Savvi said, "This is a matter of national security. If you breathe a word of what you hear or see, I'll bury you for the next twenty years in federal prison. Do you understand?"

Stuttering, he said, "Uh ... uh ... yes, ma'am."

"Did the two of you in the front hear me?" she shouted.

Two voices resounded, "Yes, we did."

"When we get to the hospital, I want these men taken to a private room. I'll handle the intake personnel."

When the ambulance pulled in front of the emergency room doors, Savvi hopped out, followed by Blake. A nurse rushed out. Savvi held up her badge. "FBI Agent Roth. This is a matter of national security. I want a private room for two patients. They are to go straight there."

The nurse blustered, "We can't do it. They have to go into ER first."

"I'm telling you. Get me a room. Then a doctor."

The medics had exited and waited at the rear of the ambulance. Savvi turned to them. "Let's get them inside."

As the medics wheeled the stretchers inside, a man in blue scrubs ran up. "What's this about a private room. It's not possible. They must be treated before we can move them to a room. Who are you?"

Savvi held up her badge. Blake walked up beside her. "Agent Roth. This is Agent Kenner. I am ordering you to take these men to a private room. I don't want to have to repeat myself."

The doctor stared at the medics, who shrugged their shoulders. "Follow me." He signaled to the nurse.

He led them to a room at the end of a hallway and held open a door for the medics. They rolled the two men through the door. The doctor stepped to the side of Frank's stretcher. When he touched Frank's chest, Frank opened his eyes.

"I'm Doctor Murphy. Lie still, and we'll get you comfortable in a few minutes." Then he stepped to look at the second man.

"Tell me what happened?" he demanded and looked at Savvi, who stood by the door along with Blake.

"There was a shooting at the lodge. Mr. Bracken was hit by a bullet. Mr. Littleton took a bad fall. His head hit the concrete."

"Nancy, get me a cart, and let's get this cleaned up."

Savvi held up her hand to stop her. "Before anyone leaves this room, listen up. You cannot talk about these two men, not even to your family. If asked, your answer is no comment. If you do not follow my instructions, you will be prosecuted. Do you understand?"

Nancy nodded, then rushed out of the room.

Doctor Murphy turned to the medics. "Help me get them onto the beds, then you can leave."

As he eased the towel from Bracken's face, the doctor said, "Do you always bully people, Agent Roth?"

"Only when it comes under the heading of national security."

"Then it's only fair to warn you, I'm an obstinate sort of guy. I noticed you've evidently been shot in the back. As you are standing here, I must assume you are wearing a vest. However, once I've finished with these two gentlemen, you will be next."

A weak chuckle erupted from Frank.

WASHINGTON D.C.

After he turned up the sound on the TV in the conference room, Scott walked to Nicki's office. She shook her head. Then he headed to the breakroom, his ears tuned to the talking head. His phone rang.

Answering, he said, "How bad is it, Adrian?"

"A hell of a mess."

While he listened, he filled his cup. When Adrian said he'd shot the sniper and who he was, Scott interrupted, "Who knows it was Roman?"

"No one. He didn't have any identity on him. The only reason I knew was from the pictures Nicki sent. There won't be anything going out on the news wires. Garnett's dead. Right now, everyone believes he was killed protecting the Chairman. Since Roman killed him, I suspect he'd have killed Headley if Blake hadn't shot him.

Not sure who Headley planned to kill—Frank if Roman missed, or Savvi. Roland, another of Halston's boys, is in custody."

"Paul has a team of agents from the Denver office headed your way."

"I can use the help. The local law enforcement is doing a good job, but they've never dealt with anything like this. It's going to take a while to sort it all out. It was a slick plan. From what I've pieced together, Blake defused one bomb. Garnett probably intended to put it in the conference room. He couldn't. Savvi was there, so he went next door. If the bomb didn't kill Frank, then Roman wanted to be sure Frank came out the front door. The exit at the end of the hallway where the conference room was located had been wired shut. The explosions, one in the kitchen and the other in the dining room, blocked the rest of the exits."

"How many people hurt or killed?"

"Roman, Garnett, and Headley are the only casualties. I don't know the number injured, but most are minor burns and scrapes. Two were transported by car since there's only one ambulance up here. Did Savvi tell you the bastard shot her in the back? She and Frank were both wearing vests."

"No, she didn't."

"When Bracken took Frank to the ground, she threw herself on top of the two men. By then, Roman had to know it was over. He'd lost any chance of getting to Frank, but he still took time to take a shot at the person who got in his way. It cost him his life. By then, I was in place to take a shot. Someone's hollering at me. Got to go."

Scott disconnected. With a thoughtful air, he walked out the door. When he heard someone say breaking news on the TV, he ran.

A banner flashed across the screen, announcing a news report from the Grand Mountain Resort in Jackson, Wyoming. The camera spanned a smoke-filled building, firemen and medics before focusing on the reporter's face. Her face flushed with excitement, she announced the shooting and probable death of Federal Reserve Chairman, Frank Littleton.

The camera zoomed on a stretcher. A man, his face covered by a bloodstained towel, was lifted into the ambulance. The feed shifted to Savvi and the blood staining her clothes, as the reporter identified her as the Chairman's personal bodyguard. The camera locked onto the single tear sliding over Savvi's cheek as she spoke to the reporter, then the hole in the back of her jacket as she walked away. The action shifted back to the talking head, who told people to stay tuned as new details were forthcoming.

A shudder rolled over him at the thought of how close he came to losing an agent. Still, he had to shake his head in amazement. Savvi had suckered the reporter.

CHAPTER
37

SEATED IN HIS office, Senator Halston hung up his phone with an air of satisfaction. He'd just garnered a hefty campaign contribution from a textile manufacturer in his state. It would, of course, be covered up so as not to appear he was paid by a lobbyist.

Sharp raps pounded on his door before it opened. An aide, his face pale, and his eyes wide with shock, babbled, "Uh … sorry to … uh … interrupt. It's all over the news. My, god, we can't believe it."

Though his voice was calm, anticipation built. "Jeff, what are you talking about?"

"Uh, the Chairman. Frank Littleton. He may be dead, killed somewhere up in Wyoming."

Even as his expression took on a look of dismay, exhilaration surged through him. Max had pulled it off. He followed his aide, who ran out of his office. Clustered in front of the wall-mounted TV, his staff watched in silence as a news reporter discussed the shocking events and the possible death of the Federal Reserve Chairman.

He tapped his secretary on the shoulder. When she turned to look at him, he said, his tone somber, "I'll be in my office. I need to contact people regarding this terrible, shocking tragedy. I don't want to be disturbed."

She nodded before turning back to the TV.

He closed and locked the door before he pulled out his cell phone. When Sutter answered, Halston asked, "Did you hear the news?"

"Yeah, everyone here is already running around like a chicken without its head. The project is a go. Holcomb's programming the computer as we speak. I need the account numbers."

Halston sat and pulled a small notebook from his jacket pocket, then read off the numbers.

Sutter said, "I'll let you know when the money is transferred." The line went dead.

Halston leaned back in his chair. Elation threatened to overwhelm him. Sutter believed he was the brains behind a plan to destroy the Federal Reserve and become wealthy in the process. But it wasn't Sutter.

It was his brilliance and vision that recognized an unprecedented opportunity when the dual currency system was first proposed. After swinging his political clout behind the legislation, he began to move players into position. With the support of the consortium, he was about to reach new heights, and fulfill a lifelong ambition to bring the Halston family into the realm of the Rockefellers, J.P. Morgan, and other banking dynasties. With money and power, nothing could stop him from winning the Presidency. The currency fiasco would ensure Larkin wouldn't be elected for another term.

★★★

Scott's phone rang. It was Savvi.

"I guess you probably heard the broadcast?" she said.

"Yes. What's the status there?"

"Everyone is cooperating, though not without some resistance. Only the doctor and one nurse are allowed in the room. Frank and Todd are both conscious. Todd had to have a few stitches, and

Frank has a small gash and a large knot on his head. Otherwise, they're fine. Frank wants to call Amelia. I told him to hold off until I talked to you."

"Go ahead and let him call. I've spoken to her. If Todd needs to contact his family, he's to tell them he's okay, nothing more for right now. No one has commented on the second man yet. I'd like to keep him out of the news for a while. How's your back?"

"Uh ... who squealed?"

Deciding to keep Adrian out of the mix, he said, "It's on all the news channels. When you turned to walk to the ambulance, the camera zeroed in on the hole in your coat."

"Damn. Never occurred to me. Hurts like hell, and my back is turning all shades of colors. No broken ribs, though the doc insisted on checking. Anything on your end yet?"

"No, but Nicki is watching. I'll call when we know something."

As he walked out of the conference room, the outer door to the office opened. Remy and Jaimie walked in. "We decided to wait here instead of the apartment."

"Did you see the news?" Scott asked.

"No."

"A reporter in Wyoming announced Frank Littleton might be dead."

Jaimie stared at him with a look of shock. "How can you say it, and ... and sound almost happy?"

"Let's have a seat in Nicki's office, and I'll explain."

"Ach! I have been hoping for another opportunity to get to know the incomparable Nicki better."

"Remy, keep your hands off my agent."

In his mocking tone, he said, "We will have to see, won't we?" then grinned.

Nicki shouted, "Scott!"

He rushed into her office, followed by Remy and Jaimie. Her face glowed with glee. "It's running. Holcomb initiated the command."

Remy said, "I must call Louie." He stepped out of the room. When he came back in, he said, "He's watching and will call when he sees the transfer is complete."

While Nicki watched her screen, Scott relieved Jaimie's concerns, with a succinct explanation of the subterfuge taking place.

The evidence mounted as Nicki tracked and recorded the program changes. Once the activation cycle completed, the alert status on the new currency changed from red to green.

Scott was as engrossed as Nicki in the process. For Jaimie and Remy, what they saw was like watching a movie in a foreign language without the subtitles. Nicki's running monologue to explain the codes and algorithms rolling across the monitor helped.

At one point, Remy protested after watching her enter command after command into the Federal Reserve computer network. "How is this possible? Surely, they have firewalls to stop hackers. Why are the alarms not going off?"

She looked at him with an almost sympathetic smile. "I'm like a ghost wandering the corridors of their computer. The firewalls don't even know I'm there. I pass right through them. I could explain, but it's complicated."

He shook his head in wonder.

"I'll be damned!" Nicki exclaimed. "I found the reason for those odd isolated sections in the program Holcomb protected with a unique set of firewalls. They're accounts, one for each bank. Wait a minute, there are seven, not five. Two more were just added."

Remy said, "There are seven offshore accounts."

Scott glanced at him. "You never mentioned the number. We may have snared Sutter and Holcomb. I'm willing to bet those are their accounts."

With a flick of her fingers, the monitor shifted to multiple screens. In five of the accounts, the bank name appeared in the header. On the other two, it was merely S and H.

"Another account just popped up," Nicki said. When it came up on the monitor, it was labeled C.

Remy said, "I bet that's my account."

"Holcomb is programming the computer," Nicki said. "He's in the account for Halston's bank, and just converted the bank's excess assets to gold dollars."

In the empty account titled, Ohio Mutual Funds, 100 billion dollars appeared with the tag line, USG, United States Gold, the new ISO currency code.

One by one, the same amount appeared in the other bank accounts.

Then a second change started. The funds for each bank decreased as gold currency dollars were transferred into the accounts for Sutter and Holcomb.

Scott said, "Sutter and Holcomb just got their cut. Ten billion each from the five banks. Remy, you just got one billion."

Remy said, "That's right. It's what Halston and I agreed on."

Then one by one, the money in each account disappeared.

Nicki said, "He's transferring the money to the offshore accounts." Her fingers flew as she recorded the transactions on her computer.

Remy tapped his phone. When Louie answered, he said, "The money's been transferred." Louie told him they knew and would call back.

"Something else is going on. Remember the file I found with five bank reports?" Her fingers flashed, and another screen came up. It was the approved file for the bank stress tests. One by one, the reports for the five banks disappeared. A few minutes later, they reappeared.

"Holcomb deleted the falsified reports and transferred the

correct reports to the approved file." She hit the print button.

Remy's phone rang. He answered, then said, "Thanks for letting me know."

He pocketed the phone and said, "The accounts are locked. If they try to move the money, they'll get a message the transfers are in queue. Bisset will move the money to a secure account until the Feds decide what to do with it."

Scott took a deep breath and began to relax. The money was safe.

As Nicki continued to record the changes Holcomb made in the computer, she said, "Holcomb has deactivated the gold currency system. It's no longer live. The tracks of the conversion and the transfers are gone." She typed in a command and looked at what appeared on the monitor. "Everything has been erased. It's as if nothing happened. Not a single trace of evidence to prove someone ripped off the Federal Reserve to the tune of 500 billion dollars."

Scott said. "No one would have been the wiser until the gold dollars hit the market with a demand to redeem the cash for gold bullion. While everyone scrambled to find out where it came from, the Federal Reserve would have been left holding the bag, albeit an empty one."

Remy's phone rang. When he looked at the caller ID, he said, "It's Halston." He answered, "Chabot." He listened, then said, "Yes, thank you for the notice." He hung up. A grin split his face. "Halston telling me my fee was deposited. Son-of-a-gun, we nailed them."

Scott leaned back in his chair, a look of satisfaction on his face. It's what he expected would happen.

Jaimie had been studying the new bank reports Nicki printed. "All the excess assets have disappeared. The reports appear to be accurate. I'm not sure I fully understand what just happened."

Scott said, "As it turned out, the plan was a simple one. Let's say

I want to give you twenty dollars. I can give you a twenty-dollar bill, which means I lose it, and you gain it. Or I can write you a check. When you deposit the check, twenty dollars is added to your bank balance. Down the line, twenty dollars is deducted from my bank account. There is, however, no actual transfer of cash. My bank doesn't send your bank a twenty-dollar bill. It's electronic money, merely a figure in the credit/debit logs of the banks.

"Let's say my bank decided, out of the goodness of their heart, to increase my bank balance by adding money. Since it's my account, I have access to the new funds. By reporting assets the banks didn't have, they simply improved their bank balance."

In amazement, Jaimie nodded. "When they did, the extra funds became real in the bank's ledger."

"More importantly, once the bank's stress test had been approved, the additional assets became real in the Federal Reserve program. A rider had been added to this year's tests. A bank's conversion of fiat dollars to gold currency was based on the assets from the bank's stress test. It was why the reports were falsified."

"That's why the approval of the bank stress tests was so important. Good lord, you're right. The answer was there all along," Jaimie said.

"Yes. The conversion had to be done before the currency went online for real. It was also the reason to kill the Chairman, create a distraction. While they pulled off their sleight of hand, no one would be looking at the computer system. As we found out, all they needed was a few hours to convert billions of electronic dollars to the gold currency. Then transfer the money to the offshore accounts, replace the false stress tests, wipe out all the computer evidence, and they were home free."

"Until all that gold currency was redeemed for gold bullion resulting in a global economic disaster," Remy added.

"If Sutter's plan was to take down the Federal Reserve, it would have worked, plus, he'd have become extremely wealthy in the process," Scott said.

After Remy and Jaimie left, Scott called Paul, who said he'd received a call from Bisset. Paul's office was already coordinating efforts with Interpol for arrest warrants of a lengthy list of conspirators. Even though there were a lot of loose ends to tie up, he left his boss in a happier frame of mind.

After another call to Savvi, it was arranged his agents would fly back with the Chairman as soon as he was released. The plane rented for Blake and Adrian would take Todd Bracken back to Austin. Scott laughed when Savvi told him Todd claimed his small scar would be a badge of honor for his role in the plot. He planned to contact Todd once he was back in Texas.

While he waited for Nicki to finish compiling her reports, he stood at the window, staring at the street.

He had no doubt the man who'd played second fiddle for so many years was the genius behind the plot. Halston didn't have the knowledge or brains to pull off such an elaborate scheme within the Federal Reserve System. Holcomb might be a computer genius, but he didn't have a financial background.

No, it was Sutter, and he'd played his cards well. If his scheme had gone awry, his hands were clean. The blame for the fraudulent bank tests would fall on Lois Barnett. Of course, there would be a stink when it was discovered she was an Interpol agent. Still, the consortium could claim they'd done nothing wrong and knew nothing about what was going on. The reports they submitted were correct.

Savvi became a bonus. Sutter could add her to the mix with his charges. While the accusations wouldn't hold up, the damage would have been done, her reputation in shreds. Her career in the FBI over. As for Remy and the Interpol investigation, well, it would have been a dead-end. Jaimie had no proof of wrongdoing, and it wasn't a crime to set up offshore accounts.

The attempted assault on Savvi and Nicki, the bombing attempt, the attack on Remy, Jaimie's kidnapping, none of it could be tied back to Halston, Sutter, Hayes or Holcomb. Sutter could claim he didn't know someone had broken into his barn. Not one solid piece of evidence existed.

Sutter had come damn close to pulling it off. What caused his downfall was the courage of Naval Lieutenant Jaimie Marston and Frank Littleton's willingness to put his life on the line.

EPILOGUE

TWO MONTHS LATER

Scott stepped out of his car and walked to a large tree. A light breeze stirred the leaves. Ahead, a cluster of civilians, law enforcement, and Army personnel gathered in front of a grave in Arlington National Cemetery.

His entire team was present. Once another serial killer was behind bars, Ryan, Cat, and Kevin had returned from Ohio. Nicki stood between Savvi and Adrian. Nearby, Blake stood, Jaimie at his side, their hands tightly clasped.

He spotted Paul standing alongside Vance Whitaker. Frank and Amelia were present, along with Remy and Louie Bisset. Kerry Branson, Ryan's fiancée, stood next to him.

While he waited, his mind drifted back. Earlier in the week, his team had finally wrapped up the Federal Reserve case. As promised, Savvi slapped the cuffs on Sutter and Hayes. Nicki had the honors for Holcomb.

At first, the cluster of conspirators denied all the charges. The first crack in their solidarity was from Roland when he agreed to a plea bargain. Sutter tried to play it cute by flinging his criminal accusations against Jaimie and Savvi. That lasted until his attorney learned Jaimie was an Interpol agent, and the FBI had computer evidence. Then one by one, they started pointing fingers at each other, wanting to make a deal. While a few received reduced sentences, they would all spend time in federal prison. Even Halston's money couldn't keep him out of jail.

The launch of the gold currency was successful, though anticlimactic for everyone involved in the case. Frank took a vacation. He and Amelia had gone to Texas, where he was treated to a grand tour of the Texas Gold Depository.

Scott had talked to Todd Bracken after he arrived home and learned his side of the story. Intrigued by finding Adrian and Blake incognito at the lodge, he'd kept a close eye on the agents. His curiosity grew when he noticed another agent hovering around the Chairman and figured whatever was going on involved Littleton. During the exodus from the building, he was behind Savvi and it was obvious she was protecting Frank. He saw a man hit Savvi, then try to drag Frank away. He ran toward them. When Savvi screamed for Frank to get on the ground, he jumped in to help. Of course, once the news media snapped to the fact that Todd had saved Frank Littleton's life, he became the hero of the day. Todd had laughed, saying he had to quit answering the phone because of all the requests for an interview.

When the crowd stirred, and the Army Chaplain stepped forward, Scott's attention shifted to the present. This was a day for a different type of remembrance and new beginnings.

The gravestone carried a new name, Sergeant Kathleen Logan. Family members were seated in a row of chairs. After the Army Chaplain finished the eulogy, rifles fired in salute. As the sound of the shots faded, a new sound rose. A bugle wailed—the mournful notes carried by the faint breeze.

An Army General stepped forward, on his arms, a folded American flag. He presented it to Kathy's mother. The flag had draped the coffin carrying her daughter's remains from Iraq. It had been returned by Jaimie's family.

After the ceremony concluded, he watched Jaimie as she

approached the Logan family. Tears streamed down her face. She spoke to each one, then hugged them before walking away.

Scott waited for the family to leave before approaching the grave. For several seconds, he stood, his head bowed. When he looked up, his gaze drifted across rows of white gravestones, gleaming under the warm sunlight. He felt a hand on his arm. Turning his head, he stared into Nicki's eyes, glistening with tears. He laid his hand over hers as they gazed at the seemingly endless gravestones. Though silent, their thoughts honored the men and women who had paid the ultimate sacrifice for freedom.

★★★

That evening another ceremony took place. A flute of champagne in one hand, Blake leaned against the wall. Wishing it were a bottle of beer, he took a sip as he eyed the elegantly clad gathering. The reception was in full swing. The hum of conversations competed with the soft sounds of the small orchestra in the corner of the ballroom.

A short time earlier, Kerry Branson and Ryan Barr had sworn to have and to hold, from this day forward, for better, for worse, for richer, for poorer, in sickness and in health, to love and to cherish, till death do us part.

Under the iridescent chandeliers, the two swirled around the dance floor, their eyes locked onto the other's face, oblivious to everyone. They'd met when Kerry rescued Senator Anthony Murdock's son from a ruthless gang of mercenaries in East Texas. The Tracker Unit had been assigned the investigation, and Ryan was sent to Texas. The rest is, as the old saying goes, history.

The list of wedding guests read like the who's who of the rich and powerful in Washington D.C., Vance Whitaker, Paul Daykin, Senator Anthony Murdock, his wife Catherine and their son Tristan, the Littleton's, along with many other politicians, friends, and family.

President Arthur Larkin had been unable to attend. His gift, though, a hand-crafted silver coffee urn and cups from Tuscany, Italy, sat in the middle of the gift table. Somehow, the President had learned of Kerry's obsession with coffee. She'd fit right in if she decided to join the Tracker Unit. Scott had already offered her the job.

Of course, the entire Tracker Unit was present. The sight of Scott nattily attired in a black tuxedo with Nicki in his arms brought a grin to his face. As they energetically twirled in and around the other couples, it almost looked like she was leading. They did make a good-looking twosome. A plait of black hair circled the back of Nicki's head, bringing into prominence the high cheekbones that bespoke her Native American heritage. The pale turquoise gown clung to her petite body as the long skirt flowed around her legs. Even in three-inch heels, Scott towered over her as he threw back his head and laughed.

Scattered around the room were the other Tracker agents. Adrian Dillard was cozied up with a luscious blonde, a college friend of Kerry's who had been one of the bridesmaids. Cat Morgan and Kevin Hunter were on the dance floor. Their expressions mirrored Kerry's and Ryan's. But then, they were still newlyweds. Remy was seated at a table, his arm draped around Savvi's shoulders.

Blake shrugged, shaking off a quiver of uneasiness. He was never comfortable around the high brass, a carryover from his military days. Then Jaimie stepped in front of him, and his discomfort slid away. He set the flute on a nearby table and held out his arms. Several days earlier, they had been quietly married. Not wanting to detract attention from Kerry and Ryan, they decided to keep it a secret. Besides, a big wedding wasn't their style, and he wasn't taking a chance of losing her again. They slipped out the door.

Scott led Nicki back to their table and spotted Blake and Jaimie as they left. He smiled, wondering when they'd announce their marriage.

As they sat at the table where Savvi and Remy were cuddled up, Remy looked at Scott. "What's this I hear about a painting?"

Nicki laughed.

Scott groaned. "It's the one Nicki bought at the gallery reception titled, *The Enigma*. She hung the dang thing in my office, where I've got to look at it every day."

"So, what's wrong with it?" Remy asked.

"It's nothing but black dots connected by lines on a white background. How would you like to look at dots every day?"

The tinkle of Nicki's laughter was joined by Savvi's as she realized the significance of the painting.

Remy looked at them in puzzlement. "Why don't you move it if you don't like it?"

Scott grumbled, "I can't. Nicki bought it for me."

Nicki had picked up her glass of champagne. Her eyes gleamed with mischievousness as she looked at him over the rim. After taking a sip, she said, "Did I mention Louie Bisset wants to meet with me to discuss opportunities in Interpol?"

Scott glared at Remy, who stared back with a mocking grin, then turned to look at Nicki. His eyes darkened with intensity and a bit of worry. "What did you tell him?"

Nicki laughed.

THE STORY BEHIND THE FICTION

NAVAJO CODE TALKERS

The use of American Indian language to create a secret military code became a truly singular event during World War II. Recruited by the Marines, the Navajo Code Talkers were assigned to the war in the Pacific Theater. The code they created to transmit vitally important information on U.S. troop movements and combat plans was never broken, saving the lives of countless American soldiers. They served on the front lines as they coded and decoded messages. During the invasion of Iwo Jima, the Navajo Code Talkers transmitted over 800 messages. Their actions played a major role in the Marine Corps' success in taking back the island from the Japanese Army.

In 1968, the Navajo Code was declassified. The Navajo Code Talkers finally received the recognition they deserved for their heroic efforts. President Ronald Reagan awarded a Certificate of Recognition to the Navajo Code Talkers and established August 14th as the National Navajo Code Talkers Day. In 2000, President Bill Clinton signed a law awarding a Medal of Honor to the original twenty-nine Navajo Code Talkers and a Silver Medal to each person who qualified as a Code Talker. In 2001, President George W. Bush presented the Medal of Honor to the four surviving Navajo Code Talkers from the original twenty-nine.

FEDERAL RESERVE

While the plot, characters, and many of the locations in OPERATION NAVAJO are fictional, many of the details regarding the Federal Reserve are factual.

On November 22, 1910, six men, prominent, influential bankers and politicians, boarded a private train car in the middle of the night in New Jersey. Their destination, an exclusive resort on Jekyll Island off the coast of Georgia. Shrouded in secrecy, their identities were a first name only. While the trip was touted as a duck hunting trip, the purpose was to draft a bill that would become the basis of the Federal Reserve Act signed by President Woodrow Wilson on December 23, 1913. The newly created Federal Reserve System gave the power to control the country's monetary policy and printing of currency to twelve regional Federal Reserve Banks, and a Board of Governors.

In 1944, representatives from forty-four countries met in Bretton Woods, New Hampshire. The meeting resulted in the Bretton Woods Agreement that established a global monetary system. The U.S. dollar became the global currency. As the U.S. dollar was backed by a fixed gold rate, the central banks of other countries could exchange dollars for U.S. gold.

When President Nixon began to lower the fixed rate for gold exchange, it resulted in a run on U.S. gold reserves by foreign central banks. To stop the depletion of the gold reserves, on August 15, 1971, President Nixon announced the Treasury would no longer exchange U.S. dollars for gold. Hence, the fiat dollar was born. Fiat dollars are based on the value of the government printing the money and have no intrinsic value.

Over the years, politicians and economists have proposed a return to the gold-back currency. While the controversy continues to rage, to date, the U.S. economy is still based on the use of the fiat dollar.

After the 2007-2008 global financial crisis, the use of bank stress tests to determine whether a bank could survive in an extreme economic crisis increased. In 2010, the Dodd-Frank Wall Street Reform and Consumer Protection Act was signed into law. The Act established a two-part process. The first step is the Dodd-Frank Act Stress Tests (DFAST). Large banks are required to conduct stress tests using the Federal Reserve's adverse economic scenarios for that year and make the results public. The second is the Comprehensive Capital Analysis and Review (CCAR). The Federal Reserve tests the banks' capital plans to make sure the banks have adequate capital under the adverse scenarios.

Each year, the Federal Reserve Bank of Kansas City plays host to the Jackson Hole Economic Symposium, an international banking conference held in Jackson Hole, Wyoming. It is attended by the top financiers in the world. The event takes place at the Jackson Lake Lodge, located in the Grand Teton National Forest. The conference was moved to Jackson Hole in 1982, and according to numerous recounts, the reason was due to the then Federal Reserve Chairman, Paul Volcker. He had a fondness for fly-fishing.

TEXAS BULLION DEPOSITORY

In 2015, Texas Governor John Abbott signed HB 483, creating the Texas Bullion Depository. The new depository and transfer of gold assets held by Texas A&M University and the University of Texas became the basis for the plot in *A u 7 9, a Tracker Novel*. I couldn't resist once again using the depository and administrator as they were a perfect fit for the conclusion of *OPERATION NAVAJO*.

About the Author

Anita Dickason is a twenty-two-year veteran of the Dallas Police Department. She served as a patrol officer, undercover narcotics officer, advanced accident investigator, tactical officer and the first female sniper on the Dallas SWAT team.

Her fictional works are suspense/thrillers, and her plots are drawn from her extensive law enforcement knowledge and experience. Characters with unexpected skills for overcoming danger and adversity have always intrigued her. Anita's infatuation with ancient myths and legends of American Indians, Scottish and Irish folklore creates the backdrop for many of her characters and plots.

I hope you enjoyed *OPERATION NAVAJO*.

Best Wishes
Anita Dickason

www.anitadickason.com

Made in the USA
Middletown, DE
15 February 2021